Contents

i **Contents**

iii **Editorial**

1 Always North
Vicki Jarrett

5 Two Ronas
Kirstin Innes

9 Bygones
Jason Donald

10 Why Nothing Works No. 2
Rodge Glass

18 Let's Buy a Keyring...
Anneliese Mackintosh

22 Edwin Morgan's Funeral
Graham Fulton

23 The Unemployable Poem
Dilys Rose

23 Books I Have Burnt
James A Irvine

24 Money Talks
Rodger Evans

24 Rats
Gordon Meade

25 The Fall of Baghdad
Duncan Muir

26 Corruption
Colin Will

27 Ghazi
Larry Butler

28 Dusting the Dark
Olive M Ritch

29 Showa, Oppenheimer
JoAnne McKay

30 The parable of the blind
Jim Carruth

31 Forbidden Texts from the Former GDR
Susan Kemp and Fiona Rintoul

36 Ways of Walking II
Johannes Jansen

37 Extract from literary magazine UND!
Gabriele Stötzer

38 Tracking Down the Skadocks
Arthur Ker

47 Extract from the novel *Leipzig*
Fiona Rintoul

51 There are no German creeps
Margaret Christie

52 Dark Matter
Brian Johnstone

53 The Mockers
Andy Jackson

54 Incision
Christine Williamson

55 The Alienist
Lesley McDowell

60 Sylvie Chandrashakar
Simon Sylvester

64 Ramon Usobiagi
Simon Sylvester

67 The Passenger
Jane Flett

72 Campground Murderer
Rose McDonagh

73 Extract from the novel *Piraeus*
Graeme Williamson

76 Four poems from *Fr Meślier's Breviary*
A C Clarke

80 Two Types of Wine
Jason Monios

81 The Temptation of Adamnán
John Douglas Millar

82 Fabulous Beast
Patricia Ace

82 On Looking
JoAnne McKay

83 Honesty
Nick Brooks

84 Elemental
Patricia Ace

85 From Light to Air
Christie Williamson

85 Late Night, February
Niall Campbell

86 Absorb
Hazel Frew

87 One for the Road
Brian Johnstone

88 Milk of Morning
Nick Brooks

89 Homesick
Cynthia Rogerson

92 Extract from the novel *Dog Evans*
Barry Gornell

97 Shoes on the road
Anne Morrison

101 10 x 10
Andrew Philip

106 The Museum of Broken Dreams
Ewan Gault

111 Extract from the novel *Eleanor's Book*
Mark Ryan Smith

115 A Kind of Loving
A P Pullan

116 The Leaving
Olive M Ritch

117 Rainbow Oil
Stephen Nelson

118 In Two Minds
Olive M Ritch

119 Extract from the novel *Burning Rates*
Helen Sedgwick

122 Limp
Jenny Love

128 Shared Conditions
Michaela Maftei

131 I am not Gary, she is not Gwen
Nick Holdstock

136 **Reviews**

153 Runners
Dave Whelan

157 Roads: M74 (Junction 21 to Junction 8)
A P Pullan

158 In the Flood
Brian Johnstone

159 Stump
Christine Williamson

160 Poem (iii)
Ross McGregor

160 Naked
Larry Butler
161 Camping
Nalini Paul
163 Trompe L'Oeil
Zoë Wicomb
171 Bloodier than Blood
Doug Johnstone
174 A Fairy Story
Frances Corr
178 Astronomy 101
Pippa Goldschmidt
181 Perfection, extract from the novel *Lost Bodies*
David Manderson
185 La casa dei doganieri
Eugenio Montale
186 Translations of two Montale poems
Allan Cameron
189 Out Of Magma, The Moon: A Witness
Alexander Hutchison
191 Blustered
Nalini Paul
192 Six St Kilda Poems
Donald S Murray
195 Mystery shopper report, with conclusions
Richard W Strachan
200 Bags I Go First...
Vivien Jones
201 I Am Not My Body
Allan Cameron
210 &
Django Ross
211 Dirty
Patricia Ace
212 The Ladies of B-Wing Topless Calendar
Andy Jackson
213 The Master
Olive M Ritch
214 The Annabel Chong Documentary
Janette Ayachi
215 Deil Tak The Hinmaist
Alexander Hutchison
217 In search of Duende
Christine Williamson
218 The Clangers on Acid
Patricia Ace
219 Manuscript
Andrew McCallum
220 Diasporran.
Catherine Baird

221 **Contributor Biographies**

Gutter
Editorial

You might not expect to find non-fiction in a magazine of fiction and poetry when its natural habitat is the journal or newspaper. But 'creative non-fiction' owes as much to fiction as it does to journalism, in the way that documentary film relates to mainstream cinema.

A good documentary will have a principal character, either the film-maker or their subject, through whose eyes the action unfolds. The setting might be compellingly exotic or, if humdrum, provide fresh insight to grab the audience's interest. And, behind it all, the director draws out the narrative, scene by scene, creating rhythm and pace, omitting what they consider unnecessary, giving particular focus to what they regard as pivotal to the unfolding story. The only difference with Hollywood: the claim to truthfulness through facts or, at least, the representation of facts.

In the same way, creative non-fiction can be deeply satisfying for both fiction reader and writer as the tools are familiar. As novelist, poet, memoirist, travel writer and *Gutter* contributor, Kapka Kassabova, pointed out in her recent *Scottish Review of Books* Diary – Jorge Luis Borges called *all* his work 'fictions', because "according to his vision of reality, everything becomes a fiction as soon as you write it down".

To this extent, *Gutter* welcomes the addition of creative non-fiction to the genres of writing we publish. Fiction and poetry will always remain our priority but we're keen to give writers of all kinds the chance to try their hand.

To kick things off, we invited Arthur Ker, whose story 'All in the Mind' appeared in *Gutter* 02, to provide a specially commissioned piece, 'Tracking Down the Skadocks', his account of a visit to the former East Germany to trace relatives previously lost behind the Berlin Wall. Like the best fiction, it's intriguing, humane, moving and feels wholly authentic.

'Tracking Down the Skadocks' is also part of our mini-feature on the former GDR within *Gutter 04*, linked to a festival of banned East German films that was part of the Glasgow Film Festival, which coincided with publication in February 2011.

Together with organisers Susan Kemp and Laura Bradley of The University of Edinburgh and *Gutter* contributor, Fiona Rintoul, we present examples of the kind of work (including direct facsimiles) that made up the *Samizdat*, underground literary magazines that were hand-produced in East Germany in the 1970s and 1980s in circumstances well beyond most of our experience or understanding. Demonstrating our *cosmowegian* credentials, we find fascinating the interplay between Johannes Jansen's poetry and Gabriele Stötzer's short fiction, provided here in translation by Fiona Rintoul, with another extract from Fiona's novel *Leipzig* (an earlier extract was published in *Gutter 01*), set in East Germany during the same era, and Arthur Ker's memoir.

*

One of the great strengths of current new writing in Scotland is the interest in, and engagement with, international themes and influences, that help leaven the dough in our literary oven. Besides Arthur's and Fiona's pieces, we're delighted to include a very timely story by Rodge Glass, 'Why Nothing Works No. 2', which was conceived in Tunisia just prior to the recent political upheavals. The international crosscurrents continue with a Murakami-inspired piece set in Japan by Ewan Gault, 'The Museum of Broken Dreams', the treat of a sneak preview from Glasgow-based South African writer Zoë Wicomb's forthcoming story collection with the tour de farce, 'Trompe L'Oeil', Allan Cameron's translations of two poems by Italian Nobel Prize winner, Eugenio Montale, Jane Flett's unstoppable New York Subway story, 'The Passenger', Dave Whelan's ➳

ambiguous, intriguing American road movie, 'Runners', and Nick Holdstock's Bonny and Clyde confession, 'I am not Gary, She is not Gwen'.

We're delighted to include *Gutter* debuts from acclaimed short story writer and novelist, and VS Pritchett Prize winner, Cynthia Rogerson, author of *Choke Chain*, Jason Donald, novelist and literary biographer, Lesley McDowell and author of *Tombstoning* and *The Ossians*, Doug Johnstone.

In poetry, we are pleased to present new work by Jim Carruth, Gordon Meade and Andrew Philip, a selection of AC Clarke's engaging poems about Jean Meslier, and Scots poetry from Alexander Hutchison, Christie Williamson and Ross McGregor. From the edge of Scotland, Donald S Murray's sequence of St Kildan poems bring a fresh perspective on the remote. There is also bold writing on love and sex from Patricia Ace and Janette Ayachi.

*

As the recession casts a shadow across the publishing landscape, with more bookshop closures forecast and a major contraction of London publishing underway, it's getting harder than ever for Scottish writers to 'get a deal'. Anything created north of Watford seems to constitute 'niche' in the minds of some editors. Whether a promising debut or a third or fourth book, the product of a steadily developing career, publishers are finding it increasingly easy to say 'no thanks' to any writer who isn't already famous or who can't guarantee a minimum of 5,000 copies sold.

Philip Pullman recently lent force to this in an online article where he said, "the greedy ghost of market madness has got into the controlling heights of publishing... the greedy ghost whispers into their ears: Why are you publishing that man? He doesn't sell enough. Stop publishing him... Why are you publishing this woman? She'll only appeal to a minority... Books are published not because they're good books but because they're just like the books that are in the bestseller lists now, because the only measure is profit".

While no one can argue against the suggestion that in the boom years some of the work that made it into print was of dubious merit, it's clear that in the next few years many deserving and culturally worthwhile projects, often from writers with decent track records, will languish because, for large international houses, the figures just don't stack up. Looking at the *Samizdat*, it's humbling to see what East German writers achieved under the oppression of a police state. And without sounding trite, sometimes in adversity there is opportunity.

In the past, when times were hard, Scottish culture had a habit of kicking into overdrive. 1992 was the year of Black Wednesday and the last big recession. It was also the year Rebel Inc was founded with the rallying cry, "Fuck the mainstream!" Now is a great time for like-minded folk to look at filling the gap vacated by London publishers. In fact it's already happening. It needn't be about profit, but if it's done professionally and with passion, profit – both artistic and fiscal – will follow.

‘...a taste for drawing-rooms has spoiled more poets than ever did a taste for gutters.’

Thomas Beer

Always North

Vicki Jarrett

IF I COULD arrange time in a circle, sit the separate moments around a table, say. Or in a semi-circle, a horseshoe shape, like teeth in a mouth, then I could be right across from the one where the bear's breath is hot on my face and the stink of his blood-wet breath is nearly knocking me off my feet. The smell so strong it nearly suffocates the fear, but not enough to stop me pissing myself. It runs hot out of the bottom of my waterproof trousers and steams over my boots. The bear grins, licks his black lips, and opens his jaws wide to show me the yellow spikes of his teeth.

*

This far north, and we're about as far north as it's possible to be, the sky comes curving out towards you from the horizon, low and flat, like a closing lid. The sky and sea rolling together like two huge wheels and the ship heading for the join, pulled in towards the meeting at that line, that vanishing point where everything is crushed together and it all becomes one pressed wafer of nothing. The sun never sets and we all crave darkness.

*

Peder, the captain, stabs a thick weathered finger at one of the display monitors and glares at Angus. 'He doesn't even know what fucking day it is,' he spits. Angus is pale. I can tell he hasn't slept for days. Stubble covers half his face and his eyes are red-rimmed and watery behind his glasses. He winces and rattles the keyboard. 'I don't know what's happening,' he says. 'The time stamps are all over the place. They keep getting out of synch. I've run the diagnostics but I'm just getting crap back. It's not just one problem. There must be multiple failures. As soon as I track one, another pops up.'

*

I sit up in my bunk and bang my head off the cabin roof. The small space is in total darkness, the one meagre window covered with blackout material taped all the way round to block out the midnight sun. I have to put my fingers to my eyes to check they are open, there is no difference between open and shut. I have no idea how long I've been asleep. Nobody sleeps much out here. The sun never sets but in the small hours where darkness should be, it lowers in the sky and hangs there, watching us, red and unblinking.

*

Nobody knows how the bodies get on deck but they appear with increasing regularity, at least one every day. We assume they are seals. They are all headless and have been neatly skinned, using some kind of corkscrew motion. The exposed tubes of flesh, a sticky mottled pink, are banded with spiralling lines as if they have been fed through some kind of machine. We heave the meat overboard and watch it vanish back into the sea, not knowing what poor manners this demonstrates.

*

Somewhere up ahead the icebreaker grinds onwards, always north, shouldering aside the smaller floes, pulverising the larger ones, pushing further into the edge of the pack ice. The shearing, scraping noise of metal on ice sometimes drifts back to us on the wind and sets my teeth on edge. The clear channel stretches ahead, laid over the moving ice field like a silver ribbon. Somewhere off to starboard is the west coast of Greenland, a distant monochrome hunch of black rock and snow. In every other direction, irregular slabs of ice are scattered across the sea like an impossible, abandoned jigsaw.

*

What is it with the pickled fish? The Norwegians can't get enough of it. Since they own the vessel and the chef, they get to choose the food. I wouldn't mind but the Russian crew have nicked all the pastries again. They can't get their heads around the idea that such luxuries will reappear tomorrow. They fill their pockets with all they can hold each day and stash it in their cabins, as if they're hoarding for a long winter. I settle for black coffee and make my way to the bridge. I don't think I got much sleep before the silence woke me.

*

We work on the problem for hours but the errors just keep multiplying. Time is swirling and looping within the sub-processes of the system. Little eddies of seconds and minutes, repeating and overlapping, when we need them to go in a straight line. Instead they form patterns as unreliable as oil on water. The data means nothing without the timing. Just so much white noise. The time between the guns firing and the receivers picking up the sonic reflections tells us everything and if we don't know that, we may as well not be here. You can't know where you are if you're not damn sure *when* you are.

*

In the distance a patch of pale yellow against the white is moving from floe to floe, sometimes disappearing and reappearing, getting closer all the time. Until he is close enough for us to see what he is. And then he stops and stares, his long neck extended, head low and level with his massive shoulders, his feet planted wide, claws hooking him into the ice. His eyes are dark magnets holding all the nighttimes captive throughout the summer. There is no doubt he's thinking, reasoning, cataloguing our size and speed, weighing up our intentions. He knows exactly what we are.

*

I listen to the silence as I pull a thick jumper over the clothes I slept in, drag open my cabin door and stumble up the narrow corridor towards the galley. There's obviously some kind of problem. The silence tells me that much but I'll be damned if I'm going to get roped into sorting it out before I have some breakfast. I just hope the Russians haven't raided the galley and swiped all the good stuff and all there'll be left is the pickled fish. I never knew there were so many ways to pickle a fish. And all of them disgusting.

*

At first he communicates only in grunts, growls and low, muzzled howls but gradually he presses these guttural utterances into the shapes of rudimentary words and we can converse. The seals, so skilfully prepared, were an offering, like a cat brings mice as a gift. He knows we are hunters. What else could we ever be? He assumes we are hunting for seal, or something bigger, better, some ultimate unending food source. He seeks alliance. Our manners improving, we learn some of his language and together we sail north, always north, through the ice with a crew part bear, part human, both parts hunter.

*

HHMMSS, hours minutes seconds, in a line, not stacked on top of each other or arranged in a circle, useful and illuminating though that could be. Moment follows moment and we are born again into each one, each time, bloody and helpless as the last. And if there is birth, there must also be death, the death of each one of these moments. We are the children of time and all time is dead. Everywhere, everything, everyone, some shade of dead. Always.

*

The door from the deck bursts open and one of the Russian crew comes in, bringing a swarm of snowflakes with him. Peder rounds on him and gives him a toxic mouthful in at least three different languages, just to make sure he gets the message. He has very strict rules about coming onto the bridge from the deck. He is also shit scared of polar bears. Who wouldn't be? But the story is that Peder has actually seen one up

↣

close. Sometimes they get onto the vessels, by the open back deck, following a trail of food smells, and the stink of our rubbish. It can't be dumped out here so is grudgingly, inadequately stored in metal containers on deck.

*

The gap is constantly moving. The channel has to be in just the right location at the time we sail over it, firing the guns and picking up the acoustic reflections, amassing our drifts of data that will reveal to someone else, not us, exactly what's down there and exactly where. Our prey hides, sliding black and silent under ice, under sea, underground. Our job is only to find it. We're not paid to think about what will happen when the others come back with rigs and drills and platforms. Not our problem. A separate moment in time, spinning off on some outer spiral arm that doesn't concern us.

*

The bear is not white. Each stiff filament of hair is translucent and amplifies the frozen light. But light is not truth. Underneath, at the roots, the thick carapace of his skin is black as ink, black as the crude oil that lies beneath the frozen sea. Black under white, he is the landscape given blood and breath. He says a bear only lives as long as his teeth and his teeth are strong. The sun will not set but hangs low and bleeds gold and fire and blood into the sky. And the sea draws it into veins between the ice creating livid flesh that breathes and groans in the swell. Ice channelling sky, channelling sun.

*

There is a sign on the inside of the door from the bridge room onto the deck. It says WARNING and underneath there is a silhouette of a polar bear which appears to be ambling along minding its own business. Perhaps the sign would work better if they showed it roaring, all teeth and claws and charging towards you. Below the bear, the sign says:

POLAR BEAR ALERT
DO NOT ASSUME THE COAST IS CLEAR
A POLAR BEAR MAY BE OUTSIDE
THIS DOOR

*

The Russian is shaking, his whole body jerking as he tears off his heavy gloves and waterproof jacket. They are slicked with blood and pinkish waxy lumps. He drops them to the floor and pastry flakes drift from his woollen undercoat as he talks. We hear the fear but don't know the words. He looks around at us and switches to English. 'Breathing, I tell you, it was breathing. And warm. I could feel it coming apart in my hands. The tail end split open. It looked like legs.' He stands shaking and staring at his own legs as if he can't trust them. His hands hang by his sides, and I see his nails are long, curved and filthy and his fingers are webbed up to the middle knuckle, folds of translucent skin strung between the bones.

*

The guns have stopped. It was the silence that woke me. Sharp fingers of emptiness poking into my ears and demanding attention. It doesn't take long to get used to the thump of the guns on a job like this. Within a few days of shooting the constant, regular noise becomes part of the fabric of reality on board, like a heartbeat. Then silence becomes loud. The air in my tiny cabin is thick with artificial darkness, but I can't sleep unless I block out the midnight sun. It never sets. Nobody sleeps much and we all crave darkness.

*

When I get there, the galley is empty. Plates and cutlery are strewn around the floor. There is nothing to eat, not even pickled fish, and the chef is nowhere to be seen. The doors on the hatch leading to the kitchen have been wrecked. One has been torn completely off and the other hangs by a single hinge and swings back and forth, back and forth, clicking like a metronome. The tables are covered in ragged score marks and the walls are running with red. I make my way to the bridge. Angus is hunched over his keyboard, marooned alone on his tiny island, hemmed in by waves of light, muttering to himself about the wrong kind of North.

*

Winter is approaching. Soon the bear will unlock the dark coils of captive night from his eyes and sleep. He assures us that we will sleep too, that we are enough bear to last the long cold months. But first we must fatten up, we are too skinny to survive a week as we are. And so he brings us more seal and fat juicy pups. We bite into the snowy fur and warm blood bursts between our lengthening teeth. Slimy thick fat slides down our throats to our bellies and makes us stronger. Blood, bone and survival are all that matters.

*

Time streams in from decaying vibrations in space and converges on us, uncorrected, ephemeral. This is the wrong kind of time. Hours, minutes and seconds are the keepers of our reality and there must be agreement. We must have alliance, or chaos will find us and push us from our footing and we are falling, falling, falling through the universe, passing galaxies yet to be born and suns long since dead. Frozen, separate, and unable to remember our world, forgetting even ourselves, putting our hands to our eyes but there is no difference. Everything is darkness.

*

The bear opens his mouth and I can see all these moments arranged like two horseshoes of spiked white, curling inwards. I can feel my blood splash down from my throat onto my chest, staining it black, and I can see his throat vibrating with a roar that goes on forever across the great white silence. The empty space between each beat of my heart expands and stretches, out and out and out, until I can't hear it anymore. The sun finally slips from the sky and sinks into the sea. Summer is over and this is the time to sleep.

Two Ronas

Extract from the novel *Fishnet*

Kirstin Innes

Blog: Do you remember the first time?

Early forties. Thin, short, unhemmed like his edges had been gnawed. Something feral about him, but not bad looking. Not really.

I'd thought he would be ugly. Old and fat and ugly. I'd thought about fucking someone repulsive, fantasised about rolled lolloping flab that'd shake as he shagged, kept my fingers and brain in place on the transaction, the power, tried to train myself into it.

Old skin touching me.

Instead, just this little vulpine man, smell of dead smoke off him. His mouth was dry, smacked as he opened it to say Hi, white flecks in the corners.

I said Hi back, and he let me in.

Just two of us in a room, a very ordinary hotel room.

'I'm Jimmy,' he said. Irish.

'Rona,' I said. That was fine. It was okay, to say that.

'Yeah – I guessed.'

'Of course.'

'So.'

'So.'

That's when I realised it was my job to break through this. My job, this, to ease him out of the nerves, to take his hand through it. Maybe it was his first time too.

All I had to do was smile at him, and say, in that voice like it was a normal thing to say

'So. Shall we discuss services?'

And I smiled at the end, a little bit, like we both knew how awful a thing it was, to have to ask, to have to reduce it down to money.

'Just the basics, please. Just the hour.'

The words flat, no expression.

He handed me an envelope without me having to ask. It probably wasn't his first time.

My phone rang, before I could check the amount.

'I'll just need to-'

'Of course,' he said again.

No, not his first time.

'So?' she said, down the line.

And I thought, well, I'm not sure. It was something you were supposed to know, by instinct, she'd said. Well, my instincts weren't telling me to run, but they weren't telling me anything at all. I was just in a room with this expressionless man, and he was skinny.

'I'm here, and it's fine,' I said.

'Okay. I've got the hotel on speed dial anyway,' she said. 'Two rings as soon as the hour's up. And good luck, hon.'

If my instincts had been telling me anything, the code was 'I'm here, and he's reallylovely.*'*

We both stood there in the silence again, and I remembered that this was also part of my job.

'Give me two seconds,' I said, taking a step towards the bathroom, 'while I go and change into something, eh-'

'Just do it here,' he said, gesturing to a space on the floor. 'I'd like to see you undress.'

I was thinking, I haven't been able to count the money yet. I was thinking, I haven't done the lube yet.

He sat down on the bed, looking at me, and I stood in front of him, and pulled at the zip on my dress. It stuck for the first few seconds, and I had to wrestle with it, trying to keep smiling, swaying my hips a little to distract him. Cheap fucking thing. It came, eventually, and I let it swish down around me, stepped out of it. See through panties and a half balcony bra, so this man, this stranger was now pretty much seeing me naked.

He didn't say anything, his face didn't change, but he unzipped the front of his trousers and pulled himself out, already mostly hard.

'Would you like me to suck your cock,' I said.

'Yes,' he said. 'I'm right in thinking I don't need to wear a condom?'

'Not for oral, no,' I said, like that was what I always said.

Eyes closed, and it's just like giving any other blowjob. Could be someone I'd met in a bar. Could be a new boyfriend. I was touched that he'd washed it.

We spoke in these clipped, formal sentences, both of us. Like neither of us were there for the conversation, so what was the point in pretending? Made sense. He helped me in a way, that wee skinny Irishman, because my response would have been to crack jokes, to ease things through a bit. And of course, with some clients you can do that, and it's great, but the first time, this one, he helped me pare everything right down, establish a rhythm and a way of being in the room. It wasn't a kindness to me, he was just a customer, waiting for a service; I was the provider, that was the point.

It didn't occur to me until afterwards that I'd crossed over, that I'd actually done it, that I was now not one of us.

Tags: clients memories irish outcalls
| **Comments** (3)

The first time I noticed what Rona could do was the year after the divorce. Mum still had the house, dad had moved to a tiny suburb on the outside of the city and we had to stay with him one week every month. The sort of place that had probably once been a proud independent village in its own right, co-opted into the city by bypasses and Tescos and housing schemes and opportunity.

It was February, the air was sharp and good for you; we'd just started having to put an extra jumper on under our coats. Thirteen. She was thirteen, for fucksake, probably hadn't even started her periods yet (not that I'd know).

There were five of us at my school who lived out that way, the only ones. Me and Rona, Jenna Anderson in the fifth year and her wee brother, and Malcy Lamont. If we made it in time, which we usually didn't, we could catch the school bus, the one put on by three city centre schools for a disparate bunch: kids from village schemes and the part-timers staying with the parent who made less money.

Anyway, that day we were on time; weren't going to shamble shamefaced into first period as usual to everyone mock-tutting, James Gibson pointing and going oooooh! We crossed the road and I went to grab her hand out of instinct. She glared right up at me.

—I'm not a baby, she hissed. I'm thirteen. And there's no bloody traffic.

Screw her. I was in a good mood that day. We sat down in the wee shelter and I leaned out the one window where someone had punched the scratched Plexiglas away completely, grinned up the hill, still a bit heathered, the sky above it blinking off the last of the sunrise.

Rona was thirteen, but I think she already had more chest than I'd ever get. Not that I knew that at the time, still clinging to old Judy Blume tales of hope and late development. Even in uniform I was nobody's fantasy of a schoolgirl; I've never really worked out how to stand. But this was the day I realised it.

Dad lived at the last stop before the bus turned and ploughed down the bypass. It usually filled up at the five earlier stops and we almost never got a seat together. Not that Rona would mind that day. After a few seconds she got up and marched down to the verge, glaring into the road, hood of her duffel coat pulled up in the sunshine, shooting the odd glare back at me. Still all pissed off because I'd tried to take her hand. Oh, get over it, you stupid KID, I muttered at her in my head.

Just the two of us there, that day. Looking up the hill again, I saw him coming.

Malcy Lamont. He was in my year, but we never spoke. What would we say? He'd been
➳

in trouble ever since he arrived, just turned up one day about six weeks into third year. I think it was just the way he looked at the teachers, default expression of solid, nasty insolence. Eyes deep set with long, black, fantasy girl's eyelashes, greasy gingery curtains over a round head, fat lips always wet and half open. Not sixteen and already sexed, sizing the female teachers up when they told him off, just standing up there, itemising them – breasts, legs, back up to the crotch, where he *stopped* – till they backed down, every one. There were whispers about who he'd poked round the back of the science building, who had let him get three or even four fingers up, who he'd gone all the way with. Nobody really mentioned whether the girls had had much say in the matter. It was Malcy Lamont. He just happened. My plain girl's invisibility cloak didn't work on him, either – I'd had to pass him in the corridor on the way to PE once and he'd put his arm up, not let me through till he'd had a good, slow look. No words. Just letting me know that he would, if he felt like it. You dreaded getting anywhere near him during country dancing, in the progressive numbers, but you dreaded it silently.

Malcy Lamont was coming down the hill to the shelter now. Soft flop of cock at the crotch of his tracky bottoms, sour smell coming off him downwind. Malcy Lamont only existed in the physical. The times before, when we'd made the bus, hulking Jenna Anderson and her brother had been there, the two of them like a barrier, soaking up some of Malcy. Not today. And he was coming over. I curled in to the wall of the shelter, carried on staring out of the window frame, ready to flinch, wondering after what neverending length of time the bus would come.

He didn't come into the shelter, though. I turned around, and saw him standing in the grass, him and Rona facing each other. Her hood was down, the coat open and slipping off her shoulders, her hair blown back from her face. Just staring right back at him, eyeballing, keeping his sightline level with hers. Her jaw was set; not the way it would be when she was going to start a fight.

I didn't understand what I was seeing, really. I'm not sure I do now. No idea what their two bodies were saying to each other, what sort of unspoken conversation happened there. Malcy Lamont didn't move. I didn't move. The bus came and Rona broke it, stepped past him and told me to come on, commanding, making her point. Schoolies spilled and burst all over us, jeering across the aisle, warmth and the fart stink on my skin. Somebody's tinny transistor playing that Robert Miles song, *Children*, scratching and fuzzy at the strings. Rona was three paces ahead of me, cutting briskly through the tangled limbs of the aisle. She got a seat beside a smaller girl in her year, turned to her and started chatting.

— Are ye getting on, then, son? the driver was asking.

Malcy Lamont walked quickly down to the back seat, where his mates were whistling at him. Head down. Didn't stop to brush his groin up against any outstretched knees, didn't look at Rona. I looked at her instead, through the seat behind. Her and thin, lank Donna Bruce talking away, the same age except one of them was a child and the other one wasn't.

Next time I got a chance to talk to her was after lunch, passing her on the way to French.

— What was all that about this morning?

— All what? You just need [patronising voice, full height] to remember that I'm not *actually* a baby, Fiona.

— You know what I mean. With him. With *Malcy*.

I whispered that bit, didn't want to get caught saying his name out loud.

— No idea what you're talking about, she said, peeling off and away from me, her hair whipping out behind her.

I wasn't even surprised when the knock on the door came that night. Dad was out at the shops and Rona was in the toilet, so I went, already half-knowing who it would be.

— Is your sister in?

He was wet through – it had just stopped raining – huddled up under a man's coat too big for him. I looked down on him from our steps and thought it was maybe the first time I'd ever heard him speak. I wasn't really sure what to do, so I just closed the door on him, softly, and went back into the living room, turned the telly up louder.

That was it, for Rona, though. I heard her new laugh in the corridors and on the bus, bright and healthy. From nowhere, she had boy friends and then boyfriends, mostly third years but once, for two terrifying, glorious weeks until the slaggings from his friends got too much for him, Chris Wood in fifth year, captain of the football team, lead actor in the school plays. Never Malcy Lamont, although I'd sometimes catch him staring at her cheek on the bus, immobilised. She was untouchable for the likes of him now. She walked taller than me, bunched her school skirt into her belt, stretched her legs out at break times to pull her socks down into thick rolls over each ankle. I'd pass her in the playground, screeching and flirting and petting with an entirely different set of friends from the ones she'd had before.

Malcy Lamont disappeared as suddenly as he'd arrived a few months after. We stopped thinking about him, like you always stopped thinking about people who had left the school, wrote them out of your history. When we were about twenty-two, Heather said she thought she'd seen him in town, with a woman and a baby on his shoulders.

— They all looked happy, she said. I think it was him.

It doesn't get decided that early, a person's character. That's a myth spun from those high school movies we used to watch, with their morals and their thirty-year-old teenagers. It was what I started with though, when I began this whole thing. The cold on my face and the damp on his lips and the wind in her hair.

Bygones

Jason Donald

ONE YEAR LATER, they met for dinner in a neutral place. She wore a tight blouse to accentuate the few pounds she'd managed to starve off. He went for the unshaven care-free image he'd spent a year struggling to create. They laughed a little too enthusiastically, convincing each other it was all in the past. Halfway through the main course she promised herself not to tell him about James, her desperate third attempt at internet dating. He mistook her guardedness for vulnerability, so felt it best not to tell her about Sue, the crush from his Uni days he'd finally found the courage to bed. When the final course was laid before them, they thoughtfully spooned dessert into their own mouths. Each smiled at the other from behind their delicious secrets. Then the time came to settle up. She offered to pay and laid her card on the table, thinking this was probably the most successful date they'd ever had.

Why Nothing Works No. 2
Rodge Glass

AFTER PEERING THROUGH the darkened doorway to see what kind of place this really was, he finally decided to go inside. He stepped off the street and felt an unfamiliar jolt in his gut as he did it. Then he leant into the chunky glass block which separated him from the world on the other side, and pushed hard. The door was heavy. It began to shift.

Once inside he stood in the purple light bathing the doorway and breathed in through his nose, smelling smoke. Then he let go of the door and watched the glass begin to slip back towards the hole. (This is how it seemed, like it was slipping.) The hole belonged to this building he'd walked by eight times in the last fortnight, but tonight was entering for the first. On a Friday night. Way past nine o'clock. Here he was a man without a history, nobody knew his profession, and this could be *his kind of place*. The man hitched up his jeans by the belt, and why not? Tomorrow night he'd be back on the couch, complaining about the cold. His eyes adjusted to the lights. They were low enough to make his skin seem darker but bright enough, perhaps, to show off the shirt he'd haggled for at the beach that morning. The shirt had a certain effect. It still had what his wife called *that fresh-from-the-designer-sweatshop smell*. If she'd seen his top two buttons undone she'd have teased him, and the two of them would have kissed. As he thought this, the door finally closed behind him. Not too fast. Not too slow. Just right, with an initial dignified steadiness, then something more like a crawl in the last moments, so no damage was done to wall, door or persons close by.

All this seemed appropriate. This was the *High Flyer Brasserie*.

It simply wouldn't do to have doors close in a rush.

The man stood in the light a moment longer. He'd not quite registered it yet but this was, for some, the hottest hotspot in town, the place where well-groomed bar tenders, chefs and waiters gathered after a long week of serving others. (Though small, the tourist industry was the primary industry here. Local elders complained it was now the only one.) Anthony Bell, not the most perceptive man, wouldn't notice this sort of thing, but the *High Flyer* was where these hard-working people came after working back-to-back double-shifts. After days of bowing, grins fixed on their faces, hoping for disproportionate tips from those who'd not yet worked out the value of the currency or were too rich to bother calculating it. Many spent 60 hours a week or more saying *please* and *thank you* in Italian, German, English, French, always making the effort to guess the customer's mother tongue and switch to it without comment. Doing all this regardless of whether it was deserved, wanted or noticed. Not that Anthony would even consider these sorts of details, (he was already far off in his own thoughts, wondering, mostly, why he was experiencing the beginnings of an erection, very unusual for him in public), but the *High Flyer Brasserie* was pretty much the only venue where these workers from the food stalls and the town's endless *tabac* stands, these children of quiet, religious men who'd grown up on these

↣

streets and now wore sunglasses at night as a statement directed at their fathers – *this* was the only place these people felt free. These people, who shunned tradition and planned to spend their only day off in full-on rebellion, these were mostly young men. Because in this town, the cooks, waiters, servers and stall holders were nearly all young men. It was a young country. It was a male country. Anthony had seen this for himself during the last fortnight, which he'd mostly spent travelling between customers of his own, taking bulk orders from the big warehouses and corner shops and family businesses. As he'd joked to Caragh on the phone earlier, apart from the odd wrinkly pensioner in head-to-foot white shawl, Anthony had hardly laid eyes on a female the whole trip. So he couldn't have played away if he'd wanted to!

He moved forward a few steps.

He picked up a drinks menu and scanned the contents.

The prices in the *High Flyer* determined the clientele. Drinks were just about affordable for locals, being lower than the town's tourist bars but higher than the average, giving what the American-born manager called *an air of exclusivity, a unique space*. The *High Flyer* was off the main track, somewhere locals whispered about, kept to themselves. It served beer with alcohol in it. It was open till dawn. And, as Anthony was just noticing, it even hosted the occasional *woman*. Ones whose dresses showed flesh above the ankle and below the neck, who wore tight jeans, dresses and high heels, who smoked, laughed with confidence and drank with the men like they were staking a flag in newly discovered land. Perhaps land they'd been inching towards for centuries. The bar area here had fluorescent pink lines underneath which also suggested something new and exciting – these lines zipped round the outskirts of the service area and flew off, unafraid, into the distance, as if making a break for foreign shores. This place, with its English-only sign out front, understated private booths and Western channels on plasma TV screens, this place let local boys and girls play at being wealthy Westerners – ones who just so happened to prefer Arabic music, and who happened to sell shawarma and pizza by day. It let them be, for the night, Hollywood Stars and New Jersey Mafia Dons. Each town waiter, now being waited upon, felt the weight of the beer bottle in his hand and surveyed the scene with satisfaction, imagining himself as a central character in a film with a dramatic, happy ending set in a country he'd only experienced on DVD. Not that Anthony was even listening but here, sons of fishmongers dropped words like *babe* and *dude* into their conversation. They modified their accents. The *High Flyer* was far from the sober café culture that pervaded this town, this country as they saw it – the sausage-fest, plastic-chair-and-table coffee places on every corner which only served espresso and shishas and hosted men who hadn't had serious hopes in decades. Who hated their leaders but never tried to change them. Between these walls, the only system belonged to a distant land. The seats felt soft to the touch. The blinds kept the outside world firmly out (or hid disapproving eyes looking in) and that was the way customers liked it. The *High Flyer* preserved the illusion of being at the pulsing centre of New York or LA right up until closing time. This was the management's unspoken promise.

Anthony was aware he'd been standing for too long.

He was keen to sit.

He nearly picked the closest table, one right by the door. But then he changed his mind, spotting a back corner booth with a view of the whole place. This looked like a spot for a successful businessman. Someone taking some deserved *me-time* after a day's serious work. So he strode over and sat, sliding his rucksack out of view in the same swift movement. (Rucksacks were not welcome here, it was obvious. Even ones containing sales reports from recent days that Walid would be very, very pleased with.) Anthony looked around. This table had a clear view of seven television screens running in tandem, on silent, while to the right of the largest one he could see three older men in good suits, deep in conversation. They looked different. They had bellies suggesting decades of success. Anthony straightened his back, stretched, and tried to work out what channel he was watching. He wondered whether these guys were the management. Then he thought: perhaps this was a brothel.

Local music played through the speakers. To Anthony it sounded like religious dance music, though he suspected this guess was based on a Westerner's prejudice. (He slipped into that sometimes. He knew it.) This sound, it certainly had the cadences of religious music, the instrumentation, the wandering lilt of the call to prayer he heard from his hotel room, wafting across the street from the mosque. Curiously, this perhaps-religious song was being delivered by a man making no pretence of being able to actually sing – a man whose tone seemed to say: *this is just my job mate, I could just as easily be an oven salesman* – but people were nodding as if finding something delicious and wicked. And actually, Anthony noticed, it did have something of that to it. A lightness, perhaps. A darkness. A sound that hinted at something filthy going on, somewhere, close by. Keyboards hummed and swelled in the background.

As Anthony settled in his seat, thinking he'd finally *discovered* something on his travels, not merely *visited*, he observed some of his fellow customers more closely. Some small groups. Two large ones, mixed gender. Couple of drunks. A few younger men, like him, sitting alone in the near darkness. But – as Anthony noted with pleasure – they all looked like locals here. Locals keen to suck up this experience as if sucking up the future, which they believed, the man imagined from their expressions, was wild, and dangerous, and uninhibited. It was a future that didn't care about the opinions of others: it was wearing impractical suspenders and probably crotchless knickers. (Or *panties*, as the Americans say. And these fellow customers of his, it wasn't London, Edinburgh, Cardiff or Belfast they were dreaming of.) A man at the next table nodded, as if sharing something. Then he looked away.

The three suits at the bar were moving their hands, and Anthony wondered if they were discussing a drug deal. (They weren't.) As he considered the details of the exchange they might be engaged in (but weren't), speculating about whether it was smack or crack or something else they were smuggling (or weren't), and thinking about just how dangerous that kind of life might or might not be, the lights changed colour and the music in the bar increased. In an instant, the atmosphere changed. The volume of this music suited somewhere tabla players were rarely heard on record or wanted in bands, and where bare skin was standard currency on the dance floor, clothing merely the optional, occasional decoration around exposed legs, arms and torsos. Here, there wasn't even a dance floor at all. And yet, it seemed like there was. Something was going on. A music video started on the screen, a new song blasted through the speakers, and three off-duty waiters at a nearby table recognised the tune. They stood, raised their glasses and clapped along, one attempting a sort of drunken belly dance. Anthony recognised the dancer. He'd served him a crêpe two hours ago.

Just then, someone new appeared at his table. This person was dressed like everyone else. It didn't seem like he was working. Actually, thought Anthony, did *anyone* here act like they were working? What did this individual want? A light, perhaps? Did he want Anthony to leave? As if answering these questions the standing person cocked his head upward slightly, and Anthony said: *UNE BIÈRE S'IL VOUS PLAÎT*. Which seemed to be right, because the person grunted then walked towards the bar. Anthony smiled at this reaction: he was in possession of a strange and exciting power. He leaned back and drew his arm across the chair next to him as if there were someone sitting in it, Caragh perhaps. No one noticed this. Then he realised something. He shifted in his chair again, wondering how people behaved, alone, in bars with loud music in the background. Then he focused his attention on one of the many screens. Inside the screen a woman danced, wearing a bikini Caragh might have described, with acid on her tongue, as *basically a piece of string attached to*

→

three small cheese triangles.

He had now been at the *High Flyer Brasserie* for nearly three minutes.

He watched the bikini woman in the screen.

One thing was obvious: this woman was not from this world, or even from Anthony's world, but from what his brother Barry called *Planet Latina*, somewhere Anthony had never visited but had heard much about. Barry had lived on this planet for a while, a place that, whenever asked, he liked saying was *anywhere south of Texas, baby*. Barry holidayed there often, always coming home looking tanned and well-fed and strangely confident. In unguarded moments – in moments, basically, of drunkenness – Barry explained it was hot and poor on Planet Latina, and full of women scouting for Westerners. These women dreamed of resettling in cold countries, where they'd be happy doing cleaning jobs and performing explicit sexual acts for white whales like him without a thought for themselves, as long as they got a passport out of it and could send money to their families. These women were angels, Barry said. They'd rescued his wavering belief in God. He said that, in the hope of escape, many of these gorgeous, angelic women – and here was the crucial detail – many of them would gamble on putting out for a night or two, on the off-chance. This was what Anthony had heard about Planet Latina. And, though he knew Barry was full of shit even at the best of times, though Barry was basically ignored or laughed at by everyone he knew, though Anthony was an intelligent enough soul who knew a made-of-crap male fantasy when he heard it, he enjoyed, just for a moment, imagining capturing this woman in the video and taking her home with him to Bexley Heath in a sack, tied up with the string from her bikini. He didn't want to hurt anyone. The idea horrified him. But in the imagination, he thought, who gets hurt? He was just waiting for his drink. Anthony wondered how long it would be till it arrived. This place was having a surprising effect on his imagination.

The world slowed.

He felt a dryness in his mouth, a bead of sweat on his neck.

Watching this woman move, this shiny-skinned, slender woman surrounded by several half-naked boys mirroring her actions, Anthony realised it had been two weeks since he had seen a belly button, either on a screen or in real life, and he'd forgotten the magic of it. This belly button danced, and the hips either side of it danced too, shifting in a kind of symmetry. He wondered whether she'd been operated on. If she had, he didn't want to know about it. She was singing to him, *at* him, her fingers making a *c'mere* signal, a cheeky smile on her face which looked entirely spontaneous and gave Anthony a tingling feeling he wanted to bottle and keep. (In reality, the woman had been required to offer up said smile, for hours at a time, on several separate shooting days. During the filming of the video, her fourteenth, she'd reproduced it repeatedly as if she'd just received some fabulous news. She did this in nine different costumes. She did it in three locations. And it was all a bit much actually. In a private moment with her PA, she complained that all this posing and pouting made her feel *more like a whore than an artist* and said that from now on she was going to take more charge of her own career. Her next record was going to be a concept album in Spanish about her ancestors.)

The news the woman in the video was pretending to be so delighted about was unclear, though Anthony imagined she'd received a passport in the post. He laughed inwardly at this, then stopped because actually, he had no one to share to share the joke with, and *she* was the one in the television, while he was an oven salesman sitting in a bar looking at her virtual stomach. (He looked.) In that moment Anthony realised, with another jolt, that he would probably leave Caragh if he believed he had a realistic chance of licking that stomach, just once. He wondered what else he was capable of. Then he wondered if, armed with this new self-knowledge, he'd ever be able to return to his quiet suburban marriage. Meanwhile, the woman's hips continued to shimmy, surrounded by members of her large and supportive local community, all partying like actually, it was fine. There were no problems. Isabella (he called her Isabella) looked perfectly happy on Planet Latina. Anthony couldn't imagine why she'd want to leave, and began to wonder whether Barry had really visited this place at all. He thought: where was his fucking beer?

Just then, the camera cut away to a muscle-bound black man delivering his lines at the camera. (He was conscious of registering the man in the screen as 'black' rather than as just a man. It was the kind of thing Caragh, whose father was Jamaican and prided herself on her Caribbean roots, criticised him for.) It looked like this man was rapping, but Anthony was now worried: perhaps that too was a racially-based assumption. (It wasn't. The man was actually rapping.) Then the video cut back to Isabella again. And then back to the man. He'd clearly invested a fair chunk of his life in a gym, this man, and acted like he had no outer body confidence issues. Isabella had spent time in the gym too, lots of it, and also looked supremely confident, though obviously, Caragh told her husband, *all* women had body issues of some sort, no matter how apparently carefree their shimmying hips. It was just a case of how well they hid it. On this screen, now: female belly button, male chest. Belly button. Chest. Belly button. Chest. Then a wide shot of the sea. Then Anthony's beer finally arrived, a cool wet bottle which somehow seemed luxurious. The waiter presented both items to him just like he'd taken the order, as if really he wasn't a waiter at all. Anthony didn't see this but he sensed it as he watched the screen, wondering for a moment whether there was some arrangement, some understanding, between workers and customers here that he hadn't quite worked out yet. (Yes, there was. And no, he hadn't worked it out.)

The thought passed.

He was back on Planet Latina.

The narrative of the music video had moved on since the arrival of Anthony's beer mere seconds ago. What first appeared to be a simple party duet was now developing into something more like a mini romantic drama. In one shot Isabella jumped onto the back of a motorbike, holding onto a strange waist, a different one to the one she was sharing the song with. She was then at a beach party, near some expensive cars, while the biker rode alone, clearly distracted. Then she was back in the city, getting changed in the street into leather boots and then they were together again, the couple, in a tight clutch, as if they loved each other, faithfully and deeply, and knew they always would. They kissed. It looked convincing. (When introduced on set, the two actors disliked each other instantly. Isabella told her agent she'd rather die than risk disease touching this individual – she'd heard he was a womanizer whose conquests numbered in the thousands. The man considered changing his agent. He'd done proper acting work now, he wasn't just a model, and was conscious of the imbalance of his CV. But they were professionals, the two of them, and they got on with it. Besides, they were both attractive. And in the end, kissing each other was easier than expected.)

After the clutch, the motorbike rode into the distance with both of them on it.

Anthony sipped his beer. It tasted good. He looked around the bar, but not for long. His surroundings seemed less interesting now.

In the next segment of the song, the climax perhaps, Isabella looked like she was in yet more mini-scenes with *lots* of men who were perhaps the same one but perhaps not. None of them seemed to be related to the rapper, who was now a less regular fixture on screen. (This was not explained.) Anthony thought: what was the message of this video? Perhaps simply that Isabella from Planet Latina was very sexy, and very horny, and potentially yours. You, the viewer. Perhaps the point was that, as a star and therefore public property, she belonged to *everyone*, really, even the guy performing the song with her – though surely no one seriously believed that, outside of the mere fact of celebrity, these two had a single thing in common. They lacked screen chemistry. (For starters, they appeared to have filmed their parts on different continents.) Anthony, who was given to outbursts of indignation about small issues he felt represented bigger ones, had a thought that made him feel drunk, even

↣

though he was still on his first beer. This song, he thought to himself. The existence of it. It stank of strategy. Straddling two international markets by gluing together bankable names who'd open up crossover potential to the other. The song was irrelevant. The hip-shimmying was a cynical ruse, to hypnotise. Anthony pictured the board meeting where the idea was hatched, and was disgusted. The screen cut back to dancing at the beach, with plenty of zoomed-in torso action. Specifically, zoomed-in hip action.

These hips were getting a lot of screen time, but despite his disgust, Anthony was prepared to tolerate them a little longer. (He had now entirely forgotten what country he was from, also that he was sitting in a small bar in a minor town on the coast of North Africa. He had even forgotten, briefly, that he was married to a woman he deeply loved, and was a really rather successful, passably attractive oven salesman attached to a medium-sized firm making serious inroads in a country where it was possible to purchase an oven at midnight.) Anthony thought: what did it matter anyway, all this? What did it matter if he stared a while? He couldn't be blamed for watching one of these many screens in a context where, let's face it, there was fuck all else to do except watch screens. This bar, as far as he could see, had been specifically designed so men like him could sit in booths and watch hips jutting, grinding, bouncing and swaying harmlessly in the ether until they were ready to go home. (The men, not the hips.) Besides, this singer, the one responsible for this virtual strip show, this singer was probably a millionaire. She probably had a handsome singer husband who probably also kissed strangers on screen for a living and mimed along to songs written by others. So really, where was *his* crime? Also, it had to be said, these were exceptional, mesmerising hips. Astonishing hips. The hips of a Goddess. Skin wrapped tight at the bone on either side but with just enough wobble at the belly, the tiniest fragment of wobble, to hold the attention of any viewer regardless of age, nationality or sexual preference. The hips on this screen in front of him, he realised in a moment of unusual, startling clarity (he was often confused), had the perfect combination of tautness and wobble. Surely even Caragh – a woman who prided herself on her intimate knowledge of the physical defects of famous people – a woman whose manic displeasure at the sight of other female bodies was almost pathological – surely even *she* could understand that. (He thought: he wanted to call her. It was her smell he missed the most. And the way she cuddled into his back at night.)

As the thought of Caragh's unique smell drifted out of his consciousness and the contents of the video drifted back in, imagination began to take him elsewhere. He thought that, really, these hips were hips to finally crack the Middle East peace process. To unite the fucking world, you know? When you considered the issue properly, these hips (he looked), these hips, and all hips like them – or even not like them at all! – were, essentially (he kept looking), all of human history. Perfected. Sculpted. *Condensed.* They were the *universe*, these hips. They were the *reason* for the universe – the reason human beings had not died out. Because, you know, people had looked at hips like that and been compelled to procreate. Was that not true? And if it *was* true, was that not a thing of incomparable beauty? (In the background, his soundtrack: more humming keyboards. More crashing strings and rapid tabla thumps.) Was it not his duty, as a living, breathing oven salesman every bit as essential to human history as anyone else, anywhere, ever – was it not his responsibility to admire these hips as you would admire Michelangelo's David or the Mona Lisa? (He'd seen both of these works of art on family holidays as a child, but was not impressed. Meanwhile his erection was now, at last, complete.) This idea, of these hips representing all of human history condensed, being the universe, the galaxy, the stars and Milky Way, the past, present and future of all experience, struck Anthony as tragic and deeply poetic. In his mind it was the answer to all questions, the question to all answers. As he thought, he realised this thought right here was possibly the only truly interesting or original or important thought of his life so far, the only one he might ever have, and he was overtaken by an urge to write the thought down before he forgot it. Which he knew he was likely to do. In fact, which he knew he was *certain* to do unless he got to a piece of paper and pen pretty fucking smartish. Anthony was not deluded. He knew his limitations, he knew he was basically just an idiot, and knew it was just a matter of time before this mind-altering, world-changing realisation flew out of his brain forever. In the following seconds he looked frantically in his rucksack, which was now no longer hidden from view. (That pretence was long gone.)

He found paper easily enough but could not find a pen.

The video ended.

As he looked for the pen, a new video began. This one was filmed live at a concert, featuring another impossible, unattainable, possibly surgically-enhanced Arabic version of Isabella, only wearing a less revealing outfit. Despite showing less leg, she was somehow more alluring.

As it played, Anthony noticed the waiter who had served him the crêpe swaggering past in the direction of the toilet, wearing a shirt very similar to his own. The waiter nodded in acknowledgement, but with a new confidence. Perhaps he was smirking. (He was not.) This thought troubled Anthony. Perhaps he was being laughed at. (He was not. Simply by *being* in the *High Flyer Brasserie*, he'd gone up in the crêpe waiter's estimations. Besides, the crêpe waiter was a nice guy and often smiled for no reason.) Anthony stopped. He went back to looking in the rucksack. He wondered what he was looking for. And then, through no fault of anyone's – neither his nor Isabella's nor the crêpe waiter's nor anyone else's – the thought about the galaxy was gone. It arrived without warning and left the same way. Anthony mourned the loss. Already, he missed the magical hips from Planet Latina, and the poetry contained within them – whatever it was – which was now gone forever.

His erection subsided.

He wanted to leave.

He looked around once more, wondering whether maybe there was only one place like this in town because everyone else was perfectly happy with life here, and maybe they didn't need any more *High Flyer*–style brasseries. Maybe there was only just enough custom for one.

At this moment Anthony really wanted to phone Caragh, who he really did love, he always had – he felt like calling her and trying to explain all about this evening he was having, these few minutes of discovery and loss which were probably changing him in ways he didn't even understand but *she* probably *would* understand because she knew him better than he knew himself. He was desperate to phone and say he missed what she smelled like. (She would consider the comment odd and ask him if anything was wrong.) But he was powerless. He couldn't. He was alone with these thoughts because tonight she was with a friend, and rules had been clearly laid out. She'd warned him that her phone would be off, all night, because the friend's husband had just left her for some penniless Ecuadorian twenty-something slut who was clearly just chasing a passport, they were having a girls night in, just the two of them and several bottles of wine, and the last thing the suffering friend needed was for a *man* to call during the conversation and remind her that the woman consoling her, the one telling her she was right there sharing the anguish and that it was all going to be okay, the last thing this poor friend needed was a blatant reminder that this *consoling* friend was actually perfectly happy in her relationship thankyouverymuch, and that, at the end of the night, after the compulsory drunken hugs and declarations of eternal friendship and statements like *all men are bastards, who needs them*, and the heartfelt appreciation for such a special night which she was convinced would really help her *pull through this difficult time*, the last thing this poor lonely woman the wrong side of thirty-five needed was the knowledge that the person who appeared to be right there with her in the struggle was now free to go home, kick off her shoes and text her husband to tell him how proud she was of him working so far from home, all alone,

➳

selling ovens to provide for their future. This desperate, lonely woman would not want to be reminded that her friend was probably going to message her loyal, adoring husband from bed that very night, in cutesy text-speak, to say that as soon as he returned she was going to reward him for his responsible behaviour by fucking his socks right off.

Now would she?

Desperate though he was, when it was put that way, Anthony understood why he couldn't phone home. And it was just this kind of thinking ahead regarding the phone situation, this attention to small practical details, the caring for others, which was typical of Caragh. As he considered this he held his beer tight and went numb around the toes, just as he had done the day they'd met at Barry's garden barbeque, the day when the storm came so quickly that they'd all had to run inside, already soaked by the time they made it to cover, each holding bowls of damp salad and smiling natural smiles. Anthony felt a pull on his cheek muscles and noticed he was smiling now too. He looked forward to going home and kissing Caragh's belly button. This desire was the only thought left in his head as he sipped some more of his beer. (Though the reason for it escaped him.)

Just then, as quickly as he'd been taken over moments before, Anthony's attention was stolen by something moving at the door of the bar. A stranger, a tourist perhaps, one hand pressed over her forehead, looking through the thick glass door, just as he had a few minutes ago. She peered inside, perhaps to see what kind of place this was. The tourist was looking at the screen, then the bar, then the seating area. She appeared to recognise something. Then Anthony smiled, gesturing for the stranger to come inside. It was okay, he seemed to be saying. In here, in the *High Flyer Brasserie*, everything was okay.

Let's Buy a Keyring So We Can Remember This Forever

Anneliese Mackintosh

HER NAKED BODY reminded me of my dead father.

Yellowing mouth.

Bruises along the arms.

Pinpricks.

Scabs.

But the way she moved: that was something else. Slow, cranky, hips groaning from side to side.

I lifted a hand to the glass, wondering if she'd raise her palm level with mine.

She didn't.

Instead, her wide black pupils flicked towards me. A sharp tongue ran across her lips. After a few seconds, minutes, maybe hours, she jerked to one side. Then she bent her knees, put her hands on her hips, and wrenched out her chest. Lank, black hair hung down her back in ropes. Medusa.

One, thick scar ran from her hip to her left nipple.

You want some, baby?

She might have said that: her lips had shuddered. They might have said anything. Or nothing. How could I tell? A pane of glass cut between us.

'Hannah! You coming?'

Rob's voice. Rob was here. Where were we?

'Hannah, it's rude to stare. Come on.'

Goodbye, my lips shuddered, then I walked away from the window.

Every window was different. The girls were fat, thin, brown, white, ugly – and some, some were beautiful. They sat, sprawled, and squirmed. Beckoned, smiled, and pouted. But none of them was quite like my Medusa girl.

'I thought we could check out the Condomerie,' said Rob. 'Be a bit of a giggle. Apparently they do over three-hundred types of—'

'Okay,' I shrugged. 'Let's do it.'

Rob ran his fingers over the map. 'Let's see... We're here... And we need to be there...'

I pointed to a cobbled street ahead. 'It's *that* way.' The thought of having to listen to Rob make a complete hash of Amsterdam's intricate streets one more time was giving me sinus ache.

'Oh. Right.' He folded up the map, neatly and precisely into exact sixths, and put it safely in the pocket of his 50-tog all-terrain anorak. Then his fingers reached for mine.

I was shocked at how clammy my hands were. 'I need some gloves.'

'Don't think they sell that sort of *glove* where we're going.' Rob choked out a laugh, so I choked one back.

As we headed down the cobbled street, we passed a shop window chock-full of cuddly toys. Hundreds of neon-pink teddy bears: each one with a big, furry, teddy-erection. A sign above them read: TEDDY BEAR'S DICKNIC.

Rob stopped and took a picture on his iPhone. 'Classic,' he grinned.

I hurried ahead and feigned surprise. 'Oh look, here it is.'

The shop hadn't changed. In the window was the same row of condoms, pegged on a line

➻

like dirty socks.

A supersized woman in a baseball cap shuffled out of the door. 'Well, honey,' she called behind her, 'that was real swell. Now let's go get somethin' t'eat.'

A skeletal man in a baseball cap trailed after her. In his hand was a bulging carrier bag. 'I thoughtcha wanted to go back to that there Souvenir Shop first, honey?' he puffed. 'Get that keyring you liked? This is your last chance before we head to the airport.'

I didn't hear the woman's answer, but I hoped that she did go back for that keyring. How else would she remember Amsterdam? Those condoms would get used up, if she was lucky, and all that nice holiday food wasn't coming back – well, not in a way you'd want to keep on your mantelpiece, anyway. A keyring on the other hand – a keyring lasts. Every time you open the door to your same-old home back in your same-old town, you'll remember the time you were abroad, having a real swell time in a Red Light District.

'You're daydreaming again.' Rob dragged me into the shop.

The condoms came in every shape and colour and flavour imaginable. They came looking like animals and people and vehicles and buildings, and they came with spots and spikes and hard bits and soft bits. All very safe and clean and tourist-friendly. I couldn't tell you if they were the same styles as the ones I'd seen here two years back. I didn't care much then, and I cared even less now.

It was near impossible to connect this Disneyfied nonsense with what I'd just witnessed a street and a half earlier. I couldn't help wondering if my Medusa girl had ever been pumped with a rubberised version of Snow White or Santa Claus or Dr. Zeus. Or if, at five euros a pop, these johnnies were too precious to waste on Red Light pussy.

For my ninth birthday I got a Cindy doll. She wore a pink meringue dress. The sort of dress that, if she were real, and it was still the eighties, she would wear to her high school prom. The sort of dress that, if she were real now, would make her look like one of those perfectly pretty but perfectly insane girls, with pencil-thin arms covered in magic-marker-thick scars.

Anyway, to a nine year-old, Cindy's look was aspirational. She wasn't as skinny as her cousin Barbie, whose waist was about twenty times smaller than her tits, and whose feet were stuck in eternal tiptoes, making high-heels her only option. No. Cindy had flat feet. She had a sturdy waist and believable breasts.

For my tenth birthday I got another doll: Paul. He had white teeth, bendable arms, and a shiny jacket. And he came with a miniature chocolate box. Ready-made romance.

I remember the moment Paul and Cindy first met. I made Paul walk up to Cindy, nice and slow. 'For you,' he said, in a deep, sexy voice, holding out the chocolates. 'Thank you,' Cindy simpered. She gazed into Paul's eyes. He gazed into hers.

Eventually, I laid the box of chocolates down on the carpet. I undid the zip on Cindy's dress and pulled it carefully over her head. I took off her tiny, flat shoes. Next, I peeled away Paul's shiny jacket, and pulled down his all-in-one-shirt-and-trouser-suit. I took off his tiny, flat shoes.

I held their bodies close together.

I made them move their heads around and kiss like movie stars.

Then I let Paul fall to the floor.

Somehow, I realised, having Paul there was making me love Cindy less. I took Cindy in both hands now, gazing at her plastic curves, wondering if one day this is what my nipples would grow into. With a small shiver, I lifted Cindy to my mouth, and held one of her curves between my teeth.

Back at the hotel, I slumped on the bed with a magazine while Rob had a shower. I was exhausted. We must have biked our way around half of Amsterdam.

I wasn't really reading the magazine; just staring at the pictures. I wondered how I would look on those glossy pages. If anyone would notice me in there. See that something wasn't right, that one of the women in there wasn't a proper model. It'd be like a game of *Where's Wally?* Or: *Spot the odd-one-out in today's LOOK magazine and win a holiday to Ibiza!*

Of course people would notice. I was five foot four. The muscle on my upper arms was turning to flab, and I had too many freckles. My hair kinked in weird places, even with straighteners, and I had permanently tired eyes.

I stared at a page consisting entirely of photographs of handbags and wondered what was in store for tonight. Rob wanted to get stoned and then eat one of those twenty-course Indonesian meals we'd seen advertised everywhere. I had one of those when I was last here, and then spent the next few hours curled up into a ball. Just me, my irritable bowels, and a world of pain.

But Rob wasn't to know I'd been here before. Nobody knew, actually. Two years ago, shortly after the death of my father, I pulled a sickie. Took three days off work and flew out here on a whim. No reason in particular, other than it was the cheapest holiday in Thomas Cook's window. Since the very first section of my tourist guide was about the Red Light District, that's where I went first.

I'd never thought about doing anything like that before.

But two live sex shows later, and I was a changed woman. I felt sensations inside me that until then I'd never known. I started using strings of dirty words. Especially all those delicious 'c' words. Cocks. Cum. Cunts. Only ever in my head, mind. I never said words like that out loud, but it burnt me up inside to *think filthy*.

'Phew, that feels better,' breathed Rob, wrapped up in the hotel's not-so-fluffy, not-so-white towels. 'Hannah,' he said suddenly. 'Are you feeling...?'

I grew aware of myself. Lying on my back, hands in my pants, with the problem pages lying open beside me.

Rob whipped off his towel.

I pushed my fingers deeper into myself and waited.

His cock began to twitch, then with one sharp spasm it yanked upright. A big pink erection, just like the ones on the teddy bears in the shop window.

Rob was quicker at the draw than any man I'd ever known.

And I'd known a few in the past two years.

'You look hot, babe,' he gasped. He almost fell on top of me, his prick nudging at my knickers.

Eventually, I took out my fingers and pulled down my pants.

'Oh, hang on a minute.' He jumped off the bed and knelt on the floor. I heard the rustle of plastic, then another sound: like a lid peeling back. It couldn't be, could it? Oh God, no. Not a chocolate box.

'Ta da!' he shouted. 'What do you think?' On the tip of his penis was a bright green crocodile. Its beady eyes were looking straight at me. 'I bought it when you weren't looking.'

'It's great,' I told him, then closed my eyes and let him in.

'Oh, fuck,' he groaned. Sex was the only time Rob ever swore. The rest of the time he was all 'sugar' and 'fiddlesticks' with the occasional 'damn', but only when he was *very* pissed off.

As I said, I'd never said a rude word out loud before. Not even during sex. Actually, I didn't make any noise during sex. I just moved quietly and obediently in rhythm with my partner, and sometimes let my eyes roll back.

'Fucking hell!' shouted Rob, pushing frantically inside me. Then he stopped and groaned.

Rob was quicker on *that* too than any other man I'd ever known.

'Oh babe,' he panted, pulling out painfully quickly and lying next to me. 'You turn me on *so much*.'

I pulled up my pants. The crocodile had hurt me. I think it might have been for novelty purposes only. 'Yes,' I murmured, running my thumb along one of his bendable arms. 'You too, Paul.'

The next day we took a wrong turn at the park and ended up spending three hours longer on our bikes than we meant to. By the time we got to the Anne Frank house our day had almost disappeared. This particularly annoyed me, since I'd never made it here on my last visit. After forty-five minutes of queuing, I practically ran up to the attic.

Anne Frank's bedroom.

I spent as long as I possibly could in there, ignoring Rob's whining, and only leaving when it was time for the museum to shut.

Imagine being cooped up somewhere like this, I kept thinking. Imagine having to be so still, so quiet. Imagine the strange, secret thoughts you'd keep inside you before sleep.

Locked away from the world. No windows.

When we left, I bought a keyring so I'd never forget it there.

I haven't forgotten it.

I haven't forgotten about my Medusa girl, either. Now, in my dreams, I refer to her as Anne. Anne Frank with windows.

At night, when I put my fingers in my knickers, I'm never quite sure which Anne I'm thinking of. And I'm even less sure why thinking about either of them should make me feel the way I do.

Edwin Morgan's Funeral

Graham Fulton

Unable to go, I had to make do
with *The Herald* announcements,
2 days before.

Alphabetically placed on page 21 –
right in between ***McDOWALL*** – *ANNE*,
PRINGLE – *ROBERT*; a squash of print.
McDowall!
                Morgan!
                                Pringle!
I think
of starlings, Riddrie, gathering leaves.
A woman's piss on the mid-day ground.
The thought exists.
                The piss exists.

And now I'm on the train to Dumfries,
rattling past high flats, scaffolded walls.

Already I am moving out, leaving the ones
                who belong
behind —
The Poets in their Thursday best,
looking around to see who's there.
            A daft cow charging away from the sound.
      A telecom mast on an upland hill.
An aggregate truck on a south running road.
Barrhead!
            Kilmarnock!
                                Cumnock!
I think
of blue toboggans, snack-bar stairs;
a young man and his girl, instamatically,
falling backwards into a window.

The glass exists. The beauty exists.

The ticket inspector inspects what I have —
a Virtual black tie around my neck,
open return, valid for weeks. 26 August 2010.
The sun burns through over Auchinleck.

The Unemployable Poem

Dilys Rose

A poem is not a rabbit's foot, a comfort blanket, a keepsake.
It is not a cause, a religion, a key to the mystery of existence.
It is not a sedative, a barbiturate, a panacea, an antidote.
It is not a recipe, a prescription, an implicitly good thing.
It is not a party membership or clubcard, a secret handshake,
an access code, a form of prayer. It offers no guarantees, no reassurance
or insurance regarding life, death or the crumbling rock to which we cling.
Though it may contain patterned phrases on the play of light on water,
the awesome majesty of mountains, on loose ribbons of geese,
the resemblance between swallows and fighter jets, herons and stylites,
though it may transform fear or frailty into cadences beautiful or sublime,
though it may light up a dark day or draw the blinds on an abomination
this is not its job. A poem does not have a job. A poem is unemployable.
It is just a poem. Take it or leave it. Either way, it won't care.

Books I Have Burnt

James A Irvine

Rhyming Dictionary of the English Language
by J R Walker
Complete Idiot's Guide to Writing Poetry
by Nikki Moustaki
Rules for the Dance: A Handbook for Writing and Reading Metrical Verse
by Mary Oliver

Money Talks
Rodger Evans

The millionaire says we should all be brave and take the hit.
The billionaire says to which channels we must switch.
The zillionaire says he plans to give away most of it.
That's rich.

Rats
Gordon Meade

Here, everything runs on time. And here,
everything is clean. So much so, that a marriage
may be annulled if either the husband,

or his wife, should make it to the platform
a few seconds late. And a love affair may be over
if either the other man, or the other woman,

should forget to floss their teeth. And yet,
here, as everywhere else, there are rats. You can see
them watching, enviously, from the side

of the tracks. You can see them polishing
their teeth underneath the neon sign of the local pharmacy.
Or you can see them, as I did, on a summer's night,

in the middle of a city, strolling, unashamedly,
through a park, with one eye on the eighteenth century
palace, and the other on the main chance.

The Fall of Baghdad
Duncan Muir

Later we heard
you'd been in the hills
looking down on the city

pointing lasers
at warehouses, office blocks,
and homes.

You selected each structure
then waited,
the sound of breath

pushed close to your face,
until your scope, your eyes,
filled with fire.

Corruption

Colin Will

The water butt stank. Sure manure
betimes smells bad – know how
fetid retted comfrey gets?

This was worse. Think pigshit,
double it and add ammonia.
Ever been to a tannery?

Ever stood downwind
of a renderer? Abattoirs
are pine-fresh when compared,

but odour words are watery
components of our language.
Too often similes have to do.

This was, then, a Gothic concoction,
a multi-layered reek, symphonic
in complexity; feculence

and putrefaction the major themes,
and no relieving leitmotif—
really not nice.

The thought of sourcing
this noisesomeness
had us gagging,

but someone had to clean
the allotment's Augean stable.
Gingerly forking, I snagged

a weight and undrowned it.
A cat, black now but forever
unlucky, squelched out

on the straw by the shed
like a birth gone wrong.
Another swirl, just to make sure,

hooked a second stinker,
further down the line
to dissolution.

It took a long time
to trust the vegetables
watered from this whiffy barrel.

Ghazi

Larry Butler

: & I was alone in the dark
in a solitary cell
for days for months
beaten, tortured
but never subdued.

This is my first passport
I am British now
my children British
I belong here
I am happy living in Scotland –

In Syria they had identity cards, they were nobody,
didn't belong, in & out of prison
: Iran, Iraq, Israel, Jordan, Syria,
20 times maybe more

: & I was alone in the dark
in a solitary cell
for days for months
beaten, tortured
but not broken.

British now
but always a Palestinian
living in exile drinking
strong black coffee with cardamom
& a big phone bill talking
every week to his friends & family,
writing poems & plays in Arabic
translating into English –
it's better being British
speaking English & Scottish.
Holding high his purple passport:

UNITED KINGDOM OF
GREAT BRITAIN
AND NORTHERN IRELAND

Last week my daughter Hanin
was kicked out of school
for fighting racism,
that's what caused it,
she needs to learn not to hit.
My son Oudi watches too much telly –
cartoon myths about good & evil.

British now
but not with stiff-upper-lips,
they shop at Asda
ride the bus to Waverley
while eating fish & chips,
catch a train to Glasgow
for Survival Awareness Training.

Dusting the Dark
Olive M Ritch

In the dark times
Will there also be singing?
Bertolt Brecht ('Motto')

As if answering Brecht,
she sings,
singing about
dusting the dark.

Showa, Oppenheimer

JoAnne McKay

this bomb a necessity a necessity bomb the reason a cruel enemy
an enemy we the enemy bomb that enemy a job this new job a necessity
we employ a bomb the a bomb the reason necessity we did a job a new job because
it was a necessity to bomb a cruel enemy we the cruel enemy we bomb the organic we
we bomb the organic the new is the organic we bomb we employ reason to bomb the enemy
that cruel enemy that organic enemy to employ reason to bomb is cruel reason cruel reason bomb
new bomb a bomb that bomb this bomb a new bomb a bomb that bomb this bomb new bomb
we did this we begun this we did this we begun this we begun this necessity bomb
the necessity bomb the bomb to employ this new and most cruel bomb
the bomb the enemy to bomb the enemy the bomb the enemy
the a bomb the most bomb the most bomb the a bomb
necessity necessity necessity
the enemy has begun to
employ a new and
most cruel bomb
the reason that
we did this job is
because it was
an organic
necessity

The parable of the blind

Jim Carruth

How right it feels
to return at this time

to Brueghel
and to this painting

though his focus
on those rural beggars

shuffling in line
to their destiny

penniless and dirty
being led by the trust

in an others' shoulder
or a long stick

seems somehow
less relevant

and the numbers
are all wrong

not six in their own
private dark

nor six hundred
six thousand

not even six billion
falling,

falling

falling.

Forbidden Texts from the Former GDR

Susan Kemp and Fiona Rintoul

Samizdat – a Russian word – roughly translates as self-publishing. For writers in the former Soviet bloc countries who wanted to write what they really thought, self publishing, *Samizdat*, was often the only option. Banned books – and books that had been published but which displeased the authorities and were therefore almost impossible to find in bookshops – were laboriously copied and distributed from person to person.

In the 1970s and 1980s a series of underground literary magazines started to appear in the former GDR. The magazines were produced by hand. Each writer or artist asked supplied the number of copies of their work required for the print run. Because of this labour-intensive production process, no more than about 20 copies of each issue of a magazine were usually made, though the readership was of course much larger. Often, writers and artists worked closely together, with the writers responding to the artworks in their texts.

Today, the surviving copies of these *Samizdat* magazines are both beautiful hand-created objects and a fascinating document of a vanished state. The GDR is unique among the former Ostbloc countries in that it simply disappeared after the Berlin Wall fell in 1989, being subsumed into the Federal Republic of Germany. These magazines provide a record of a rich artistic life lived behind what the old GDR regime used to call (without a trace of irony) the 'Anti-Fascist Protection Wall'.

The magazines are attracting increasing attention now that, with the benefit of distance, the history of the former GDR is being ever more intensively explored. And to celebrate a special strand at this year's Glasgow Film Festival focusing on banned films from the former GDR – entitled 'The Stasi are among us: film censorship in the former GDR' – *Gutter* has reproduced some pages from East German *Samizdat* magazines. Two texts, by the writers Gabriele Stötzer and Johannes Jansen, are here translated into English for the first time, and appear in this issue of *Gutter* alongside contemporary writing set in the former GDR: a second novel extract from Fiona Rintoul's *Leipzig*, and, for the first time, some creative non-fiction from Arthur Ker.

FLUGSCHUTT

OKTOBER 198

```
PQR]¤*);^¬/STUVWXYZ|,%¯>?0123456789:#@'=" ABCDEFGHI[,<(+|&JKLMNOPQR]¤*);^¬
PQR]¤*);^¬/STUVWXYZ|,%¯>?0123456789:#@'=" ABCDEFGHI[,<(+|&JKLMNOPQR]¤*);^¬/
R]¤*);^¬/STUVWXYZ|,%¯>?0123456789:#@'=" ABCDEFGHI[,<(+|&JKLMNOPQR]¤*);^¬/
]¤*);^¬/STUVWXYZ|,%¯>?0123456789:#@'=" ABCDEFGHI[,<(+|&JKLMNOPQR]¤*);^¬/S
¤*);^¬/STUVWXYZ|,%¯>?0123456789:#@'=" ABCDEFGHI[,<(+|&JKLMNOPQR]¤*);^¬/ST
*);^¬/STUVWXYZ|,%¯>?0123456789:#@'=" ABCDEFGHI[,<(+|&JKLMNOPQR]¤*);^¬/STU
);^¬/STUVWXYZ|,%¯>?0123456789:#@'=" ABCDEFGHI[,<(+|&JKLMNOPQR]¤*);^¬/STUV
;^¬/STUVWXYZ|,%¯>?0123456789:#@'=" ABCDEFGHI[,<(+|&JKLMNOPQR]¤*);^¬/STUVW
^¬/STUVWXYZ|,%¯>?0123456789:#@'=" ABCDEFGHI[,<(+|&JKLMNOPQR]¤*);^¬/STUVWX
¬/STUVWXYZ|,%¯>?0123456789:#@'=" ABCDEFGHI[,<(+|&JKLMNOPQR]¤*);^¬/STUVWXY
/STUVWXYZ|,%¯>?0123456789:#@'=" ABCDEFGHI[,<(+|&JKLMNOPQR]¤*);^¬/STUVWXYZ|
|&JKLMNOPQR]¤*);^¬/STUVWXYZ|,%¯>?0123456789:#@'=" ABCDEFGHI[,<(+|&JKLMNOPQ
&JKLMNOPQR]¤*);^¬/STUVWXYZ|,%¯>?0123456789:#@'=" ABCDEFGHI[,<(+|&JKLMNOPQR
JKLMNOPQR]¤*);^¬/STUVWXYZ|,%¯>?0123456789:#@'=" ABCDEFGHI[,<(+|&JKLMNOPQR]
KLMNOPQR]¤*);^¬/STUVWXYZ|,%¯>?0123456789:#@'=" ABCDEFGHI[,<(+|&JKLMNOPQR]¤
LMNOPQR]¤*);^¬/STUVWXYZ|,%¯>?0123456789:#@'=" ABCDEFGHI[,<(+|&JKLMNOPQR]¤*
MNOPQR]¤*);^¬/STUVWXYZ|,%¯>?0123456789:#@'=" ABCDEFGHI[,<(+|&JKLMNOPQR]¤*)
NOPQR]¤*);^¬/STUVWXYZ|,%¯>?0123456789:#@'=" ABCDEFGHI[,<(+|&JKLMNOPQR]¤*);
PQR]¤*);^¬/STUVWXYZ|,%¯>?0123456789:#@'=" ABCDEFGHI[,<(+|&JKLMNOPQR]¤*);^
QR]¤*);^¬/STUVWXYZ|,%¯>?0123456789:#@'=" ABCDEFGHI[,<(+|&JKLMNOPQR]¤*);^¬
R]¤*);^¬/STUVWXYZ|,%¯>?0123456789:#@'=" ABCDEFGHI[,<(+|&JKLMNOPQR]¤*);^¬/
]¤*);^¬/STUVWXYZ|,%¯>?0123456789:#@'=" ABCDEFGHI[,<(+|&JKLMNOPQR]¤*);^¬/S
¤*);^¬/STUVWXYZ|,%¯>?0123456789:#@'=" ABCDEFGHI[,<(+|&JKLMNOPQR]¤*);^¬/ST
*);^¬/STUVWXYZ|,%¯>?0123456789:#@'=" ABCDEFGHI[,<(+|&JKLMNOPQR]¤*);^¬/STU
);^¬/STUVWXYZ|,%¯>?0123456789:#@'=" ABCDEFGHI[,<(+|&JKLMNOPQR]¤*);^¬/STUV
;^¬/STUVWXYZ|,%¯>?0123456789:#@'=" ABCDEFGHI[,<(+|&JKLMNOPQR]¤*);^¬/STUVW
^¬/STUVWXYZ|,%¯>?0123456789:#@'=" ABCDEFGHI[,<(+|&JKLMNOPQR]¤*);^¬/STUVWX
¬/STUVWXYZ|,%¯>?0123456789:#@'=" ABCDEFGHI[,<(+|&JKLMNOPQR]¤*);^¬/STUVWXY
/STUVWXYZ|,%¯>?0123456789:#@'=" ABCDEFGHI[,<(+|&JKLMNOPQR]¤*);^¬/STUVWXYZ|
STUVWXYZ|,%¯>?0123456789:#@'=" ABCDEFGHI[,<(+|&JKLMNOPQR]¤*);^¬/STUVWXYZ|,
|&JKLMNOPQR]¤*);^¬/STUVWXYZ|,%¯>?0123456789:#@'=" ABCDEFGHI[,<(+|&JKLMNOPQ
&JKLMNOPQR]¤*);^¬/STUVWXYZ|,%¯>?0123456789:#@'=" ABCDEFGHI[,<(+|&JKLMNOPQR
JKLMNOPQR]¤*);^¬/STUVWXYZ|,%¯>?0123456789:#@'=" ABCDEFGHI[,<(+|&JKLMNOPQR]
KLMNOPQR]¤*);^¬/STUVWXYZ|,%¯>?0123456789:#@'=" ABCDEFGHI[,<(+|&JKLMNOPQR]¤
LMNOPQR]¤*);^¬/STUVWXYZ|,%¯>?0123456789:#@'=" ABCDEFGHI[,<(+|&JKLMNOPQR]¤*
MNOPQR]¤*);^¬/STUVWXYZ|,%¯>?0123456789:#@'=" ABCDEFGHI[,<(+|&JKLMNOPQR]¤*)
NOPQR]¤*);^¬/STUVWXYZ|,%¯>?0123456789:#@'=" ABCDEFGHI[,<(+|&JKLMNOPQR]¤*);
PQR]¤*);^¬/STUVWXYZ|,%¯>?0123456789:#@'=" ABCDEFGHI[,<(+|&JKLMNOPQR]¤*);^
QR]¤*);^¬/STUVWXYZ|,%¯>?0123456789:#@'=" ABCDEFGHI[,<(+|&JKLMNOPQR]¤*);^¬
R]¤*);^¬/STUVWXYZ|,%¯>?0123456789:#@'=" ABCDEFGHI[,<(+|&JKLMNOPQR]¤*);^¬/
]¤*);^¬/STUVWXYZ|,%¯>?0123456789:#@'=" ABCDEFGHI[,<(+|&JKLMNOPQR]¤*);^¬/S
¤*);^¬/STUVWXYZ|,%¯>?0123456789:#@'=" ABCDEFGHI[,<(+|&JKLMNOPQR]¤*);^¬/ST
*);^¬/STUVWXYZ|,%¯>?0123456789:#@'=" ABCDEFGHI[,<(+|&JKLMNOPQR]¤*);^¬/STU
);^¬/STUVWXYZ|,%¯>?0123456789:#@'=" ABCDEFGHI[,<(+|&JKLMNOPQR]¤*);^¬/STUV
;^¬/STUVWXYZ|,%¯>?0123456789:#@'=" ABCDEFGHI[,<(+|&JKLMNOPQR]¤*);^¬/STUVW
^¬/STUVWXYZ|,%¯>?0123456789:#@'=" ABCDEFGHI[,<(+|&JKLMNOPQR]¤*);^¬/STUVWX
¬/STUVWXYZ|,%¯>?0123456789:#@'=" ABCDEFGHI[,<(+|&JKLMNOPQR]¤*);^¬/STUVWXY
/STUVWXYZ|,%¯>?0123456789:#@'=" ABCDEFGHI[,<(+|&JKLMNOPQR]¤*);^¬/STUVWXYZ
|&JKLMNOPQR]¤*);^¬/STUVWXYZ|,%¯>?0123456789:#@'=" ABCDEFGHI[,<(+|&JKLMNOPQ
&JKLMNOPQR]¤*);^¬/STUVWXYZ|,%¯>?0123456789:#@'=" ABCDEFGHI[,<(+|&JKLMNOPQR
JKLMNOPQR]¤*);^¬/STUVWXYZ|,%¯>?0123456789:#@'=" ABCDEFGHI[,<(+|&JKLMNOPQR]
]¤*);^¬/STUVWXYZ|,%¯>?0123456789:#@'=" ABCDEFGHI[,<(+|&JKLMNOPQR]¤
¤*);^¬/STUVWXYZ|,%¯>?0123456789:#@'=" ABCDEFGHI[,<(+|&JKLMNOPQR]¤*
*);^¬/STUVWXYZ|,%¯>?0123456789:#@'=" ABCDEFGHI[,<(+|&JKLMNOPQR]¤*)
);^¬/STUVWXYZ|,%¯>?0123456789:#@'=" ABCDEFGHI[,<(+|&JK
;^¬/STUVWXYZ|,%¯>?0123456789:#@'=" ABCDEFGHI[,<(+|&JKLMNOPQR]¤*);
^¬/STUVWXYZ|,%¯>?0123456789:#@'=" ABCDEFGHI[,<(+|&JKLMNOPQR]¤*);^¬/
```

!!!! UND!!!!UND!!!! Nr. 12 / XXX Oktober 19hunde

```
STUVWXYZ|,%¯>?0123456789:#@'=" ABCDEFGHI[,<(+|&JKLMNOPQR]¤*);^¬/ST
/STUVWXYZ|,%¯>?0123456789:#@'=" ABCDEFGHI[,<(+|&JKLMNOPQR]¤*);^¬/STU
¬/STUVWXYZ|,%¯>?0123456789:#@'=" ABCDEFGHI[,<(+|&JKLMNOPQR]¤*);^¬/STUV
^¬/STUVWXYZ|,%¯>?0123456789:#@'=" ABCDEFGHI[,<(+|&JKLMNOPQR]¤*);^¬/STUVW
;^¬/STUVWXYZ|,%¯>?0123456789:#@'=" ABCDEFGHI[,<(+|&JKLMNOPQR]¤*);^¬/STUVWX
);^¬/STUVWXYZ|,%¯>?0123456789:#@'=" ABCDEFGHI[,<(+|&JKLMNOPQR]¤*);^¬/STUV
```

Gangart zwei (Richtung Schönhauser Allee)

Mögliche Richtungen
Zwischen Schiene und Strang
Gehst du
Vom Ausgangspunkt
Zum Ausgangspunkt
Mit der Entfernung
Nimmt deine Größe zu
Und ein Wort
Gibt das andere
Das Gangbare
Auf der Landkarte
Die Sternenhimmel heißt
Hast du
Weiter nichts
Weiter oben
Faltest du die Zeitung
Siehst du
Unter dem Graugrün
Die Wurzeln
Unter dem Gelb
Das Fleisch
Unter den Pflastersteinen
Den Strand
Unter den Wörtern
Die Hast

Im Schritt
Den abgehaunen Fuß
Wir reden davon machen
Mit der Sofortbildcamera
Ein Loch in die Landschaft
Es ist weiß
Wie der Tag
Und einfach
Wie die Vergangenheit
Perfekt war
Im Buch
Unter dem Schrank
Der Staub die Stadt
In der Mitte
Richtung Schönhauser Allee
Mit der S-Bahn zur rechten
Ein Stück
Verrostete Brücke

Berlin Marz April 85

Ways of Walking II (Destination Schönhauser Allee)

Johannes Jansen

Possible directions
Between rails and rope
You walk
From starting point
To starting point
With distance
You increase in size
And one word
Leads to another
What's walkable
On the map
That's called the starry sky
You still
Have nothing further
Further up
You fold the newspaper
You see
The roots
Beneath the grey-green
The flesh
Beneath the yellow
The beach
Beneath the paving stones
The haste
Beneath the words
The chopped-off foot
In the step
We talk about it make
A hole in the landscape
With the Polaroid camera
It's white
Like the day
And simple
Like the past
Was perfect
In the book
Beneath the cupboard
The dust the city
In the centre
Destination Schönhauser Allee
With the S-Bahn on the right
A piece
Of rusted bridge

Extract from literary magazine *UND!*
Gabriele Stötzer

The die is cast.
The cards are dealt.
The bell has rung,
the game is in progress, all bets are off.

Tamara Reinhard is standing in front of me in a dream, saying: I wouldn't have done it again (she's talking about her brother; he was in jail). I don't know where the boundaries lie between fun, pleasure, vanity and joy; naïvety is the starting point for every action. Euphoria washes over me; flight pushes the blindfold over my eyes; we take off in the blackest darkness; my outstretched arms don't feel the wind, but my legs bear no weight. We are flying in circles, constantly returning. The runway and landing strip fuse into one. Staying and leaving will, in the end, have amounted to the same thing. It was this path from the start; the coordinates cannot be changed now.

I won't have to run along behind. It'll catch up with me. Love is the slightest excuse and our only weak point. We always betray ourselves first. Naked chest, parted lips: they expect reciprocation, and we always hope that we will be able to free ourselves gently.

Experience is nothing more than always starting again.

To have arrived at the bottom and to have learnt nothing apart from discovering that everything comes round again. Present, past, future. Each moment is a melting point. And the person who says I today becomes a thing tomorrow, a case – political, criminal – that's one of the possibilities. Their peace is disturbed, their light is extinguished, their silencing shroud is spun from a thread of darkness.

To be silent and still act, to be silent and to act no more. To become this dark person who has unleashed their deepest, blackest desires on the world and therefore fills up the space.

We always betray ourselves first; we always recognize ourselves first, in symbols, words, moments of terror.

The iceberg has an underbelly. Not visible but finite. And it swims because it is melting.

Tracking Down the Skadocks

Arthur Ker

MY FATHER, ARTHUR Putschker, an ex German POW, died in 1988, the year before the fall of the Berlin Wall. He had lost all contact with his family around the time of its construction in 1961, and never, to my knowledge, made any serious attempt to find them again. It was a taboo subject in his later years.

A decade on, sorting through my mother's effects after her death, I uncovered a wallet of photographs from the fifties. They were of my father's uncle and aunt, Fritz and Grete Skadock, their children Erwin and Elli, and their grandchildren Hans-Peter and Hartmut. In October 2004, after years of procrastination, I set out with my daughter Verona to track down any surviving relatives in what had been the old GDR. We had no correspondence or addresses, our only clues as where to begin the search were the town names Stassfurt and Hecklingen stamped on the backs of the photographs.

18 October, Berlin. This morning Verona and I make it down to breakfast for about 8.15. We are confronted with a feast: muesli, cream, four flavours of yogurt, brambles, oats, almonds; followed by scrambled eggs, bacon, sausages, fried tomatoes; rounded off with breads, rolls and croissants. By the time we've finished sampling what's on offer, we can hardly get up from the table to help ourselves to more coffee.

I savour my second cup and watch a tiny middle-aged blonde woman in tight leather trousers tuck into a fry-up of Desperate Dan proportions. A worry that started niggling at the back of my mind last night as we taxied through the Berlin streets reappears and rapidly blooms into full-blown terror – I don't want to drive a hired car; at least not here in Berlin. Driving on the left is scary enough, but watching our taxi driver cut across four and six lane roundabouts at sixty miles an hour had my blood pressure soaring. My city driving is bad enough at home in Glasgow. I could never navigate my way across Berlin.

I confess my fear to Verona, hoping she'll spare me the scorn I deserve for being such a coward, and notice that she too is staring at the tiny frau in the lederhosen posting morsels of her massive fry-up between her perfectly painted lips.

'I'm amazed you even considered it,' she says, as the woman slices a sausage with near surgical precision. 'Ask at reception and see if they can give us any information about trains. We can hire a car in Stassfurt if we need one.'

An hour later, we're in the bustle of the Hauptbahnhof, running to catch the 11.22, which will get us to Stassfurt for 14.00. As we pull out of the station, we watch the buildings and streets glide past, followed after a time by sprawling, picture-book housing estates, then the functional retail and industrial parks that border all big cities. When we reach open country, it is featureless, flat as a billiard table, and strangely empty. We are headed deep into the old GDR, a country notorious for imprisoning and spying on its own people. Will we see any lasting effects of that regime fourteen years

➻

on from unification? The further south we go the more neglected the towns appear, and the people boarding the train look shabby as well, their clothes chosen for durability rather than style. Verona remarks that few of the kids wear recognised brands of trainers.

In Stassfurt we book a hotel through the tourist information office. They direct us, I suspect, to the most expensive in town – it's certainly the swankiest building and the first where we see any buzz of human activity. As young people enter and exit a door next to the reception, we can hear the trundle of bowling balls followed by the smack and clatter of pins being struck. Clearly, the bowling alley and the neighbouring pool and gym are *the* places to hang out in Stassfurt.

We check in, dump our cases in the room and go for a walk to get a feel of the town. The buildings are run down, and many of the shops are empty, as if half the population had suddenly upped and left. A constant stream of cars cruise the streets. As we make our way to the centre, Verona points out a white convertible and a customised vintage Beetle that she's certain have passed us three times. I start scanning the cars. She's right; a lot of them appear to be making endless loops of the town. Verona says it's like *The Truman Show*; they're only there to persuade us the town's real, and not a set in some weird German reality show. Down by the river there's a huge funfair. The stalls and rides are manned and open for business, but there isn't a soul about; the machinery of cheap thrills stands idle while coloured lights flash and chase round the gaudy signs. A fairground organ cranks out a cliché.

Before going back to the hotel, we drop in to Tourist Information again to see if they can offer any advice on where to start our search. In my basic German I manage to explain to the woman at the desk that we are looking for the descendants of Fritz and Grete Skadock who lived in Hecklingen, particularly their daughter Elli and her two sons who we think lived near her parents. The woman says she is from Hecklingen and tries the name Skadock in the computer. She pulls a blank expression and shakes her head. Nothing. I show her some of the photographs. She says if we leave the photos she'll take them home and ask her father who has lived in Hecklingen all his life.

'Come back tomorrow,' she says.

I *danke* and *danke schön* in what must be the most awful, hammy show of gratitude. The woman removes her rather stylish glasses, snaps down the legs and gives one brisk nod to acknowledge my fawning thanks. She switches off her computer and starts throwing things into a black leather shoulder bag. When she looks up and sees me still standing there, she raises her eyebrows in surprise.

'*Morgen?*' I say.

She nods her head slowly.

Back at the hotel, Verona and I have a couple of drinks next to the bowling alley and watch the play. Everyone is incredibly skilled and takes the game seriously. The younger people, who could only have been four or five at the time of unification, are as rowdy as youngsters at home, but the older people are reserved, their facial expressions blander. There's none of the boisterousness you find in Germans on the Costas. Perhaps this is the legacy of the old order where everybody had to watch their backs?

When we go up for our meal, there are only two other diners in the huge restaurant, businessmen in suits and loosened ties. They're already on coffees and cigarettes, their tables cleared. It's only 6.30. Verona reckons we're back in *The Truman Show* and they're extras, drafted in to make the place look less creepy and put the town's two tourists at ease. Whoever is directing the show is rather extravagant with the cast this evening; at least three different waiters attend on us during the meal.

After dinner we take an evening walk. The town is deserted, whole streets in darkness, without a single light shining at a window. Again, there are all these cars prowling the centre. Where are they going? There are no bars, no clubs, no diner/restaurants that we can see; just the funfair and that's as dead as it was in the afternoon, only now the flashing lights seem almost psychotic in contrast to the sullen town.

On the way back to the hotel we take a shortcut across waste land. Verona points to a forlorn light in an otherwise blacked-out building. At one side of the window the thin curtain is caught up and a silhouetted figure is peering through the gap. As soon as we stop to look the curtain drops and the figure disappears. Every time we look up our snoop is back, and every time we stop the curtain drops and the figure disappears. We play a game of peek-a-boo till we are just under the window. Then the light in the room goes out.

19 October, Stassfurt. In the morning we go back to Tourist Information to see if the woman has been able to find out anything. She tells us her father wasn't able to identify Fritz, Greta or Elli Skadock.

If her father, living in Hecklingen all his life, doesn't recall them, I think our chances of tracking them down are pretty slim.

The woman hands back the envelope of photographs, keeping one and holding it up for me to see. It's of a terrace of houses with a field of crops, probably potatoes, in front. She starts speaking very slowly.

'Mein Vater,' – her father, something something – 'das Gebäude,' – pointing to the building, something something – 'kleine Dorf' – little village – 'Gänsefurth.'

Flushed with success I turn to Verona and tell her the woman's father says that the building is in a little village called Gänsefurth. Verona rolls her eyes; she had worked that out for herself. I'm a bit miffed and it obviously shows on my face because the woman smirks as she waits to continue. She suggests we go to Gänsefurth and contact two families, the Wartmanns and the Schiekes, whose addresses she supplies, and if that doesn't work we should try the Archive Museum in a town called Cochstedt. I thank her, a simple *Danke* this time, and ask for directions to the nearest car hire. It's just round the corner, so we are in a car and on our way to Gänsefurth within half an hour.

We approach the village down a long straight stretch of road with flat fields on either side. From a kilometre away, Verona spots the terraced houses. We stop just outside the village and study the photograph to make certain; there's no doubt it's the same building. We drive further up the main street and park. We look out the addresses the woman at Tourist Information supplied and find we are right in front of the Schiekes's house.

When we knock on the door there is no response. We can't hear any sound of movement within the house, so Verona suggests we try the Wartmanns' and come back. Just as we are about to move off, we hear a bolt slide back and the door creaks open. It's an old man with Einstein hair. He has a slight cast in one eye, which makes it difficult to tell where he's focussing; it also makes him look nervous, almost fearful. He stands, holding the handle of the inner glass-panelled door as if ready to make his escape.

In pidgin German I explain why we are here but when I finish I'm not convinced he understands. I show him the photographs of Elli and her children, thinking he must be about the same age as her and might remember her rather than her parents. He shakes his head saying *'nein'* every photograph I show him. I try one of Fritz and Grete and say *'Das ist ihre Mutter und Vater,'* thinking I'm saying, that is *her*, meaning Elli's, mother and father.

It's as if poor old Herr Schiekes has been jabbed with a cattle prod. He jumps back, his cross-eyes wide with alarm, and screams *'Das ist meine Mutter und Vater!'* He keeps repeating that they are not his mother and father in a rising scale of hysteria, his eyes swinging back and forth between me and Verona.

'Ich weiss, ich weiss,' I try to reassure him. '*Ihre Mutter und Vater*,' I repeat, pointing to the photograph of Elli.

How the hell do you distinguish *her, your, their* in German?

Verona is no help. She says she's forgotten all the grammar, but somehow she doesn't think fine-tuning my accent or grammar's going to help here. The old guy's in meltdown.

Herr Schiekes is gibbering. He withdraws behind the inner door and slowly pushes it shut, keeping his eye, his good eye, on us till

→

the gap closes. We hear one final plaintive '*Das ist nicht meine Mutter und Vater,*' before his shadow vanishes from the textured glass panel of the door.

Verona and I stand on the doorstep, not sure what to do. Should we try and allay the poor man's fears? How? We decide the best thing would be to leave him to calm down. Up until fourteen years ago, anyone coming to your door asking questions wasn't a welcome thing.

At the Wartmann's when I ring the bell a woman sticks her head out of an upstairs window. She has a ruddy-brown, weathered face and her peroxide hair is tucked up in a floral turban. As she leans out further to get a better look at us, I can see she's wearing a floral pinafore that matches her turban, a sort of housewife's uniform of the fifties. Our whole interview is conducted through the window; she doesn't even consider coming down to the door. When I finish my garbled explanation, she leans further out the window and bawls 'Franz' towards the corner of the house. There's a high wall with large wooden double doors which must lead to a courtyard or work yard. After a few grunts and growls behind the doors, we hear a bolt screech and clunk and a small door cut into the larger door opens. Herr Wartmann's scowling face appears, twisting round and up to see what his wife wants. When he sees us his eyebrows rise and he steps out the door and stands, leaning forward, with his hands clasped on his stomach. He remains in this nervous, servile stance, smiling and frowning at us while his wife rattles through some explanation of why we are here. Her job done, the window crashes down and she disappears to resume whatever chore we've interrupted. Herr Wartmann waits, dropping his arms and drumming his fingers on his thighs.

I tell him I'm looking for the Skadock family who lived here in the 1950s and show him the photograph of Fritz and Grete. He peers at it but there is no flicker of recognition. He mutters the name Skadock a couple of times, shaking his head. I show him the photograph of Elli and her two boys; again nothing. I continue showing him the snaps although I feel I'm wasting my time. I'm about to retrieve the photographs and thank him when he mutters something then flicks through the stack, pulling out three and handing the others back to me. He holds up one of the photographs and points to buildings in the background and does the same with the other two. He starts talking quickly but I pick out the words *Haus, hier, Dorf*, and realise that he's saying that these houses are in this village. He points to various quarters of the village, indicating where they are. He hands back the three photographs and turns and shouts up at the window of the house. Frau Wartmann's head appears from another window. She listens, stony-faced, as he talks. As soon as he is finished she says '*Auf Wiedersehen*' to us and slams the window shut.

Herr Wartmann says something about an *alte Frau* – old woman – and disappears through the little wooden door into the yard. He reappears with an old black pushbike and walks off down the road, indicating with a jerk of the head that we are to follow. He is suddenly very jaunty and confident, waving and calling to neighbours working in their gardens. He gives us a running commentary of some kind; a monologue I presume, because he never looks round for any response. He keeps it up till we arrive at the terraced houses in the photograph.

He knocks on the second door. A very tall, imposing old lady answers. She listens to what Herr Wartmann has to say, looking Verona and I up and down. When I show her the photograph of Elli she nods and holds her hand out level with her ample bosom saying something about 'eine kleine Frau'. Elli was tiny, almost a head shorter than any other woman in the photographs. The old woman points next door and tells us Elli lived there.

'Where is she now?' I ask.

The old woman shakes her head and says something I don't catch. She starts talking about a daughter, I think, called Gabi who lives in Stassfurt. Her name is Stakalies and she and her husband run a household electrics business. I'm not sure if she's talking about her own daughter or Elli's daughter. We have no photographs of any daughter, just the two boys Hans-Peter and Hartmut. I show her some of the photographs from 1958 when Hans-Peter was eight and Hartmut five.

'Keine Tochter,' I say, indicating the absence of any daughter.

The old lady tells us Gabi is much younger than her brothers and wasn't born then.

This is an unexpected turn in events. I'd hoped that our first contact would be someone in the photographs. There's a good chance this woman will never have heard of my father if his contact with the family ceased before she was born.

The old woman signals that we are to stay where we are. She disappears into the house and when she comes back she has a phonebook and a cordless phone. She lays the phonebook on a little table just inside the door, flicks through it and then punches a number into the phone. As she prattles to the person at the other end she waves me into the doorway.

'Gabi Stakalies,' she says, handing me the phone.

Every word of German I know deserts me. I stand with the phone to my ear, my mouth gaping. The old lady flicks her hand in front her mouth, urging me to speak.

'Mein Name ist . . .' I start, and somehow in my plodding German manage to say that I'm from Scotland, my father was Arthur Putschker, her mother's cousin, and can I visit her this afternoon. There is a very curt reply consisting of the time, 2 o'clock, and the address, 66 Langestrasse. I hand the old lady her phone back and thank her.

'Bitte. Auf Wiedersehen,' she says, bowing and shutting the door.

'Auf Wiedersehen,' says Herr Wartmann, who gets on his bike and cycles off back to his house.

I'm beginning to sense foreboding about this whole venture. I don't understand why my father stopped writing to his family and wonder if there was a rift of some kind. Communication would have been difficult after the wall went up but other people managed to stay in contact. He said his half-sisters both married East German policemen and stopped writing. A friend, Karen Froebel, who also had family in East Germany said this would have been true; police were not allowed contact with relatives or friends in the West. But it doesn't explain why he stopped writing to Fritz and Grete.

On our way to meet Gabi Stakalies, Verona, very tentatively, and sensitively, suggests I might try smiling when I'm speaking German. She appreciates it's difficult when I have to scrabble for every word, but if I could just top and tail each question with a brief flash of the gnashers it might help.

The shop, when we eventually find it, looks run-down, like a lot of the shops in the town. The boxed items in the window display are all bleached by the sun and coated in grime; you would think the business had gone bankrupt and closed doors years ago. A bell jangles as we enter. Inside, a high wooden counter cuts right across the shop and the merchandise is stacked on shelves behind the counter; there is almost nothing in the narrow customer side. A middle-aged woman with short mousy brown hair appears from the back shop. I have my best smile in place but something puts her on her guard. She stops about six feet short of the counter and folds her arms across her stomach.

I ask if she is Gabi Stakalies and she nods her head. I ask if her mother was Elli Skadock and she nods her head again. I repeat what I told her in the phone call, who I am, where I'm from, and explain my father's relation to her mother.

'Wir sind Cousins,' I say, remembering to smile.

There is no reciprocal smile, if anything she adopts a more stony expression and locks her arms tighter.

I get the envelope of photographs out, select those relating to her family and spread them on the counter facing her. 'That is your mother and father and brothers,' I say, pointing to one. She takes three steps forward, still not coming right up to the counter, and peers at the photograph. That is her mother and brothers she tells me but the man is not her father, it's

➳

her uncle Erwin, her mother's brother. I ask where her mother lives and she tells me she died in a house fire in 1993. I remember when I asked the old woman in Gänsefurth where Elli was I couldn't understand her reply – she was telling me about Elli's death in the fire. One advantage in Gabi's curt responses is they are easier to translate. I can see that she has no real interest in the photographs; she only glances briefly at those I point to and never unknots her arms to pick one up. I keep waiting for some response, or some gesture of welcome, but there's none forthcoming. I ask if Erwin is still alive and she nods her head and tells me he lives in a place called Salzgitter Bad.

'Do you have his address?'

She disappears into the back shop.

I look at Verona and shrug my shoulders, stumped for what to say when Gabi comes back. Verona shakes her head.

'I don't think they'll be stringing lights along the Langestrasse or killing any fatted calf, Dad. There's nothing else you can do or say; the woman just isn't interested.'

When Gabi comes back she slaps a scrap of paper on the counter and retreats to her usual distance and folds her arms. The expression on her face seems to say: Okay now we've established who I am and who you are, what is it you want?

What do I want? What did I expect – a big party with beer and schnapps and people singing German folk songs? I don't know.

As I gather up the photographs and the slip of paper with Erwin's address, a young girl appears from the back shop, jabbering away to Gabi. I hear her say Mama, so she must be Gabi's daughter. When she sees us, she stops talking, smiles and apologises for interrupting. In the silence that follows she looks at us then her mother, obviously waiting for some introduction or explanation of what is going on. Gabi says something to the girl quickly which I don't catch but which makes the girl pull an exaggerated puzzled face. She probably told her I was some crazy Scotsman and not to encourage me.

The next thing I know I'm saying '*Danke*' and '*Auf Wiedersehen*' and Gabi is saying '*Bitte*' and '*Auf Wiedersehen*', and that's it; we're back in the car barely five minutes after having left it.

After that experience, I'm not sure I want to drive however many miles it is to Salzgitter Bad to have another door slammed in my face. I think my father must have fallen out with his family. They were in regular contact up until I was seven or eight, then it all suddenly stopped; no more letters, no more photographs, no more cards or presents. I think we should abandon the search and just enjoy the remaining time in Berlin. When I voice the idea, Verona gives it short shrift.

'We have nothing to lose. There's no point coming this far then giving up,' she says.

20 October, Salzgitter Bad. The journey to Salzgitter Bad is relatively stress-free. We negotiate three autobahns and arrive in the town just before noon. I don't want to turn up at the house during the lunch period, so Verona and I go for a coffee and take a stroll round the streets. The centre is very quaint with a lot of old half-timbered buildings, all beautifully conserved. There's an air of affluence here that there isn't in Stassfurt, and the people in the shops and tourist information are much more open and friendly. They appear to have embraced the opportunities afforded by unification and adapted to the lifestyle and aspirations of their old enemy with ease. Stassfurters, in comparison, seem locked in a communist time warp.

I'm still apprehensive about this visit after our reception from Gabi. I agree with Verona that we have nothing to lose; if they slam the door in our faces, at least we'll know we tried. It's the language thing that bothers me. Not fully grasping what people are saying and knowing that what I'm saying completely lacks any subtlety or nuance of feeling, whether I flash my gnashers or not.

At two o'clock we consult a street map and find Heinrich Von Stephan-Strasse. As we drive down the street, counting off the numbers, I look ahead and see a woman sweeping the garden path of number sixty-four, the house we are looking for. She is wearing slacks and a thick jersey and looks in her early seventies. I draw in and park just before the house.

'That must be Erwin's wife,' I say, pointing her out to Verona. 'I just want to sit for two minutes and rehearse what I'm going to say.'

We watch the woman sweeping right down the path to the garden gate. As we get out of the car she notices us and stands, leaning on the brush, watching us. There's something wary in her expression, and her eyes narrow as we approach.

'*Entschuldigung*,' I say.

She looks even more wary now. It's going to be a repeat of yesterday's meeting with Gabi, I'm certain, but before she has the chance to retreat, I blurt out my prepared introduction: my name is Arthur Ker, I come from Scotland, my father was Arthur Putschker. Finally, I ask her whether Erwin Skadock lives here.

The woman's eyes dilate, her mouth gapes wide and she stares at me, her face a caricature of amazement.

'Arthur Putschker?' she whispers.

I nod my head.

She steps forward, opens the gate and ushers us in. All the way up the path she keeps repeating 'Arthur Putschker' under her breath and laughing.

In the house she shows us into the sitting room. The first thing I notice is that the walls are covered with the same family photographs we have, and next to the door there is a little colour pencil drawing of a church, identical to one we have at home. My father told me his Uncle Fritz drew it and sent it to him as a reminder of the village church in Straupitz, Silesia. Through the open door we see Erwin's wife standing at the top of a flight of stairs leading down to a basement. She calls on Erwin to come up and laughs as she explains something to him as he climbs the stairs. Things seem more relaxed here.

Erwin is small, but not as small as his father or sister. The handsome, angular face from the photographs is still recognisable but he is frail and very deaf and has to position himself so that his good ear is towards us. After we introduce ourselves, he introduces his wife as Christa, which isn't a name I remember from the backs of the photographs. I start to show them all our photographs and they laugh and nod, pointing to the same pictures framed on their walls. At one point I hand over a snap to Erwin, saying that is him and Elli. He shakes his head and points to Christa who takes the tiny photograph from him and nods to confirm it's her. When I look at it again it's so obviously her. It's then I realise I've always confused her and Elli in the photographs, thinking they were the same person. And later, when I hand over a picture, naming Elli's sons Hans-Peter and Hartmut, I'm corrected again: they are Erwin and Christa's sons Edmar and Norbert. I had always assumed it was the same two brothers in all the photographs. The mistake was easy to make, because the boys all have the same blond straight hair and look incredibly alike, and for some strange reason there are no photographs of all four of them together.

The conversation moves by fits and starts. Anytime I string together a coherent sentence Erwin and Christa overestimate my ability to translate and rattle off anecdotes I can't keep up with. But there is no doubting their warmth or their pleasure at meeting us. Christa keeps shaking her head, saying 'Arthur Putschker' and laughing. She explains that she knew my father well as she grew up in the same street in Straupitz. She, Erwin and my father all went to school together. One thing that is becoming clear is that there was no falling out or bad feeling between my father and his family. Christa says they talk about him often. There are regular reunions with all the people moved from Silesia and they can't wait for the next one to tell everyone about us.

Christa serves us coffee and beautiful home-baked cake and Erwin produces an old photo-album belonging to his father Fritz,which he tells us was one of the few things that survived the fire in the family home that killed Elli.

We flick through the album and there are lots of shots the same as ours, or taken on the same occasions. Towards the end of the album, I turn over a page and there are photographs of a pipe band and people in kilts, and on a stage in

➻

the background what looks like the then King, George VI, and Queen Elizabeth. On the facing page are various snaps of my father doing the high jump, long jump and pole-vault. I realise it must be Ballater or Braemar Highland Games.

I explain to Erwin and Christa where the pictures were taken.

I turn the next page and there are photographs of a smiling baby, in a pram and in its mother's arms. I feel an immediate emotional rush, almost before my conscious mind has processed and identified the mother and child.

'That is me,' I laugh, showing Erwin and Christa the page. 'And that is my mother.'

Erwin and Christa are amazed. They say they had never seen the album till they found it in a cupboard in the one room that wasn't completely gutted by the fire. They'd often wondered who the woman and baby were.

When I flick over to the last page in the album, Verona and I burst out laughing, and every glance at the spread of photos fuels further laughter. We end up almost helpless, tears streaming down our faces. Erwin and Christa look at one another, completely baffled at what has set us off. I wipe my eyes with the back of my hand and turn the page of the album round for them to see. They start laughing as well.

The cause of the outburst is a series of eight photographs of my father. He's in swimming trunks, striking beefcake poses in front of what looks like an army blanket pinned to the side of a log cabin, which I guess was one of the huts in the POW camp in Aberdeenshire. His body is impressive. To quote a starlet describing Johnny Weissmüller: 'He's got muscles in places other men don't even have places.' The shots of his back are incredible; every muscle outlined and shaded in a way you only ever see in anatomical illustrations. Where did he find the means to build that body? It must have required protein as well as exercise, and those were still the days of strict food rationing. My father was vain, obsessed with his fitness and appearance. I remember him, stripping off his shirt as soon as the sun appeared or he had any physical task to perform, especially if there was a captive female audience. But this is narcissism of a kind I would never have suspected. Who were these photographs intended for? I've never seen them. He'd obviously sent a set to Fritz, but I wonder if he carried a set about with him for years, showing workmates and drinking buddies. I shudder thinking about it.

'*Verrückt*,' I say, twirling my finger at the side of my head.

Erwin and Christa nod their heads. Christa goes into a sideboard and brings out a huge pair of scissors. She cuts the page from the album and hands it to me.

Two days later in Berlin we met Erwin and Christa's son Norbert and his family. Over dinner I told them about our search around Stassfurt, Hecklingen and Gänsefurth and described the frosty reception we got from Gabi Stakalies. They were shocked at her behaviour, and Norbert couldn't believe that she didn't give us her brother Hans-Peter's address who lived in Hecklingen.

At the end of the evening, I sensed, from a few pointed questions, that Norbert was perplexed about something. As we were leaving, he came straight out with it.

'Why didn't your father keep in touch?'

'With you all living in East Germany,' I said, 'surely communication became difficult during the cold war.'

'But we have always lived in the West,' he said.

'Salzgitter Bad was in West Germany?'

'Yes,' he said.

I was devastated. I had no idea that as we drove from Stassfurt to Salzgitter Bad we had crossed the old border. My father was convinced his whole family were in the GDR.

‘Poetry is like fish: if it’s fresh it’s good; if it’s stale, it’s bad; and if you’re not certain, try it on the cat.’

Osbert Sitwell

Extract from the novel *Leipzig*

Fiona Rintoul

HENTSCHEL'S ATTITUDE HAS changed. He doesn't look at you as the Stasi men take you downstairs. He walks in front of the men, whistling a well-known pop tune under his breath. After a moment, you place it: *Pretty Young Girl* by Bad Boys Blue. He's wearing the brown plastic jerkin you know he likes. It doesn't suit him and it's too hot for the weather. He clears his throat and squares his narrow shoulders. He looks like he'd rather be anywhere than here.

When you reach the door to the Hinterhof, one of the younger men goes ahead – you assume to check the coast is clear. He comes back and gives the others the nod. As you cross the Hinterhof, you glance up at the apartment window. You can just make out the hand-painted pottery vase that Kirsten made for your twenty-first birthday – a rare and precious splash of colour and fantasy in a centrally planned economy firmly focussed on the utilitarian. Visitors always admire it. Want to touch it. Ask where you got it. Probably, you'll never see it again. Probably you'll never see the apartment again. Once this matter is cleared up and they've released you, it won't be sensible to come back here. That means you will never again rummage through all the weirdly wonderful clothes in the trunk to find something to wear – five years' collecting down the drain. Or maybe Kirsten will be able to save them for you. You shake yourself. It doesn't matter. None of it matters. You have a new life ahead of you.

Outside the building a van is waiting. The slogan 'Fresh Fish' is painted on the side panel alongside a picture of a happy, jumping herring. Without saying a word to you or the Stasi men, Hentschel starts walking up Shakespearestraße away from the van towards the main thoroughfare of Karl-Liebknecht-Straße.

'Where—' you begin.

'Silence!' one of the men hisses.

The men glance up the street to make sure no one is around. Hentschel keeps on walking, not looking back. The men ignore him. Where is he going? Why is he leaving you? You feel oddly bereft. In that moment, for the very first time since you saw these men on the stairs leading to the apartment you contemplate the idea that things might go wrong. But you quickly dismiss the notion. They don't have the most important information. If they did Hentschel would have mentioned it already.

Shakespearestraße is dark and empty. The light from the street lamps is as weak as piss and barely penetrates the black night sky. The men steer you across the pavement, keeping watch the whole time, then yank the van's side door open and bundle you in. Inside are several tiny cages, each with a narrow metal seat only just big enough for an adult human being. They shove you into one of the cages. You bang down hard on the seat. The older officer handcuffs you to a bar inside the cage.

You look at him. 'What are you doing?'

He bites his lip, looks almost embarrassed. 'Purely a precautionary measure, comrade,' he says. When he's done, he slams the cage door shut. Total darkness descends. You hear the men pile into the van and ram the door to.

Then the van sets off at a lurch, and you nearly fall off the tiny seat.

The journey is interminable. The driver is moving fast and not taking any particular care. Even in the pitch black you can tell that. At this time of night the roads in Leipzig are quiet. He's speeding along. You think he might be jumping the lights, a crime punishable by an on-the-spot fine even for pedestrians. You try to follow where he's taking you. He turned left out of Shakespearestraße, you think, heading for the suburbs rather than into town. But then he turned right and right again. That would mean you were heading into town after all. Soon you've lost all track. For a time you occasionally hear the comforting rattle of a late-night tram. Then you don't any more. Every time the driver takes a corner, you are thrown against one of the cage's metal walls. Every time the van brakes, you have to clench your leg muscles and brace your arms to stay on the seat. You hear the men talking and sometimes laughing, but you can't place exactly where in the van they are. You wonder if they'll help if you fall off the stool. You wonder if they'll even hear you.

After what feels like a very long time, the van comes to an abrupt halt. You are nearly thrown to the ground this time and you jar your arms badly. As you struggle to right yourself, the engine is turned off. You have no idea where you are or what time it is. There is not a speck of light in the cage and you can't read your watch. Even if there were light, you wouldn't be able to move your wrist enough to see your watch. You guess you have been in the cage for at least three hours. It could be more; it could be less. The cage has no ventilation. You're gasping for air. You're parched. Your tongue is gooey and it sticks to the roof of your mouth. You shift on the hard metal seat. You hear the van door being opened and and you hear voices: men. Somewhere a dog growls. Then you hear a key in the cage door. Thank God! They're going to let you out. The door is pulled open and harsh bright light floods in. You blink as your eyes struggle to adjust.

'Aussteigen!' barks one of the young officers.

But you're still handcuffed. The older man shoulders him out the way with a tut and unlocks the handcuffs. You rub your wrists. They're red and sore.

'Aussteigen!' the young officer shouts again.

You stand up as best you can in the tiny cage. Your legs are stiff and weary. You have a strange pain in the small of your back. Crouching, you make your way across the van and clamber out of the door. As you step down from the van, you catch a glimpse of the sky beyond the blinding searchlight and see that dawn is breaking. You are in an anonymous courtyard with high cement walls. (Many years later, you will learn from your files that it was the entrance to the prison block at the back of the Runde Ecke. You hadn't even left Leizpig; they drove around for three hours to disorientate you.) The young officer who shouted at you to get out of the van grabs your elbow.

'Walk!' he screams, steering you forwards.

He leads you into a building, up some stairs and along a corridor lined with cream-painted metal doors. The smell of a powerful disinfectant bites into your nostrils. Halfway along the corridor, he stops.

'Wait!' he shouts.

He is about your age. Average build with fine features and sandy-coloured hair. You want to tell him he could just speak; he doesn't have to shout. But you know already what would happen if you did that: 'Silence!' he'd shout.

The young officer knocks on one of the metal doors.

'Enter,' says a man's voice, and the chesty rasp of the long-term chainsmoker is already apparent in this one-word utterance.

The young officer opens the door, then takes your elbow and half-guides, half-pushes you into a smallish square office. The back of the door is padded. The walls are a dirty yellow colour. The brown linoleum is cracked. The blinds are drawn. An electric fan whirrs by the window, ruffling the blind's vertical slats as if teasing you with the possibility of a view outside. Behind a wood-veneer desk that takes

➻

up most of the room sits a man of perhaps 50. He has the lined and puffy face of a *bon viveur.* His thinning hair has been inexpertly dyed black and is plastered to his scalp with hair oil. He wears a grey army uniform with braided epaulettes and claret lapel stripes. A row of medals marches across his chest pocket. His cuff band reads: Wachregiment F. Dzerzhinsky. All the Stasi belong to the guard regiment named after, Felix Dzerzhinsky, the Cheka founder. On the desk next to a dove-grey plastic telephone sits the man's army hat. It has a black visor and a double strand of silver braid, and it bears the insignia of the GDR bracketed in golden oak leaves and acorns. You get the feeling he's dressed up just for you.

The young officer lets go of your arm, salutes and says, 'Comrade Oberstleutnant.'

The man behind the desk looks up, as if he has only just realised you're there. 'Yes. Hmm,' he says to the officer. Then turning to you, he says, 'Won't you sit down, Frau Reinsch?'

He nods to the young man, who pulls up a chair for you. You sit down across from the Oberstleutnant. The chair is very low.

'Cigarette?' he asks, offering you a packet of F6.

You nod eagerly. You're gasping for a smoke. You have to reach awkwardly across the desk to take the proffered cigarette because your chair is so much lower than his. He slides a box of matches across to you. You light the cigarette and take a deep, grateful drag. You can't remember the last time you went so long between cigarettes. You get a head rush and feel dizzy for a moment.

'Ashtray for the lady,' say the Oberstleutant to the young officer, who is still standing in the doorway, awaiting instructions.

The officer takes an ashtray from a shelving unit by the door and brings it to you. It's made of red glass and adorned with a green enamel badge showing the shield of the Ministry for State Security: an arm holding a bayonet from which flutters a red flag carrying the compass-and-corn ear insignia of the GDR. You flick your ash in the ashtray, wondering what they'll do to you if you stub your cigarette out on their shield when you're done with it.

The Oberstleutnant gives a second meaningful nod to the young officer, who salutes, says, 'Comrade Oberstleutnant,' and leaves the room. The Oberstleutnant watches him go, keeping his eye on the door until it clicks shut. Then he turns his attention to you.

'Ah!' he says, sitting back in his padded, imitation leather chair. It's as if a great burden has been removed from him; as if he's really been looking forward to a cosy tête-à-tête with you; as if you are alone at last. He smiles at you, revealing a mouthful of long, stained teeth. 'So why do you imagine we've brought you here today, Frau Reinsch?' he asks in a conversational tone, lighting a cigarette for himself.

'I suppose it's about Herr McPherson,' you say.

'Ah-ha!' He nods. 'Yes. Good. Very good. You display an admirable capacity for honest assessment, Frau Reinsch. Would you like a coffee?'

You say that you would. And, encouraged by his friendly tone, you ask if you could you perhaps also have a glass of water and something to eat.

'The journey was very long,' you say. 'There was no air in the van. I felt quite ill by the end and I'm dying of thirst.'

'Is that so?' the Oberstleutnant says, and his brow creases in what look likes concern. He lifts the telephone receiver and gives instructions for two coffees and a carafe of water to be brought to the room.

'We'll sort out something to eat later,' he says to you, replacing the receiver. Then he leans forward across the desk, hands clasped in front of him, and looks you in the eyes. 'I once had the pleasure of meeting your father, you know. I'll let you into a little secret. I thought he was a simply wonderful man. A true hero of socialism! Yes! He's been an inspiration to me throughout my working life. I don't mind admitting it. Indeed no.'

You smile. 'That's nice,' you say.

This is no time to share your own views about your wonderful father. You see now how it's going to be. A paternal chat. A little light admonishment. You'll admit your mistakes and ask for forgiveness. Perhaps you'll offer to write a self-criticism. Then the Oberstleutnant will ask you to write out and sign a commitment to work as an unofficial collaborator for the Ministry for State Security – 'The Sword and Shield of the Party!' he'll say, trying to inspire you – just as Hentschel did that day in Grünau. This time you'll do it. They'll be mollified, not realising they'll never get anything from you. That it's too late. That you'll soon be gone. They'll bring the food then and perhaps a glass of Schnapps. You and the Oberstleutnant will enjoy a drink together and another cigarette. He'll reminisce about the time he met your father. When he's had a couple of drinks and his face is a little flushed, he'll make a cheesy remark about how very pleasant it will be to have such a good-looking young lady reporting to him on a regular basis. You'll chuckle dutifully, and he'll perhaps allow himself to touch your hair or your cheek. Shortly afterwards you'll be back outside, your commitment to the working class no longer in doubt.

There is a knock at the door.

'Enter,' says the Oberstleutnant.

The young officer from earlier wheels in a hostess trolley with a coffee pot and cups on it, a carafe of water and two water glasses. You suppress a smile.

'Thank you, Comrade Hauptmann,' the Oberstleutnant says.

He gets up and pours you a glass of water. 'You'll be needing that,' he smiles as he arranges the coffee cups on the desk and pours the coffee. 'Milk?' he asks. 'Sugar?'

You gulp the water. 'Could you possibly tell me where I am?' you ask, as you turn your attention to the coffee, which smells remarkably good.

'Special blend for officers,' the Oberstleutnant says, reading your mind. 'Cuban.' Then, 'Didn't they tell you where they were bringing you?' He sounds shocked.

You shake your head. 'Nobody told me anything.'

'Really? Ah well, one thing at a time, I suppose.' He rubs his hands together and sits back down at the desk. 'Well,' he says, 'I suppose we'd better get the interview underway, don't you think?'

'Yes,' you say, taking a sip of coffee. It really tastes good. 'I suppose that would be best. Might as well get it over with.'

The Oberstleutnant smiles and presses a button on the large reel-to-reel tape recorder that sits on his desk opposite the dove-grey telephone. He gives the date, the number of the interview room and your name: Reinsch, Magdalena Maria. He smiles apologetically as he reads out your name is this bureacratic inversion, as if to say: such nonsense, but what can you do? Then he turns towards you, and the expression on his face abruptly changes.

'You're quite an arrogant young lady, Comrade Reinsch, aren't you?' he says. 'Rather convinced about yourself?'

He tells you then some of the things he knows about you, and you begin to realise how incredidly stupid you've been.

There are no German creeps
Margaret Christie

I used to find him a bit creepy, I said.
You didn't know that word in English. Creepy.
I looked it up in Oxford-Duden.
It gave *unheimlich, gruselig, schaurig*.
I looked them up the other way round.
Eerie, uncanny, dreadful, frightful.
They're much too strong. It seems no German word
conveys the way I felt about this man.
And now I know him. Know he's not a creep.
But something's missing in the world of words.

Dark Matter
Brian Johnstone

It's the look of panic
we glimpse
moments before the fall,

legs a Catherine wheel
of thwarted hope
spinning against the gravity

that drops the body off the cliff
seen too late
to hear our silent, inner cry;

it's the silhouette outlined
in glass
whose jagged edges hint

at some attempt to stop in time,
arms thrown up
to break momentum,

as speed and motion hurl
the object
of our attention

through the surface
only clocked
seconds before impact;

it's the figure invisible
but for a hat
suspended by illusion

in space above the manhole
tumbled down,
attention wandering

from the present inexorably
lost now
to this idler found out

deep in someone's coal hole,
hatless, black
and bruised by time and pace.

The Mockers

Andy Jackson

It could be that you didn't cross your fingers,
or perhaps you missed that hopeful puff
into your palm before you cast the dice,

or maybe you neglected to salute the lonely
magpie sentries on the bypass. Maybe
something in your prayer wasn't right,

a presumption your petition would be heard.
Perhaps you should have worn the lucky
shirt again. It worked last time, your team

three up in half an hour. Remember when
you failed to take the normal route to work,
took the rat-run past the Cats Protection League,

Sandy Denny turned up loud? The soot-black tom
that ran across the road outside, that jelly-thud
below your smoking tyres. The time you missed

the space above your shoulder, scattered salt
all down your suit? You laughed so hard
it turned the milk. That time the brolly opened

by itself, your windmill flailing, trying to contain
the blossoming eclipse before it fell across
you, eating up your shadow. That bastard

owl in the early afternoon, his whit-to-whoos,
eleven, twelve, thirteen. The surgeon with
your file who does not frown but does not smile,

who takes his shoes off, puts them on the table.
The sweating horse that shelters in the field –
what does it suspect, indeed, what does it know?

Incision

Christie Williamson

Dir taen da A
oot a JSA –
da jobless is allooed
naetheen noo,
dir choost seek.

Invalidity benefit
isna valid ony mair
dir fun aniddir wye
o cuttin doon da bill
tae disgust

o middle hell
wha froth at da mooth
aboot economic migrants
on dir daybrakk commute
in dir fower wheel drive

disgrace o a excuse
for a ecological conscience
ta charge whit dey
can gjit awa wi
fir wark at could
be wheeched fae da faes
o wir human existence
an be missed as muckle
as a sair plook.

Cut da pack, higher,
lower? Dey dunna want
casino bankers. Why pit up
wi governments gambling
wi bairns lives?

The Alienist

Lesley McDowell

LONDON, 1823

I couldn't have known what it was, not the first time. I wasn't to blame, though later I believed I was, and for a long time after that, too. But it was the wood smashed him down onto stone. It was the chair that tipped and the basin that clattered out of my arms, like they had lives of their own. I didn't make them. I didn't make the blood bubble blackly from his burst tongue and his irises roll, or the dough splatter yellow and thick on the stone slabs.

I didn't make my girls scream out. Yet I don't blame him, I can say that honestly: it's not why I still want to leave him. Their fright wasn't his fault: something else was pinning him down that day. Something we couldn't see made him monstrous, thrashed his arms against my newly-scrubbed kitchen floor and bucked his legs out at the toppled chair. I might have moved with the heaviness of a woman three times my age but it wasn't from fear, or reluctance to help. I had to consider, slowly, that was all: then a rush, sliding on the dough, and I sent a footstool flying that just missed Izzy who was at the back door, rattling at the doorknob and crying out to leave. But I wouldn't let her go. A demon had my husband: it might take hold of all of us. Still: I couldn't let her go.

I used to think about demons a great deal. In Broughty Ferry, when I was growing up, we thought about them every Sunday. Kail-kirk to fill our bellies and cold church walls, on those bright, fierce days, to protect us from the sea outside. The sea lured men from the town: some never came back. Drink called to them, too, on a Saturday night, when the taverns bulged. The sea and the drink were demons both and only prayer and abstinence could save us. When I was young, I thought they were enough.

But demons are everywhere and prayer and abstinence are useless. It was natural a demon should have been in my own house, inside my husband, that morning: a punishment for unwifely thoughts. Six years late, maybe, but here at last. The relief of it made me clumsy: I pushed Izzy too hard at her sister, and she fell, crying out as I tried to clear the way, still his head. I got my reward when he flattened my fingers twisting this way and that. If I could have made a fist out of my crushed hands I'd have struck him but Izzy's wails called me back. The demon is no match for my girls.

My sister's silver tea-urn crashing down; her copper pans, her wedding china, the mortar and pestle she brought back proudly from Pisa. I didn't try to save them. Tiny, bloody darts splintered in his cheeks and my fingers flickered at his face because I didn't know what to do. I know now, though, how much time I wasted. Telling my girls to stay, to run and fetch help, to stay after all. I waited for it to show me the way out, my instinct for escape, but it let me down for the second time. I sat beside him instead, as still as he was restless, as though by my stillness I could force him to be quiet.

When at last he was, it was little thanks to any action of mine. The demon left him as it had entered him, of its own accord, and the shaking stopped. I took a deep breath, then, and laid my palm on his chest, to feel for the heartbeat I knew I wouldn't find.

The second time I'd found the courage to think about leaving; the second time I'd failed. Just as before, he persuaded me to stay: perhaps it's as well. I've not thought about it until today. There have been many more fits these past four years, though, so I doubt my wickedness is to blame after all. Just the same, it's nipping at my neck, the need to decide. Wanting it isn't enough.

Because I am the expert in his disease, that is the problem. No-one knows the warning signs better than I do. The torpor in his eyes just before the eyelids begin to flutter; the lolling of his head; the grey pallor of his skin. The bite-marks on the smooth little bar of wood I always carry in my pocket are an eager pupil's good grades, but I didn't earn my marks today. How often it comes on him in the mornings! I've never understood why, and no-one can tell me, not the pamphlets I order or the chapters in David's books, or the articles in journals that make a kind of sense, before slipping away. Watching for it is all I know to do.

When I first complained about him, my father sighed as though he'd anticipated this all along. It was only to be expected. 'An older man's jealousy of his young wife, that's all. There's thirty years between you, Bella,' he said.

I'd already considered that. 'He has ways that are not... he gets angry, for no reason...' The fits hadn't yet begun. My father was working at his ledger in our windowless little box-room: in a few days he'd be gone to London, although I didn't know then that we were bound to follow him so soon after. It wasn't the best time to speak to him, when he was working out his accounts, especially after all that he had lost, but it was rare for us to be alone now I had Kathy. I seemed always to have her in my arms and when I did, I wasn't looking to speak to anyone else.

My father had the kindly tone of a fair man. 'We're all angry occasionally, Bella. He's bound to get impatient with a growing family to keep and times being what they are...' But I wanted escape, not fairness.

'You've heard nothing, seen nothing, while you've been here? You think he is... as he should be?' My tally of excuses just beginning.

'David's a good man, Bella. There's no man I have known longer, or better.'

I persisted: David *was* a good man. 'He's different from what he was; he has moods, I don't understand them.'

My father scratched at his ledger. I shivered with no June sun to warm me. Petulance doesn't keep the cold out. 'Different from what you *think* he was, maybe.' He chuckled at that, his head still not raised. 'That's what marriage is for. To find out. You are so young, you have a lot to learn.' My father is a compassionate man, a good father. But he believes too many in the world are like him, when they are not, and he should know this better.

I tried again. 'You know they called him Devil, in Broughty Ferry. They were scared of him.'

My father looked up at that: his clear brow and even features, tricked into a shocking, rare frown and meant for *me*. My guilt and apology only muddied more the mess I was making. 'Don't whisper like that, Bella,' he said, sounding worse than he looked, but I couldn't be surprised at his impatience. 'You of all people can't be cowed. You! My Bella – the best of them all? No wonder he's suspicious if you don't speak up. *You* know better than to be scared of him.'

My father and my husband. Praise that jabs the way condemnation might. They're not alike but they are in cahoots, I think, sometimes. I raised my voice. 'I try, every day. I try to talk to him but it's impossible. Sometimes I think...'

'What? Come now, my girl. You're a Baxter. We don't hide away. Tell him what's on your mind.'

I am not a coward.

'I've tried, but it's more than his work that keeps him from me... how can I make him hear me?'

'I told you: it's what marriage is about. Talk to him again.'

'You make it sound so simple... I think he forgets who I am.'

'How can he forget? Only if you don't speak to him as a wife and an equal should. You weren't brought up to think otherwise,

Bella. I didn't raise my girls to think they were lesser beings.'

'I don't mean he thinks I am lesser... he thinks *I am not there*. He doesn't *see me*.'

He turned back to his ledger. I am a spoilt little girl: if I touch the grey curls, tug on the tweed coat draped across his shoulders, I can confirm it. 'Don't let things fester between you,' he carried on. 'It's bad for your marriage, Bella, and bad for you.'

Was I mad to marry him?

But I only whispered those last words to myself as I slid out of his study. Diabolical is a word from the Greek, 'diabolos', meaning Devil. My father wouldn't recognise the diabolical in anyone. I am different: I know the diabolical when I see it.

And I should have seen it this morning. I missed the signs.

Recrimination lures like those wicked sirens of the sea and I welcome the chance to punish myself for my carelessness. How best to effect it, I wonder. What method shall I use this time? I like to feel guilty, even though it's sinful to like it and I'll be punished for that, too. I was good, though, this morning at breakfast. The moment he fell I swooped down onto the carpet behind him like a voluptuous grey swan, bolstered his head and shoulders and gripped his back with my hips and thighs as tea spattered patches on my skirt. I fixed on them while he shook and shuddered against me.

I concentrate now on my guilt even though I shouldn't and pour David some water once he's calm again. I smile as I reach round his chest and I smile as I clasp my hands and wrench him up from the floor. Now, as I fix my shoulder under his arm and we shuffle out of the dining-room together, I am smiling still.

He'd warned me our cottage was ugly on the outside and too small on the inside, but I didn't believe him until I saw it and prayed we'd walk by and it wouldn't be ours. But he stopped and I knew it was our new beginning, with its poky front parlour and mean little dining-room at the back. I like to keep to the kitchen: its awkwardly shaped S makes it difficult for more than one adult person at a time. I've never gotten used to living so close by others: I had room growing up, more than I needed. And more possessions, never mind our vows of poverty. I used to complain about practice on my mother's old harpsichord: how I'd like to hear my girls making such a complaint one day! But that's long gone with our old house, and dreaming of new paper hangings and velvet chairs won't help me.

Our house is deceptive, though: for all it's so small, it must hold more paper than the great library of Alexandria ever did, I say to him. Parchments, manuscripts, letters, leather-bound companions to this or that exhausted-looking volume are scattered on the floor of his bedroom, or balance on the mantle. Some piles reach the tip of the fireplace, others almost touch the ceiling. There's no space for the man himself: even the bed is spread with his own papers, spidery black letters scored across white. He told me long ago to sleep with the girls in their room so they don't come in here and only rarely do I. Except last week, when Izzy cut some roses for him. Jammed into an old jug and balanced on a book on the window-sill, they're turning brown and pulpy. They still make me smile though, and for her sake, I enjoy taking a kick at Hume and Locke before settling David carefully on the bed. But then Thomas Reid catches the edge of my toe and I squeal like a cat with its tail caught. I don't cry: when my husband first cried in front of me it shocked me and I cried with him. It takes more than an old philosopher lying in wait to bring tears to my eyes now, though.

'Be careful,' he snaps, as I stumble and catch my cuff on his collar.

'There's a bruise here,' I notice, suddenly. 'Where?' he blinks, panicking. 'At your temple, close to your eye.' His long fingers quiver at the sore spot and he winces, so I bat him away as gently as I can and dab around the sooty edges, smears from the dining-room floor where he fell. He sulks like the boy I imagine him to have been once. 'It's only a little bump,' he mutters. 'Don't be silly,' I tell him, briskly. 'These can do more harm sometimes, you know that. Worse than a broken bone.' But I'm not paying proper attention: the slightest change in my tone can upset him, and it does now.

'Don't speak to me like that. I'm not some cretin!' He's up on his elbows, now; I make a feeble attempt to restrain him. 'David, I wasn't – you need to lie still...' Thirty years older he may be, but he's still strong. 'Leave me alone!' he spits out the words. 'Abandon me forever like I always knew you would. Whore! Slut! Where's my wife? What have you done with her? I want my Bella! Give me back my wife!' Spittle hangs from his lips as his eyes bulge and his eyes search for something to strike me with, as he's done before. I step away but he grips me hard around the waist, stabs his thumb at my back. *'You know what I can do!'*

My friend, Mary, has written about monsters. About a yellow-skinned, yellow-eyed creature galvanised by an unseen power into mimicking the movements of a human being. What makes a monster? Mary's never witnessed what I have. The monster a man becomes when reason deserts him and he thrashes about, insensible, on a stone floor. When nothing his wife says or does brings him back to himself. What mother might tell her daughter this on her wedding night – if I had had a mother to warn me on my wedding night? I would have listened to her. Wouldn't I?

At last he leans back and closes his eyes: pale lashes and heavy, withered lids. Resentment can take a material form, like a piece of coal that warms and glows inside the body. It burns inside me when he is this way. I know the fit won't kill him when it happens now and I wonder if that knowledge makes the glow burn brighter, makes me the wicked woman he tells me I am.

I try not to frown because that annoys him, too. He once told me he loved my frown: not what I was expecting. To love my frown and not my smiles? 'Looking like you're always right about everything,' he'd said, then. Was that another sign? How many of them I must have ignored, misread.

'I'm not a man,' he sighs suddenly and sinks down against his pillows. 'I'm no husband to you. You don't want me. I can see it, I know.' He wheezes a little and I pat his shoulder gently.

'No more, now, David. Excitement makes you worse. Please lie still. I can't get the rest of these clothes off you if you won't be still.'

A faint smile shimmers on his lips. 'You're a good wife, I know you are.'

But he won't charm me so easily. He finds me clumsy and uncaring, more often, and says so. His tone this time, though, becomes melancholy, self-pitying as he continues, 'I don't earn enough to keep us all. I've failed in every way. Nothing I do is good enough. Nothing works.'

'That's not true. Don't get upset, you only make it harder for yourself.'

'I'm sorry, Bella. Forgive me. You should leave me; take the girls. You'd do better without me.'

How do I leave you now?

His stilting whispers come always after a fit. His vulnerability snakes round, squeezes my treachery out of me to leave nothing behind except *how can you leave him now?* His hands are stretched out, the veins standing up thick and black and I wonder, suddenly, about the colour of his blood. Then I see it.

'Don't speak, there's something...'

'What are you doing? What's this?'

'Your hand is scratched, torn, it looks bad. I need to bandage it...'

'It's not a catastrophe, woman. It's not a twisted thumb. I can still write! That's all that matters.'

'You need to rest it, trust me, please.'

He mutters more protests but lies back all the same. Uneven bones jut through his shirt. I wind calico round his wrist and wonder if it's feeling or a sensation; which I will cause him, which he causes me. I tuck in the loose ends of the calico and place his wrist against his chest. 'I have so much to do,' he grumbles. 'You'll have to write the paper up for me...' I shake my head. 'I don't have time to copy down everything you dictate for a week, David. The house needs me.' He reaches for my waist with his good hand again but friendlier this time, and pleads, 'Maybe I was lucky this time. Is it getting worse? Did it last longer than usual?' I shrug off his questions and his grasp, turn away to put the calico back on the dresser. 'No, not so long,' I say. 'But you know you shouldn't

➻

talk.' He persists, 'Did I hurt you, Bella? I didn't hurt you, did I?'

'No, no, not at all. I'm fine.'

'And did I say anything...'

'Nothing, nothing at all. Shhh. You have to rest now.'

'But I've got things to do. Important things... my paper... my lecture for the Society...'

'Don't worry about your work. You must sleep. I'll look after everything.'

'But don't touch anything, not in here, I don't want you in here. I've told you that before but you never listen to me, I know you come in here when my back is turned...'

He's excited again: I pull up the blankets, reign him in.

'Shhhh, please, David. Go to sleep.'

'You never listen to me. You stay out of here...'

'Stop it, now. Really, please. You need to rest.'

To my surprise, he gives in at this and shuts his eyes once more. For now, his shame and my own inability to offer anything more than a few soothing words and some liniment to rub his feet, nearly blue, prick something inside me at last. Not my heart. Not that. I lighten my pressure after a while and wait for him to smile, complain as usual that I tickle. But it's only when I stop and cover those long, white toes that look artful enough to hold a brush or a pen that I realise he is asleep.

And that I am alone.

Sylvie Chandrashakar / Highgate, London / November 2003

Simon Sylvester

DURING BREAKFAST IN the old house, I used to watch the bugs that gathered on my bedroom window. There were tiny brown mites crowded on the rubber seals, and the wood was flocked with mould. Old cobwebs hung in the corners of the room, long wispy things, but I never saw a spider. In the average square mile of British countryside in the summer, there are half a million spiders. I never saw one in the city, though they leave behind their webs to gather dust. This became very important to me, this idea of traces left behind.

I'd spend so much time watching the mites that my tea and toast would go cold. I even tried to draw them, right up close to the sill, my breath fogging the glass, but they were too tiny and moved too steadily. The condensation inside the window looked like scales so the trees outside were fractured in the beads of water, and this I did draw a few times. Then I'd realise how late I was for college, and throw on whatever underwear and dress and coat that came to hand the quickest. Finish my tea in a swig of the last half a mug, slop it over my chin, down my shirt. Find my bag and keys and leave, grate the door shut, step out into autumn, winter, spring. I'd do my mascara in the bus stop.

I used to think, when I first moved to the city, that every travel card needed to be completely exhausted. It cost so much money, about twenty pounds a week, but it was still the cheapest way to get around. I felt the need to wring the value out of every card. Any day without a journey was a wasted day, shaving pounds and pence from what I'd spent to buy it. So I'd go to see friends in new parts of London. Up to Manor House, down to Crystal Palace. Mile End, Goldhawk Road for the markets. Once or twice I took the bus to Abbey Road, and sketched the faces of groups of friends as they waited for traffic to clear at the famous zebra crossing. I found unnecessary things to do, like going to see new shows in galleries that opened in warehouses in Holloway for two weeks before closing again. House parties afterwards. Night buses to my place. Or to someone else's place. Morning buses, going home in rush hour with a hangover. Standing at the stop and waiting, folding the travel card into seven sections, one for each day, a little orange concertina with each segment showing what I'd used and what I'd wasted. Sometimes the machines would spit the card out because of the folds, and the attendant would tell me off.

I kept all the old travel cards in an A4 envelope, filling up a week at a time. As the envelope gaped fatter, I started looking for more tickets. Stuffed down the back of seats, dropped beyond the turnstile, crowded in dusty heaps of cigarette butts beside the kerb, on top of ticket machines. Each one was the ghost of a journey, stamped out with times and dates, corners ripped for cigarette filters, mobile phone numbers, times, initials. I kept trying to think of something to do with them, and eventually I made a giant face, stapling all the tickets onto a piece of plywood I found in a skip. I used them back to front, so the black magnetic strip made thick lines and the small print of Terms & Conditions worked as shading.

➳

All I really cared about back then was contrast. I was obsessed with the shadows in a person's face and what the shadows told you about the real person. I had this saying: absence is presence. I wrote it everywhere. My pictures were all called Absence 2, Absence 14 and so on. Sometimes it was Presence 9, Presence 20. I liked the idea that it was impossible to go somewhere without leaving something of yourself behind. Shadows were the nothing, the void you carried with you. There can't be a shadow without something to cast it. Absence of light depends on the presence of light. I was getting into Lee Miller pretty heavily.

My favourite tickets were the ones with the holes punched through them. The holes were a perfect absence, giving me the presence of the inspector, bored, I'd imagine, hungover in new shoes and two-day underpants, marching up and down the aisle and punching holes in tickets. I loved that. When I'd finished stapling all the tickets onto the wood, this gigantic shadow face in white and black, I didn't know what to do with it. I took it into college and discussed it with my tutors. They all went crazy for the absence is presence idea, but the face took up too much space, and eventually the wood began to stink. I took a dozen photos, and developed some properly, and others in negative, then pried off all the tickets and carried the board back to the skip. The tickets went back into their envelope. I guess I must've forgotten them when I moved house. I travelled light by accident.

This was when I was studying at Goldsmith's. Three mad years when I lived all over London. Ten months here, three weeks there, two months there. For however long it took before I got itchy feet. I lived in a front room in Greenwich where the double mattress filled the entire floor, so the door couldn't open properly. That was with an incredibly tall Zimbabwean girl. She was really Amazonian, tall and broad, but once or twice a week she'd knock quietly, squeeze through the door in tears, wanting a cuddle. Then I stayed with my auntie in Twickenham. She had a wooden box in the loo packed with a lifetime collection of postcards. I'd sit and leaf through cards from Borneo, Alaska, Belgium. You could travel the whole world while having a shit. The ones from India looked nothing like my father's India. Absence is presence. I crashed in a friend's place off Brick Lane for a while, and shared a flat behind the Bethnal Green fire station with some boy. We flirted but I can't remember his name. Sometimes I'd house-sit for a family friend in a tiny cellar flat in Dulwich Village, watering plants and feeding cats and sketching. For a few months I lived at this huge half-built place in a backstreet of Southwark. It was skeleton rent in exchange for some wallpapering and painting, but the whole situation got pretty heavy. The girl who owned the flat started schizing out and staring at me. She was always waiting outside my door in the morning. Either in a chair in her room, waiting for my door to open, or actually standing there, as though ready to knock. She'd always ask me if I wanted to use the bathroom, if I wanted into the kitchen. She screamed at me when I fixed a lock to my bedroom door. She had some kind of eating disorder, and ate my food when I was out, then called me a liar when I tried to talk to her about it. She moved around at night, her presence betrayed by creaking floorboards. After a few weeks I started finding her tooth marks in the butter and cheese, and I realised she was sleepwalking and eating in her sleep. That really freaked me out, so I moved up north to Angel, sharing with this Australian nurse. She played for a women's touch Aussie-rules football team on Tuesday nights and sounded like a foot pump when she was shagging boys. West Acton was not so good, a cold winter in an attic room, nylon carpet and a creaking ladder. That old house in Highgate was okay for a while. The house had these gigantic pot plants in it. They must have been there since before I was born, getting bigger, outgrowing their pots, crawling up the walls and across the ceiling. I think that's where the bugs came from. The flatmates were alright, I guess. There was an admin guy for Haringey council, a floor manager at Harrods and a runner at a famous Soho sound studio. When he was logging rushes, he'd take a sleeping bag into work and sleep beneath a desk. I only ever saw him eat crispy pancakes, half a dozen at a time. The guy who worked for Harrods had a broken nose and kept my cookbook when I left. They told me how Pink Floyd used to live in the house. It was owned by this weirdo next door. He had blinding white hair, and he'd let himself in without knocking, wander around in his dressing gown. They said he used to be a concert pianist, and an architect, and that he'd rented it to three members of Pink Floyd late in the 1960s. Apparently there was a concert documentary made of the band around then, and you could see them rolling spliffs in our front room on a gigantic glass-topped coffee table. The table was still there, a monster of a thing, chipped and cracked in a metal frame. We rolled spliffs on it, too. I guess the pot plants must have been smaller in the 1960s. The place was a dump. I could stick a finger straight into the wooden window frame. The mites would go crazy. But the view was good, onto a garden that looked twenty years overgrown. I watched that garden for hours, listening to Joni Mitchell, sketching the trees, the mess of branches in a bust-up trellis. It was a decent neighbourhood but the embankment from the railway line was covered in footballs, trolleys, builders' helmets. That's the same everywhere in London.

I had the room at the end of the upstairs corridor. There was a single bed, a tiny desk, a stack of old wooden wine boxes and a hanging rail, bowed in the middle. There were shelves in an alcove where I put my books and some CDs. I could just about cram all my dresses onto the rail, and packed my knickers and jeans and shirts into the boxes. I was even messier back then, and the boxes were always spilling legs and bra straps and shirt sleeves. Pinned some of my drawings to the wall, some of my mum's drawings. My auntie was always taking cruise holidays, and I put up some of her postcards, too, building my own collage of the world. In the end I was there for maybe half a year, over winter.

Back then, I was still trying to work out if I was gay or straight. Sometimes I'd try to hook up with girls, which was hard, and sometimes with guys, which was easy. I was pretending to be bohemian, but only because hipster girls were easier to get with, hanging out in the Foundry in summer dresses and deliberately mismatched tights. I guess everyone was faking, but some of us were more convincing than others. I was pretty prudish by their standards. I'd get them drunk, chat them up, make all the effort, but they'd have to kiss first, and they'd have to guide my hands between shirt buttons and up tops or into knickers. Once that line had been crossed, I could relax a bit and enjoy it. It was weird. The idea of having sex with another girl really turned me on, but not the reality so much. I'd come most of the time, more often than with guys, but it never seemed complete, like half an orgasm. It was flattering and curious to give a girl an orgasm, to watch her face, but it never gave me the satisfaction of making a guy come. I found guys rough and sore and clunky and selfish, but loved the energy, the commitment, feeling so needed. And girls weren't enough afterwards, when I'd want to put my head on a bigger chest and listen to his heart. But I loved to lie facing the girl, mirror her body, shuffle up the bed to align our hips and breasts and watch her sleeping. I was still working it out. It was a very long time before I realised that I didn't have to choose, that it was okay to be bisexual. I never told my mum. I think that would have upset her more than being outright lesbian. She liked everything black or white. She liked to know everything for certain.

It was only when I lived in Highgate that it started to bother me. I really wanted to know, to build my world around it. Straight or lesbian. What's wrong with you. Be happy, try to be happy. Make your mind up, choose a team. Make your bed, and lie in it. There were times I'd be talking to people, but felt so wooden. A sculpture, chiselled away, my own self reduced by chips the more I tried to fit in. I'd lie in bed, staring at a woodchip ceiling until evening turned it black, getting colder. Then I'd climb under the covers in my clothes and shiver myself to sleep.

We had a party once. It was the only time I ever took magic mushrooms. Some posh boy was handing them out. He had hundreds in a tupperware box. They were rubbery like shiitake mushrooms, and nothing happened.

➻

It wasn't fancy dress, but the administrator from Haringey had told his workmates it was, and they'd turned up like cowboys and zombies. One of his friends showed up with a long coat. When she took it off, making sure people were watching, she was wearing only underwear. My throat went tight. She'd done her hair like the 80s with a black hair band, and she was wearing a bra, knickers, stockings, a suspender belt and high-heeled shoes. That was it. I don't know what she was supposed to be dressed up as. And she swished about the party with a perfect swell to her stomach and perfect fold to her waist and perfect arse and perfect tits and perfect white face. But I worked out right away she wasn't queer, and the sadness came back. No matter where I went in the party, skinny geeky me trying to talk to girls and boys I didn't know, she was there. I couldn't shake her off. She was always in the background, this woman turning a finger through her hair and laughing in her underwear and talking only to guys. After an hour of cheap red wine, I walked past her. Deliberately let her hair brush my shoulder, sucked her perfume deep into my lungs. But up close, I could see the coats of foundation on her face, the spots and blemishes buried underneath. Her face was caked in the stuff. It was pitted and cracking in places. The elastic from her underwear cut into her. But that saddened me even more, knowing she wasn't perfect, after all, but I still couldn't have her. I started feeling sober and really depressed. I went for a piss. Sitting on the loo, not really knowing why, I reached out and drew on the bathroom wall with a permanent marker. Half a face, the shadows of a girl like me. Shadow girl, absence is presence. She and I watched each other until someone hammered on the door.

I couldn't sleep for the music thudding in the floor. Sometimes there was perfect laughter floating up through the floor but all I could think of was the blemishes, coated in powder to make them go away. I sat up flicking through a shoebox of photographs, found some from an old school art project. Nude photos I'd taken of Andrew when they wouldn't let us do life drawing. He'd taken some of me, too. He had a really thick cock, beautifully shaped, and I'd taken loads of photos of it, his square cock and balls, lines of muscles between his stomach and his thighs. I laid them out on the bed in front of me and tried to masturbate but couldn't get turned on. Next morning, the buckled photos of Andrew's cock were scattered all over my bed and the floor. One or two people were still dancing to the shit music downstairs, quieter now, though more were slumped in the corners or sharing spliffs. I went to the caff and drank lots of instant coffee and sketched faces in my book. When I got back the guy from Harrods was ranting about what cunt had drawn on the bathroom wall. I'd forgotten all about my shadow girl.

'Never mind,' I said. 'I'll do the bathroom.'

I tried to say it lightly, but I don't think they bought it. We only had non-smear window cleaner and J-cloths for cleaning, and as I tried to wipe my face from the woodchip, ink smeared everywhere and no matter how hard I scrubbed, it spread deeper into the wall, becoming thinner, stretched wider and thinner. It was the very first time in maybe ten years of making work that I'd completely destroyed something of my own. Grey streaks of soapy inky water rolled down the wall. Maybe it was the mushrooms, but I thought the shadow girl was crying because I was killing her. Then I started crying too, stuffed my fingers into my mouth as sobs shook me hard enough to hurt.

That afternoon I started flat hunting again. And that's how I wound up living with Pab.

Ramon Usobiagi / Barcelona, Spain / August 2004

Simon Sylvester

I HADN'T BEEN down La Rambla for a while, as you don't crap where you eat and pickings were always pretty good at the old fairground. But I was getting sick of candy floss. Every day I'd buy a candy floss and eat a couple of mouthfuls before I remembered how fucking shit the stuff is. And every day I chucked the candy and got a cola instead. Walked around, pretending to be interested in the rides but really checking out the punters. Pickings were always good so long as you didn't get too greedy. I knew a lot of guys who'd been busted for getting greedy. It's a senseless way to go. There's plenty enough for everyone.

I was hanging out by the art museum on Santa Monica, because that's where the punters go. I was pinging the ringpull on a can of cola and smoking a cigarette. This was a disguise. Really, I was looking for pretty much three things. First, a cluster of tourists with a guide. Second, some mug with a loose bag. And third, no cops. There were plenty of tours and plenty of mugs, but it took maybe forty minutes before I saw them both together. A large group of maybe forty were heading from the waterfront towards the museum, and a couple were looking at a street map, pointing in different directions. They were older than me, which pretty much means slower than me. She wore a miniskirt and vest and thin sandals fastened round her ankles, he had a rucksack and camera bag on one shoulder. I stubbed my cigarette and wandered towards them. As the group passed the couple, I cut straight through. The herd of tourists jostled each other, forced to move around me, and the guide started yelling to stay together. The couple were distracted. I walked right behind them. Popped open the camera bag, took out the camera and dropped in the cola can. The weight was about the same. I kept walking. At the corner of de la Banca, I risked looking back. The couple had folded their map and were walking up La Rambla towards the plaza. His camera bag swayed on his shoulder.

Fucking beautiful.

I always scanned through the photos from cameras. It was cool seeing where all these people had been on their holidays. Kinda like seeing Barcelona for the first time, you know? We live in such a beautiful city, but it's easy to forget, and these tourist snaps would always remind me how lucky we are. And this camera was pretty much the same. There were some great ones taken round the Placa Catalunya. Sometimes there was the guy and his woman pointing the camera back at themselves. They were always smiling. They looked a good couple, you know, really good together. Then some of the Dali Museum. After the Museum, a couple of landscape shots from the train, and then there was this sequence taken in their hotel room. The woman was sitting on the edge of the bed, wearing pretty much the same stuff she wore at Santa Monica. She was looking right at the camera with this half-smile I couldn't quite figure out. The curtains were drawn, so it was a bit dark, but there was some light coming in through a gap, and the bedside lamp lit one side of her body. In the next picture, it was pretty much the same and it took me a moment to realise that now she was sitting with her legs

➳

apart. In the next one, they were totally wide apart, but it was still too dark to see properly. In the next one, she was standing up, taking off her shirt, her ribs standing out. She was an older chick, maybe 40 or something, but she was pretty hot. She took off her bra in the next picture. After that, with her tits out, she was looking down as she unfastened the top button of her skirt. Pretty soon she was wearing no clothes and posing on the bed. I don't know why, but it was hotter because she kept her sandals on. It was like porn only not so much in your face, and I was getting this fucking big erection. A couple of pictures later, she had her cunt out, using her fingers to spread it wide for the camera. I pulled out my cock and started beating off even though I don't usually like older chicks. She kept changing positions as I scrolled through the camera. It was fucking great. I started getting really close to coming, and just as I was about to come, the sequence ended. The next picture really freaked me out. It was the guy. His face, close up. And he was staring at me. Right at me, me, Ramon Pedro Usobiagi, right here and now. Shit, man, he was looking through me. He was looking out of the camera and right into my soul, I swear. I completely lost my erection. I sat on my chair with my cock going soft and this devil looking at me.

There was something about that shot, man. Something really freaked me out. It was so completely clear that I'd taken something that belonged to him. Not the camera. Maybe not even beating off over his woman. It was more that I'd dared to take something from him at all. The principle of it. Like I'd fucked with the devil or something. You don't fuck with the devil. And that was how I felt, I'd sailed so close to the wind with this one. I couldn't shake that face, staring. He was a black and white face in the newspapers, all shadows. A dead man. A murderer in the papers. It really fucked me up, that face. And I don't know for sure why, but I couldn't bring myself to fence the camera. Could've sold it easy, maybe a hundred, maybe a hundred-fifty Euros, but I didn't. I kept it. I wanted to use it. When the batteries ran down, I went out for a charger from the photo store. Bought a new memory card too. Couldn't bring myself to delete the old pictures, to wipe them away like it had never happened. I tried to chuck it in a bin a few times. But the guy, the guy and his woman. I couldn't wipe them away like that, like some fucking shit stain on the wall. My finger hovered over the delete button so many times, man. But I couldn't do it. I was scared of what would happen if I did. How can you kill a devil? It's impossible. He'll only wait for you in the next life. That memory card burned a hole in my fucking jeans for weeks. I felt like such a crook. So in the end, I got some random address in London off the net and sent it there. Just popped it in an envelope and posted it. It was a fucking albatross, that thing. Jesus. That guy and his chick.

After that, I started taking loads of pictures with the camera. It turned out to be a shit-hot piece of kit. There were so many controls like flying a jet, all these dials and buttons, digital menus. Back then I didn't know jack shit about aperture or exposure or ISO or anything. To begin with, I took a bunch of pictures at the Baobab. And it was clear that they weren't quite right, but Lupe sees the pictures and says they're pretty good, man. You should take more. I did, I took loads, but most of the controls were a mystery. Then Lupe told me there was a night class in digital photography at the college, I should go along with her. The place was full of bachelors and students, but they showed me what all the controls were for. The tutor said I had the eye for it. 'You have a good eye, Ramon.'

Man, I was fucking pleased with that. Then we got set this assignment to take stolen portraits. That tickled me. Steal pictures with a stolen camera. I got this amazing Sigma f3.5 180mm long lens for the job. Cost me a fortune, but it was worth it. All the way along the boulevard, man, camera steadied on a wall at the Sagrada Familia, or against one of the trees on La Rambla where we used to carve our names and look at the caged birds. I'd take these shots of tourists looking up, nothing but blue sky behind them. Or pictures of the fucking pigs, dozing in the sun. Tour guides herding their sheep with that weird mix of concern, disgust and boredom. Kids. Pigeons with stumps for legs. And I was good, you know. I got this knack of always getting one detail in amazing focus, so quick it could be an accident, these tiny slices of time. I was the one who caught them. No-one else. Single moments, half-moments. One-offs, man. Streetlights reflected in sunglasses, single cigarettes glowing. Half-smiles. It was fucking beautiful.

Lupe's brother hung some of my pictures in the Baobab, and then I took some to the other bars and cafes in town. It was pretty cool. Everyone loves a photographer. Also, talking to the other guys on my class gave me a much better idea of what all the gear was worth. The fucking fences had been ripping us off for years. But I guess that's nothing new. Easy come and easy gone. You have to learn to live with that.

By taking pictures, making myself a tourist in my own city, it was so perfect. It's better camouflage than a cola can. It's much easier to steal from tourists who think you're a tourist. I could get right up close to them. Then I realised that they would come to me. For college, I was taking a picture of a worker on the basilica roof, smoking his cigarette. I stood for ages, waiting for him to turn his head a little, to get it just right. Then I realised some son of a bitch was standing near me. I thought it might be a fucking thief, but it was another tourist.

'That's a nice shot,' he says, in English. 'Mind if I steal it?'

Then he points his camera up and starts shooting. His jacket was open. His wallet was ostrich leather. I was dumbstruck. He was giving it to me. It was so fucking simple. I started doing this all the time. Hanging out in the hotspots, taking perfect pictures. Wait long enough, and the amateurs would come to steal my shot. Then I'd take their wallets or their phones. Just reach over and take them out, pretend to be guiding their photo. Sometimes they'd even pat me on the back, shake my hand in thanks. Gee, thanks, pal. Cheers, mate. My favourite was an open camera bag. They'd have their eyes glued to the camera, and I'd be murmuring guidance, then reach over and lift out the spare lens. Just lift it out. Best of all is now I know what the fucking things are worth.

The Passenger

Jane Flett

YOU BOARD THE F train at Broadway-Lafayette, even though the coffeehouse is closer to Second Avenue, even though you're exhausted by the day. If someone asked why, you would find it difficult to articulate, you'd probably shrug. Somewhere though, you're thinking it's a good omen for the tiresome midweek, this pleasing name. It reverberates with Franco-American relations, Sinatra scooping Charlotte from Serge's arms, running her into the sea himself. It's fun to say in an accent, rolled on the tongue like bitter ristretto, chin tilted in Givenchy and silk scarves. Sometimes, you like to eschew geography and let more poetic forces dictate your route: there is never any telling where that might lead. However, no one cares to question your station choices. The train is grumpy and silent, the commuters are not seeking friends. You hide your face in a *Mĕtro*, tuck your feet up on orange plastic and murmur, *Lafayĕtte, Lafayĕtte*.

It is a stupid habit, this reliance on romantic notions. Alan has always told you so. It isn't something which will get you anywhere; it doesn't gel with progress. There is a way to do things – a way to bone a fish, to wire a plug, to ensure the straight lines of skirting boards – ways which are, in fact, *the* way. So: it would be churlish to act otherwise. It is churlish to indulge in the small rebellions you sometimes do. It would be sensible to board the closer train.

Either way, you are here now, slumped and daydreaming in the corner, and this train finds its cantankerous momentum, pulling into the dark tunnel. You wish the lights were dimmer. The faces in the fluorescence seem obscene, like the final songs of discotheques when everyone looks up, glistening. You press your cheek against the windowpane, aware if he were here he would chide you, horrified by germs, but the pane is cool and blocks out the worst of the light, the people, your grease and their eyes. Second Avenue pulls into sight. The platform is thick with crowds and you realise when they swamp on you will need to move your feet, curl tighter. You would prefer the train whisked through, ever onward, and took you straight home.

This thought is not vocalised, but it seems the gods hear it anyway. The train slows to a tease, then gathers itself and moves on, the doors steadfastly closed. The faces on the platform are furious; you turn away, lips bitten in a smug grin. Passengers mutter, shuffling back to their seats —

'Huh, I thought the F stops here?'

'Usually yeah, we can walk from Delancey though.'

'Whatever.'

This may be so, but as the train approaches the station's mosaics it shows even less inclination to pause, rattling through with panache. Those who were supposed to get off here, or earlier, are now hunched at the doors with fists, full of expletives and scowls, pointing at the map where the white dot promises the train will stop. But it hasn't, and you are quietly head-down pleased. Soon, you will be home. You can undo the pins from your hair and clean the coffee granules from beneath your nails. You can make dinner of that goggle-eyed sea bass you brought home from the Chinatown market last night, which ogled you from the fridge shelves at breakfast this morning. You can go to sleep early: tomorrow you have a double shift.

By the time the train skips East Broadway and hurtles under the East River towards Brooklyn, uneasiness is beginning to catch beneath the exasperation, a low burbling panic like the sound of scuba tanks exhaling, emanating from inside and outside all at once. It was supposed to stop, the train was supposed to stop, and it's not so long ago that those planes taught the skyscrapers not to aim so high. People are wary now of surprises, particularly those sprung in tunnels and transport. They do not want it rammed home that they are here, in a metal box, hurtling through shafts carved in the foundations of the city. Strapped in this ride; the bar has come down, the music has started. At this thought, a man shakes his fleshy head, yanks himself from his seat, and stomps through the carriage. He makes for the front of the train. It is time for someone to find out what the fuck is going on.

You pay little attention to the man's mission, something in your brain is convinced his attempt will be fruitless. The train is moving with an intent which undoubtedly trumps his own. You are distracted by an old woman who is rummaging through a loose-leaf notebook. Her arms are scrunched up into her sides like crippled chicken wings. As she scribbles in the pages, she shrugs her shoulders, darting and juddering in her seat. You wonder what she is writing, what inventions could possibly justify this panicked dance. It might be the story of her life, making its way into posterity down a lined page. She could be inventing maps, creating cities and populations in neat columns, a secret world made real in the retelling with ragged scrublands and battered firths stretching long into the land. Perhaps it is only a shopping list.

When the fat man returns, the first riot kicks off.

'There's no one there. No driver. He's...'

'What?'

'You heard me! There's not even... I can't... Oh god.'

The man paws at his chest, his breath rasping. His eyes scan the carriage accusingly, unwilling to admit that this is a crisis, still clinging to the supposition that this is some elaborate hoax played on him by friends who will wait for his panic to slap him on the back and laugh, 'You believed it, you asshole!' This is not the response he is given.

'What do you mean, there's no driver?'

'What the hell is going on?'

'Daniel, don't shout, the baby...'

'Don't shout? The man says there's no driver. We're in a tunnel going god knows where and there's no one at the controls and you're telling me not to... I mean, is he in the bathroom? Is he... Where are we? What was the last station? Shouldn't we be at Jay Street? Be passing Jay Street? Oh God, where do these tunnels go, oh god, oh where? Oh...'

'Shut UP!'

A number of passengers are jostling through the Do-Not-Open-Unless-In-Case-Of-Emergency door which leads between the carriages, pushing forward to the front of the train where the small room of buttons lives, where there should be a sullen man in a peaked cap who leans out at stations to yell 'Stand AWAY from the doors.' The train is still moving, you realise; although the windows are black there is the sound of a steady canter and a cool wind blows through the open door, tickling your hair. It is a small doorway and no one is willing to wait for an orderly queue.

'Get out of my way!'

'Ah fawk you, mister.'

'Ow!'

'I need to, I need to...'

'Let me PAST!'

The boy swears again and turns to the man, whipping out a small blade he brandishes like a fist, eyes dark beneath a lank fringe. For a moment, it seems as if this will bring the momentary calm of threats upon the crowd, but then a fist flies into his gut and he crumples, the knife skittering across the floor and under your seat.

'Hey!'

And then there are kicks and scuffles, the shrieks of women, a dull thud like files dropped on desks. There are yells like questions and knees which find groins and the 'stop it stop it stop it stop it, my *baby*, stop it stop it, *please*, I...' and a puckered woman with brown roots like a skull-cap in her bleached hair scratches her diamanté nails down the cheek of a dark teenage boy dressed in baggy Diesel jeans, and a shambling drunk emerges from his layers of pus and grime to head-butt the smooth Armani chin of the banker who yells 'FUCK', and a Hassidic Jew lets loose with a kick, and they scream and tussle, and the train hurtles and you sit and you watch and —

'AaeeeeeeEEEEEEEEEEE!'

And suddenly the noise is lathed by this keening harpy scream, loud beyond all proportion from those crumpled lips of the bird lady. The idea that noise could be produced in her withered lungs is impossible, and the shock stills the crowd instantly. It is as if an innocuous draped sackcloth has been yanked away to reveal a gleaming cage, the tiger prowling inside. Everyone stares. She stops screaming and looks back at them. A mitt unclenches a handful of hair, muscles relax, the coiled mob shuffle apart, silent but for mutters. Suddenly, eye contact is impossible. The carriages sop with the embarrassment that follows the shaken hat of beggars. For your part, you already suspected this ugliness lurking beneath the veneer of manners, though you never wanted to get involved. Now everyone is in agreement, and quiet. The train lurches on.

'Listen.' It is the fat man who first investigated the situation. He is slumped against the window, his features slack and defeated. 'There's nothing there. There's no driver, but that's not it, there's no... no... controls. There's nothing. There's two more carriages but they're empty and then the train, it just... stops. It, the door, it's gone, or wasn't there, or... I don't know.' He exhales heavily with the exertion.

'Well, what are we going to do?' asks the woman with the baby, rocking it back and forth on the seat, bouncing her knees like a child waiting for the bathroom. The carriage is silent. 'We have to do *some*thing.'

'I'll call the authorities. They'll come. Or they'll stop it.' A man pulls a Blackberry from his pocket, triumphant. 'Quiet, a moment, everyone,' although the carriage is already silent, all eyes trained on him. He punches some numbers determinedly, a collective breath is inhaled, but the phone beeps in protest. Of course, there is no reception embedded this far beneath the city, no signals penetrate the pavements. He drops his technology to the floor and blushes. 'There's nothing.'

You are watching this all with a curious detachment. Although logically there is cause for concern, it as if the panic of the others has removed that responsibility from you. You sit patient as a character in a play, convinced that events will unfold. Secretly, you find something intoxicating in ceding control. There is nothing to be done, and you cannot be blamed for not going home, to bed, to work again. You needn't apologise. The train bobs gently and the gaggle of voices recede. You fall asleep.

And in your shadows, the bird lady is pecking around an empty lot, worrying at the dry earth. She holds sheaves of paper which she crumples into balls and rams underneath stones. The soil catches beneath her fingernails as she furrows deeper in her paper graveyard. You are trying to make yourself invisible, though her attention is elsewhere. Crouched behind a wooden stile, you shift from one foot to the other. You watch her pause, remove a pen from her folds, and add more words. Whatever is written is clearly the crux of the matter, undoubtedly she is spelling the secrets.

You wait until nightfall, which happens sudden as the flicking of switches. She is gone. She left no markers where the papers are buried, but you move with certainty to a spot where the earth is barely disturbed, and begin to dig. Once you break the surface the earth becomes hot and moist, inhaling and exhaling primordial whispers. Your arms sink into it, scooping great hunks of mud. There is dirt everywhere; your face is smudged, you can feel grains between your teeth. You feel like a warrior, face-painted and heroic, and dig faster, gasping. You catch a glimpse: there! A corner of white paper gleams and you brush away the remains of earth like a crack-addled archaeologist hunting for the final tinfoil remains. You make to close your hand around it. With a rustle, the paper scurries deeper. You claw after it, but the paper is faster. You are digging frantically, panting on your knees. You are sinking, headfirst, into the hole. Your arm reaches over and you follow it tumbling, plummeting, into a moist and filthy abyss.

When you hit the bottom it is like a slap. You are wrenched back and open your eyes. You are on the train.

By this point, much of the hysteria has dispersed. With no active plan, the other passengers have settled, like refugees, to wait. Small camps have set up, food is shared. People sit cross-legged on the floor, no longer bound by propriety to remain upright. There is still the occasional rippling of discussion, but the stones cast are smaller now and quicker to settle. You are all, for the time being, inert.

Time moves differently. In constant motion, you think about the conundrum of the twin ageing differently in the spaceship to his brother on earth. Time is dilating. You wonder if you walked backwards through the carriage would you be standing still, you think about the earth spinning through space, you think about home. If everyone there is growing older, the food in your fridge decomposing. If Alan misses you, if he's noticed. Maybe there's a search party hunting for your corpse; you can't imagine he would entertain the other implication of your absence. You don't think that you're losing your mind. There is a simplicity to decisions you lacked before; in fact, decisions are few. You open your hands and let the weight of intention be lifted from your palms. Sit tight, and wait.

Time passes, and some of your fellow passengers begin a pilgrimage to the carriage with the *Dial 1-800-IMMIGRATION* adverts, mutter at the sign in low confessional tones. Church services to a laminate god. You find it hard to believe that visas and paperwork will be required where the train is taking you, but perhaps they still believe in returning home, and worry without custom stamps they will be trapped endlessly behind borders. Or maybe they just like to talk to the poster, with its definitive fonts. Personally, it offers you little relief. You find your own solace balanced on the gangway between carriages, breathing a damp tunnel air in the momentum of clatters. You like the confirmation that, as suspected, the train is in constant motion, ever-forward. Sometimes this is forgotten in the lull of carriages. You spend many hours chin poked into the air, watching the walls whip away. You try not to think too hard about where you are going. Just this, the journey, seems enough.

When you're not standing outside, you tend to sleep. Despite everything, you have never felt better. You sleep soundly with rich, textured dreams, curled up in a plastic corner. Unlike at home, you don't toss and turn for hours. The tightness in your throat has abated and you no longer wrestle through a long fug on waking: your eyes open and your mind is instantly alert. It would be strange to say you are happy, but when you wake and find everything is still the same, you are.

In fact, you realise, as you wander into another nap, this is the best you have felt in a long while. You are not ditzy nor frivolous, no. Whatever is happening, you're doing fine. You are coping, you are confident. In your small life, you feel almost in control.

And then a noise wakens you, a sound like the scream of a mechanical bat. You look instinctively at your watch, although it could be 3am or 3pm and neither matters. Your stomach is unsettled: something has changed. The train is not moving. You are not hurtling. After the sound of brakes, there is silence. Passengers look to one another with wide eyes like open palms. Those who are standing reach out for bars to clutch, for windows to lean against. It is like stepping off a ferry onto solid ground after months on a tempestuous sea. You feel sick. Strangely, of all the endings, this wasn't the one you tended in your mind.

The more vocal passengers decide to lead an expedition back through the tunnel, back to the city, the world beyond the train. They will walk as long as is necessary, they will find

↣

help, rescue will blaze through the tunnels. Salvation will arrive. You find yourself on your feet, tissued with indecision.

You could follow, join the trailblaze to the city, make your way back to where home is waiting. You could sit tight here and wait for the turning of the world. The bird lady twitters to your side, squeezes past down the carriage, and you notice she has left a single folded sheet. You lunge, unfold and read the message she has left. It is, of course, exactly as you have come to realise. You sigh. Then, you think of the other options and a grin begins to tease at your lips. Humming, you clamber from the carriage, past the others, to the front of the train, the darkness of the tunnel. You fold the paper into your back pocket, take a deep breath, and carry on alone.

Campground Murderer
Rose McDonagh

THEY ARRIVED LATE at the camp, parking between two neat metal pins tied with red tape. The sun poured thick yellow beams between the trees. Rob helped his dad to thread the poles through the lining of the tent while his mother got the little stove spitting and cooked sausages which split with pink, wobbly flesh.

When it grew dark, his mum took him along a path through the woods to show him a gap in the trees. Below the sea was pure black, above the moon shone round and white as a torch beam. The more he stared up at the sky, the more the stars revealed themselves.

In the sleeping bag at night his feet were cold and he woke up four times, once thinking he was on a sailing boat in the middle of a storm. The next day, patches of sun shifted over the campground grass as if the countries on a map had come alive and started to migrate.

In the doorway of the tent next door, a girl with bob-cut black hair was using two pans as drums. During breakfast, she came over to Rob shyly. She was only nine, he learned with scorn. But after he'd finished eating, they went into the woods a little way, pretending to be highwaymen and she told him an incredible secret. 'I killed someone once,' she said. Her eyes had wide, black pupils like plugholes.

For the whole week they played and each day she revealed more of how she carried out the murder. On Tuesday, she told him, 'I cut his throat, I cut out his eyes.' On Thursday she said 'I burnt the body and then I buried the ashes.' He moved between scorn and nervous awe. In the highwayman game they would watch the pathway for victims; each family was a stagecoach filled with riches. On the second last day he slipped on the steep bank and grabbed a bunch of nettles to break his fall. His lower eyelids filled with tears and he had to bite into his cheek to stop them coming. It burned him up to think she might have seen.

On the last day, he went to find her but when he got halfway through the trees he saw her dad had caught her by the arm. He was shouting something about a broken chair. Rob watched from behind the trunk of a pine as her dad hit her with his belt. He imaged her skin under her t-shirt becoming striped like a zebra crossing. He returned to his tent and sat for a while, drawing with a stick in the earth. When she appeared back in the clearing, he wandered up to her but her eyes narrowed. 'You're too much of a baby for a highwayman,' she said and turned on one heel.

The time came for his family to leave. He sat in the car with everything packed around him, his feet up on the cool-box. The girl was nowhere to be seen while they packed, but as the car pulled away, he glanced out the rear window and saw her, staring silently at the bumper. Her look was steely and in that moment he felt sure that she must have killed someone. The thought filled him up with wonder like a jar in a rainstorm.

Extract from the novel *Piraeus*

Graeme Williamson

Here there are no shadows
to tell us where we are.
Paula Allen

PHILIP IS FLOATING in space inside a beautiful room. Everything glows the colour of moonlight and sunlit milk. Above his head an opaque mist extends into infinity. Voices mutter from behind an invisible partition. He suspects he is being observed and that someone is discussing his case.

At some point he has become transparent although he cannot remember how or when. Through the back of his skull he sees the warm sheets of an undisturbed bed beckoning him earthward.

He tries to explore the room but this is difficult. The air becomes heavy, a transparent, viscous fluid. He holds his breath and swims along the wall into a corridor. The shadows of invisible people pass by and the sterile imprints of their bodies shiver in the air around him like rainbows. At the far end of the corridor he arrives at a dead end. In an alcove an icy waterfall shatters into an ornamental pool.

After a time the effort of swimming exhausts him. He returns to his place above the bed and hovers. Air enters his body through his pores and his fear of suffocation subsides. As he floats he wonders why he no longer knows himself. He has become a vast, shapeless embryo, without provenance, floating alone in the womb of space, uncertain even if he is alive.

A woman sits on a chair in the corner of the room. Her hair is dishevelled but her uniform is immaculate, as if she's chosen it for a special occasion. As night falls she reaches across to the table beside her and clicks on an anglepoise lamp. The dim aura cast by the lamp and the firefly illuminations from the machines by Philip's bed glimmer in the darkness.

The woman, whose name is Annie, is studying a journal in preparation for an exam. *The use of opiates for analgesia in patients suffering from dementia is not recommended.* Information dissolved into a sea of fatigue. She yawns, shivers, glances up at Philip's bed, but does not raise her eyes to where her patient is floating.

Why can't she see me? Philip wonders.

Philip needs to be washed several times a day. Although he's been unconscious for a week he never stops shitting. Keeping Philip clean is one of the tasks associated with Annie's job but she does not mind. He might come back at any moment and she wants him to wake up fresh, in sheets as clean as a spring morning.

She approaches the bed, smoothes the blanket, lifts the pad from its slot, records the observations, examines the tubes that sprout from Philip's body, shines a penlight in his eyes. The pupils inexplicably respond; his reading is still 3 on the scale, although his limbs are no longer rigid.

'Where are you, my dear?' she whispers in his ear.

The lights blink, the filter shunts away like a mill. Rain batters at the window and boiling silver clouds fly along in the moonlit sky.

Annie goes to the room next door and asks

for help. Frankie, the auxiliary, joins her with all the necessary materials. She unscrews the top from a bottle of Hibiscrub, splashes the pink liquid into a plastic basin, runs water from the mixer tap on the sink, swishes the froth around. The two women position themselves on either side of the bed, lift Philip by the shoulders, slip the soiled pad and the sheets out from beneath him, peel off his sweaty pyjama jacket, bathe his arms, face, chest, armpits – replace the sheet, lay him down, wash his legs, groin, feet, turn him over, wash his back, wipe his asshole with aqueous ointment, apply cream to his entire body, lift him to a sitting position, pull on a new pyjama jacket and comb his hair. To finish off, Frankie shaves him. In the process she nicks a slice of parched skin from his chin. A thin, urgent trail of blood trickles down his neck. *Low platelets*, Annie says. She sits beside him on the bed, holding a clotting stick against the cut. Twenty minutes pass before the flow finally ceases.

When they finish Frankie leaves the room and returns with coffee for Annie, which she drinks in silence.

The window rattles. The wind rushing by outside sounds cold. Annie takes her cardigan from the back of her chair and wraps it tightly around her shoulders, even though the radiators are on full and she is sweating.

In order for the filter to work Philip must remain motionless at all times. Even the slightest twitch activates the alarm. When this happens the pump stops working and Philip's toxic blood begins to poison him. When Annie is on duty however, he lies peacefully for hours at a time without moving a muscle.

A nurse walks into the shadows at the far side of the room. She stands by a steel trolley. Philip's arm is laid out on a surgical tray. The nurse unwraps a procedure kit, dips a cotton ball into a tray containing a creosote-coloured liquid and cleans the skin. She discards the cotton into a yellow incinerator bag and draws up a syringe of heparin, squirts out a misty plume of excess liquid and injects the remainder into his fistula. Philip is frightened that the nurse would do something so dangerous, so irresponsible. He fears he may have been getting on everyone's nerves and now they want to kill him.

Annie is never sure if Philip hears her but once the ward lights have been extinguished and they are alone together in the wilderness of the dark, she talks to him to cheer him up. She tells him about a field in the North where years before she watched a meteorite fall to earth in a ball of flames.

The hill rises steeply at first, then you come to a pasture, which is usually empty. A burn runs through it with yellow water that tastes of sulphur. You can't drink from it because sheep fall in further up and drown. I got really sick once from drinking the water there.

There's a brilliant view over the loch. Every moment something changes. People think there's more to look at in the city, but that's rubbish. The country is never monotonous. Shadows the size of mountains fly over the hills in a single breath. Light comes up out of the ground like a living thing.

At first I thought the stone was a firework, then a comet. I was sure I knew where it landed, but I was wrong. I looked all day but found nothing. That was five years ago. I camp there every summer but still I've never found it.

Philip wanders, pulled this way and that by every word.

Fields
Sky
Wind
No one is on the road
There is no one in the village
The door of the house is open
No one lives here.

One evening he is awoken by a steely scratching at his throat. A necklace of barbed wire encircles his neck. Movement is painful and frightening.

He tells Annie: *This is no life for a human being. This is barbaric.*

There's no alternative, Annie replies.

Fuck, Philip shouts so loudly he wakes a patient in the next ward.

Fuck!

→

Fuck!
Fuck!

For the next twenty-four hours he repeats the curse, loudly, over and over. Frankie, a devout evangelical woman who has only worked in the ward for a few days, is a little shocked but Annie explains.

On top of everything else, dying is extremely irritating.

Fuck!
Fuck!
Fuck!
Fuck!

Voices murmur from the nurses' station. It is dark in the corridor but a glow from beneath the door attracts him like the lights of an inn. Annie appears from around a corner, a revenant in surreal white.

I'm expecting some ice cream from America.

At this time of night? Are you sure?

Of course, I'm sure.

Well, go back to bed and we'll let you know when it arrives.

Don't patronise me.

I wouldn't think of patronising you.

He turns back along the hallway to his door, shuffles into the windy chill, slips into bed, draws the blanket up to his chin. Throughout the night Annie returns again and again. Each time something is different and he does not recognise her. She has changed her uniform, or grown taller or dyed her hair or put on a mask or become a man, or a child, or transformed into a terrifying machine.

One night the angel of death appears at his bedside. Slender, suave, black eyes, black shirt, black trousers, black shoes, black hair. The sound of the pump fades, the wind dies, the darkness deepens, a chill rushes through him like a vast wave into a breached ship. He shivers, takes a deep breath, steps out of himself into thick, hollow silence, but after a long pause the figure turns away, creeps to the door, and is gone.

Every night, the cool, steady gaze of Annie's blue eyes goes with him into the dark.

Philip says goodbye, goodbye to everything. The chaplain, having been here before, is not afraid to help him. Philip begins with the place of his confinement. He lets his eyes dwell briefly on the blemishes in the paintwork, the imperfections he hasn't noticed before, which now seem as personal as the idiosyncrasies of a face, the sinuous chrome curve of the mixer tap, the military grey drugs cabinet on the wall by the door, the shadows in the sheet, the geometry of painted steel and plastic, the leaves flashing past beyond the window, the bending treetops, the pure, uninhabited emptiness of colour delineated by roofs, trees, the pleasing or unsettling angles and intersections; aerials, phone lines, scaffolding. Next he turns his attention to the pathology of scars, indentations, marks, skin tones, and the shapes of faces, patients, young and old, other white-coated personnel, *'and this is what I want to happen when I'm dead,' he* says. The chaplain nods, agrees to conduct the ceremony, even though the patient has no beliefs to speak of, has never in all this time thought of praying, suggests a reading. A spot on a hillside, no marker, a few friends present, the senseless whimsicality of the demented man dictating everything, and then finally, goodbye to the human, mother, father, dissolving others, Annie. There is a composure about these arrangements. Having prowled his labyrinth for months, he is no longer searching for a loophole.

Four poems from *Fr Meslier's Breviary*

Fr Meslier's Confession
A C Clarke

Roll up! Roll up! Get your souls laundered here!
No sin too stubbornly entrenched, too trivial. Instant relief
guaranteed. Just a mutter

of dog Latin, a brief
wave of my magic hand and you're whiter than white.
I won't give you grief

(I'm light
on the penances). I come cheap too,
a tenth in cash or kind all I require. I might

as well turn huckster, peddling quack remedies as I do.
It wouldn't stop the laity.
How they queue

for a turn in my booth! It sickens me
more than their black
teeth, the breath of poverty

through the grille. I've been slack
in 'duty' – no wonder! If I offered salves at least
people could take them back,

proved dud. I'm a priest.
I have the keys.
They're being fleeced

in the name of the Church. I've brought them to their knees
and they're weeping for joy. It's a disease.

Fr Meslier's Quill
A C Clarke

I sharpened a new quill today
shaving the pliant bone
fallen from the wing of a sky-
wanderer, its feathers shaded
mist-grey to rain-grey,

gave thanks so lovely a thing
had come into my keeping,
its balance between finger and thumb
the poise of flight.

In that moment I was out
of myself, the sky above me
drawing me on and up
blue on blue on blue
without end.

Fr Meslier At His Desk

A C Clarke

Day is into its stride. The beasts at pasture,
my own flock bent to toil.
The Lord is my Shepherd.

To everything its time. To me the task
I laid upon myself that April evening

(and that at Easter or thereabouts)

with branches, new in bud, dancing their pattern
against the windowpane.

She thinks I'm writing sermons, my housekeeper.
I dip my quill in copperas and gall.

My hand, hunched familiar
crawls across the page
a spotted toad

smeared with holy fat
slimy as soap
never a day's work, not so much
as lay a fire.

They run to kiss their curé's hand
torment

My *zeal has eaten me up.*

Would they hear?
Or hearing understand?

– poor Father Meslier he's studying too hard –

the letters dance like fever
no sense in them

dizzy my brain with empty syllables

Take from me this cup.

Fr Meslier's Reproaches

AC Clarke

O my people what have I done to you?
how have I offended you?
Do not answer

I would have led you from slavery to freedom
but you have nailed me to the cross of myself

For twenty years I have led you through a desert,
fed you with lies, as you desired

O my people what have I done to you?
how have I offended you?
Do not answer

What more should I have done for you that I have not done?
You could have been the grapes of a choice vintage

Because you would not move from exhausted soil
you chose to be thin, sour wine

I would have opened a path through a sea of confusion,
you closed your hearts before I could dare to speak

O my people what have I done to you?
how have I offended you?
Do not answer

Do not answer. You have no need to answer
Your small accounts are right with the small god
you worship. Mine
are deep in debt. I am the creditor
who gives himself no quarter

O my people
I have done worse than nothing
I have offended you
by not offending

Two Types of Wine
Jason Monios

There were two types of wine
on the table. He mixed them together,
uncaring. They were the same colour.

A glance warned him, too late.
He was always doing things like that,
in front of people, in front of her.

She forgave him, instinctively,
berating herself for her angry look,
seeing only his shame now.

She took the glass from his fingers,
held it and gulped the twin fruits,
forcing their union into herself.

She pledged silently never to judge him
nor to want someone different,
not to lie to herself again and again.

He poured more wine for himself.
A different type, a different colour,
a new glass now that the old had been dirtied.

The Temptation of Adamnán

John Douglas Millar

Sea rich as blood and blood
taste on lips sere with scour of salt
breeze and sun.

The saint bundles his bark
through tangle and sloke and bladder
wrack, and on

across rock and bog tarred
with steaming peat and raw iodine
stench. He rests,

rowan and fir berries
burn like stars in the canopy.
his body

a galaxy of aches,
nerves as raw as winter trees
his rags rich

with blood and sweat but no
tears. His small sack of barley roped
over a bone raw shoulder.

In a copse of apple-wood,
                    hazelnut and cedar
                                    stands a single cherry
                                                in blush of bloom

and below, a girl, her flesh open to the sky
eating
        a crimson apple.

Fabulous Beast
Patricia Ace

No, I'll not worship at the foot of this altar – the days
when it was nothing but rows and making up from rows,
heads locked in mortal struggle like two skinny strays
grappling in an alley over scraps the butcher throws;
panting under pressure, spines dipped then flexed
in a bid for the prize, each rib visible through pastry-thin
skin; heavy paws scuffing the dirt, thick-set necks.

No, make me instead a fabulous beast, something
lifted from the margins of a medieval text with the trunk
of a lion, part eagle, part dragon, shark-toothed and winged
that can change shape at will – and the reek of a skunk.
Or failing that set me to slither in the dust, jaws unhinged,
my body shapeless and sassy and strong – yes, I'll swallow
you whole before I'll honour and obey, before I'll follow.

On Looking
JoAnne McKay

I am a badly-peeled grape of girl,
having lost my good face at twenty-one.
I lived, briefly, as a smooth-skin lustre pearl,
then my flirtation with beauty was done.
The face that replaced it I choose to forget,
except it appears the choice is not mine;
I see it in every reflected glance yet,
the veiled pity eyes that cloud me unblind.
But distorted as any fairground mirror,
truth lies like a gypsy fortune teller
searching pockets to see the future clearer:
people look not at, but in. So do tell her,
the world is not as cruel as we can be;
be kinder to what mirrors what you see.

Honesty

Nick Brooks

My other half spits
the word honesty
into my face
as though not in her right mind.

That's what I think of your honesty, she says
the word dripping
salt and sour
over my lips.

Honesty is a club you use to beat me,
she says.
But you wouldn't know real honesty
if it kicked you up the arse.

You wouldn't know real honesty
if it grabbed you by the throat,
her consonants a blade working
between my ribs.

I savour
their sweetness.
The quickest way to a man's heart.

Elemental

Patricia Ace

At first you were air to me —
essential, invisible, blue.
A breeze blown through an open window,
riffling papers, lifting dust motes to spin
in sunlight like planets, racing.

Sometimes you were water to me —
necessary, untenable, clear.
A spring in the hills where a lone walker
pauses, parched, filling her tin cup
from the source of the river.

And then you were earth to me —
mineral, secretive, black.
Black as the seed bed where the spore
takes hold, splitting into growth;
black as the burial ground.

But mostly you were fire to me —
incendiary, untouchable, red.
Flames licking the stove where our words
turned to ashes. But oh they burned
brightly, my darling, and well.

From Light to Air

Christie Williamson

I breathe you, you
leave nothing to chance,
dance like the wind
in the yellowing sycamore
leaves, sit like the stone
beneath the cypress tree,
a shelter for the shattered
shell of a crustacean
who crabbed too far
for him to chew.

The seat I've carried
in my heart was built
for two, for me and you
to sit and taste
the time of day in.

Check your watch. Today you waft
yourself into my top notch.

Late Night, February

Niall Campbell

Then like the blind astronomer
I've only memories of those nights.
And memories of mostly nothing;
just poses in the dark: out late,
side-by-tender-side, a thrilled light
where my hand held the small of her back.

Absorb

Hazel Frew

I could live
inside your mouth,
no kidding

quite easily
move in
and make myself at home

rest my toes
on soft flesh

hear your breath
long and short and wet

smell your smell
use your tongue as a blanket

wrap me roll me
lap me all over
I'm naked

teeth portcullised
barring escape
(as if I'd want to)

and if you saw fit
you could swallow me
whole just like that

I'd gladly go deeper,
all the way

sliding from gullet
stomach to ileum

absorbed like food
disappearing
for good.

One for the Road

Brian Johnstone

The headlights beam into the dark,
illuminating silence the vehicle moves into,

distant till it dopplers past, a fan of light
that breaks upon a sky so full of stars

it's nothing but the swipe of us
intruding for a moment on the pitch of night

much as a match flares till it's shaken out,
or as we try to make our mark

but stumble, spill its substance, light up
our surroundings only briefly, see

there's nothing more than we'd steered into,
find we're fumbling for the map.

Milk of Morning
Nick Brooks

I retire early   set up camp
on our habitual battleground
my Culloden   times four
your Agincourt
the site once more   of so many
noble defeats
the quilt that   divides retreats
a patchwork territory
of tangled limbs
      severed
          nights
  then
the bugle blown
a surrender with
the first milk
      of morning
and toast crumbs
      at peace
        between your tits

Homesick
Cynthia Rogerson

IZZY HATES HER mother. She has hated her mother as long as she can remember. It isn't anything in particular her mother says or does – it is everything she says and does. Izzy supposes there must have been a time when things were different. She has a vague memory of opening her stocking one Christmas morning to find dozens of miniature presents – fairy gifts – and she'd played with them for hours, weeks, months, till they were worn out, and still she'd not wanted to share them. Of cuddles she can remember none. This is odd, because there is plenty photographic proof of affection. And happiness. It must have happened, yet there is not a scrap of it left in her fourteen-year-old heart. Even the sound of her mother's voice, even the word mum coming up in text on her phone, has the power to set up little waves of repulsion.

So when her mother is killed at milk crate corner – a clear and cold October afternoon, with the blackbirds at the rowan berries and the geese all revving up, round and round – Izzy feels none of the things she ought to. Except surprise of course, because no one expects sudden death on sunny days. She feels intensely annoyed with her mother – stupid woman, what was she doing driving home just at that moment? Typical. Oh! Izzy is so angry! Angry, but excited at the same time, because whatever else this is, it is not boring. A shameful and secret joy twists with her hot irritation, till she doesn't know if she is coming or going.

She does not miss her mother one bit. In that place in her life – that continuous surrounding place – where she had become used to feeling repulsed all the time, witnessed all the time, is now a resounding and resplendent relief. Izzy used to love to swim, back when she'd loved things, and this reminds her of diving into water deeper and warmer than the shallow chilly water she'd braced herself for. Sometimes the loch was like that, on a July afternoon after torrential rain. Mother-less, she is able to unclench now, and just be.

The evening of the funeral day, she goes out to find a boy who lives down the street, the one everyone calls that ginger-haired loser from down the street. Still in her new funeral clothes, she walks over to the bus shelter – his home, basically – where he is smoking with his mates. She finds she is walking very slowly. All her limbs feel heavy, as if gravity has increased its pull on her. She asks for a puff of his cigarette and tells him: 'Hey, I'll do it with ya.' She says this in a flat, serious tone, and her eyes are dead under the orange street lamp. The ginger-haired loser from down the street looks like he'd rather not, but then all his mates are watching, so he takes her to his uncle's empty place across the road. They both slide through the half open kitchen window at the back. The window ledge hurts her belly, and later he hurts her too, but not much. The whole thing takes less than fifteen minutes. It is not at all like she'd expected. She can't understand what all the fuss is about. She is angry about that, too. She doesn't think she'll be bothering with that again anytime soon, thank you very much.

'Where have you been?' her father asks, after she walks in her own back door, with sticky knickers and aching thighs.

'Nowhere,' she answers.

Then her father says: 'Sit down and eat.' That's all he says, and he looks back to his own food. Izzy feels as if she's put her foot down hard on a step that is suddenly not there. Into this alarming void she falls. Thwump! And suddenly there is her mother's grating voice, loud and sharp: Where exactly is nowhere, and what do you think you're doing, worrying everyone on a day when they've enough to worry about, selfish besom that you are and always have been. You'll be at the washing up tonight, my love, because you've done nothing else all day but suit yourself.

Ears ringing and dizzy, Izzy notices all her siblings are already at the table. Not a lot of eating seems to be going on – mostly mash getting pushed around on plates. Becca's long blond hair has not been properly brushed in a week, and looks like cutting it might be the only solution. Ian's chin looks swollen where he has stitches from the big fall off his bike yesterday, and his nose runs right into his mouth. Annie, the eldest, sits silently crying without looking any less pretty – a mean feat, impressing Izzy, who can't decide if this takes practise or if some people are born this way. Annie has always been perfect, her mother's angel, so probably it is genetic, and there is no way on earth Izzy is ever going to be able to cry prettily. Or perhaps at all.

Her auntie is sitting in her mother's chair as if she has a right to, and eats with great efficiency. Blow your nose, she tells Ian, and passes him her own cloth handkerchief. Izzy flinches at both the sight of her auntie sitting in that chair, and the tone of her voice. Even the fact of her proper hankie is appalling. They'd all grown up knowing ingenious alternatives to hankies.

Her father sits woodenly shovelling the steak pie in. His eyes look small and his hands tremble. He seems much older than he did last week, and he does not seem very substantial. Izzy wonders if perhaps both her parents were killed last Tuesday, but God has decided losing both parents is too much of a cruel shock for the family, and so has allowed her father back for a bit. She looks hard at him for traces of encroaching invisibility.

In the kitchen, the radio is on, as always. No one ever listens to it, but tonight no one is talking and everyone hears it. Who had tuned in that naff channel? No one ever thought about it. Like the way clean clothes and wholesome broths produced themselves. Now a man with a rich pouring voice sings about a pussy cat, and asks the pussy cat what is new. He keeps asking in a coy tone, as if he already knows the answer, as if he expects to be told that something happy is new. Izzy hurts down there, and she can smell herself now, in the warmth. Sweet, but rank too. The food in her mouth has no flavour, and takes great effort to swallow. She watches the clock on the sideboard slowly shunting the minutes. Something unpleasant has happened to time, and even the clock seems to know it. The sideboard itself is piled up with new toys, like Christmas. Izzy, who is too old for toys, feels a giggle rise up – the same laugh that's been riding around inside her for days. But the laugh is too big, way too big. If she let it out now, it might finish her off. She pushes her plate away and stands up.

'Where are you going?' her father asks.

'I'm tired. Needing a bath.'

'Okay. Goodnight.'

Again, the plummeting feeling and her mother's voice: Aye, well that's a fine thing. Don't let us stop you! Don't feel you need to keep us company in our time of despair and grief. Just go on then! Hey, exactly where do you think you're going, young lady? You march right back here this minute and sit with us for a while. Who do you think you are? The Queen of Sheba?

Izzy locks the door and runs the bath. There's only one bathroom, and she knows she has ten minutes of privacy, tops, so the taps are on full blast, and she strips off and slips in while it's filling. The water is a blessing. She turns off the cold with her toes, and lets herself be scalded. She is stinging inside now, and her inner thighs ache and her mouth feels puffy. She tenderly inspects her body, as if it's been plundered while she wasn't looking. As if it is not even her own body.

➳

The water slowly turns pink and she closes her eyes. Feels her breathing and heartbeat slow, and slow, to almost nothing, and she thinks of all the things that have happened in her life so far that have led to this pink bath. The sequence of events is confusing, and she has to keep going back again and again as she remembers more. It seems important to remember it all, in just the right order. What had she last said to her mother? What had her mother last said to her? These words elude her, though she has a clear memory of shouting at her lastWednesday, about her red top that her mum had put in the dryer and shrunk.

'I hate you, you always have to ruin everything.'

These were pretty much her exact words. And they were true. Everything was her mother's fault. Everything still is. Now, in the bath, she can still hear the kitchen radio, and it's playing a song she likes, one that she's liked since she was wee, about a yellow submarine. She knows all the words, and that's because they used to sing it on the long car journey to see her gran. At her gran's house, she was always put to sleep on her own in the attic room, which smelled of cat pee and had spooky wallpaper. She'd often woken with an ache deep in her belly, and also lodged in her throat – a sort of all-pervading pre-tears angst. She'd creep down the stairs – *she'd forgotten this* – to the room her parents slept in. Her dad would never wake, but Mum would always wake instantly, pull open the duvet and in Izzy would slide. Hush darling, you're only feeling a wee bittie homesick. Scoot in here. Then her mum would yawn, roll over and her snores would lullaby Izzy to sleep. That had really been her mum, and that had really been her own self. She even remembers her nightie – pink daisies on blue, brushed cotton, and how she would curl into her mum's warm back and breathe in her mum smell.

Well!

Izzy closes her eyes, sighs deeply, sinks down under the water. She wonders for a second if you can be homesick for someone you hate. Impossible, and yet there it is. There is the same deep swollen ache in her belly and throat. And then, while she is worrying about this, as well as all the normal things that keep popping up as if nothing has changed – like what to wear for school tomorrow – there is a scuffle on the landing outside the bathroom door. Becca is shouting at Tom: 'Sod off, you wanker, that's mine!' There's the clear sound of a slapping hand landing on flesh, and Tom automatically shouts, in the summoning bark they have all used since the day they could call her:

'*Mum!*'

For a second, then another second, silence. Then footsteps and her father's voice:

'Bed. Now.'

Extract from the novel *Dog Evans*

Barry Gornell

NEITHER OF THEM had spoken on the walk away from the burial. As they got closer to home they could hear the whimpering, cutting into the quiet of the night.

'Shit,' said Nugget, 'listen to that. He must be wondering what he's done wrong. Has he ever been locked in on his own before?'

'You tell me, he's your dog.'

Lynne strode past Nugget into the house as the dog jumped up to greet him, licking his unshaven neck and jaw-line, causing Nugget to laugh and push him away, back to the floor. When Nugget stood up from stroking Bru, the smile was knocked from him and he was forced to take a step back as she threw his work bag at him. He caught it. He looked at it, he looked at the dog, he looked at her.

'Lynne?'

'Well, come on then,' she said. 'What are you waiting for?'

His eyes widened as he realized what she meant.

'Really? You think I should go now, so soon?'

'Well, he won't be going home anymore, will he?'

'But.' He shifted from foot to foot as he thought. 'Lynne, don't you feel bad, even a little bit?'

'Nugget, I feel poor, a lot.'

'But.'

'No buts,' she said, sliding the frosted glass door on the dresser open, revealing their drink store. Lynne dropped a half bottle of whisky into the bag. 'You know it's there. Everybody knows it's there. Be the first. Go and get it,' she said, patting the bag.

He was still looking at her hand when it stopped and he knew she was staring at him.

'Doesn't it feel disrespectful to you,' he said, 'so soon?'

'There was no respect in the killing and the burying, was there?'

'I suppose not.' They were silent. The only sound was the clicking of Bru's claws on the linoleum floor. 'You think it's wise though? Really?'

'Oh please, tonight of all nights, show me some of the old Nugget magic,' she softened her voice as her hand crept up his leg and she placed it on his crotch, 'some of the old spunk.' Her filthy smile spread wide in response to his dirty grin. 'You still got it in you?'

'Oh yes.'

'You're still the guy, the one who told me he was going to be somebody, aren't you?'

'I believe I am that guy.'

'The guy I'll do anything for when he gets back?'

She plucked her thumbnail up his zip and felt the throb behind it lurch. He groaned.

'Anything?'

'When you get back. Plus things you haven't even dreamt of. You my guy?'

'Absofuckinlutely.'

His tongue was thick and his throat was dry as he spoke to the dog.

'What do you think Bru, should we go?'

Bru wagged his tail. Bru always wagged his tail.

'Good dog,' she said. 'Here, something to

keep you going.'

Nugget opened his mouth and took the tablets. He couldn't swallow them and needed help from the bottle to get them down, one gulp for each tablet. When he put the bottle back into the bag he kissed Lynne, before leaning down to run his hand across the smooth fur of Bru's head.

'Come on then Boy.'

Bru was a mongrel, shaggy haired and bright orange. Hints of labrador and collie dwelt beneath the overwhelming blanket of red setter that followed Nugget back out of the house.

Adrenaline, amphetamine and alcohol sped through his body as he sat watching the house. His right knee bounced up and down while his left knee supported his left elbow. His chin rested in the palm of his hand as he forced the stumps of fingernails over his lower incisors, gnawing them clean. He took another sip from the bottle. The rough blend stripped his windpipe and scalded his stomach, burning along the fuse-wire of his veins to his extremities. Goosebumps crackled across his scalp like fire through stubble after harvest. His face prickled with growing sweat beads. He screwed the lid back on and bagged the bottle. Patting Bru a couple of times, he stood up and he approached the dead boy's home.

Nugget gripped the tarnished brass of the back door handle. It chattered in its casing like a clockwork bite.

'Fuck.'

He let go, glaring at the curled fingers of his hand as though they had dropped the golden apple.

He took a step away from the Evans house. Over his shoulder, marsh water caught the moon and the village feigned sleep. His nose ran. He wiped his sleeve across his face, before snorting the slimy remains into the back of his throat to be spat straight onto the porch floor. The two upper panels of the door glared at him. Nugget twitched, willing himself not to think of the house as a living thing.

'Glass and timber,' he said, nodding, rocking from heel to ball, 'glass and timber.'

He scooped the half bottle from the empty postbag slung over his shoulder. He sucked a mouthful out, then another. He took a deep breath, held it and released it slowly. Stepping forward, he finger-tipped the handle. His touch was steady. He grasped, turned and pushed in one breath. The door stopped after a few inches and he collided with it comic book style, the slapstick splitting the skin above his eye. He stood up and straightened himself as he glanced around for anybody who might have seen. Nobody had. It was quiet and still. A barn owl ghosted by. Bru was motionless.

Exploring the cut, his fingertips came away wet and he could feel the blood trickling through his eyebrow.

'Shit. Nugget, come on. What is wrong with you?'

Bru whined.

'Shh boy, keep that down.' He crouched and held the dog's head in his hands, his blood streaking its fur. 'You don't want them all to hear, do you Bru? Don't you want your share? Steak every day; think about that. All for a little shush and for helping Nugget with the search. Steak every day, my God, it even sounds good to me.'

Pulling a used handkerchief from his pocket he applied pressure to the wound as he pushed against the door again, using his meager body weight to steadily increase the force. There was some give, before it stopped again.

'What do you think boy, winter damp?'

Partially open, he pushed his head into the gap to try and see inside but snapped back as he inhaled the interior smells that now seeped out to blend with those of the nearby bog. The rank cloud of bad air that escaped wrapped itself around him and slammed him back against the wall as he gagged at the stench of butchery and cooking, or maybe rendering. Bru backed down into the corner behind Nugget's feet and lay his head on his front paws as though to keep below the smell, only standing when Nugget pushed himself off the wall.

'Come on boy, let's get this thing done; go home rich.'

When he thought he could deal with the

smell, he took a few steps back before throwing himself at the door. He shouldered it open enough to be able to get in, scuffing a fresh arc into the grain of the floor. Looking down, he saw that it was wedged on paper. Hovering between the moonlight and the interior, he peered in, trying to make sense of the room. Taking his head torch from his pocket, he turned it on and held it high. Like the probing searchlight of a police helicopter it lit upon a flotilla of tiny origami boats. A densely packed column, about a foot wide, sailed across the floor, away from him, like an exercise in perspective, towards the pale light of the rear window. Bending down to pick one up he realized it was currency, crisp and clean. They were all identically folded bank notes. It was the last of the fleet that had caused the door to jam.

'Well, looks like he didn't use this door, wouldn't you say?'

Strapping the torch on, he used the handles as a pivot and attempted one long swing into the room, aiming to avoid the boats. One crunched beneath his foot.

He was still holding onto the handles when he saw that Bru had stayed outside, framed in the tall slit of partial doorway, a burnished copper statue in the night's light.

'Come on boy.' Nugget bent his fingers towards himself, calling the dog. The dog leant forward. 'That's it, good boy, come on.' Bru crept in, head low and tail down.

Once inside, Nugget saw that the boats bisected the room in a line of unchanging width and direction; passing over a low coffee table, one of the dining chairs and an upturned box, straight as a Roman road, determined as a cockroach migration. To the right of the line was what he took to be the living area. A large sofa and a leather armchair faced an open fireplace. Embers still glowed in the hearth. To the left, the dining area, table and chairs, next to what he assumed to be the kitchen.

Curiosity bounced the erratic beam of light around the room without method, each movement corresponding with the pop of a thought in Nugget's head. It wasn't dirty, as the smell had suggested. Although it was a world created without recent adult guidance, a kind of order was in place. But the manner of things gave a sense of the awful. Animal traps, both gins and snares, against the back wall. Pelts draped over the sofa gave it the look of a sleeping bear. Worst of all were the skeletal remains. Piled in the space beneath the stairs on the left hand wall, pale collections, with the look of both ossuary and shrine; the charnel house contents of some other way of life-size graded cairns of skulls, limbs, ribcages, the awkward shapes of pelvis and scapula; the tiny disassociated links of tails, feet and spinal columns of all manner and size of beast.

'Jesus.'

He covered his eyes against it but he still had the retinal print of what he had found; his own gothic diptych. He turned away and opened his eyes to journey with the boats toward the pale square of the far window, to be somewhere else. As he became fully accustomed to surrounding gloom, his attention came back to the boats.

'Just look at all that fucking money, Bru. It's why we're here boy. And there's more, lots more.'

He held some of the notes to Bru's muzzle. 'Let's find it. Search, Bru. Search.'

His mission back on track, he ransacked the place, pulling drawers open, smacking cupboard doors back on their hinges and slapping the lids off any boxes he found.

'I know for a hand delivered fact that this fucking navy is but a small part of the boy's, no our treasure.'

He had pushed monthly packages through the door for years now. They were always the same size and weight. Occasionally, the envelopes changed colour, when a packet had been finished maybe, or when the sender couldn't lay his hands on his usual supply. The postmark was rarely the same, coming from anywhere in the country, although predominantly East coast. It was obvious what they contained, so obvious that one time he had opened a package to check. He had found a slim bale of banknotes wrapped in a piece of paper, plain save for the line, 'buy a good thing,' and the swirl of an 'S' in the bottom right corner. Maybe the message had changed with each package but

↣

the contents hadn't, he was sure of that, utterly convinced. The delivery had become a talking point amongst the three postmen. Soon, the whole village suspected what he knew. Lynn was right. Sooner or later, others would come; probably sooner. The temptation would be too much. Even conservative estimates made his head dizzy. The money had come to dominate his thoughts to such a degree that he rejoiced when the office was downsized and he had the fortune to become the sole full time delivery man, responsible for every property in and around the village.

Nugget knew the boy had never bought anything, good, bad or indifferent. On the rare occasion he was seen in the village, he was avoided but watched. He never once stepped into a shop. Clothes they had seen his father in came to fit him and he seemed to have no need for bought food. The one display along Main Street that did attract him was the bookshop. He would stand for hours looking at the books the way others would watch a bank of televisions, smiling, as though imagining the lives and journeys within each volume. It struck Nugget as strange that the boy never bought a book. They all knew he could read. Maybe the possibilities that they offered were enough thought Nugget. He scanned the room for a bookshelf, his heart pounding, his breathing shallow and quick.

'She's right Bru. I was stupid for leaving it this long to be thinking about taking the money. I don't know what I'll do if someone else got to it first. Every delivery was an investment, banking once removed. I'm here to withdraw.'

The circle of his light flashed across the wall, stopped and backtracked to the fireplace. On the mantelpiece was a low neat pyramid of packages, offset like brickwork, their placing so uniformly precise that they had looked to be part of the fireplace surround, an intricate carving, the peak of which obscured a small section of the mirror that hung above the fire. Nugget grinned.

He ran his hands down the paper sides of the money mound. He was gentle, barely touching the unopened packets. Something half-way between a sob and a whimper escaped from his chest. For the second time that night, his cock pushed against his trousers. Wiping the dust away, he looked into the mirror. There were tears in his eyes. The three gold teeth that gave him his name, one each of incisor, canine and molar, shone in the torch beam. He kissed his fortune. He had anticipated this moment for so long but never pictured it like this. Hidden in a drawer, a cupboard, a box in a wardrobe or a bag under the bed maybe, even buried. Not on display, there for the taking, unprotected. It was too much. He yanked his zip down and pulled his erection out. His vigour overcame his distraction and in less than a minute wanksplash sizzled on the coals. His scrotum hung soft and warm in the heat of the fireplace as he subsided. The base of his shaft rubbed against the nylon zip of his work issue trousers as he eased the final spurts out, dribbling over his fingers. He began to weep. His nose ran. He wiped his hand across his nose but only succeeded in swapping snot for sour ejaculate. Forced into his nose, the smell was even stronger than that of the house. His innards lurched. He leant against the mantelpiece.

A glistening far behind him caught his attention. It came from the bottom of the bleached mound. Deep in the reflection he saw the ivory dome of a human skull. He vomited, sluicing his nostrils with whisky and bile, spraying the sleeping bear. The acid boiled in his throat. Sweat iced his body as he hunched over, leaning on his knees, spitting. He used the strength remaining in his shaking frame to scoop the money into his postbag. He closed the flap and hugged it like a lost child.

Nugget shivered as he stooped to inspect the skull. He knew that it had been the starting point, the foundation; that the rest of the skeleton was at the bottom of each pile. A silver chain was threaded through both eye sockets, wrapped a couple of times around the ridge of bone that separated them. The large crucifix attached to the chain leant against the skull, partially occluding one of the sockets. Nugget moved the cross to reveal an irregular dent in the forehead. Hairline cracks radiated from it in all directions. Nugget shook with wheezy laughter.

'So that's where you got to, you fucking mad bastard.' He knelt. 'Father Finnegan – Fireball Finnegan. Just look at you. Here all the time. Jesus. And the company you're keeping.'

Nugget brushed the dust from the crucifix. He lifted it. It was heavy, solid silver. It wouldn't fit through the eye socket and he couldn't find the end of the chain so Nugget tried teasing it undone with gentle pulling. When the whole pile of skulls shifted he jumped and let go. Bru backed away, growling.

'It's okay, boy. It's okay. It would have been a bonus. We've got what we come for. He can keep it.'

'Keep it.' Nugget relaxed with the skull once he knew who it was. He sat back on his heels. 'The fucking trouble you caused. You fucked with this village more than anything else, you know that? Poor Mary, she still thinks you're coming back. Can you believe that? She wrote to the Pope, asking where you'd been sent. No reply. She had another boy; he's got your hair.' Nugget made the sign of the cross. 'Bless me, Father, for I have sinned; but not as much as you did.' Nugget stood and took a few backwards steps away from the priest's skull. 'You look better without the moustache though, I'll grant you that.'

Shoes on the road

Anne Morrison

LIKE I TOLD you when I answered the advert, I insist on confidentiality. It's all over now and I only contacted you out of curiosity, to see if my shoe was one of the ones you'd found.

I couldn't help myself.

As well as the shame, you see, there's something else. I think it might be pride. Knowing I'm capable of something as reckless as that.

How's your espresso? You won't find anything as good around here. This place used to be a record shop. We kept the name, my husband and I, but that was all.

So. The shoe. I was in his car down by the harbour and I said to him, not here, I can't. There was nowhere for me to put my knees: the handbrake, those tricky sports car seats.

You're smiling. You know what I'm talking about.

He was kissing me and I could feel cold air on my back where my shirt had ridden up. I was, still am, married, and he was the coffee salesman. Fairtrade organic. I put my hand on his chest, pushed gently, not too hard; this wasn't rejection, not really, not yet.

I asked him if we could slow things down a little, go for a walk. That was before I learned that you either do these things or you don't. He pulled away from me then, straightening his jacket.

Sure, he said. Why not. A walk.

He opened the driver door and the internal light came on before I'd had a chance to sort myself out. He slammed the door shut and I heard him walk away. It felt odd sitting there on my own with the car light fading so I got out quickly, closed my door too softly and had to do it again.

I told him I was sorry. I wasn't used to this sort of thing.

He lit a cigarette, shielding the tiny flame with a cupped hand. Then I followed him into the darkness. I think that's when I tried to make a joke about it being such a cliché: misted windows; industrial estate car park; salesman. He didn't answer straight away, sucking so hard on the cigarette I could hear the tobacco fibres burning up.

It's called being spontaneous, he said.

I thought he hated me then, so I slipped my hand into his and squeezed it gently. He fired his cigarette end into the darkness the way you might throw a dart. His hand didn't hold mine terribly firmly, but he didn't let it drop away. We walked to the edge of the parking area. There was a fence. The kind of metal fence you get around playing fields, high and made up of interlocking diamond shapes. Heavy enough to lean against. I leaned my back against this fence, opened my jacket and unbuttoned my shirt. I could learn to be spontaneous.

He hesitated long enough to let me know I'd upset him, but not so long I could really doubt he still wanted me. He gripped the fence with one hand and me with the other. The metal was slippery with frost and as bouncy as a well-sprung double bed. It left me with marks like burns across my back and my bum.

The fence. That's where we were when the lorry swung into the turning area, lights on full beam.

We ran for the car and it was only after

we'd got onto the main road and I was half a mile from home that I realised I'd lost a shoe. The shoe was made by Clarks. It was black leather, slip-on and looked a bit like a clog. I bought another pair exactly the same the next day and put the odd one in the bin.

*

You are so very kind to call me back at the requested time. I can give you twenty five minutes before I must leave for luncheon club. So where would you like me to start?

It still pains me to think about it. But I'm glad you found them. Or one of them at least. Was it terribly damaged? I've often thought about the shoes lying on an embankment next to the A9 and I've worried about the conclusions people might jump to if they happened to come across them.

I suppose you could call them *suggestive*.

I bought them in Debenhams, not on the high street as such. Peacock blue, patent leather stilettos. Beautifully shaped. Gorgeous. Absolutely gorgeous. And such a vibrant, showy blue they made me feel joyous.

I tried them on, looked at them from every angle. The teenage shop assistant smirked but I wouldn't have, if I was her, with those thick calves and ankles. They have a word for it now, don't they? *Cankles*. I've always had good legs even though I carry more weight around my middle these days. Good legs are an asset, you know. I was always popular at the tennis club and the golf course. That was back in the days when Geoff's business was still on the up.

I paid £89.99 for the shoes and left the shop with my heart beating wildly. I put the box on the passenger seat of the Rover and had just crossed the Kessock Bridge when I suddenly thought about home. I thought about my husband, finishing work at the Mission. He organises the transportation of donations abroad – clothes, blankets, baby things – you know the place. I glanced at the box and knew I'd made a terrible mistake. I could never wear these shoes. There really seemed no point in keeping them or passing them on to anyone. I didn't want to be seen to encourage that kind of flamboyance, not now, not when we've made a decision to turn our backs on all that and live a different kind of life.

I'll be honest with you. I felt horribly jealous at the thought of someone young and beautiful slipping on the shoes and going public in them. I rolled down my window and I threw the box out. Yes, you're right, it probably was a dangerous thing to do, but I wasn't thinking about other motorists at the time.

No-one saw me.

I actually feel better now that I've told you about it. The whole thing left me a bit depressed, if you must know. Thinking about what a waste it all was.

If you don't mind me asking, why are you doing this? Is it an art project?

*

My name is Cal. And it isn't my trainer, it's Jamie's. But I know how it got there and I said I'd talk about it because there are lessons to be learned. Nobody thinks they're going to die. Not really. I know it's a fact of life but as far as I was concerned, it was something that happened to old people. Unlucky people. And I wonder what the point is in telling you about this. You might stop and think for five seconds but I doubt you'll change a thing. I didn't. Jamie didn't.

We'd spent all Saturday afternoon down by the beach, watching the sea, watching the girls, listening to excellent sounds on the stereo. We got a load of attention that day, because of the car. It was his first car.

You could say his only car.

We had a couple of beers and a few smokes to celebrate, but nowhere near the limit. Jamie wanted to go into town. By this time it was eight o'clock and it was still hot. It was going to be a creamy night, one of those nights when anything can happen, everyone's home from college and there's a kind of hysterical happiness in the air.

We had the windows down, hatch open, stereo cranked right up. It was amazing, it really was, he'd only had the Astra a week and here we were making for the city, laughing about how we'd never have to stand at the bus stop again.

I could hardly breathe for the pure rush of wind. Hills rose up and fell away. It was all so smooth, so green and blue, like flying, like

➳

a dream. We were headed for the centre with Jamie's foot to the floor and I could feel the bass through the soles of my feet, the whole car throbbing and alive with wild energy, no time to lose, we didn't want to miss a thing.

I have no idea how it happened. Lost control? Is that what they told you? It didn't feel that way at the time. Crest of a wave. And riding it.

I don't want to look at the trainer anymore. It shouldn't have been left lying about. Like people putting flowers at the spot. I don't agree with that. He didn't live his life on a verge on the A9. I hate that verge and I don't want to be reminded of it every time I pass. The police said it would be good for me to talk about the accident, get other lads to go easy on the accelerator, don't drink and drive and all that.

They say there are lessons to be learned and they're probably right but I don't think I can tell you what they are.

*

I've got you here under false pretences. I don't recognise any of these shoes, but in a way I recognise all of them. It took a while to get the visitor pass sorted out but you're here now. I don't get many visitors unless you count the lawyers.

You could say that lost shoes have been something of a theme in my life but that makes me sound like some sort of fetishist. It's a novel idea though, reuniting people with their lost footwear.

You seem a little annoyed. Don't worry. Hear me out and you might solve a bigger mystery than you intended.

The first shoes I found weren't by the roadside at all but on a gritty beach in Fife. I was with a girl I'd never met before and never saw again and we were digging a hole all the way to Australia as children do. It was getting to the point where the sides kept caving in but I was sure we'd soon hit rock and I'd drill straight down by twirling my plastic spade round and round and round until I broke through the earth's mantle and the digging would then be as easy as spooning out blancmange.

I scraped a spadeful of sand up the side of the hole and it snagged on something on the way up. I dug off to the side and the sandals fell out of the wall one after the other in a quick easy tumble like how I imagine twins are born. I shook off the damp sand and looked at them closely. They were made of a stiff yellow mesh material, edged with white and open-toed with toffee-coloured plastic soles and little buckles on the sides. They were small and very neat.

New. A pair.

I couldn't decide if they had been hidden, abandoned or lost. There's a big difference. I think you must know that, must have found that out by now. Some things are deliberately hidden away. Others are thoughtlessly abandoned. Of all the stuff out there, only a fraction of it is genuinely lost. Of course, there are things which are hidden and then can't be found again and items people say are genuinely lost when in fact, they've been deliberately abandoned.

I stopped digging, afraid of what else I might find: a tiny foot; a matching yellow and white summer dress with a broderie anglaise frill; soft pink fingers wriggling in the cold sand.

It feels like an admission of some kind, the fact that I still have the sandals.

Later, I began to notice how many leather soles there are washed up on rocky shores and beaches everywhere. You should go and look. You'll find them. The heels I often find separately: elongated semi-circles of liquorice coloured leather, tiny tack marks around the edges. The soles lie stranded in seaweed, caught up in unravelling lengths of rope and heather roots, something about them reminding me of those flimsy magic fish you get in Christmas crackers, twisting oddly and revealing secrets about your inner self if you study them carefully. I study them. I study them very carefully. Uppers are less common, I don't know why.

Then there were the running shoes. I saw them every day I travelled on the high school bus, always sitting on the left hand side, a window seat. As the bus began one of several long, slow climbs, the driver changed down through the gears, and at about the moment we dropped into second gear, the running shoes came into view. Someone had placed them inside a small hollow next to the road, the kind of dry hollow overhung with grass where sheep sleep in bad weather.

The running shoes were brilliant white with angled blue stripes and as was the fashion at the time, they were fastened with Velcro, not laces. They looked brand new and far as I know, no-one touched them over the course of the two years I travelled on the bus until the day the council widened the road.

I cycled along that road a few years later and went looking for the running shoes.

Why?

I suppose it was important to me to find out if they were still there, to see if a workman had put them carefully to one side. They were gone, of course.

You could say that the running shoes got lost twice even though they never belonged to me and I never wore or even touched them. I found it reassuring to see them and I felt a little bereaved by their absence.

Every time I see a shoe by the side of the road now I feel the owner's loss. I can still picture the running shoes, sitting side by side in that dry hollow. The picture gets distorted when the digging starts. The sides cave in. It's difficult to breathe.

*

I saw your advert in the Press and Journal and as soon as I read it, I felt sure you'd have them. Thanks for coming round. Getting out of the house is an exercise in logistics these days.

They look awful, by the way. I told Eddie we should tell you our story, though you've probably had a few like ours.

I remember asking him to stop the car. He told me I couldn't be serious. I think I shouted at him, *Just stop the bloody car!* or something like that. He pulled over into a lay-by, a big one with a yellow container full of road and an oversized wheelie bin stuck on a concrete slab. Funny how objects you wouldn't look twice at on a normal day take on this kind of 3D sharpness.

Anyway.

The passenger seat was as far back as it could go but I still couldn't get enough space. I was being pulled apart from the inside. Not slowly. Fast. Way too fast. Trying not to hold my breath, trying to relax like they'd told me. Relax! Can you believe that?

I remember Eddie taking my seatbelt off and I told him to open the door. He wasn't having any of it. He told me it was snowing, I'd freeze to death.

I think I got a bit nasty at that point. I opened the door myself and sort of crawled or fell out. Eddie was round in a flash, shaking from head to foot and looking really cold and pale and young.

A log lorry sailed past covering us both in brown slush. I could hear Eddie on the mobile, telling the hospital we were in a lay-by near Achnasheen. They must've asked him for landmarks or something because he came out with a long list of things like trees, railway line, wheelie bin. Not helpful, looking back on it.

I started groaning. Well, roaring, actually, and then Eddie really began to panic. They kept talking to him on the mobile but I knew he was pretty desperate. There was a tiny pain-free window, a wee lull, and I let him move me onto the back seat.

And that's when I saw my feet. For a second, I didn't recognise them as mine. Ridiculous feet in fluffy pink and white Christmas slippers with bunny ears and little black button eyes. I could hear someone laughing like a drain, a filthy laugh, a brothel of a laugh. Eddie thought I was losing it and told me so. I stopped laughing and screamed like I was about to kill him.

THE SLIPPERS! GET RID OF THE BLOODY SLIPPERS! I CAN'T GIVE BIRTH IN THESE SLIPPERS! For a second he didn't seem to understand, then he grabbed a sodden slipper in each hand and threw them, one after the other, as far as he possibly could, great big pebble-into-the-ocean throws, javelin throws, champion throws.

Oh how I loved him as I watched the bunnies soar and tumble, loved him, the man throwing Christmas slippers into the sky for me as I hauled off trousers and pulled down underwear. That's how Alex was born. In the back of a Peugeot 306 near Achnasheen.

Did you get what you were looking for?

Andrew Philip

for Judith

1. ORIGAMI

You are a folded deer quick-stepping
the bog-cotton muir of a how-to book.
Hind for the white hart whose leathery heart you have
smoothed to bleaching linen or a page
freshly rolled in the mill, I adore you

for every crease unironed in your nature.
Not for me the copper-bottomed überbeauties,
those bronzed denizens of the glossies
who are glazed like fine porcelain and just as vacant
as washed tins dropped in the recycling.

2. SUMMERTIME...

Backlit by a Balkan sunset, in your denim skirt
and well-worn sandals you sit by the water's edge:
it's a favourite snap of mine. The gloaming heckles
dark from the evening, turning the trees across the bay
to pig-iron sculptures of themselves. In that light,

your hair becomes a metonym for fire, as if
burnishing the air around to a deep bronze sheen;
your smile becomes a kiln for happiness. As if
we could can that for the years ahead! Still, while possible,
let's linger in the moment's printed afterglow.

3. SHAGREEN

Imagine us old: wrunkled cowhide faces,
me in linen trousers at some summer festival,
one of us walking with a stick, both chatting
with the bittersweet, gentle irony of the aged,
all trace of copper faded from your hair.

Our younger heads, cast in bronze by a friend,
may occupy a prominent spot beside your Dutch vase,
prevailing over the tinpot fears of aging
as we recall fondly the days of cheap paper,
inexpensive cotton and less heat.

4. THE RAVELLING

A certain group of flaxen-haired wee boys
has breached the doors of pre-school nursery.
We spy them through the railings and experience
a kick like power surging down the wires—.
Grief is no monolith. It's more like molten bronze

or a potsherd dug up in unexpected tilth.
It speeds like a tinfish out of sonar range.
It's a crack that can't be papered over
for long, a snapped thread left to hang,
a belt to scourge our each essay at happiness.

5. DOVETAIL JOINTS

I could never have lifted you over the threshold.
And let's not count the ways I've dropped the iron,
or mention the nail you hammered through a hot water pipe,
the sun screen I slaistered on well past its use-by. Let's not
enumerate the plates and bowls that clattered from our grasp

this past 10 year. That's all in the can. Instead,
I'm leafing through the future's wide extensions,
its beds replanted with pear trees and cotoneaster.
A suede-upholstered future, our coming years together
unfolding like a brand new pack of king-sized sheets.

6. FERROUS SULPHATE

Dark chocolate, Guinness and steamed asparagus.
Your thickened hair basting in the summer sun,
your skin not burnished, browned or slightly burnt.
Casseroles and other one-pot dishes sitting by the door.
Tinned apricots crowding the kitchen cupboards

as if on free prescription. Red books and birth certificates.
Fitted cot sheets, muslin squares and body suits.
My footwear worn from pounding the surrounding streets.
The linens on our whirligig and no space left for drying.
How mighty oaks we hope from little acorns now are growing.

➻

7. SMALL CHANGE

Every red penny we save these days
is technically bronze, so nothing — not even
the humble piggy bank, or the chugger's
rattly plastic collecting tin — is quite
what it looks on paper. Nor are we

who we were when we first shared the sheets,
my kilt and sporran tossed with your dress,
the hotel linens wrapping us tight. But I
don't pine to buy those times back, not even though
what we've shared since then would temper steel.

8. COMING THIRD

Never was it gold or silver in the medal stakes.
Never bone china, always the bargain-basement crockery.
Never the full spectrum, always the tinnier speakers.
Always paper-thin ham instead of the juicier cuts;
static-filled synthetics rather than Egyptian cotton.

But now we're talking genuine Italian leather,
an Irish linen garment cut to fit just so,
African ebony inlaid with mother of pearl,
pure Ossetian free of loans and calques,
a sunstruck copper roof devoid of verdigris.

9. A CUT-PRICE SET OF CROCKERY

Barely six months' use when the glaze cracked.
It felt as smooth as a fresh roll of kitchen foil,
an unsigned marriage certificate or
the new sheets on our first, rented bed but looked
more like withered shoes under museum glass.

We traced the daily strains with our dishtowels
and at the table over breakfast or dinner.
Iron sharpens iron it is written. We felt more like
a copper cup already turning green. But no:
we were a new-minted penny ready to shine.

10. NOT BEING THE WOODSMAN OF OZ

I once played the cowardly lion; a coward
not only in the script, whispered some who'd not
cottoned on — seeing how feart I was
of a playground leathering; of muddying my
clothes on the pitch; of the opposite sex — that courage

to weep could compensate. Bit of a cross to bear.
You had your crosses too, hard as nails and heavier.
They may mean you feel no Venus, but to me
you're a bronze shield cast by Vulcan or a new
earthenware goblet brimming with wine.

Note
This sequence is organised by direct or oblique reference to a list of the first 10 wedding anniversary gifts. Each poem moves through the 10 gifts in turn line by line, each successive poem beginning with the gift for the corresponding anniversary. The list is: paper, cotton, leather, linen, wood, iron, copper, bronze, pottery and tin.

‘The worse mutilation you’ve got is a crime of the Christian commandments, STINGINESS, CHEAPNESS, PURSE PRIDE! Your rosary’s in the gutter with your GUSHER! Goddam, you got me thrown out, out, out!’

Tennessee Williams, *The Mutilated*

The Museum of Broken Dreams
Ewan Gault

Travëlling sick
My dreams roam
On a withered moor
Basho, 1694

PLUM BLOSSOM, THE two words lolling about on my tongue like something vaguely voluptuous. I was there, in the land of the rising sun, to see day break over the horizon as it had done every morning since the world began. And the golden walls of the temple did glow while a dragon fly dipped to kiss the lake that reflected a world which seemed better than the real thing. Reverential children momentarily looked up from their mobile phones and one or two elderly people actually shouted, 'Banzai!'

I felt like I had been watching life on an old pixelated TV that had just been replaced by a 32 inch plasma screen set. Amateur photographers most of whom wore sunglasses and military inspired clothes pressed buttons with a nervous intensity. I wanted to see what they were seeing and raised my own camera but the memory was full.

'That's it,' an American whose chin sagged into his droopy man tits said to his boxercised and botoxed wife. She smiled while her man fondled the camera on which he had just captured *the* defining picture of a sunrise over *the* most famous temple in Japan. 'It looks just like it does on the postcards,' he confirmed. 'Just wish the plum blossom was out. It isn't complete without the plum blossom.'

I didn't want to miss anything. At the entrance to the temple complex was a stall selling seaweed crackers, fortune cookies and cheap disposable cameras. Twenty-four photos. There was something final and beautiful about that. I turned, aimed, fired. The camera clicked, like a distant mouse trap or a full stop on a typewritten letter that will never be sent.

Despite getting what I had came for I milled around for a bit watching the scene swell with colour until it seemed I'd have to buy a pair of sunglasses – and this for me who has never worn sunglasses, in all his known life. Had all those people bumping into each other on the underground not daring to lift their shades had a moment like this, when they felt the sight of the normal world might blind them?

The golden pavilion looked almost new, which was unsurprising as it, like many of Japan's historic buildings, was a replica. In Kyoto however, most of the temples and shrines were originals as the city had been considered too beautiful to bomb. Strange how considerate men who dropped nuclear bombs could be about architecture but that is another story.

This temple had been burnt to the ground by a monk deranged by the perfection of the place. Five hundred years, gone up in smoke. Unlike the man who took a hammer to Michelangelo's La Pieta he at least went on to try and kill himself. He was after all Japanese. His mother on hearing of her son's actions did the same thing. He failed, she didn't. The pavilion was rebuilt some claimed more perfect than before – more perfect? You might say this is impossible, but how can you be sure?

I took another photo of the reconstruction, blinked and blushed as if it were me and not the

➻

building being photographed. The thick gold lacquer, sky a cooking gas blue and Spring doing its thing everywhere. I rubbed my eyes, I was still getting used to all this colour.

The previous night I'd taken the bullet train from my home in northern Honshu where the winter still covered the fields, the snow going on for ever until you saw blue veins, pink eyes, pulsing beneath the white. We had shot down the country, a streak of lightning, through mountains, over rivers, countless paddy fields, their patchwork patterns lost in the night. I imagined Haiku poets sitting down to contemplate ruined Samurai castles, broad hatted peasants carrying impossible loads over bridges spanning improbable chasms. I strained to see something more than the reflection of my carriage with its ranks of salarymen reading newspapers and drinking bottles of green tea. But what did I know of this country's night, nothing of the spirits that crowd it. The dark continued until we reached the bright claws of Tokyo and could see how fast we were really going. And then the lights shot past like ball bearings in a Pachinko machine. Millions upon millions of people and I didn't, perhaps couldn't know one of them. So many times I had dreamt of this - the thrill of travelling through a foreign land at night on a trip you've taken on a whim. The giddy feeling that no one knows where you are, that you could drop totally and utterly off the radar.

A few hours later I was at another temple sitting on wooden boards soothed smooth by centuries of shuffling feet. A Japanese girl kept looking at me and smiling. She was wearing a short navy blue hokey skirt and white ankle socks, which made her look like a school girl but she was older than that. Her T-shirt sported a picture of an elephant dancing on a ball and the slogan 'Are we acting weird! Sometimes I feel I don't belong here.' As time went on it was becoming clear that some poetic genius in the clothing industry was having a great laugh at the expense of the Japanese.

I had come to the country after reading too many Murakami novels, fully expecting that in every coffee shop would be a girl with a broken heart and unusual eyes marking out the minutes with cigarettes, waiting for someone like me to save her. When I got there I found that smoking was banned in cafes, that all the girls had the same dark brown eyes and that when I tried to talk to them they said I spoke Japanese like Tarzan.

A guide passed us loudly telling a squabble of tourists that this was a place of tranquility where monks could meditate. A Japanese man took photos of his young family. Every time he pressed a button the camera shrieked, 'Hai, cheesu,' and the little ones smiled and made peace signs. The Japanese girl was still looking at me but I was focusing all my attention on this stone garden and on stroking my chin and looking thoughtful. I had been told it was important – the garden as well as the looking thoughtful. What I could see were about a dozen mossy rocks that had been dumped in a bed of neatly raked gravel.

The girl waved at me and asked, 'How many rocks are there?'

'Fourteen,' I replied after dutifully counting them.

She shook her head and in an infuriating game show host voice said, 'Try again.'

There were definitely fourteen, but I really didn't want to get into an argument.

'Really, I can only see fourteen.'

'Come over here,' she said.

'Are you sure?'

'I am not biting.' I bum shuffled across. 'Had you seen that rock before?'

I had not, and slipping back to my original place realized that it would have been impossible for me to have done so as it was totally obscured. Just as it slid out of view however another rock appeared hence keeping the number fourteen.

'There are fifteen rocks,' the Japanese girl started saying.

'But you can only ever see fourteen.'

'Exactly. And that one there is meant to be a whale.'

'Really.'

'And this group a tiger with her cubs.'

'Now that you mention it.'

'Or they could all be mountains poking through the clouds. Or islands in the sea. If you like a tour could be taken.'

She stood and walked off one hand trailing behind her, like I was going to hold it or at the very least follow. She had very thin legs that bent inwards at the knee. A lot of Japanese girls' legs were like this. One woman had told me it was due to all the time spent sitting in the Seiza position, others that it was a genetic problem and still others that it was simply a fashion.

I followed her round to the back of the temple and stopped in front of a water fountain.

'Let us begin. This is a square water bowl, around it are four Kanji characters. In English they mean, 'I only know plenty.' Or 'All I have is all I need.' Something like that.'

'Be content with one's lot?'

'If you say so. Also please note that there is no cup so you must bow to the bowl, you must make humility.'

The water tasted mossy and was very cold. 'Are you not going to drink?'

'No, I had a coke before meeting you. Here, I would advice you to take one or at least two photos. This is the famous sight.'

We strolled on with her pointing out painted sliding doors, a lake, a tree that people had tied wishes to. I took photos of them all and this seemed to please her.

'So where else have you seen?'

'This morning I went to Kinkakugi.'

'For the sunrise?'

'Yes.'

She laughed. 'Did you read about the monk that set the temple on fire? I don't believe someone could do that. For me it was probably an accident. I think they just made an escape goat out of him.'

'A scapegoat.'

'Really? And I've been going round saying escape goat.' She covered her mouth, wide eyed and shocked as an anime character. 'Ok then shall we take a look at Ninna-ji Temple next?'

I should have suspected something but it was turning into a day that made you suspect some bearded and benevolent being who looked after things was for once on your side. So I collected my shoes and the girl her multicoloured wellies and we continued on to the next temple complex. 'This one is famous for its avenue of plum blossom trees. In two weeks time thousands of people will take picnics here with the sunshines. Today however there are no plum blossoms and the place is void.'

'Do you ever feel you keep arriving at places too early or too late?'

'No,I am always punctilious.' She shrugged modestly. 'It is just my nature.'

At the bottom of the avenue men with luridly coloured vests and baggy trousers were setting up scaffolding around a stage with clunks of clamps and cleats. Occasionally a monk deep in meditation would walk past. There was something mournful about the dull metallic sounds, the workmen toiling without conversation or instruction.

'They are building a stage for tonight's pop concert. Come,' the girl said. 'There is something I am obligated to do.'

We walked away from the cherry trees, the girl pointing out the four level pagoda and another rock garden.'

'Tomorrow I have very important English exam. So today we visit a shrine to make prayer.'

'You mean there is a god for exams?'

'In Shinto there is a god for everything. Always I pray before the exam. Also we eat green tea flavoured Kit Kats, there are many ways to good fortune.'

The shrine was surrounded by a pine forest so silent that but for the smoking incense sticks you would have thought no one had been there for years. The girl led the way into a semi-circle of small statues wearing what looked like baby's bibs and hats. Around the shrine students had left pencils, sharpeners and tangerines, their gaudy colours at odds with the moss covered statues. The girl closed her eyes and put her hands together. She had what the Japanese call egg shell cheeks, by which I took to mean cheeks that were white, smooth, unblemished. After all of 5 seconds she opened one eye and caught me looking.

'Pray,' she ordered.

'For what?'

➻

'For me,' she replied. Twenty seconds later she made a rude noise and started laughing.

'That's all?' I asked.

'That's all, we Japanese don't believe in these things that much. We're not crazy you know.'

'So, where to now?'

'How about high tea? I know you English are nothing without your tea. There's a cafe near here called The Museum of Broken Dreams. But before that can I make your picture, I want a reminder of the boy who taught me about the escape goat.'

She waved a disposable camera that was identical to mine at an elderly white couple. Despite it being the most basic camera in the world the old man managed to fuss and fidget with it allowing the girl to go through a series of peace sign poses while I held my hands firmly behind my back.

The old man returned our camera and told us what a beautiful couple we were. I blushed and the girl giggled, covering her mouth. We navigated the beautiful paths of the temple, our hands occasionally brushing, hips accidently nudging. A group of photographers ignored us, busy as they were hounding a tree to see if the blossom would come out and they could capture the first pictures of the season.

The Museum of Broken Dreams was cluttered with rusty or deflated children's toys from previous decades like something the sea might have thrown up after a particularly rough night. On the walls were dozens of posters advertising gigs from decades ago in venues that probably no longer exist. Hollywood stars held cigarettes in black and white the creamy smoke frozen, their faces never aging.

My friend swept her arm at these objects as if they were part of some grand gallery. 'Recognise anything?' I nodded and she smirked, clearly delighted with the place. 'Just you wait and see.' We ordered our tea and she complemented me on my Japanese.

'I've only been here a week,' I lied, 'But I think I'm picking it up.'

'You're doing fine,' she agreed.

Our tea arrived the cups and saucers endearingly mismatched.

'It's like they have a problem with uniformity.'

'Yes, no two things are the same.'

'I don't know about that. The skateboard on that shelf is just like one I had as a kid. I left it in the park one night and by the morning it had gone.'

'You missed it?'

'I'd plagued my mum to buy it but I had no balance and was always falling off.'

The girls shrugged and blew on her tea.

I fiddled with my camera. 'Twenty-three photos done. Can I make this the last one?' I clicked, her face partially obscured by a cup decorated with the badge of The Scottish Football Association. 'This is too strange.'

'Unique?'

'No, there must be thousands of them but how this one ended up here.'

I placed the camera on the table and went in search of a toilet. I recognised the Kanji for man and opened the door. To my left was a hat stand from which hung a trenchcoat that I had borrowed from my dad and left at a party. A much loved and maligned Trilby lay on the floor and that mountain of mismatching socks and gloves that we all know must exist, somewhere filled far corner. I lifted a familiar looking tartan scarf that I had forgotten all about to my face. It smelt like home.

I slumped down on the toilet seat. In the corner I spotted my first full sized football lost in a neighbour's garden, phone numbers on scraps of paper, an acoustic guitar left on a train when drunk, marbles vanished down drains, a memory stick filled with lyrics of genius! I felt filled with neon, the excitement that all these things would once again be mine, that with them I could somehow be the person I should be. My eyes flitted down the spines of books abandoned at airports to comply with weight restrictions, obscure records stolen at a party, watches whose straps had actually broken.

I started picking things up but there was no way I could carry them or even explain to the owners of the café why I was taking them. I needed help so scuttled down the passage but the girl had gone leaving only a saucer of coins and my disposable camera. The café door made an electronic beep bop like the sound on a quiz show when you give the wrong answer. I clattered past tables and chairs. A moment later and I would have missed her as she turned onto a busier street. She was no longer doing her pigeon toed walk but was bouncing along purposefully enough. I dodged grannies bent at right angles from decades of rice picking, man handled monks pleading with me to slow with the calm of their eyes. By the time I was behind her I barely managed to muster a, 'sumimasen.' The girl turned and looked at me with shockingly green eyes that she immediately lowered knowing what they could do to men. She was smoking a cigarette and had that abandoned look I had been searching for everywhere. 'One moment,' I shouted, noticing the tour girl elegantly mount a scooter. I ran after her but it was useless. I hadn't even bothered to learn her name.

The green eyed girl had ghost-slipped into the crowd of Saturday shoppers and I turned myself in the direction of The Museum of Broken Dreams. After twenty minutes of trudging streets that repeated themselves like the background in some manga cartoon it became clear I was totally lost. Typically I refused to accept this, or take a map out. Instead I remembered that the café was near a temple in which the girl had told me a pop concert would be taking place. All I had to do was follow the strains of some string instrument. The music was coming from back down the hill. I let it lead me in a merry dance before arriving at a neon lit space ship like building proclaiming 24 hour karaoke. I listened for a bit. The high pitched nasal wailing of some salary man letting out the anguish of a 60 hour week, ripping off his shirt and wrapping his sensible tie kamikaze style around his head. I could hear proper pop music mixing with this sadness and headed in the opposite direction. After zig-zagging through the mazy streets I arrived at a crossroads where 4 karaoke bars and the cries of a man in a panda suit trying to usher in more singers made a jingle jangle mash up. Everywhere I went that night the same thing happened. The night and its flashing lights were goading me like the smell of a perfume that evokes lost memories before slipping, slithering away.

A year later I got the film from that camera developed. I was back in Scotland by then surrounded by familiar faces and objects suffocating and smothering me. No one I knew got films developed anymore and I had forgotten the excitement of opening a package, not sure if I would recognise or even like what I would see. At first I thought they'd made a mistake but then I recognized my tour girl posing in every picture with a succession of awkward looking white men, each shot taken in front of a shrine that she visited to help her pass English exams. The westerners came in all shapes and sizes but we all shared that confused, hopeful look, that romantic dizziness which confounds lonely men when far away from home. My photo was the last one. It showed a lost soul, pleading with the camera to tell him something about himself.

Extract from the novel *Eleanor's Book*

Mark Ryan Smith

THE MAN SEES himself in the mirror. It's the first time in a while he has seen his reflection. In his hand, a hairbrush. He doesn't remember picking it up. The boy asleep in the next room. Nothing can be heard, but he imagines his son's breath pushing its way into the humid air. Should he open the window? He looks at the hairbrush, following the loops of her hair as a canoeist would follow a river on a map.

These things, these female things, they'll have to go, like an old currency to be taken out of circulation. Hair straighteners, perfume, all the mysterious pots of cream and bottles of liquid, they'll have no place in their new economy and, as time goes on, the flat will become more and more the province of men.

Not yet. The boy would notice in the morning. He can't even bring himself to dump her toothbrush, so there it sits, just as it's done since she last replaced them, a green Scylla next to his cherry-red Charybdis.

He opens the window in his own room to cool the air before he goes to bed. It's been getting later and later. There's a match on. European cup. That means some noise when the pub empties. He hopes the boy won't wake and reminds himself to close the window. If Celtic win he'll be able to tell. When it comes to the football scores, a post-pub Glasgow street is more efficient than the News at Ten.

He rests the hairbrush back in its place, the handle protruding over the edge of her dressing table as if anticipating the hand of its owner. Unplugging the hairdryer, he neatly coils its flex before putting it away in a drawer then turns and goes through to the living room.

The TV is still on. The program the boy was watching – some sort of science fiction adventure – has finished and there is now a documentary about obese Americans in its place. The man picks up the remote control to switch it off but watches just long enough for it to catch him.

There is one woman who, unable even to turn from front to back, lies all day in bed watching TV, whatever happens to be on, waiting until somebody comes to roll her over and feed her. This happens four times a day. She can wear no clothes and, as it is hot where she lives and they have no air conditioning, she is always naked. There are various pipes and devices jammed here and there to service her bodily needs, as if she's a bus or a car raised on a lift for its annual bout of maintenance. Her husband, who obviously wants nothing to do with the cameras moving around his house, watches another TV in another room. He has given up. Whoever she was when they met is gone, and he looks battered and beaten by the grotesque mass of flesh sprawling in the next room.

The man lays down the remote and sits on the arm of the sofa. How can a human being possibly get so big? He aims the remote and changes the channel.

The football is on – Celtic are one down to the Spanish side Villarreal – but he decides not to watch it. There is another documentary, about crab fishermen in the Bering Strait, which he lingers on for a while. Then he starts to jump through the channels, looking for something, he doesn't know what, that he's happy to stay with.

There are adverts for air freshener, a channel selling earrings, another shopping channel where a singer he doesn't recognise is trying to sell her latest album. There is a film which has Jean Claude Van Damme as a time-travelling lawman. There is a preview of a wrestling tournament where the wrestlers are fighting in the aisle that runs through the crowd and one of the characters is called the Undertaker. There is motorcycle racing, a program which lists the top 100 rock anthems, a program in which some of the methods of building the great pyramid of Giza have been reconstructed. There are adverts for washing powder, shampoo, vegetarian microwave meals, Vauxhall Astras, aftershave, sofas, computers, a magazine which includes a different piece of a plastic model of H.M.S. Great Britain every week, mobile phones, bagless hoovers, holidays to the Caribbean, weedkiller, whisky. He keeps going, firing out commands in infra-red like a gunslinger spraying bullets, hardly stopping to look at what each number contains, letting the onslaught wash over him like a wave.

Eventually he comes back to the football. Celtic are two down now. He decides to watch until half-time so he can see the goals.

A car with a loud exhaust drives along the street too quickly. The street is part of a network which, to the initiated, offers a short-cut between two busy roads. Cars come this way to try and defeat the undertow they are caught in every night, every morning. There was talk of having speed-bumps in the street but there's been nothing more since the last letter a year ago.

Somewhere across town an ambulance blares. Eleanor, his wife, who grew up in a place where the appearance of an ambulance was an event, would have looked out the window and, if she had seen the vehicle, would have commented on which direction it was going. She had been fifteen years in the city but she still gave him opportunities to rib her about her country ways. You can take the girl out of Shetland, but not the Shetland out of the girl.

There are five minutes to go until half-time. He wonders about taking the boy to a football match. He is old enough and would enjoy going. Maybe going to a match could become something they do. A tradition of their own making. A Scotland match might be the thing to go to. Or maybe Partick Thistle. Closer to the action there. He remembers hearing a comedian do a routine about how he thought 'nil' was part of Partick Thistle's name.

He knows that rituals of their own will be important. Football, the cinema on a certain night of the week, going for a pizza, meeting for pints when the boy is older. They will have to survey the islands that offer themselves and find one able to accommodate them both.

Celtic have a penalty claim in the last few minutes of the half. The man sits forward in the chair to study the replays. The commentator, abetted by a former Celtic player who provides analysis of the action, howls for the penalty to be given. The referee, as if he and the commentator were in league, points to the spot. The crowd goes wild.

Then, after the protests of the opposing team have subsided, there is a lull in the rhythm of the crowd. The player who was brought down takes the ball and places it on the spot. A Villarreal player makes a fuss about the ball being placed incorrectly, causing the former Celtic player to comment on the gamesmanship foreign players are prone to. The penalty taker looks down at his boots, wiping his nose and brow, waiting for the whistle, not allowing himself to be put off.

When the whistle goes, the player looks up, runs forward, and side-foots the ball hard past the keeper's left hand. The noise from the crowd and the commentators erupts hugely, like the long-willed consummation of a great love affair. Replays from various angles follow in quick succession, catching the expressions on the faces of the penalty taker, the goalkeeper, the crowd. The scorer runs to the advertising hoardings, holds his arms out cross-wise, allows himself to be pulled into the mass of people who have pushed to the front. Stewards step in and disentangle the player from the fans.

After the goal, the Spanish side keep the ball in benign areas until the whistle goes for half-time. Celtic have scored at a crucial time,

➻

the commentator states. The former Celtic star agrees and offers some ideas on the strategy his team should follow after the interval. The man thinks about going to the fridge for beer to accompany the second half.

The phone rings. Somebody else watching the game. He turns down the volume and lifts the cordless phone from the coffee table.

'Colin?' says the voice, 'It's Mimie here.'

The sound tips him into the cadences of his wife's voice. Like an archaeologist he sees the layers she gathered come away to reveal this same accent at her core, the metamorphic foundation she could never entirely conceal.

In the last few years she found the sound of her voice easier, as if she could recognise the person she had become in the rhythms and syllables of her speech. When she first started teaching, there was little of her Shetland accent left. This suppression, she once admitted, begun when she first went away to university. In one of her classes she had to give a talk on Tennyson's poem 'Ulysses' and, so self-conscious and bumpkinish did she feel about her way of speaking, she made a decision to exorcise the Shetland elements from her voice as much as she could.

During her first trip home this change in her voice, and in her clothes, her hair, her attitude, drew comments from the uncle and aunt she lived with. She didn't feel as if she had changed too radically but, to them, she was almost unrecognisable from the girl they had waved to on the ferry a few months before. Her uncle, embarrassed but resolute, stumbling when certain words had to be said, tried to give her advice about being careful with boys. She tried to be confident and forthright, but afterwards felt she had pushed at the scab of his discomfort, rather than accepting the well-meant advice as it had been intended.

But, despite knowing that her aunt and uncle were unsure about the changes in her, she felt excited when she viewed her metamorphosing self. She was free to wear what she liked, speak how she pleased, drink, smoke, stay out late, sleep with whoever she wanted.

Not that she had done much of the latter.

When he first started to see her, court her as she said, quaintly, underneath the bravado and thick black eye-liner, she was still the naïve girl from the isles. He wasn't the first boy she'd been with, but the first time they did it, in her single bed in her halls of residence room, her room-mate, who had smuggled him in, tactfully spending the night elsewhere, they felt a kind of joining that was new to them both.

'Are you doing OK?' asked Eleanor's aunt.

'No too bad. No too bad. Trying to keep busy. You know the way.'

Eleanor's aunt had taken to phoning him every week. They always had the same kind of forced and awkward conversation but he had come to appreciate the reliability of her calls. It wasn't always on the same night she phoned, but knowing her call would come gave something to anchor himself on.

'That's fine. That's fine. We're all fine here too.'

Mimie, in her quiet way, always made the best out of any situation.

'Billy was wanting me to say that young Andrew, his sister's boy, was going to be coming away to Glasgow, to the college, and he was wondering if you would maybe be able to see him?'

'Yes, Mim, no bother.' He had picked up Eleanor's name for Mimie. The first time he went to Shetland, after a week, he had called her that, so used had he become to Eleanor using the name. Mimie, looking up from her knitting, smiled at him, catching his eye, and, as her attention returned to the jumper, he felt that she had given approval to his boldness. Ever since then, and for the boy too, that was how he spoke to her. She minded even less, now.

'So what is it he's going to be doing?'

'I'm not sure what it is. Something to do with computers. And no at the same college as you and Eleanor.'

'Yes, I see. It'll be a big trip for him.'

'Yes yes. He's a sensible boy, though. I think he'll be all right. He did awful good at school'

'Well, give him my number and I'll meet up with him.'

'Sure sure. I'll do that. I'll phone tonight.'

The task of arranging a soft landing for

young Andrew out of the way, their conversation fell into its usual channels. Colin related all the little triumphs and the knocks the boy had met over the last week. He promised to send Mimie a copy of a story the boy had written and won a prize for at school. He told her that he was thinking about taking him to a football match, and listened to her well-meant advice about keeping clear of the tribes of feral maniacs who ruled the terraces of Parkhead and Ibrox. Then the weather, in Glasgow and Ustaness, then a report on Billy's travails with fixing the car, a digression into the health problems of Phyllis Simpson, Mimie's neighbour, then a reminder about Andrew, Billy's sister's oldest boy.

'And you phone if you're needing anything. Whatever time of the day it is.'

'I will. And I'll get Daniel to phone. Maybe at the weekend.'

'Splendid. That would be splendid. And mind and be careful if you take him to the football. So, ta ta then.'

The phone bleeps twice as Colin squeezes the end button. He drops the handset into the waiting billows of the sofa, where the TV remote is trying to force its way into deeper waters. He picks up the remote again and, as it's still a few minutes until the second half starts, he sets off again through the channels. CNN is the first landfall, where, moving slowly along the bottom of the screen... *Actor Marlon Brando Dies... Actor Marlon Brando Dies... Actor Marlon Brando Dies... Actor Marlon Brando Dies...*

A Kind of Loving

A P Pullan

And you said you'd been followed by shearwaters
that crissed and crossed low at your stern
as if they were carrying gossamer to stitch up your wake.

I said the wife saw a magpie at Kilwinning station once
and sure enough she and I shared the toilet that night;
a prawn curry from the Taj.

You said you rounded the Kyles of Bute
on a night when the moon was a bulb,
the sea a smoked-glass table and you
up the main sail, dimming the light.

Me, pissed up, tripped over the cat during a power cut
and woke tucked up, glass of water by my side.

You said you'd seen the fluke of a humpback
wave to its mate who not only waved back
but curled up her finger, summoned him to her side.

Mad that she still had it, I'd thrown out pages of her diary
from the bedroom window then in guilt rounded them up,
the last one flapping its whereabouts from the gutter.

You said you'd dived naked for scallops at Barra
then fed them to kelpies, the day just coming up through its gears.

I said there was that time it rained for seven days
and seven nights at Prestonpans caravan site,
so I bravely set out for a multibag of Wagonwheels and a box of Nambarrie
to see us through such harsh times.

You said you were halfway across the Atlantic
and all God had to watch was you
like a flea on his quilt, yet you've never known loneliness,
that your craft is your place of worship,
the sea and all her moods; your reason for being.

I said I missed my wife when I'd run out of milk
the third night she was in for that ectopic pregnancy.

But you didn't know about love, you conceded,
what to do lest it cross your bows,
breach you, take you onto another course.

So I said let it just come,
come like a standing wave you can't run from
to feel its depth, the hot musk of it, the dry taste of it
then note the direction of the wind

it leaves you breathless in.

The Leaving

Olive M Ritch

Don't look back,
says the echo of a Voice
as I stand alone on the bow,
south-bound, looking forward.

I've had enough of tied-tongue
and skin-snipping wind-torture.
I've had enough of sowing,

and reaping, and the upright
shining order. I've had enough
of hands waving, drowning.
Don't look back. Don't.

A solitary tern swoops and soars
overhead. I long for beauty
and the terrible peopled place.

Rainbow Oil
Stephen Nelson

I knew an old man once
who told stories about
his years as a drunk
in the gutter
before he met
the Lord.
I imagined
his wino body
laid out in puddles,
stained with oily
rainbows, rank alcoholic breath
toxicity befouling
clean air (he stank of
garlic which he used to eat raw
as a defence against bacteria),
grit teeth hissing breath &
bubbles of saliva
foaming at
the world's disdain.

Now he wears
a rainbow body,
light as laughter
sailing on the wind
above high mountains,
& knows the scent
of weather angels
shifting clouds for
the amusement of
solitary yachtsmen.

His life as a fox
is the birth of a
bear willing to learn
from polyphonic
river preachers
the mushroom dance
of heaven.

Whenever I see
a deer skip back from the
railtrack between
Newton & Blantyre,
I can understand
eager ascent from
wild transition &
the need to discard
toys below bridges
where stories accumulate
as musk in a
field of bees.

In Two Minds

Olive M Ritch

I am homesick after mine own kind
but not the clicking tongues

at the mouth of narrow closes.
I am homesick for my friends,

my family with wings clipped.
There are folk about me, flocks of them,

don't get me wrong; I am surrounded by strange
voices, tall grey buildings, and wide streets,

but not green fields, and sheep,
and big skies. I long for

lilting voices, spoken softly
on private piers, and I long for

the meeting and the parting.

Extract from the novel *Burning Rates*
Helen Sedgwick

CHERRY TREES IN blossom. White-pink petals falling like confetti. A round yellow sun in the morning sky and a bold bright blueness everywhere. The world is made of crayon colours here – the grass is too green, the bricks too red, and there is a pavement made of square paving stones in lightly different shades of grey and a hint of pink. Amber's mother is holding Amber's hand tight and, on the other side of her body, Toby's even tighter.

Amber's hair is longer now than it was before, she has a fringe that tickles her eyes and she blows it out of her face in a way that she thinks looks sophisticated. Years later, she will see the same gesture performed again by kids who are nearly teenagers and realise it looks the very opposite of sophisticated. She does not have a natural elegance. Elegance is something she will try to learn one day, but she'll never think that she's succeeded.

They turn as one towards a closed iron gate that leads to a neatly ordered front garden, and Amber's mother drops Amber's hand to lift the latch and push open the gate. The path is made of big slabs like stepping-stones over gravel; the flowers are fuchsia and gold in a sea of green.

Step.

Crunch.

Toby takes big wide steps to reach from one slab to the next.

Amber crunches her way over the gravel and avoids stepping on the slabs.

The doorbell makes a ding-dong sound. And they're in.

The mother's are talking over tea at the kitchen table. Big wide windows look out into a garden that has swings and hand rings and is edged with a border of flowers. The tablecloth is plasticky, because kids make a mess. On top of it is a mat that's made of lace, and on top of this lace mat is the teapot, steaming hot. The tea china looks thin and fragile and is only for use by the adults.

Run along and play now, they say.

Amber and Toby share a second of unity here; neither wants to run along and play. Not here. Not with them.

Upstairs Amber goes to play with Michelle and Toby is supposed to play with Natalie, but he doesn't play girls games and he doesn't like Michelle and Natalie, so instead he sits in the corner and watches them. There is a bunk bed and the room is very pink, clichéd two-girls pink, double cutesy.

Michelle's got a secret.

'Tell me,' Amber says.

Michelle leans forward to whisper in her ear.

'Natalie wants Toby to be her boyfriend.'

Amber doesn't believe the secret, but goes along with the game anyway.

'Why doesn't she prove it?' Amber says loudly to the room.

'She doesn't want to.'

'You should make her.'

'Fine, I will.'

Michelle and Natalie both have long straight hair. Michelle's is blonde and Natalie's is brown. It is totally straight and very long, and it has been cut so that it falls down their backs and makes a perfect straight line. They are wearing skirts that match. Michelle says they have to close the curtains for this game and Natalie gets up and closes the curtains. Toby is sitting on the bottom bunk bed and he doesn't say anything. His blond curls are darker now than they used to be, but they still frame a round face and blue eyes that blink at the girls. His socks have got Thomas the Tank Engine on them.

'We have to have rules,' Michelle is saying.

'Okay.'

Amber thinks that Michelle has done this before. She can tell.

'Number one. We all have to do what we're told when it's our turn.'

'Okay.'

'Natalie?'

'Okay.'

'Toby?'

Toby shakes his head. 'I'm not playing.'

'Go away then.'

Toby stays where he is.

'If you stay then you play. The forfeit is a Chinese burn on both arms. Rule Number Two. Nobody's allowed to tell.'

The room seems quieter now; Amber can hear her mum's voice and Michelle's mum's voice downstairs in the kitchen. It is dark but not that dark because it's a bright day and the sun is spilling through the closed curtains. It makes the room pinky-rose coloured because the curtains, like everything else, are pink.

'I'm going to start, and I'm giving the dare to Natalie.'

Michelle and Natalie look at each other and for a second they are like twins but one is bigger and one is smaller, and the smaller one wants to make herself bigger, and it seems almost as though they are in this together.

'You have to kneel down over there and pull up your skirt.'

Natalie crawls over towards the window. Michelle looks at Amber and smiles. It is not a nasty smile, it is a sugar and spice smile. Her eyes move fast across the room to Toby.

'And you have to look, Toby.'

Toby looks.

His lips are pressed into a pout and his blue eyes blink but don't look away.

'Leave him alone,' Amber says. Too late.

Natalie is kneeling on all fours. Her head is resting on the ground and her skirt is pulled up over her back. She is wearing white cotton pants with pale blue dots on and a matching pale blue ribbon laced around the top, and her pure white socks have grass stains on the heels. She lifts her head up and looks over her shoulder to the three children looking at her bum.

'Now pull down your pants,' Michelle says.

'Okay.' Natalie leans on her head and pulls her pants down around her ankles.

Amber knows that she is never going to do a dare. That if Michelle tries to make her she will pull her annoying long straight hair and give her Chinese burns first. Michelle is weaker than Amber, and prettier, and she cares about her hair too much. She wouldn't want Amber to pull it out. That's her weakness. Amber knows it.

Suddenly Michelle squawks, 'Look look!'

Amber looks. So does Toby.

Michelle is giggling now, hysterically, no not giggling, she is laughing, almost cackling, and now she's shouting, 'Look, look, there's poo! Poo! Look!' And Amber looks and can see little brown specks on Natalie's bottom, but suddenly Natalie is trying to pull up her knickers fast and she's crawling away from them as she does it, and she's up and crying and running out of the room and Michelle looks at Amber and they both know Rule Number Two is about to be broken.

Footsteps running up the stairs.

Voices shouting their names.

Amber stands. Michelle stands. Toby lies down on the bed and pulls up the blanket and makes his eyes fill up with tears.

Amber's arm is pulled hard and it hurts (but only a bit) and her mum's face is purple fury and Amber tries to pull her arm away from her mother's tight grip. There are the vague sounds of Michelle screaming and Natalie crying but it's mostly silence she'll remember, which is weird. Silence, and Toby just sitting there smiling, sobbing, with his golden hair and his podgy round face and the knowledge that he

↣

won't be in any trouble. He never is.

'You looked too,' Amber hisses at him as her mum drags her by the arm out of the room to somewhere else; when she's older she won't be able to remember where, but she'll always remember that *she* – most definitely – was in trouble.

Limp

Jenny Love

BEFORE WORK EVERY morning I put on my tracksuit and trainers, come out of my front door, down the path bordered with lavender, I shut the gate behind me and start running.

Today, today, what have I got on today?

I hear the sound of my breath moving in and out. It keeps me focussed and I enjoy watching the scenery rush by. I go on, past the post office.

Remember to pick up George's prescription.

Must write that report.

Is it Sally's birthday this weekend, or next?

I breathe in and out and run past the church.

That poor man she is with, he's a good looking guy too, but she's letting herself go. I saw him looking at Sandra Porter at Helen's party.

Helen.

Now there's a woman who could do with a facelift...

Round the back of the primary school and down the lane.

I get home and have a good stretch. I don't want to end up with pulled muscles. I take a shower and put on my smart clothes for work. I eat two slices of toast and marmalade and kiss George on the cheek.

'Bye love, see you tonight.'

'Can you remember and pick up my prescription?' George reminds me, brushing toast crumbs off his shirt and tie.

The Salvation Army centre is tucked behind the train station, across the road from Tescos. My office is a boxy little room right at the back of the building. It has one grubby little window, facing onto the train station. Sometimes, when the trains are coming in, I can hardly hear myself think.

The carpet is brown; the tall filing cabinet is brown. In the corner there is a small coat stand where I hang my jacket and my favourite red scarf. I would put a plant on the windowsill to try and cheer the place up, but there is so little light I'm not sure it would survive.

I'm forty-six years old,

Forty-seven next month.

and on the whole I enjoy my work. I've been the welfare rights officer here for fifteen years. The punters come in and tell me tale after tale of woe and I help them and together we get through the umpteen pages of forms needing filled out.

It's been a busy morning, but my next appointment is late. I'm just thinking maybe I can nip out and get Sally's birthday present when a man appears at the office door. I've seen him before. He's a bedraggled old bloke, only in his fifties but you'd never think it to look at him. He has scruffy, yellowing-grey hair and a straggly beard. He's wearing a shaggy overcoat and leaning heavily on a wooden walking stick.

'John isn't it?' I motion for him to come in and take seat.

He hobbles through and sits down.

'Sorry I'm late. Slept in, didn't I?'

He smells of pee.

'Yes well. What can we do for you today, John?'

What about a nice cup of tea,

↣

or perhaps some male grooming products?

'It's about my money, they've fucked it – beg your pardon Miss – I mean they've made a mistake or something. I went to the Post Office to get it this morning and it wasn't in.'

'That's no good, is it? Let's see. So what kind of benefits are you supposed to be on?'

'I've got a letter here,' he says and fumbles about in his pocket. He pulls out a folded up bit of paper that looks like something has been spilled on it.

Please let that be coffee.

I read it.

'John, it says here you missed sending in a sick note. You need to make an appointment with your doctor.'

'I see, Miss. I was thinking I should.'

'I think you should too,' and I start scribbling down some of his details.

'I've been having a bit of trouble down there though.'

I don't look up from writing but I say, 'They'll be fine with you John, we just need to get your sick line and then we can get this all sorted out.'

'But it's been like this for weeks,' and he starts to stand up.

'What has?' I say, still writing.

'Well. Just look at it.'

I look up.

What the...

John is standing with his trousers and pants half-way down his legs. His flaccid penis is hanging out over his testicles. His pubic hair is thick and grey and looks like a bird's nest.

It looks like a one-eyed baby vulture.

Part of me wants to laugh. But I feel sick. I just stare for a moment. My mouth shut tight. I'm afraid to breathe.

'It's been like this for nearly three weeks,' says John

Did his eyes just glint?

He's directly between me and the door.

I'm going to have to touch him if I want to get past.

I stand up and very calmly say, 'Well now, let's see if we can get you that appointment. What doctor are you with?'

'Dr Carruthers,' he says. He is still standing with his penis out. I'm trying not to look at it.

Think about something else.

'Right. Well. I'll just need to go and get his number.'

Somehow, I stay calm. I carefully squeeze past him, breathing in so I don't have to actually touch him, though I still feel his coat brush against me as I pass.

Don't think about the smell.

Don't touch him.

Just get out.

I almost run down the corridor, past Mr Jones, the manager.

I...

but how?

Nevermind.

I force myself to smile. I reach Janine's desk at reception. She's in discussion with a balding, overweight man who keeps giving excuses as to why each appointment she's offering him isn't suitable.

I can't say to her? What would I say?

I don't want a fuss.

I interrupt her briefly for the telephone directory and look up the number for the doctor.

Doctors,

A.

B.

C.

Cunting

Carruthers.

Even though I know there is a telephone in my office I stay here to make the call.

Come on, answer the phone.

Finally, I get through. I write down the details and force myself to go back to my office.

John is sitting down. He has his trousers back up again.

Thankfully.

But I stay by the door.

'Here you go.' I say, holding out the piece of paper with the appointment time on it.

He takes the piece of paper and stares at me.

I hold the door open wide and gesture for him to leave.

Just go.

John stands up, nods at me and hobbles down the corridor and out of the building.

I breathe out. I open the small window at the back of the office. The noise of the trains is now pleasantly deafening. I get the can of air freshener out of my desk drawer and spray the room liberally. I escape to the kitchen.

The kitchen is painted pastel blue, making it feel cold even in the middle of summer. There's a short worktop, with a sink at one end and a small fridge at the other. There's a cupboard above with mugs and tea and coffee. On the worktop is a cheap white kettle. On the other side of the room is a Formica-topped table set against the window (also backing onto the blasted train station) and three mismatched chairs. I get a mug.

Why don't we have Gin or Vodka in here?

I make myself a cup of tea and sit down. For a long time I just sit and stare. The trains pull in and out of the station.

Mr Jones comes in.

'Cup of tea?' he says.

'Yes,' I say, 'Please.' I'm still staring out the window.

He pours two mugs of tea. 'Are you okay?'

'Yes, yes I'm fine, thanks.'

No.

I don't think I am.

He sits down beside me. 'Heather, what on earth is it?'

Please don't ask me that.

'Heather?'

Try him.

'That last appointment. John Smith. He...'

Don't cry.

I start to cry but in between sniffs I manage to tell him what happened.

'I mean, it sort of seemed plausible, and I just froze. And of course I made him an appointment for his doctor but it's just not appropriate and... I should have just told him to get out. I don't understand why I didn't.'

Mr Jones says, 'Oh.'

Oh?

What do you mean, oh?

A man flashes his dick at me and all you can say is oh?

'Do you think we should ring Social Work or something?' I say.

'Okay, yes, but let me ring them. See how it lies, I mean, it might just have been an old man, you know, a misunderstanding maybe?'

A misunderstanding?

How could it possibly be a misunder-fucking-standing?

I misunderstood – oops – and my dick just fell out?

I say, 'Thanks,' and wipe my eyes on the back of my hand.

I don't know what's worse.

What happened in the office or what's happening now.

I just want to go home to George and a hot bath.

Fifteen minutes later Mr Jones comes back in looking grave. He sits down and says quietly, 'Heather, it seems he's been doing it to several female members of staff up there and at the council offices the other day too.'

I'm going to throw up.

Mr Jones lays his hand over mine. I pull my hand away. He pulls his hand back and takes a sip of his tea.

The way his eyes glinted.

He says, 'Anyway... um... you're fine. It wasn't as though anything really awful happened?' And he smiles at me.

I'm fine.

I'll be fine.

Fine.

I get home as usual at five-thirty. George is home before me and has already got dinner going. He has a tea towel flung over his shoulder like a TV chef.

'Lasagne okay love?'

'Yeah sure.'

'Did you remember my prescription?'

Shit.

'No pet, sorry...'

'You okay? You look a bit funny?'

Please don't ask me.

'Heather?'

And so, for the second time today I have to explain how a stinky old man revealed his penis to me in the middle of an appointment.

I'm not going to cry.

I start sobbing and George tries to wrap his arms around me but I pull away from him and pretend to busy myself, taking the salad veg out of the fridge. I start chopping cucumber.

Don't think about it.

It's long and phallic and I'm trying not to think about it.

I chop and chop and chop.

Later, we go to bed. George undresses with his usual swagger. Shirt pulled off up over his neck (only half the buttons undone). Trousers off. Pants off. I wriggle into my longest nightdress whilst he brushes his teeth. He sits on the edge of the bed, has a stretch, and then stands back up to turn off the light. I turn over so I'm facing away from him. I can feel him looking at me in the half-light coming through the bedroom curtains but I don't look round. He climbs in and tries to cuddle in behind me. I can feel his erection prodding at the small of my back.

I say, 'I think I need a glass of water.'

I don't want you to touch me.

I want you to touch me, but I don't.

'I'll not be long,' I say.

I pad downstairs to the kitchen. I pour myself a large gin and tonic and look out of the window. The moon illuminates the garden in shades of dark blue and grey. Eventually, I hear the low rumble of George snoring and I go back to bed.

The next morning I go out for my run. I come out the front door, down the path bordered with lavender, I shut the gate behind me and start running.

Am I just over-reacting?

Mr Jones seems to think so.

I listen to my breath moving in and out, and I watch the scenery rush by. I go on, past the post office.

Remember to pick up George's prescription today.

Why didn't I say something?

Like 'oh look, just like a penis only smaller'?

Or wallop him and tell him to put it the fuck away?

I breathe in and out and run past the church.

I'm not sure I can face work today.

Round the back of the primary school and away down the lane.

Back on the horse that kicks you, as they say.

Whoever the fuck 'they' are.

I get home and have a good stretch. I take a shower and put on my clothes for work. I eat two slices of toast and marmalade and kiss George on the cheek.

'Bye love, see you tonight.'

'Can you remember and pick up my prescription?' George reminds me again, brushing toast crumbs off his shirt and tie.

I go to work but it's not the same. Every time a man comes in who smells even slightly of alcohol, I feel my guts tense up. And this happens a lot.

By the end of the week I feel like my entire body is coiled into tight springs.

Try not to think about it.

The following week is a little better, but then at lunchtime one day I hear a load of shouting from reception. Instead of going to help Janine, I close my office door and leave her to deal with whatever the problem is all on her own.

Mr Jones can go help her sort it out.

More weeks pass. Every day I seem to be more nervous and jumpy than the next.

And things at home aren't much better. I stay up late, unable to sleep. I barely let George near me.

Still, I go out for my daily run.

It's raining hard today, but that doesn't stop me. I come out the front door, down the little path bordered with lavender. I shut the gate behind me and start running.

It's been weeks now.

I miss him but I just can't.

Even though we've never went this long without...

I listen to my breath moving in and out, and I watch the scenery rush by. I hear the splash, splash of my trainers hitting the wet pavement. I go on, past the post office.

How would men like it if we ran around throwing our bits in their faces?

But that's the thing isn't it?

They'd love that.

I breathe in and out and run past the church and along the lane. I hit a puddle and skid slightly.

Woah! Nearly...

Round the back of the primary school and down the lane.

But I step in a huge patch of mud on the kerb and I fall. Hands out in front of me, and I'm on the ground.

My hands are covered in mud. There's mud in my hair. My ankle hurts. I try to sit but the pain shoots up my leg. I can feel my ankle swelling.

I let out a frustrated yell.

Slowly, I manage to stand up, and I limp and hobble home. No stretches. No shower. No slices of toast and marmalade.

Tears are pouring down my face.

'George?'

He has toast crumbs on his shirt and tie. His mouth is a large O. 'What the hell happened?'

'I fell.'

There was no-one to catch me.

'Come on,' he says, 'let's get you out of these wet things.'

He takes my hand and gently helps me up to the bedroom. He pops through to the bathroom and comes back with a clean towel and a facecloth. I can hear the sound of running water.

'Here you go. It's okay.'

I sit on the edge of the bed with tears streaming down my mud stained face.

Dirty and filthy.

Gently he wipes away the mud, towels my hair. I let him take off my T-shirt; my bra. He carefully helps me take off my trainers and socks. He eases me out of my running trousers and my pants. He lets me lean on him and helps me hop through to the bathroom. The bath is now full of steaming hot suds. He helps me climb in.

Dirty.

So gently, the same way he did with the kids when they were just tiny, he takes the shower spray and wets my hair. I shut my eyes and he rubs shampoo into my head. Carefully he rinses the soap suds away without letting the water run into my eyes.

'Don't go to work today,' I say.

I miss you.

We go to bed and I cuddle in against George's chest. I can feel the heat of us both, hear his heart beating under my ear. He strokes my hair.

You feel warm and clean.

I can feel him stirring against me.

But I don't know if...

I try anyway.

'Just do me, I'll just lie here.' I say.

He pulls back from me, looking at me all concerned. 'It's fine,' he says, 'we can just cuddle.'

Don't wait for me to start.

I don't think I can.

'But I want you to. I need you to.' I look right at him. I'm not cross. I'm sure.

'I don't know...'

'Yes you do.' And I lie on my back. 'Please. I'll just lie here. Please? Let me just lie here and let you.' My voice is trembling.

I want to, George,

I just don't know how anymore.

I can't remember...

He waits, like he's thinking about it.

Please George.

It's easy for you.

He leans across to kiss me but I freeze. Jagged. Rigid.

'No, please. Just do it. Just pretend I'm not here or something.'

He looks confused but he climbs on top of me anyway, closing his eyes. I put my arms round his back and try to concentrate on the feeling of him naked. I can feel him getting hard but I'm trying not to think about this.

He enters me and starts to thrust. I'm gazing at the ceiling.

Think about

↣

when we were younger and
that time we did it on the couch
when the kids were away.
And the first time we danced.
He's thrusting.
How handsome he was
in his suit
the day we got married.
The way he looked at me that day
on the boat
in the Lake District.
His shoulders.
Remember his kisses.

I'm kissing his neck and breathing in the cleanness of him. He's thrusting harder.

This is safe.
And he makes me safe.
And his mouth
and his skin
and...
Harder.
Warm
and clean
and.
Home.

He cries out a little when he comes and I bury my head into his neck and sob. I have been so sad and so alone for so long. George just holds me.

Shared Conditions

Michaela Maftei

THE WOMAN BEFORE me used to be much closer to me than she is now. At first this was a relief but now I am starting to miss her. I thought solitude would be preferable to forced companionship with someone I didn't know, hadn't chosen to be around, who could barely speak intelligibly and had poor dress sense. But I'm starting to think that I was mistaken, that you get to a point where almost anyone is better than nobody, a point where you're willing to overlook elements of a person's character that would normally mark them out as unsuitable for friendship.

I became aware of her in the night. Here, there are degrees of darkness, a pulsing turquoise that is the equivalent to day, contrasted by the velvet navy putting pressure on my eyes, which is the real night. This is my version of her background: a soft blur of lightlessness, unclear border between shapes, a deep plush cushion against which she materialized one day.

For the first few weeks I was terrified into stillness. I was unused to not being alone. I wasn't sure if she had seen me or not, but I thought by silencing all my movements I might escape notice. Eventually I knew she saw me and she knew I knew, though I could still take comfort in our inability to move physically closer to each other at will. We were fixed in our positions, more or less; occasionally a sudden wave or thrust or force would jostle us, distancing or bringing us together in a hushing rush, a period of intense discomfort, regardless of whether it neared or widened us.

'Are you really so small?' I eventually asked her, phlegm in my throat from breaking silence.

She widened her eyes.

'Haven't you ever heard of perspective?' she asked me in a high, pretty voice: less arrogant than me; arrogant.

I was shamed into silence; I entered into a period of unwillingness to communicate. I damn well knew about perspective. I had taken an evening art class after finishing university and I knew it was about what an apple looked like when it was placed twelve inches in front of a banana on a table that you had to draw. Of course I knew about perspective; I had spoken before realizing it applied to us. I hadn't thought of perspective as a law governing this strange night-time blue world. I withdrew with this new knowledge, into it. I turned my back on her. It seemed important that she not see me think; if she knew how I did it, it would empower her. I turned this exchange over and over in my mind, reading into it things that were and were not there, worrying it like a pebble, smoothing it into a round little piece of grit that I placed in the toe of one shoe as a reminder. This one's sharpish. Don't give her any rope.

It was seventeen days before she broke the silence. This seemed to be her limit of standing about, furtively looking at me.

'I like your hair,' she said lamely. This means about as much to me as the weather report. The sounds of these words bring forth a thousand images of lame come-ons, boyfriends' mothers, cashiers making small talk while a colleague price checks my avocado or box of

➻

cereal or clearance sale bra. But I was willing to latch on to it now. Seventeen days can be a long time.

'Thanks. It's nice,' I said.

I watched her for signs of calculation, for pre-emptive strikes, for excessive deliberation. But she really seemed to want to make friends. I fell for it, into it.

'I like your shoes,' I did not really like her shoes, but that wasn't the point. She told me where she got them, how long she'd had them, how they'd given her a blister for a while until she bandaged it and kept wearing them, and then it was alright between us. I stayed encouraging, and she deepened, telling me a significant day she'd worn them, what had happened, it was to see her brother, his birthday. So I told her about mine, made comparisons, brought up things that seemed relevant and important and interesting, at least for her. We shared. When the conversation ended, a morning-glory paleness grew, signifying day; we were tired, dry-mouthed, smiling for no particular reason, intimate.

It was a false indicator. We were never able to reach the same level of closeness, ran out of things to say with depressing reliability. There was nobody else around in this cool, dry atmosphere, and we still couldn't get it together enough to form a relationship. You'd think we would do the best we could with what we had – each other – but our edges didn't meet, our tastes never meshed.

At least until we started talking about him. It was an accident, of course; I would never purposely invite discussion about him. But I slipped, or I misinterpreted something she said, or I was caught thinking aloud one day: either way, I cracked him open like a walnut, and we dug out the wrinkled meat of him, toasting it and crunching it in our back teeth; dense like a walnut, he provided hours of chewing. She was forthright, until she wasn't, at which point she would switch off like a streetlight. She used the past tense; I used the present. Nothing was left undigested: his eating habits, that infuriating habit of letting the fridge door swing open, morning or night preferences, leather shoes with a flapping sole, the imbalances between us.

'The thing he does with the ties,' I shared, eager to make a connection even though there was not one to make.

Abruptly she stopped. 'I don't know anything about that. I don't like that.' You can hardly go on from there.

He brought us closer together; he brought us close together in the first place. He muted the awkwardness and made it seem only logical that we two would form a bond, rather than pure chance that we had interrupted each other's silent blue space, filling the misted air with our chatter. Nobody else existed in this universe but the two of us, or so I thought.

I hadn't spent enough time thinking of it, but I should have known that what I could see, and what was, were not necessarily the same thing. I had simply jumped into the assumption that what was before me was all there was. To be fair, she made no reference to anyone else, she did nothing to suggest the chain of us.

I discovered it for myself, when I became distracted by a speck in my eye. It moved and faded in and out, some days it would be more pronounced, some days it didn't bother me. It grew and I tried rubbing it and rubbing it out with my fingers, but eventually it grew, swollen, far ahead in the distance. It was the shape of a woman, a beautiful woman, dark-haired, like me, poor dress sense. That should have tipped me off. She stayed in the distance, minute and blurred, though sometimes sharper, sometimes disappearing for a few days at a time again.

I asked her if she could see this third woman.

'No,' she said, but she wasn't even looking in the right direction. I pointed this out to her.

'It doesn't matter. I won't be able to see her.'

'You're still looking in the wrong direction.'

She shook her head impatiently and pointed somewhere behind her. 'Can you see this one?' she asked.

'There's nothing there,' I told her.

I didn't get it, not for a while longer. The woman up ahead slowly, slowly got bigger, until I could see the drop of her shoulders, the tight spread of her clothing. I described her to my friend, insistent that she could see her if she only looked hard enough.

'She's not tall.'

'Ok.'

'Sort of... top-heavy.'

'No surprise there.'

Days passed, life was difficult for a while, storms were weathered, or I imagined they were. The third woman grew larger, moved more confidently into my field of vision, could not see my first friend anymore than my friend could see her, sprouted a voice that I overheard one day, rich and heavy and thick, a voice I tried to imitate for my friend, who could not hear her either, could barely hear me as she travelled backwards in the distance.

'She sounds like you.'

'No she doesn't.'

The third woman saw me one day. She had grown to half my size, her movements were fully discernible, she knew to look in my direction. She judged the distance between us, considered my height, weighed her words, then spoke.

The voice was somehow richer, heavier, when it was directed at me. A voice that could cast spells, lure. She did what I must have done, only she did it weeks earlier – brought him into it, discussed him. It took a few moments for me to recognize she was talking about him, knew him. Maybe she had a need, a neediness, that I had made myself lack. The icy wash of realization was worsened by the sudden clarity: I had done the same thing to my friend, thrown this discovery in her face. She was gracious; I was simply shocked into silence. She knew him. She knew. He knew her. I turned away for some privacy and came face to face with my friend. She offered no comfort, and I suddenly didn't want any from her.

The third woman grows more pronounced by the day, though she is also subject to these flinging forces that sometimes bring her terrifyingly close to me, sometimes remove her entirely, though not from my mind. Last week she was up to my chest, soon she will be full-size. My friend is receding, melting into the blue silk landscape. Only I am the same, remaining in a stasis of dread. I can watch my replacement grow strong and assured, trilling with laughter when she speaks of him, ignoring me when it is convenient. Movement goes in one direction only, without much control on my part; the shimmering blue distracted me from this knowledge. We are not resident in the same landscape.

'You'll feel better,' my friend tells me, her voice becoming tinny and distant.

'Soon you won't feel bad at all.'

I am not Gary, she is not Gwen
Nick Holdstock

AFTER A HARD day's ride we arrived on the outskirts of Plate. We fed the horses and pitched the tent; after a frugal supper, we slept. It was a deep, refreshing sleep. In my dream the President shook my hand after pardoning us. He said, 'O my son and daughter! How greatly you have suffered!' Then he hung gold medals round our necks and named a park after us.

In the morning we put on our masks and rode into town. When we passed someone, I said, 'Hello,' and after they returned my greeting, I added, 'We're on our honeymoon!' Then I waved my beak, and Ethel waggled her horn, and after we'd gone through this a few times, it was more or less true.

We spent the rest of the morning in the ceramics museum. It wasn't big, but there were some nice pieces, especially the jugs. It was while admiring these that I struck up conversation with a redhead in a wheelchair. After we'd laughed about my mask – *not* the most convincing ostrich – she said, 'Nothing else matters if you're in love'. She paused to spit mucus into a container. Then she asked where we were from. Usually I say we're from some place like Frant, New Hampshire, or Reptile, Florida (though you'd be surprised how people from these places get around; more than once we've had to use the 'I-moved-away-when-I-was-young' line). But I found myself telling her the truth: that we'd come from Arkady, New Mexico, where we ran a hardware store that belonged to my father and his father before him; that although it was good to get away, we couldn't wait to get back. And as I spoke I saw us pushing the door against a mountain of mail; the two of us sweeping, scrubbing and washing; cleaning a years' worth of dust.

I wasn't the only one who forgot himself; Ethel started going on about how much she wanted to sign up for a pottery course. She kept on throughout lunch – the hot dogs were some of the best I've had – then during our time at the zoo. She ruined the zebras, the mongoose, *and* the kinkajou with her prattle about glazes. The only thing that shut her up was the face of the tapir: I do not think I've ever seen a gentler-looking creature. We could have stared at its innocent features all day, but the sun was too damn hot. Both of us were thick-lipped and sweating, muttering only 'water' and 'shade'. But I would have never suggested taking off our suffocating masks. *That* was all her idea. At first I was dead-set against it, till she said, 'Come on, there's only the monkeys.'

I must confess that when we took them off, it *was* a relief. We strolled and felt the breeze on our faces, maybe even felt free.

We were enjoying the gibbons when the shooting began.

'Not again,' she sighed then dove behind a bench. I followed, and for several seconds, all we did was cower.

'*Why?*' she said. 'Why? We were having *such* a nice...'

I could only mumble back; I guess I was too upset. To my mind, they were shooting at us for no reason except that they had guns, and guns have bullets, and bullets itch to be fired. I've never seen so many guns: pistols, revolvers, rifles, shotguns, tiny ones inlaid with mother-of-pearl that were clearly polished with love. A blunderbuss that spat nails and roots, which was wielded with such aplomb that if I absolutely had to be killed by one of the firearms present, it would have been this too charming antique. Of the three girls in command of it, two were beautiful flax-haired twins; the third was a vicious little pug with a hideous underbite. She did her job with admirable zeal but the twins' aim, despite the steadying aid of a gopher-shaped trashcan, was no better than the other citizens of Plate (pop. 289). In the four or five minutes it took us to get from the bench to the snake house, through the gift-shop and into the car park where our horses were tethered, they must have fired over a thousand rounds at distances ranging from hopeful to downright embarrassing.

The closest they got was a ricochet that tattered her horn; this was what made Ethel so cross she began to return fire. According to the paper the next day, her few seconds of marksmanship were enough to rob the town of its mayor, its hot-dog vendor, a postman on the eve of retirement, two mirrored side windows of a pink stretch limousine and finally – though she denies it vigorously – two of the zebras as well.

But this was only a fit of pique, nothing compared to her anger when I abandoned her. 'Wait,' she screamed, but I had already cleared the fence. As I galloped down the central reservation, bullets still flying, car horns blaring, I asked myself what the *hell* I was doing. This was, after all, the woman I loved; who had been my high school sweetheart; who had worked side-by-side with me in our small-but-respectable store.

When the answer came back, it was a shock. Even though Ethel's cute as a pistol (and a terrific shot), I realized I *wanted* her to get caught. Then we couldn't be mistaken for Gary and Gwen (who are still as inseparable as they were on that day, three years ago, when he shot her parents in front of their wedding guests). If it was just me, I'm pretty sure I wouldn't get mistaken for him. She, after all, is the one with the birthmark in the shape of Wyoming. If I look quite similar to him, it's only from a funny angle that crops up more than it should.

So, yes, I suppose they *were* shooting for a particular reason, albeit one that was insufficient *and* poorly thought out. Because I don't think part-resemblance is reason enough. If they had stopped to think (which I reckon would be deadly with Gary and Gwen, who have a very professional approach to witnesses) the good people of Plate (pop. 286, not counting the zebras) might have come to the life-saving conclusion that those two outlaws wouldn't be seen dead in their tiny, crappy town that only has a zoo thanks to some gibbon-lover's bequest. *They* prefer the major towns, the larger banks and shopping malls. They don't care how busy the place is, how many people they have to shoot, so long as they get a big score. Last month they hit a bank in Austin. Although there were no reports of a struggle, no signs of anyone trying to be a hero, they still killed the manager, three tellers, a rent-a-cop six weeks from his pension, and five of the seven customers (the two survivors were a boy with Downs Syndrome and his almost blind grandmother). Ethel and I, by contrast, have never shot anyone unarmed (barring an incident involving a Frisbee and one of her migraines).

If, by some twist of fate, Gary and Gwen *did* end up in Plate, it would only be for the kind of innocent reason that led us to visit. All we were trying to do was unwind from life on the run. To feel like the normal, law-abiding citizens we honestly and truly were until the first Wanted posters went up. And if that meant spending a weekend in Plate, Arizona while wearing masks, then, we said, so be it. It would be like getting back to our roots. We'd find a nice hardware store; talk shop with the owner; shake our heads at the price of lumber; covertly tidy his shelves.

We certainly weren't going to lock the door, pull the blinds, put a sign in the window that said, 'Sorry, Back at 3', then truss him with his own rope. Although things are tight, they'll never come to that: there'll always be a liquor store, or failing that, a church.

Ethel was still pretty angry when she made it back to the tent. After she'd spat in my face

➻

– and this is a girl with a *lot* of spit – I didn't try to speak. To cap it off, it was raining hard. We sat at opposite ends of the tent, her still wearing the mask, me under the leaky spot, and even after it got dark I couldn't think of anything to say except that I was sorry. She didn't reply or move for a while. Then she wiggled her shredded horn and moved down to my end. I held her and she sobbed like a child that wants a present they know they can't have. I don't know if it was the drip, or her tears, but my neck got really wet.

'How is this gonna end?' she said. 'They'll kill us or we go to jail. I'm sick of camping and riding on horses because you don't like to drive. Last week when I called my mother she put the phone down. None of this is our *fault*.'

All I could do was hold her tight. I thought of Gary and Gwen. I'm certain they know about us, we're in the papers as often as them, these days even more. They probably think it's all a big joke. I doubt they're even the least bit grateful for the diversions we provide.

'Don't worry,' I said. 'It won't be much longer. Somebody'll figure it out. They'll be in one place, we'll be in another, and then someone will think, 'Hang on'. They'll put two and two together. They'll realize it's been a mistake.'

'But it's been a *year*,' she wailed, and I had no reply. It will be difficult to claim to have killed twenty-eight people in self-defense. That although we pulled the trigger, it still wasn't *us*.

The rain continued and pretty soon she fell asleep. I sat and listened to the sound of her grinding teeth. Their awful scrape and drag made me scared, so I started cleaning the guns. I usually do this in order of age – not how old the gun is, but how long we've had it. I begin with the Colt automatic that belonged to the policewoman in Tuscon. After all this time, and all the bullets, it is strange to think it was her gun that started it. If its trigger hadn't been squeezed; if the hammer hadn't eased back, lurched forward, detonated the charge that blew the bullet from the chamber, down the barrel, out into the bright May air towards us, Ethel and I might not be in hiding in a leaking tent.

But it's easy to get lost in *ifs*. If we hadn't been in town that day to visit Ethel's parents; if Sgt. Montoya Dawson, 32, loving mother to three daughters had been a better shot; if she'd bothered to look both ways before crossing the street; if the driver of the Buick that killed her had been going slower – then we'd both be dead. That we aren't, that the gun left her hand, flew through the air, landed just where we were crouching in terror, is, like everything else that's happened, only a matter of chance.

She should have made us throw her our IDs before she opened fire. She should've tried to arrest us. If she had followed procedure instead of the surge of blood and adrenalin that must have accompanied the 'realization' that the innocent, minding-their-own-business couple pushing the trolley was none other than the fiends who'd shot up the bank (and her sister) only the week before, not only would she still be alive, we wouldn't be in this mess.

It was blind, indifferent fortune that let us get away. We had no idea what we were doing. We gave no thought to roadblocks; just drove in a state of animal fear till the car gave up on us. We didn't understand how much trouble we were in till we picked up a paper next day. OUTLAWS KILL MOTHER OF THREE, it said, above a photo of what we had to admit looked incredibly like us. That was when we realized we couldn't just go home.

It was dumb luck that gave me those shooting lessons as an anniversary present (though Ethel still maintains I expressed an interest at the Clarkson's BBQ). Without these, we wouldn't have made it through the first few weeks. It was equally dumb luck that made the FBI agent (who'd done *so* well to creep up on our camp) trip on a branch and in his falling, in his flailing, blow his own head off.

After I finish cleaning the Colt, I do the Smith & Wesson. Then the Sig Sauer, the two Rugers, and finally the Heckler she grabbed from the hot-dog guy. I am oiling the barrel when it occurs to me: what happens when Gary and Gwen want to stop? They'll lie low for six months, maybe a year. When they think it's all blown over, they'll go to a movie or be at a store without so much as a pistol between them.

Because that's part of a life they're trying to leave, a page they want to stay turned. This is when some jackass will suddenly open fire. If they survive (and I pray that they do), they'll realize it's no good unless *we* stop as well. Because Ethel and I will still be trying to make ends meet (what with the price of fodder, bullets, and masks, the amount of work Ethel's had on her teeth, we'll be lucky to break even this month).

Somehow they'll get word to us, and then we'll meet for dinner. Probably in some fancy place where the waiters are trained to never look at people's faces. She and I will wear the masks, and though it might be awkward at first, I'm sure we'll soon be getting on, given how much we have in common. We'll compare flesh wounds and scars, our brushes with death, and as we're waiting for dessert – I'll have cheesecake; she'll have mousse – Gwen will lean across and say, 'Listen, we're so, so sorry. How can we make this up to you?'

And there will be a pause while Ethel and I exchange looks. Even though we're wearing masks, Gary and Gwen will comprehend the magnitude of our suffering. How their greed and selfishness have perverted our decent lives. When they realize all they've made us do – these dreadful things that just aren't us – their guilt will be so intense as to be almost unbearable. They'll think their heads are about to explode; that they're going to scream.

This is when I'll shrug and say, 'It was all just a misunderstanding.'

They'll be so relieved. We'll laugh and shake hands. We'll order cigars, brandy, coffee, a bottle of scotch. I'll raise my glass and smile and then propose a toast. We'll drink to each other's health, then new beginnings (or rather, how things were). When I say, 'Here's to the future!', Ethel will drop her napkin, slowly bend to pick it up. Her hand will travel down her thigh till it reaches the pretty black strap. When she straightens up she'll shoot them both in the chest (*not* the face) at least two or three times. During the ensuing panic, we'll empty the tills, but only to make sure we've enough to get home. Then we'll both ride joyously off with a sense of wondrous lightness. Although we'll have to lay low for awhile, it won't be long until we're back home – back to being ourselves.

All in the Words

Archie and the North Wind
Angus Peter Campbell
Luath Press Ltd, RRP £8·99, 176pp

"The old story has it that Archie, tired of the north wind, sought to extinguish it."

From the start – from that poetically succinct sentence – anyone reading Angus Peter Campbell's first English-language novel is told that what's to come is a fable, a story, but that stories and how we tell them now are important. Why? Well, as if to drive the point home, Campbell at one point has his hero Archie and his old mentor Gobhlachan stitting by an old warm forge: "...making nothing but stories which in the end proved more durable than even the iron, which now lies rusting in forgotten fields." The message is clear: for good or ill, stories last.

Archie's picaresque journey (denied to be Homeric, or "even Joycean") might seem naive to 'sophisticated' urban eyes, given that he leaves his home on a 'remote' Scottish island fully intending to block up the hole at the North Pole through which the North Wind blows. During his journey, however, Archie encounters a suitably diverse range of vividly drawn, enticingly iconographic characters: the beautiful deaf girl Jewel, who teaches him sign language, "to communicate with more than mere words"; the Russian sailor Brawn, who farts cigarrette smoke rings, "dealing with grief through black humour"; and Ted Hah, the Isaiah-quoting oil field chief searching for his "Oil of Gladness" in Alaska.

No simple slave to 'realism', then, Campbell underscores Archie's progress by the inclusion of several traditional Scots/Gaelic tales which reinforce the author's main interest: how we all, as individuals, communities and nations, create stories, myths and histories, often with little regard to 'authenticity': "Somehow Archie knew that the actual magic was in the words themselves, not in the events. The stories were the iron, to be shaped and moulded."

Though these stories date back generations, Campbell is well aware of his duty, as a 'seannachie' (bard), to show their continued relevence to ourselves today, which is why "...every time he saw a new horror, or a new marvel, (Archie) knew that it was just a modern version of his own old story".

Archie and the North Wind may be too idiosyncratic and meandering for readers looking for the simple, unthinking 'realism' which the colloquial language of the book at first suggests. Yet, almost from the start, this is a world seen through different eyes, where human and animal metaphors are used to describe land, sea and air: "Archie walked down through the winter fields to the edge of the nachair, where the mating was remorseless, the huge Atlantic waves thrashing on to the shore, the beach strewn with the debris of the thrusts." This is a book closer in spirit to the 'magical realism' of Jorge Luis Borges and Garcia Marquez, and yet it delightfully remains both specific and utterly contemporary – a "coalition age" where "ideology (is) nameless"; a world of Gore-Tex, the inter-net (sic), terrorism and the Hadron Collider. Yes, in this book you'll read tales of dragons, princesses and magic swords, but you'll also read of Yankee oilmen, Angelina Jolie and potato peelers, and you'll perhaps ask yourself what, fundamentally, has changed?

"All was alchemy. Words of course into stories, and stories which bent and altered time and history. He had a tale for every occasion, thought it may just have been the other way round: that, like a modern spin-doctor or ancient houngan, every occasion generated its myth."

Most of Campbell's earlier published fiction and poetry have been in Gaelic but this turn to English is no cultural selling out; it is grounded on his reality as a multi-lingual Scot and shows a confidence akin to Archie's own to show the world from his own unique perspective. An undoubtedly compelling and beautifully-crafted novel.
Yeti

The One That Nearly Got Away

The One That Got Away
Zoë Wicomb
Five Leaves Publications, RRP £7·99, 188pp

There aren't many writers living in this country with the support of Toni Morrison and JM Coetzee, still fewer admired at the New York Times and the Wall Street Journal. So you might expect this writer, whoever they are, to be widely celebrated in Scotland too. But Zoë Wicomb, brought up in South Africa and resident in Glasgow for most of the last three decades, is that rare thing in these self-aggrandising times – a writer who doesn't promote her writing. She hardly ever gives readings, avoids the festival circuit and publishes only occasionally, leaving her assured, reserved writing to speak for itself. So she often goes unnoticed. Even this, her first collection since 1987's *You Can't Get Lost in Cape Town* and only her 4th book in 23 years, appears in Scotland two whole years after The New Press published it in the USA. All of which suggests Wicomb has been marginalised. Which is a shame for Scottish Literature.

That shame is not due to tartan sentimentality: it's because Scotland is a hugely important element in her work. These stories continually link South Africa and Scotland, with characters often migrating between the two places. Ideas and characters also move between the stories, adding another level of migration. This makes for a refreshing mix, one which focuses on personal relationships but also draws out elements of Scottish history and culture in a way rarely touched in the books of many writers born here.

The title story follows Jane and Drew, a South African couple who honeymoon in Glasgow, an exercise which is really an excuse for Drew to pursue an art project. In a later linked tale, 'The Bird That Never Flew', the narrative focalises through the 'easily distracted' Jane, drifting around Glasgow, where she discovers the famous Doulton Monument, now on display outside the People's Palace. This celebration of the British Empire, created for the 1888 International Exhibition and showing Queen Victoria at the apex of figures representing various colonies, comes to fascinate Jane. She names the South African figure in the monument Kaatje, and imagines a whole life for Kaatje as she looks on. She continues to circle the monument, thinking about home, and about Glasgow, a city where she says "the opulence is awesome". She wonders whether art needs to provide any answers. Wicomb's assured description of Jane in these quiet moments will surely stay with many readers of this book for a long time.

Elsewhere in the collection, stories examine people in post-Apartheid South Africa – rich and poor, black and white, servants and the served – trying to come to terms with their place in this new shaken-up world. But these tales reject tidy narratives about the journey South Africans have gone on since Mandela's release, both for the citizens who have remained and the ones who have left. Zoë Wicomb's writing uses subtle internal monologue to illustrate how sometimes people feel held back even when they are told there are no longer any chains holding them. Her characters cling to their old perceived role in society, no matter which side of the old divide they were on. In Wicomb's newest story, 'Raising the Tone', added especially for this edition, teenager Miriam, now resident in Glasgow, complains that "even a shopping list can't escape the palimpsest of the old story of Africa". It is everywhere, always, even when unstated. Which also applies to this whole book.

The One That Got Away is finally being published in the UK by Five Leaves Publications of Nottingham, a small independent gaining a reputation for taking clever risks. Readers who find this slender book, and this startling writer, will be pleased someone close to home has finally got around to recognising one of our finest.
White Tiger

The Personal and Political

The Liberation of Celia Kahn
J David Simons
Five Leaves Publications, RRP £8·99, 240pp

Simon's second novel is set in Glasgow during the Great War, against a backdrop of Red Clydeside, the Rent Strikes of 1915, and the women's movement. Celia is 16 when she meets Agnes Calder, a suffragette schoolteacher from the West End. Celia's 'liberation' begins with Agnes, but, as the book subtly makes clear, this would not have been possible had Celia herself not already been interested in socialism and feminism. As her uncle puts it, "a socialist is not something you become, it is something you are." Celia's homelife is not quite ordinary, her mother has spent time interned in a British camp for German Jews, her younger brother has not spoken a word since the war broke out, and her own experiences of being a Jewish alien in Scotland are in opposition to her mother's stance on her traditional duties to marry and have children. Celia has therefore had reason to think for herself and to act on her own before Agnes came on the scene. Her influences are gently drawn, and the reader is given space to reach their own conclusions; Simons is never heavy-handed in his characterisation. The novel takes this approach to large events as well, Celia is raped by a stranger in the Botanic Gardens, but it is not until much later in the story that we learn the full consequences of this. This makes for a thoughtful and subtle style to the novel, bringing out the gradual development of Celia's independence.

Celia is a participant in many of the formative events in the women's and socialist movements in Glasgow, such as the Rent Strikes, and Bloody Friday, where a riot broke out during the strike about the restriction of working hours to the 40-hour week. Simons manages to weave in the history with the narrative in a natural, unforced way, with the historical events always contributing to the development of the characters. Agnes's incarceration for setting fire to a recruiting office is mentioned after the fact, and the focus is never placed on the action itself, but on the effect on Celia. Agnes resolves to hunger-strike for release under the Cat and Mouse Act, but instead of being released, she dies from it. Celia is never sure if she herself was culpable in this death, as Agnes has asked her to contact a journalist friend of hers and publicise her hunger-strike, therefore preventing the jailers from brutally force-feeding Agnes for fear of a media frenzy, but Celia forgets to speak to the journalist until it is too late. This focus on the psychological effects makes for an interesting narrative drive, there is plenty of drama, action and adventure, but it is rarely the action one would expect.

Following the death of Agnes, Celia is given a life-rent in her house, on condition that she use the property to continue in the struggle for women's rights, and, specifically, contraception. However, Celia discovers that even her feminist friends are split by this aspect of women's lib, where religion and family intersect. It is her uncle who, despite his increasing reliance on religion for answers after becoming disillusioned with socialism, is able to recognise that controlling family sizes would tackle overcrowding, poverty and female mortality rates. Celia's own reactions to the freedom offered by contraception are to be curious, as shown by her voyeuristic response to her friend Charlotte's sexual adventuring, then to experiment. In this, her character reaches its 'liberation', and she is able to break free of the rape. More tellingly, she loses her certainty that she should fight Glasgow's women's battles; she is 'freed' of the terrible problems that Glasgow still has. This is an occasionally funny novel and a very good read, which explores feminism and socialism with subtlety and intelligence.

Maltese Cat

My Own Story

The Last Warner Woman
Kei Miller
Weidenfeld and Nicolson, RRP £12.99, 246pp

A Light Song of Light
Kei Miller
Carcanet, RRP £9.95, 69pp

"Sometimes you have to tell a story the way you dream a dream, and everyone know that dreams don't walk straight." This idea is at the heart of Kei Miller's second novel, *The Last Warner Woman,* a narrative that becomes a poetic meditation on storytelling, on ways of telling and the texture of voices and perspectives that make up a life.

The novel begins in 1940s Jamaica with Pearline Portious trying to sell her 'ugly' purple doily to prove her mother wrong. Pearline insists on knitting in colour and "considers herself an artist, and of the kind whose chief aim was to please herself." Pearline's rebellious spirit eventually finds a home and expression as bandage maker in a leper colony. Here she helps the maternal Agatha Lazarus run the colony, who will eventually bring up her daughter, the protagonist Adamine Bustamante, when Pearline dies in childbirth. Like most of the women in the story, Agatha has experienced the violence of men. Brutally raped as a child, this event is echoed later in the novel with 'the Pads', the soft-walled cell of solitary confinement in the asylum that Adamine finds herself in, where she becomes a victim of sexual abuse: "Satan, let me tell you, was just a regular man. He did have a regular name and a regular job... Everything you ever wanted was always on the outside of that room – your clothes, your bed, your dignity. And I find out then that a man with a key is a man with terrible power."

The resilience of the women in the story is often expressed through their particular gifts and sensibilities. Guided by the strong women around her, Adamine discovers her own calling through the Revivalist Church, as the simultaneously loved and despised figure of a 'Warner Woman', that is one who warns against disaster, who cries "Warrant! Storm & Hurricane & Flood! Earthquake!" but whose warning is also about the utterance of the conscience: "The cry of the Warner Woman is Consider. She draws you into contemplation, saying, Consider that, and then consider this. Consider yourself, and your deeds." Later in the novel, it is this outsider gift that has her sectioned and labelled insane.

The theme of multiple interpretations is reflected in the form and structure of the novel. It is a fragmented telling but it is to Miller's credit that the reader is not abandoned in the process, but instead we are invited in as an active presence, listening being an inherent part of a story's telling. It is the intimacy and originality of expression surrounding the address to the reader that helps sustains our interest and patience with a narrative that is constantly interrupting and re-forming itself: "I have said to Mr Writer Man, it don't take no great skill to write down a story. All you have to do is put one word after the next and you continue like that until it done. But it take a special skill to hear a story – to incline your ears towards what may seem like silence. For nothing in this world is silent, you just have to learn how to hear."

In Adamine's complex relationship with 'Mr Writer Man', who is "taking his own sweet time to tell you" his version of her story, we witness something of the tension between a biographer and his subject. We experience the ethical difficulties that surround the ownership of stories and lives, and the omissions and distortions of history and its official records. This is poignantly felt when Adamine says of her mother: "She never important to the world, and so the world ongly write down her name three times: the first, on her birth paper; the second, on mine; and the third, on her death paper." It is the joyfully experimental quality of the novel's wayward journey towards a presentation of truths and tellings, and through which the nameless and silenced are rescued, that is perhaps its most enjoyable aspect. The magical work and skill of the narrative is in the way it clears a space for a story to be told, in how it explicitly shows the workings and difficulty of finding a beginning for any story, any life.

Like *The Last Warner Woman*, Miller's third poetry collection is comprised of a rich mix of voicings and testimonies. Divided into two sections, day time and night time, *A Light Song of Light* travels a broad and imaginative sweep through the possible manifestations and occasions of song. It asks how a song, and by extension, poetry, is possible "in dark/ times, in wolf time and knife time, / in knuckle and blood times" ('Twelve Notes for a Light Song of Light').

Perhaps the major strength of Miller's poetic voice is its range, from the restrained humour of 'a found poem' that is 'Notice to the Public, Please Observe' to the prevailing lyricism and addictive incantatory rhythms of much of his poetry, to the striking imagery and directness of examples such as 'Some Definitions for Light (II):'

> - (noun) The lungs of butchered animals are called lights. I have sometimes wondered if they pray – if, before the blade falls, cows and sheep and ducks fill their lungs with the weight of their dying, the nothingness to come, if their final sounds are light calling out to light.

The weight given to the words and thinking here – the three perfectly measured and delicate 'ifs' that the poem is poised on – demonstrate that Miller possesses a fine ear and has no fear of the prose poem. It is this quieter, more reflective mode that is behind the power of a poem such as 'Unsung' and the way it plots, carefully manoeuvring the reader towards the moment of its final lines: "There should be a song / for the man whose life has not been the stuff of ballads / but has lived his life in incredible and untrumpeted ways. / There should be a song for my father." Similarly, in 'The Longest Song' inspired by John Cage's composition, *As Slow as possible*, a piece of music intended to be played over 639 years, it is the clarity and restraint of Miller's writing that allows his ideas their fullest emotional power:

> The longest song begins like a comma, a rest that lasts for eighteen months. Long enough that when the first chord is heard, surprising as an extinct bird come back to life, many cannot stop their tears. And one man has told his wife he plans to weep until the music has reached its next rest.

Again, Miller's writing works best when meaning and sound are married in the line, as they are here, in the straining and desperation shadowing "reached its next rest".

The collection benefits from its eclectic gathering of voices and forms, drawing upon praise songs, charms and anecdotes as well as creating smaller sequences within the larger structure. The latter include the beautifully observed detail and intimate moments of 'A Short History of Beds We Have Slept in Together', the compelling riffs of the opening 'Twelve Notes for a Light Song of Light', the haunting figure of the Singerman connecting the two sections and who is based on a figure from 1930s Jamaica hired to sing to gangs building roads, as well as a sequence of mini narratives/ biographies, entitled 'De True Story of...' These character sketches make the collection feel more like a communal voicing. Indeed, as with his novel, it is Miller's skilful and varied use of lyric address, through the second person voice, that draws the reader into this community, to witness – most obviously with poems such as 'Until you too have journeyed', the elegantly moving 'A Parting Song' and 'Brochure', with its final invitation "Please, when you visit Jamaica, drive / on the Singerman's roads". It is the colours and tones that Miller discovers and invents in song here that makes this such as a joyful, dark and ambitious collection.
Moomin

Magic Beans and a Wee Red Hoodie

Glasgow Fairytale
Alastair D McIver
Black & White, RRP £9·99, 182pp

"There's two Glasgows, Ella," explains Jill (of Jack and Jill fame) to Ella McCinder, who's trapped in foster care and in love with the Celtic star striker Harry 'Charming' Charmaine. "There's the wan ye walk through every day and never really think aboot; where ye live, work, go clubbing, take abuse fae bus drivers and laugh at drunk people. Then there's the other Glasgow, which lives in a' the wee alleyways that don't seem to go anywhere; a' the amazing architecture folk never see because they'll no look up; a' the treasures this city likes to hide in plain sight." And so, in his sword-sharp debut, Alastair D McIver takes us on a tour of the other, magical Glasgow.

A giant beanstalk is growing out of the River Clyde. Jack, planter of the beans, is in love with Rapunzel, who's come to Glasgow seeking asylum but has been detained in Dungavel. Meanwhile, Karl 'Snowy' White – a strikingly beautiful albino boy from the Highlands – is hiding from the evil Reginald King with a group of magical misfits who "don't mind being called the Freaks, the Mutants, the Mutant Freaks, the Five Freaks, the Five Mutants or the Five Mutant Freaks."

The different fairytales intertwine with a fun and feisty wit, and there's no shortage of Glasgow banter from the cast of familiar characters. My favourite is the Big Bad Wolf, who gets some of the most subversive chat and makes a disturbingly convincing argument that humanity's hypocrisy can justify his murderous tendencies. There are plenty of political undercurrents too; in a pointed parody of immigration laws, BBW proudly confesses that he has been awarded his "Minimum Standard of Humanity," a coveted certificate only given to talking animals who have proved they are "human-ish" enough to deserve basic human rights. The real bad guy of the book, though, is the mirror (mirror on the wall) who manipulates human weakness and vanity to destroy as many lives as he can, and gets some cracking one-liners in the process.

Occasionally the jokes feel a little too familiar and the politics a little too light, but McIver is not aiming for weighty debate and these fairytale characters are not above laughing at themselves. When the giant in the castle at the top of the beanstalk cries "Fee Fie Fo Fum, I smell the blood of an Englishman" and Jack leaps out of his hiding place to shout "I'm no English," Thumbelina was quick enough to pre-empt my world-weary sigh by remarking "To thick to live." Indeed.

The ending is a bit of a disappointment, having the sort of fairytale schmultz that is inevitable when a writer turns to a quadruple wedding as the setting for his dénouement. Happily ever after just doesn't say anything new, and I'm not afraid to tell you that in this fairytale face-off I was most certainly rooting for the Big Bad Wolf; with 'true love's kisses' fixing lives all over the city and an absurdly symmetrical matching of women and men, McIver's magical twist on Glasgow was a little too traditional in places for this reviewer's taste. That said, one of the grooms-to-be is transspecies, and *Glasgow Fairytale* is packed full of quirky ideas, gutsy characters and a genuinely affectionate humour. As Jill says, throwing her arms wide to take in the glory of the city: "How can anyone look at that and no see magic?"
Golden Monkey

The Quest for Truth

Da Happie Laand
Robert Alan Jamieson
Luath, RRP £12·99, 388pp

Robert Alan Jamieson's *Da Happie Laand* plays with the notion of truth, through documents representing facts about a fictional place, which closely resembles a real place, its history and its people. It is fascinating, sometimes confusing, and above all, a very worthwhile reading experience.

The book is structured by the presentation of various documents, which are excellent vehicles for the development of the plot, though the reader has to rise to the challenge of this fragmented approach, and work hard to keep hold of the various threads that weave the story. The novel begins with an 'Editor's Preface' where the provenance of the documents in the pages that follow are explained. There is ambiguity here, created by the knowledge that the editor is RA Jamieson, almost the novel's author, but not quite. Alert to the question of this 'not quite' and, as a consequence, the question of truth, the documents are introduced in the form of a letter to a Mr Jamieson from the Reverend Archibald Nicol.

A stranger, who has stayed at the home of the Reverend, disappears and leaves behind a manila envelope, which has now been offered to Mr Jamieson. The Reverend Nicol asks him, knowing he is a writer, to make sense of the contents, telling him that the fragmented documents contain an interesting story concerning the mystery death of a man, Rod Cunninghame, and the disappearance of his son David. The novel consists of diary entries, correspondence, extracts from a text entitled *A History of Zetland*, transcriptions of interviews and vikipedia entries. Once again, the 'not quite'. Zetland and her people may be a fictionalisation of Shetland, but the reader isn't free to assume this. The order of the documents ensures that the reader feels continually pulled between the worlds of truth and fiction.

The diary entries contain the thoughts of David Cunninghame as he goes in search of his missing father. The appearance of his character comes at just the right moment, bringing life to the narrative. His voice gains strength as the novel progresses, even as his life seems to become chaos. It seems that the story unravels through the fragments, while also being pieced together; the chaos of life reflected in prose.

Themes of landscape and a sense of place are poignantly expressed in the documents concerning migration to New Zetland and those left behind, reflecting on the inherent human need to belong. This is linked to, and explored in, the notion of faith, in particular Christianity, which is central to the characters' lives and their development, to varying degrees. Reverend Nicol's transcription is presented with words he has scored out, though remaining legible for the reader. There is a strange attraction in reading something which appears not intended to be read. The reader learns of his distress, his faith has weakened, he didn't recognise the stranger in his home as David, a child he baptised. He questions his faith and he questions the facts of the history he is writing, arguing with, and exploring the notion of, truth by faith and truth by reason.

Interspersed with these significant considerations are amusing details. The Vikipedia entry (set out as you find in Wikipedia) on the creole language of Alroki is playful and entertaining on the subject of language. For example, the future tense in Alroki is expressed 'mibae'. The repeated stories, from different perspectives, voices and dialects, use poetic language and elegant turns of phrase, creating a rich musicality. Detailed settings are drawn, sublime and mysterious, reflecting nature's cycle, just as the outcomes for those who inhabit the story reflect the cycle of the individual and communities, with inherent questions of truth and faith, things lost and things found.
Jabberwock

Boo Boys and Belters

Bob Servant – Hero of Dundee
Neil Forsyth
Birlinn, RRP £7·99, 160pp

In 2007 Neil Forsyth introduced Bob Servant in *Délĕte This at Your Peril* where the 62 year old 'retired gigolo' from Broughty Ferry documented a series of demented email exchanges with a variety of internet scammers. Servant's autobiography, *Bob Servant – Hero of Dundee* charts the eventful life of its delusional subject from his troubled childhood – "For a while Mum and I clung to the theory that Dad was a visionary. Unfortunately for us he was a bigamist." – through his abortive Merchant Navy career and on to his entrepreneurial successes: the largest window-cleaning round in Western Europe and his central role in the Dundee Cheeseburger Wars of the early 1990s. With him throughout are an assortment of ludicrous associates (chiefly the unsubtly titled Frank the Plank), a voracious appetite for 'chasing skirt' and a passion for the life and work of Terry Wogan.

The madcap humour that Servant first displayed in *Délĕte This at Your Peril* is intact here and Bob Servant's surreal take on life means *Hero of Dundee* certainly has its share of 'belters' but there are a few difficulties this time around, although Bob Servant is well used to dealing with the 'boo boys'.

While *Délĕte This at Your Peril* benefited from the simple structure of reproduced email exchanges, *Hero of Dundee* is a more sprawling proposition. It lacks the 'stand-alone' qualities of its predecessor and is much less suitable for dipping in and out of.

But there are greater problems arising out of the move away from the email exchange format. In *Délĕte This at Your Peril* many of the funniest moments came not from Servant or his observations but from the sheer desperation of the scammers being manipulated. This 'non-fiction' element essentially meant half of the laughs, and many of the better ones, were written for Forsyth. The absurd and deranged Servant was actually the straight-man of the operation, setting up the gags and leaving the scammers to bring the house down. *Hero of Dundee* has none of this interplay. On his own, Servant must provide all the laughs himself and, on occasion, the pressure proves too much. The strongest comic moments in *Hero of Dundee* come when Forsyth moves away from the straight autobiographical form and includes various 'documents' (letters, newspaper reports, drawings) to substantiate Servant's claims.

In an introductory note Bob Servant declares that on account of his many deeds, "I should be the Hero of Dundee but it's just not happened. Any here's why." But throughout *Hero of Dundee* this premise proves repetitive and inconvenient. Towards the tail end of each chapter we get a couple of lines tenuously linking what's gone before to Servant's thesis that although he should be Hero of Dundee, he isn't. During the mid-section even Forsyth seems to have tired of the device as he omits it from several chapters but it returns in the final chapters and is as jarring as ever.

Forsyth's presence in *Hero of Dundee* – he writes an introduction, the footnotes and the acknowledgements – is also troubling. His dry narration of Bob Servant's antics in these sections is much less amusing than Servant's own delivery, and instead of offering contrast seems like an inferior way of going about the same thing. The footnotes are especially puzzling. Rather than correcting mistakes in Servant's manuscript, Forsyth, the 'editor', merely comments on them. As is often the case, when something funny draws attention to itself as being so, it seldom is any longer.

A reader who enjoyed *Délĕte This at Your Peril* and is anxious for more will certainly be interested in reading *Hero of Dundee*, but the uninitiated might be best advised to read the previous book first, or seek out the radio adaptations of *Délĕte This at Your Peril* broadcast on BBC Radio Scotland and BBC Radio 4.
Macavity the Mystery Cat

Movie in the Making

I Love You, Goodbye
Cynthia Rogerson
Black & White, RRP £11·99, 256pp

I Love You, Goodbye is a book I would happily read on a beach or an airplane or a delayed train; it's also the kind of book I'd be petrified if my impressionable teenager got their hands on. Evanton, a small Highland village, hosts a cast of characters who purport to be finding out how complex love is, the many forms it can take, and its breathtaking force, but the real power of love, both painful and joyful, is hiddden by the comedic caricatures and situations. Evanton is believable as a small community appearing by turns cosy and insular, friendly and isolated, but the individuals in it could breathe more life and originality into the things they do.

Ania, a marriage counsellor, feeds her clients platitudes of the life-is-a-journey, knowing-yourself-is-a-journey, marriage-is-a-journey, some-journeys-are-not-straightforward type; the ironies of her own personal experience balancing two relationships with two men (firmly drawn as Opposites and refused permission to move, especially her husband Ian) are thus not allowed to develop subtly but are pushed forward in often ungraceful ways. Her clients in the book, Rose and Harry, play out the roles of a past-middle-age couple facing a relationship crisis (*Did I ever love him? Is this all there is? I thought things would be different*), and, while the combination of boredom and deep comfort that mingle in most long-term relationships is well-drawn, their thoughts and actions lack nuance, and do not deviate from characteristics seen in many Hollywood movies – the bitching wife, the man who reacts to the dissolution of his marriage by going for a pint and pretending not to care, the couple refusing to have sex with each other even though it's at the forefront of both their minds, the ceaseless bickering that they seem to think is some sort of necessity or inescapable fact, the sick pleasure taken in prodding just the right sore spot to cause pain, learned from years of experimentation.

Like many such blockbuster movies, the book appears to assume a level of agreement from the audience about the terms on which it presents: Ania's confusion over her affair with Maciek is a good example. She seems genuinely perturbed by the fact that she is married to one man yet thinking about, and having, sex with another. How can one man not be all she needs? Why are her sexual thoughts not limited to the man she married? And, come to think of it, what are these sexual thoughts doing anyway, all intense and bothersome and clouding her mind when she is trying to explain to Rose and Harry why the libido is like a muscle that needs to be exercised? Actually discussing this with either man appears out of the question. The text resists moving from this angle – honesty is never put forth as a plausible reaction to problems, and characters are not permitted to deviate from these patterns: sex dies, romance dies, a relationship traps a person, and love is a funny thing that is never understood but whose name can be used as an excuse for almost anything.

There are some nice details about Maciek's life in Poland, and the best parts of the book lie in its sensitivity to Scottish peculiarities – an element that Rogerson, a native Californian, may be more alert to than natives. The surprise ending tests the characterisation more than the rest of the text, and is a genuine surprise; the climax also serves to tie up loose ends, and by the close of the novel everyone has returned to their initial positions, except for teenage Sam, who has begun his initiation into this combative game of miscommunication that love seems to be. This book is ready to be lifted to the big screen.
Cheshire Cat

From Spain to Scotland

The Songs of Manolo Escobar
Carlos Alba
Polygon, RRP £10·99, 256pp

Antonio, the protagonist of *The Songs of Manolo Escobar,* is in trouble. His wife appears to be leaving him for his best friend; he seems incapable of maintaining a meaningful relationship with his teenage son; the newspaper where he works as a political editor is, as part of a cost-saving exercise, being re-located to China; and to top things off, his dad has been diagnosed with terminal cancer and is suddenly keen on a speedy trip to his native Spain to lay old bodies to rest.

It is the issue of unresolved business in Spain that is the catalyst for Antonio to reassess his upbringing as part of a Spanish family on a Glaswegian council estate. As the story shifts between the present and his childhood we get an idea of what it might be like to grow up as a foreigner. We witness a young Antonio so keen on not standing out that he refuses to speak Spanish even though it is still being spoken in his home. It is thus from this position on the fence, being neither Scottish nor Spanish, that Antonio tells the story.

To a large extent the story is one of a dysfunctional family, and although its members are clichés (the mother who shows her love through her cooking; the stubborn father who always knows best; the swaggering older brother who keeps insisting on being on to something while his swagger becomes less and less pronounced and he slides into alcohol abuse), it is for the most part very funny and very readable. The dialogue is good and moves the plot forward effortlessly.

If the family is dysfunctional it is largely because of lack of communication, and nothing is more imposing yet unspoken than the question: what happened in Spain that caused them to move to Scotland? It is with the urgency brought about by Antonio's father's terminal illness that the silence is finally lifted and we start to dig into the past. The digging, at one level quite literal, is the attempt to find Antonio's grandparents, who were executed during the Spanish civil war, and give them a proper burial. However, it is also the attempt to gain some sort of understanding of what happened during that conflict. What Antonio finds in Spain, however, is the same reluctance to talk about the past that he knows from his own family.

The novel's attempt to provide a slice of Spanish history is less engaging than the family story from Glasgow. This is partly because one of the novel's key qualities, its humour, disappears the moment attention is turned towards the Spanish civil war. While the stock characters work in a comedic setting, they work less well when the subject matter becomes serious.

One is also led to suspect that the writer was asked to cut the manuscript significantly. Towards the end of the novel, many issues regarding the family's history in Spain are resolved rather quickly. Some of the holes that must be filled out are done so by a 'surprise relative' who materialises after Antonio has posted a message on a website for people who lost touch with relatives during the civil war. Other cracks are papered over by letting Antonio take up a narratorial position a few years in the future. The story ends in Africa with Antonio chancing upon a photo of Humphrey Bogart that his father had mentioned earlier. However, like many other events in the novel, the incident has been signposted so far in advance that the magic is slightly subdued and the surprise fails to materialise. While the story in Glasgow is humorous, the excavations in Spain remain unsatisfyingly shallow.
Gregor Samsa

The Literary Life

Klaus, and Other Stories
Allan Massie
Vagabond Voices, RRP £10·00, 187pp

Allan Massie has quietly carved a niche for himself as one of Scotland's best writers, bringing an ironic and sophisticated understanding to questions of Scottish and European politics and history. Unfairly, he has also become one of his country's most culturally marginal writers, for reasons that I am convinced have little to do with the quality of his writing. Conspicuously unionist, an old-fashioned Scottish Tory, he seems estranged from the dominant James Kelman and Alasdair Gray schools of Scottish literature. He lacks Kelman's gritty modernism, and keeps his flights of fancy closer to the ground than Gray. This does not in any way mean that his work is dull, or 'conservative' in the worst sense of the word, however. His recent *Evenings of the World* trilogy was a masterpiece of mythic and historic fantasy, proper romances that examined in wholly original ways the wider problems of European unity, and posed serious questions about the roots of the post-Roman dream of European integration.

This collection, a novella and eight other stories spanning his career, demonstrates more clearly Massie's cosmopolitanism, the pan-European gaze (from the perspective of Edinburgh and the Scottish Borders) that aligns him as much with writers like Robert Musil or Thomas Mann, as John Buchan or Walter Scott. Moving away here from his dominant concerns of history and politics towards a reflective and rueful appreciation of the literary life, Massie channels that European spirit more successfully than at any time since his 1986 novel *A Question of Loyalties*. The comparison to Thomas Mann above wasn't disingenuous either. 'Klaus', the main piece in this collection, follows the last days of Klaus Mann, novelist son of the far more famous Thomas, whose talent and success has dominated his son's life. Crushed by personal and political failures, haunted by Germany's moral degradation and bereft of a cause now that the Nazi 'brown plague' of his home country has been defeated, Klaus is fighting a listless battle against alcoholism, drug addiction, and a seemingly inevitable urge towards suicide. Massie is alert and sympathetic here to the misery of a writer in decline; unable to work, his books going out of print, and aware that while he still has much to say, he is losing the means to say it. Avoiding any hint of the sentimental, this is an unsparing portrait of literary, political and sexual defeat. These themes run liberally through the rest of this elegiac collection, to the point where you hope sincerely that this is not Massie's summing-up of his own career. Particularly good is 'Forbes at the Festival', where an elderly, half-forgotten Scottish writer is eclipsed by a brash, younger compatriot at an Italian literary festival, and 'In the Bare Lands', where a BBC researcher tracks down a Scottish nationalist writer in self-imposed exile. Exile and loss dominate these stories, as well as the consolations of old memory and the stoic acceptance of current predicaments. In his historical fiction, Massie has an uncanny ability to inhabit the sinews and the *mentalité* of a period; this move inwards, to interrogate his own beliefs about writers and the writing life, displays similar skill. It is perhaps unexpected, but at this stage of his career it feels natural and entirely welcome.

Montmorency

Leading the Mob

One O'Clock Gun Anthology
Introduction by R A Jamieson
Leamington Books, RRP £10·00, 227pp

Pax Edina is the cry emblazoned on the cover of this anthology – a call to arms for the literati of Scotland's capital city. Based on Edinburgh's *One O'Clock Gun* periodical (distributed in select Edinburgh taverns since 2004) the pieces in this volume celebrate the first UNESCO World City of Literature. However, its aim is clear – to rise, roots first, against the "culture of literary apathy stalking the capital". Such duality is presented openly on the cover and the introduction and is a key theme of the anthology and the accompanying art work.

An introduction by RA Jamieson hails the 'Situations Vacant' entry from the columns of the first issue: "Edinburgh desperately requires a Leader of the Mob, a position last held by 'General' Joseph Smith (?-1980). The ideal applicant will be boisterous, energetic, unruly, and have a wealth of relevant experience in the ancient art of rabble-rousing. Duties will include storming the barriers at Hogmanay, disrupting the Tattoo, and harassing the Council and the Lady Provost. An ability to bang the drum loudly is desirable but not essential, as full training will be given." The tone is set and indeed it seems that any of the contributors to this volume would have been qualified to apply.

There are the literary heavy-weights such as Alasdair Gray to provide social commentary in 'Billy Semple, A Vignette' and eulogies to other literary giants. Suhayal Saadi's 'The Hour of the Witch', a paean to Lilith adds mythology to the mix while Angus Calder takes the reader to 'Upcountry' across the world in South Africa. Newer writers also fill the columns, adding to the vast mix of literary genres. Of particular enjoyment is Jenny Lindsay's rhyming poem 'In Scotland We Know We're Fucked' where amusing polysemy brings an element of cheer to the traditional Scottish pessimism.

Another favourite is 'The Slaughter of St Stephen Street' by Gavin Inglis. This is one of the shorter pieces and deals with another recurring theme – Edinburgh's haunted streets. As is to be expected from such a publication, the majority of the contributions refer to the city from which the anthology takes its name. Stone Rogues whisper to each other, Presbyterianism tightens and loosens its grip and plotting, scheming and drinking consumes the capital.

It is the final piece, 'Duality: Come In, Your Time is Up' by Kevin Williamson accompanied by the cover illustration for Number 17 showing the cure for Edina's plague that draws the volume neatly together. Throughout, contributors and editors alike have openly encouraged and dissected Edinburgh's, Scotland's and a wider duality. It is this historical analysis that discusses its various facets, from a simple 'good' and 'evil' medieval Duality 1.0 to the modern state of multifarious being. This small serving allows the complex mish mash of modern literature to be understood as a unified body.

One O'Clock Gun is one of the few anthologies where so many different types of writing; poetry and prose, fact and fiction, pessimism, optimism, tales of home and abroad sit so easily together. Whether reading from cover to cover or dipping in and out, it is this variety, held together by strong themes that make this book great.

The anthology not only offers fantastic writing but also acquaints the reader with the original periodical complete with its cunning folds and intriguing columns. A full illustrated User's Guide can even be found in the appendix. Each entry is set out in traditional columns and almost all conform to the archaic house style symbolic of the Gun. Even the most discerning reader will find enjoyment within these margins. This book is testament to Robert Alan Jamieson's claim that "the mob is out there. And still kicking".
Bagheera

Cold, Clean Prayers

Tomorrow, We Will Live Here
Ryan Van Winkle
Salt Publishing, RRP £9·99, 59pp

The debut collection by the Scottish Poetry Library's American-born Reader in Residence is nothing short of excellent. There is a small-town, downtrodden, careworn feel but as Van Winkle bumps the reader along the back roads of country America – and Scotland – his urgent narrative voices rapidly dispel any air of despondency. These are compelling, self-assured, driven poems that shine a longing, elegaic laserbeam at their subjects.

Like a Bill Callahan lyric, the poems tackle the grave stuff of human existence – love, loss, lust, religion, dislocation (spiritual and topographical), guilt – with a tenderly sardonic, noir-ish humour. Subjects from road kill, a fat boy, through a pastor's son, deceitful lovers on September 11th, to the rain-soaked wishes of a condemned man are each addresssed by narrators who are edgy, uncomfortable and acutely aware of their failings.

It is hard to determine exactly how Van Winkle's poems do their work, but they burrow into the reader's skin like a mite to leave a persistent itch in the memory. The language is clean: WC Williams's 'plain American that cats and dogs can read', but with syntax that is at times polysyndetic and mesmerising: as if a character out of Faulker, Twain or Cormac McCarthy has stepped off the page to charm, disarm and then shock the reader.

Three poems particularly stand out. 'The First Time I Touched Her' is a coarse love lyric narrated with tenderness ("My wife is a purple scent / the whole table can see") by a man unaccustomed to fine living: "Never am I a man / who hasn't tinned, deboned. / Sometimes I rough perfume into my palms."

'They Tore The Bridge Down a Year Later' is an affecting depiction of a murdered child in Southern Gothic style: "I found her in a blue dress /... / with ropes around her wrists, / her neck, her ankles. / It's how we would tie a hog, / when there was money for that type of thing", by a father who laments the bridge's replacement: "Nowadays I don't pass the creek much. / There is no reason to walk my quiet boy / across metal into Louisiana. / If the bridge I knew still stood / maybe I could bring him down, / ... Tell him / his father wants to pass the time. / ... / But the bridge is not there anymore."

'Ode for a Rain from Death Row' references Kenny Ritchie's wish to be soaked by Scottish rain before he dies: "The rain is a cold, clean prayer, / the only light I want to see /... / The priest only offers a glass / where my throat wants a holy rain that pours in sheets and hoods and lasts for forty days, / till it floods and floats my sins away."

The collection closes with three poignant poems that evoke the wanderer's eternal dilemma of displacement: 'Also, it is Lambing Season' places the foreign narrator in a Scottish landscape, hemmed in by ewes protecting their offspring, "And I wanted to put my hands and knees into the mud, / ... / be a lamb again. Easter was coming. / I was not in the country of my birth. / Shadows / were all around me. My mother's milk was sepia."; 'Unfinished Rooms' builds on earlier themes of *Heimweh* laid down in 'The Apartment' (source of the collection's title).

The final poem 'And Table, You are Made of Wood', ends with a resonant couplet that underpins all the quiet revelations contained in the preceding pages: "I too have been cut, had my meaning moved / far from where I thought it was." This is a rich, incandescent book to keep at your bedside for dark winter nights.

Moby-Dick

Whisky Galore Gore

Smokeheads
Doug Johnstone
Faber and Faber, RRP £12·99, 304pp

Whisky is the drink of choice for Scottish non-fiction. A single Amazon search returned 60 in-print companions to our national tipple before I stopped counting. The industry is bigger business, contributing £2.7 billion to the Scottish economy per year and employing 10,000. There's money in them there hills. But the *water of life* has held little interest for fiction writers. I can't think of a single 'great Scottish whisky novel' beyond Compton Mackenzie's 1947 *Whisky Galore*, a significant contribution to the tartanalia that has exercised our self-image for the last 150 years.

Perhaps that's why novelists have given whisky a body-swerve. Ironically, considering how potent its mythology proves abroad, for the Scots, it's deeply unsexy. That's not to say we're not proud of whisky's success, but for many it's an old man's drink, the choice of the wife beater and milky-eyed pant pisser.

Doug Johnstone is to be commended for taking another look at our greatest export. While *Smokeheads*, his third novel, conforms to the tropes of high-octane *Deliverance* style thrillers, there's something interesting lurking at the bottom of the literary mash tun. The story follows four thirty-somethings on a lads' tasting trip to Islay, the modern, fashionable face of whisky tourism. The action is seen through the eyes of Adam, the whisky equivalent of Comic Book Guy in *The Simpsons*, a flabby boy-man still working in shop floor retail who's prone to anxiety attacks but possesses a near supernatural ability to identify obscure malts by taste alone. There's safe salaryman Ethan, mellow musician Luke and coked-up but über-successful fund manager Roddy.

Adam is in a rut but dreams of opening his own distillery on Islay. Wracked with self-doubt, he's ultimately a good egg, as evidenced by his tentative relationship with distillery guide Molly. Roddy on the other hand is obnoxious, narcissistic, over-sexed, amoral and rich. He also gets all the best lines. At the heart of *Smokeheads* is the quintessential Scottish neurosis running like a peaty burn from Hogg and Stevenson through to the present day: be good and fail, win and lose your soul to the Devil.

As with Johnstone's memoir of fictional Scottish indie also-rans, *The Ossians*, it's this fault line in Scottish identity that interests him most. Whisky provides a useful metaphor for what's good and bad in Scottishness. On the one hand it represents "the release from the humdrum... into something more... spiritual", acknowledging "the beautiful complexity of the world", but mostly it's about "getting pissed". Whisky is also a potent symbol for Scottish creativity: "no other drink borrows so much from outside influences, really absorbs those tastes and flavours and sensations then transforms then into something utterly new and original". But be reassured, Johnstone is light on the philosophising and heavy on action, which comes thick and fast: high speed crashes, psychopathic coppers, exploding illegal stills and frantic chases across snowy moors. He returns to the gut-wrenching violence of his debut, *Tombstoning*, and there's a similar body count.

Smokeheads is wholly successful as a gripping page-turner, Johnstone's prose unpretentious and Islay a suitably claustrophobic, hostile backdrop. Accepting the implausibility of it all goes with the territory. But if there's one criticism it's in the rather downbeat ending, considering the high-jinks that have come before. After the principal dénouement there's a hint of conflict to come, which fails to materialise and is instead replaced by a relatively introspective epilogue. But with a switch in publisher and uisge beatha's global popularity, it's likely that *Smokeheads* will bring Johnstone's brand of rough but potent peatreek a whole new audience.
Behemoth

War of the Hoses

Bleakly Hall
Elaine di Rollo
Chatto, 362pp, RRP £12·99

Elaine di Rollo's second book, *Bleakly Hall*, lends a refreshing perspective on the comic historical novel, a form enjoyed by other Scottish writers from George Macdonald Fraser and Alasdair Gray to Michel Faber and Chris Hannan. Part satire, part farce, di Rollo takes the *Blackadder* approach to writing about the Great War and its aftermath where straightforward tragedy would have been less memorable.

Nurse Monty, a veteran of World War 1, arrives at Bleakly Hall in search of answers following the untimely death of a friend. A run-down hydropathic sanatorium owned by brothers Curran and Grier, Bleakly Hall is a decrepit Gormenghast in miniature, where unpleasant, often painful and allegedly health preserving water therapies are conducted on surprisingly willing, elderly guests. Some treatments have more than a hint of steamy torture chamber about them.

Ada, an old wartime acquaintance of Monty's from a less privileged background, has also washed up there. Once an ambulance driver on the frontline, she seems the only one capable of keeping the place running, despite the threat that the clanking Victorian plumbing will blow at any time. Enter stage left villain-of-the-piece, Captain Foxley, and quack, Dr Slack, and it's clear that di Rollo is not above letting a bit of slapstick tell the story. But making you care about the characters is di Rollo's talent as they charge around the creaking, claustrophobic set, each driven on by his or her own personal traumas.

Di Rollo's debut, *A Proper Education for Girls* (originally *The Peachgrower's Almanac* in hardback) was shortlisted for the Saltire First Book Award. It was praised for its use of Victorian pastiche as a vehicle for examining women's struggle to break free of 19th century society's restrictive corset. In the post-war age of *Bleakly Hall*, Monty and Ada are dealing with the loss of freedoms gained through the expediency of war and snatched back at the Armistice. Like the men, they feel alienated from both younger and older generations who can't understand what they've been through.

Di Rollo's gallery of rogues is vividly drawn. The stories of men fighting in the trenches, and the terrible toll on their physical and emotional lives, are presented sensitively. It's clear that di Rollo, who has a doctorate in the history of medicine, has the knowledge required to depict the endless horrifying circumstances of war, not through the familiar tropes but in domestic detail that offers alternative insights and delivers real pathos.

Bleakly Hall is highly entertaining and has some great moments of comedy. The scene where Ada attaches a kite to Curran's wheelchair and takes him for a sail along a local beach is joyful and exhilarating. Inevitably, things don't go to plan: "She screamed as her feet scraped across the sand. One of her shoes came off, but the chair did not stop, or even slow down. Should she let go? If she did, Curran would career onwards with no means of stopping – perhaps he would take off into the sky, disappearing towards the sun like Icarus."

Di Rollo is to be commended for choosing the post war period as her backdrop, a fascinating fault line in British history where the familiarities of the old order rub hard against the dissatisfactions, hopes and desires of the oppressed. There are echoes of MacDonald Fraser's *Flashman* here, particularly in the complexities of the brave but callous Foxley. But ultimately *Bleakly Hall* most resembles that American classic, *Catch 22*, in its depiction of war's purposelessness, the waste of young life, and the acceptance that no one really knows what's going on.
Sharik

A Life Re-Pictured

A Life in Pictures
Alasdair Gray
Canongate, RRP £35·00, 303pp

Alasdair Gray has been writing autobiography for years. With *A Life in Pictures*, he puts aside the metafictional trickery of his novels since *Lanark: A Life in 4 Books*. This time, the pretext is to collect his graphic and pictorial work. Gray intended his first novel to be his only one, and to follow it with single volumes of plays, poems and short stories. *Unlikely Stories, Mostly* was meant to be his only collection of short fiction, but he found it habit forming and went on to publish five more, while another story grew into his second novel, *1982, Janine*. The plays and poems have appeared recently. Gray's largest mural, at Òran Mór in Glasgow's West End, is in part a replacement for the mural in the subsequently demolished Greenhead Kirk of Scotland in Bridgeton, whose painting *Lanark* describes. While that particular work remains incomplete, you get the impression that Gray is trying to finish things off while he still can.

Gray has described himself as 'one of those interesting second-raters'. Few of those get the chance to publish a book like this. Gray's visual art ranges across different media, from murals through portraits of Glaswegian characters made during his time as Artist Recorder at the People's Palace, to the book designs that have become his trademark. As you would expect in a survey like this, Gray details the influences on his art, from Kipling and Blake through the Japanese print makers, Hokusai and Hiroshige, to the popular art of Walt Disney and DC Thomson. He also devotes whole sections to the art of unfairly neglected friends and in particular to Alan Fletcher, an Art School contemporary who died young and who has haunted Gray's work ever since.

Many of the techniques that characterise Gray's fiction can be found here too. Gray has never seen the point of writing a good sentence twice and so phrases, formulas, even whole passages recur throughout his written work. Similarly, the same motifs, figures and heraldic symbols crop up again and again in Gray's visual art. His relaxed attitude to plagiarism is also on display. More revealing, though, is his attitude to perspective. He describes how he deliberately flaunted convention in an early work 'The City' (later 'Two Hills'), by combining different perspectives within a single image, something which has characterised all of his novels. Gray gives the impression of having emerged as a fully-formed artist in 1981. That is in part an illusion created by his late appearance as a novelist, the art form on which his reputation rightly depends. Some of that development can be seen here, though again Gray seems to have reached artistic maturity remarkably early on.

A Life in Pictures is a beautiful book. It is also Gray's fullest work of autobiography to date. It provides detailed accounts of his childhood, his experience as a war-time evacuee and his time at Glasgow School of Art which have not appeared before as well as fleshing out parts of his later life story with which readers of his fiction will be familiar. Throughout the life his latest book describes his commitment to art has been a political commitment. His dedication to murals – works of art which cannot be bought or sold – is an expression of his belief in public art and the public role of artists. In an early chapter, Gray writes, "If I stay mentally healthy and live long enough I will write a book explaining why most Scots in the first half of the 20th century stopped noticing they could govern themselves locally and make fine works of modern art". These 'connected failures' are challenged once again in *A Life in Pictures*, a challenge which Alasdair Gray has made in many art forms throughout a remarkably productive life.
Pangur Bán

'The thatched roof rings like heaven
where mice
Squeak small hosannahs all night long,
Scratching its golden pavements, skirting
The gutter's crystal river song.'

Norman MacCaig (from 'Byre')

Runners
Dave Whelan

HE RESTS THE cup, white, Chinese, blue little pattern of flowers and mountains on the side, gently on the grass. A little bit of tea, cooling now from excessive blowing, swirls up from the contents and drops down the side, creating a faint brown streak down the side of the cup, white, Chinese. The cup and the tea is all we have.

'If I ever wanted to give you a job, I would ask.'

That's what he says to me, through thick moustache and accent, Irish. He's burly and about thirty, gingery, bearlike. His face is pot-holed from childhood acne, slightly pink and bubbly, fairly repulsive. His lips, those large wormy things that crinkle and squirm at the end of his face, turn up into a sneer.

'Don't ever ask me for a job, Robin. Don't ever ask me.'

He's a lowlife, in many ways. Big lumbering bear, with spiky fur that hibernates all the time and expects me to earn money for him. Get him food. Lumbering little massive fool, with ginger tufts and worms for a face. But mother said I should stick with him, so I do. And, besides, he doesn't order me around like some sort of animal, dog, cat, horse, whatever, like most people.

'I never – ask – for a job. This is what you ALWAYS say.'

That's my voice. Fairly high-pitched, feminine, American.

'Look, I can't ask a wee girl to go do it. So forget about it. You look after yourself and I'll look after both us.'

He's sweating a lot; yellowing pale streaks fall down his face. Like the cup. We've been running for days. Literally running. Trying to go from one side of America to the next. Like that Tom Hanks did.

We have no Money, like Tom, and just as much sense. We're stupid visionaries with nothing to say, so we move. In our actions we flatter ourselves to believe we're changing the world. People ask us if we're doing it as a statement against cars, if we're some sorts of crazy activists against pollution. I always tell them NO. We're running simply because we can't speak. We can't articulate what we care about, so we run from it. In our running, I hope, we'll change the world.

'Look, I'll go to that little bar we saw down the way. Maybe see if they'll give us some food.'

'And why exactly would they do that?'

See, he's interested. He didn't actually want to go out and get us some food. Stupid little massive man. He just wanted to ease his small conscience. To say the right things so that when I leave and come back hours later tired and weary and sometimes crying, he can coo and not feel guilty, when I put food in front of his louse infested face.

'I'll go help them wash the dishes, or maybe waitress. Anything.'

'Hnn. Don't make me laugh, girl. You're a skinny type, with mud on your face and sarcasm in your eyes. Who's going to want to see YOU serve THEM food?'

*

I go into the bar, empty, old and faux-swanky like something out of a Humphrey Bogart flick, smells like dried out cider I think, as the saloon doors open and the originally empty bar fills with three men, directly in front of my face, looming. Their bodies move at once and only their heads, which look at me then at each other then back at me, seem to move independently.

One of the heads says 'Who's this little slice of muffin?' to the other two, who scrutinize me and say in unison, 'Some homeless girl, by the look of her'.

'What a shame, poor girl.' 'I know, what a pity.' 'People should never be ending up like this.' 'What do you think happened to the mother, hmm?'

Always blaming mother. That's what my brothers did. Blaming her for everything. Leaving me alone, unattached, with them. They never treated me properly. I was never their sister, not to them.

'I don't know. Oh my, we need to feed her.' 'Oh, yes.' 'Definitely.' 'Food is definitely what is needed.' Their heads turn and they look at me as if they're talking to a puppy, patronizing and insulting.

'Hey there, girl.' 'Do you want something to eat?' 'You look starving.'

They turn around without waiting for my response, which was obviously going to be YES even though the way they're talking to me makes my skin crawl and makes me think that at least the ginger bear talks to me as if I'm a fucking human being, and go back into what I suppose must be the kitchen.

I take this opportunity, fleeting, to inspect the bar, which is oddly spotless. I'm the only dirty thing in the place, I can tell. I'm a festering little ball of hair, dirt and sweat. I am a dog, I think. A little scruffy puppy that has crawled into their home, on limp all fours, begging and whimpering to be fed. I look at my hands, all bony and scarred, two identical rings (both stolen) on each hand, 'FAITH' embossed upon them; I'm lower than a dog.

'Here you go.'

'Sweetie.'

'Some nice hot food for you.'

They've actually gone and put a bowl, clay, English, rustic, heavy, of food on the floor, very clean, for me.

I'm a bit confused as to why, but the warm, doughy, homely smell draws me directly above the bowl and, even though to their credit they have set me out cutlery, I drop my face into the bowl and ravage the contents. Broccoli, lamb, gravy, potato, saliva, snot, skin, sweat, and kibble are churned into a paste in my mouth, quickly washed out by water, and then replaced with a fresh batch. Over and over again until I suck the bowl clean, dry. I hang above the bowl, clay, English, rustic, heavy, for what feels like hours but what is surely seconds, before slumping to the ground, fat and exhausted.

'She was a hungry girl.'

'Oh, wasn't she?'

'So very hungry.'

'Didn't even use the cutlery, poor girl.'

'Didn't even use the cutlery, poor girl.'

'Didn't even use the cutlery, poor girl.'

'Maybe we should give her a bath? Wash out all that dirt from her hair.'

'Oh, yes.'

'Definitely. We'll make her look pretty.'

'Hey. I'm not a damn BITCH.' I shout as I get onto all fours and push myself up straight with my hind legs. But they're already looming above, chatting mechanically, absently, to one another with brush, shampoo and grins directed, threateningly, at me.

In the next room I can hear the sound of running water.

*

Where's she gone now, damn her. Such a small little pup of a girl. Big ego and bouncy legs. Leaving me here all alone under this tree with nothing for company but this cup of tea, which is now empty if I'm being honest, and the little critters that live in me beard. Can't just admit that she needs my help sometimes, poor thing. Can't ever admit it when she's out of her depth. Always trying to run ahead of me too. Hm. I let her. Not because I can't beat her because I definitely can beat that wiry thing, but because I know it'll break her damn heart if I run too fast and leave her behind. She's not one to lose, I don't think. No not one to lose AT ALL.

I remember the first time I ever laid eyes

➳

on her. Fresh out of JFK I was, with nothing in the world but me small cup I found in Dublin before I took off, unshaven and feeling a little bit in need of a piss, tight underwear I reckon always ends up pushing a bit too hard on the bladder. So I look for the privy, you see, but there ain't none available at all. Not a single pisser in the whole of New York City without someone's arse set in front of it, I swear it. So there I am running around park and fifth or some such street and before I know what's going on this little thing is running beside me asking me all sorts of questions like who I am what am I doing here why am I running all over the place and for some reason I don't want to tell her it's because I'm in serious need of personal relief so I just tell her I'm running to change the world and she's excited about that, oh yes, and she jumps around a bit and starts yapping away about how she likes me because she knows I'm a good person as she's got a great eye for detail apparently and how she's always wanted to change the world and that now that she's met me she's going to do it because she's always known she'd meet me as her mammy told her so before she died.

So there I was, sack filled to the bloody brim, needing to offload as soon as possible, and with this little cute orphan thing alongside me telling me I'm the one she's always been waiting for. Because her mammy said so. Only got her three brothers left, she says. Only because she hates them because they ain't very nice to her, making her do all sorts of things for them. Lazy she says. So I don't know why but this girl has got to pulling my heart-strings looking so pitiful and thin and I can't bear to let her down, so I just smile and tell her Aye and then keep running down the street. To be honest, I didn't really have anything better to do in the country or at home. Bit of an exile, lonely orphan myself. New start, American dreamer. That's what I was. Unattached. I was a bit lost, you know, so this girlie with her big eyes and her faith made me want to do something, so I ran for her. To change the world, you know.

But before I know it I'm out into Connecticut, still fucking running, and I've damn well pissed myself on the street, right in front of her. I don't think she noticed, as she's always running way too far ahead, but I remember smelling so bad for days. That yellow patch on me jeans still hasn't faded.

God I'm hungry. Where's she gone now, damn her.

Is that a dog collar?

*

So I burst out of the bar and run straight to the bear, who's falling asleep under the tree, oak. He's clearly finished his tea as the cup, white, Chinese, is lying rejected on the floor beside his lumbering foot.

I've got a load of food in my hands, bread, cheese, cold meat, some chicken, turkey and pâté, and I'm being chased out by the three men, mechanical, who don't seem happy that I've stolen food from them. The thing around my neck hurts like hell but at least I've finally been able to have a bath.

'Stop her!'

'Stop her!'

'Stop her!' I hear them shout. The bear just sort of wormlike slithers up and looks scared at me.

'Run! They're crazy!' I shout. He's well trained these days and slips into his running stance quite effortlessly. He scoops the cup up with his foot in one swift motion. His wiggling lips curve up in a sort of half-smile as his big tree-trunk legs begin to move.

'How was your dinner, Rob?'

'I've had better.' I say as I nip past him and break into what feels like a 10km/h run, creating a space between me, the bear and the fading calls of my short-term masters:

'Come back here, girl!'

'Come back here, gi–!'

'Come back he–!'

*

We're running again on the way to Hartford and the three men are still chasing us, but it's been five days now so I think in fact they've joined us on our mission. I sometimes hear their chat echoing in my ears as I turn a corner. Other times we wake up and there is food at our feet.

I'm thinking, reflecting, on the comfort and enjoyment I've found in the constant rhythm of my feet, seven year old Nike LunarGlides, on the road, dun-dun-dun-dun-dun, and the company that the ginger bear gives me, how I've never been this happy since the day mother died. There is something in the open road, in the abandonment of departing, that I can't help but love. I'm running away from my past and into my future. I think it was that day, in the bar, when, after dinner and midst forced bath, when the men clipped the collar (with FIFI written on it in pink italics) how much I really do love that big oaf and the release he has given me, even if it was really because he needed to go for a piss. I won't tell him I know, and how goddamn awful he smelt for days, because I reckon that'll break his mammoth heart.

And I think, deep down, that I don't care if we don't change the world anymore because I don't cry anymore, in the day, at night, alone. With every dun-dun-dun I get a little bit happier, and every time I look back and see the bear smiling at me with those lips I can't help but feel a bit warmer inside, and I look forward into the sunset setting behind Hartford and I feel like singing.

Because, I'm finally changing my world, like mother said I would.

One step at a time.

Roads: M74 (Junction 21 to Junction 8)

A P Pullan

yet.
know
don't
You just
away?
or
Home
a significance.
and feel
Your back
hill.
that
up on
breaking
Like clouds
change.
Thing's
Abington Services.
think.
to
you seem
So
difference?
A
Beattock. *Moffat.*
it's here.
and
It's there
the blood.
the air,
which changes
That something
Lockerbie.
something.
you'll not notice
If you don't look
Ecclefechan.

In the Flood

Brian Johnstone

for Andy Goldsworthy

These stupa-like cairns that punctuate the gorge
are Goldsworthy's in spirit, if not
in name. We add to them
a stone, a pebble, waymarking the route
to lead those that the coming autumn will permit
the better down the course
of what will be a river come November
with the start of winter rain,
a torrent from the snow-melt in the spring.
The permanence of what resemble Henry Moores
in all their form and bulk,
shore up every fly-by-night route marker
stacked upon these eddy-sculpted rocks
but subject to the coming wash
of water Goldsworthy might welcome, were he here
in more than spirit, when the force
now dormant in the gorge sweeps
all – direction, art, intention – before it in the flood.

Stump
Christie Williamson

No raekin as high
as hit eence did
hit points a brokkin finger
ta whaar hit wis wint ta be.

Gray broon bark strips aff
sinks doon an doon
wi ivviry passin year
laivin a whicht shadow
anunder da lift.

A dry damp nae life
emptiness fills da air,
taestin o green fruit
at'll nivvir turn black.

Dis endin o things
is nae escape.
Hit comes on wis
fae naewhaar,
an takks wis back dere
fir langir as we'd laek.

Poem (iii)
Ross McGregor

Sometimes
ye cannae even luik
at the sky
the beauty ae it
burns ye
like biled peens
in yer een
so ye turn
luik doon
anywhaur
but that sky

Naked
Larry Butler

at last after a long walk
waist deep in water
willow above mirror below
ready to dive – poised on the edge
of decision to swim or not to swim:
cool legs – warm torso – hot head
waiting in the space between breaths
or insight for courage, a push.
Fingers ripple the still lochan
distorting any hope of certainty
making a blur before the splash
before swimming with the swans.

Camping

Nalini Paul

I lie among Hoy's Sitka spruce
the earth a bed of welcome.

Soft ground yields to my yawning form;
mounds of memory stretch back.

Patches of sky
blur the high branches
where dreams of longing return...

Sleeping outside
in British Columbia,
horizons shaped by mountains,
bears lurk behind trees.

Sitting round the campfire,
the kerosene lamp attracts moths
like lost souls disturbed in slumber,
magnetised by light.

The smell of Cedar wood burning
chopped carefully from kindling.
Waves of orange on black rise
before embers fade into night...

The sun shifts and so do I.

Pine needles jag me awake:
the forest is planted.

‘It is difficult to establish any relationship between the price of books and the value one gets out of them.’

George Orwell (‘Books v. Cigarettes’, 1946)

Trompe L'Oeil

Zoë Wicomb

ONE KNOWS WHAT to expect from a man who wears a blazer, for the blazer is designed to announce the wearer's unassailable authority. The brass buttons and double-breastedness confer both authority and probity upon the wearer, and what is more, they keep a man on his toes. The double-breasted blazer does not brook investigation. Just as it does not permit slouching, a leaning this way or that; rather, it bellows a no-nonsense clarity of purpose guaranteed by the combination of sober navy-blue with sportive brass buttons that declares its difference from the staid traditions of the suit. Thus does the blazer blaze the wearer's ready-made integrity. In its signifying function, it is not unlike denim, which once spoke so unashamedly of permissiveness and subversion, of a brazen disregard of order, that it had to be rescued and recuperated by the fashion industry. There is of course no danger of the blazer being appropriated in that way.

The two men in representative blues are discussing secularism. They stand at the railings of the grand house, admiring the sublime view, the tie-dye blue of the sea into which a bloody sun is about to plummet. X, in denim, shifts his weight, bracing himself for a lecture from the blazered man by his side. He ought to have found an excuse to leave when Y arrived but, never having met anyone like Y, he is at the same time fascinated by the man.

Gavin deplores this kind of thing, fiction that claims to say something significant about the real world. These people should stick to stories, events and characters, rather than rummage through stale stereotypes and imagine that something new has been forged. He has no objection to a good old-fashioned yarn, that is, when one can find the time for reading fiction, but this pompous stuff... Why on earth does Bev think that he would be diverted by it? She ought to know that he sees through this kind of thing – platitudes passed off as profundities.

It is the beginning of a short story by Roddy What's-his-name, the Scottish writer they met at the Study Centre in Italy – at least RP are his initials, and the story appears to be set at just such a place. That, presumably, is why Bev, who knows that Gavin has neither time for nor truck with fiction, thinks he would want to read it. Bev, who unfortunately had nothing much to do at the Centre, was rather taken in by the chap with his funny, sing-song Glasgow accent and the olde-worlde 'ayes' and 'buts' which, if you asked Gavin, was pure affectation. Surely educated Scots don't speak like that.

You're a colonial at heart, Gavin teased Bev. He could not quite bring himself to say so, but her interest was surely in the young man's parentage – a Scot with a South African mother – as if they did not have enough of all that tiresome stuff at home.

So, should we be reading you? What is it you write about? Gavin had asked Roddy loudly across the expanse of dinner table. The young man seemed taken aback, embarrassed, as if it were a faux pas on Gavin's part, which was of course a piece of nonsense. He was only asking him to speak of something that already existed in the public domain; besides, that's why they were there, to get on with their work and, surely, to speak about it.

Och, this and that, you know, Roddy stuttered. Nothing much, nothing other than you'd expect but.

They sparred regularly over dinner. The young chap, like most young people nowadays, had astonishing gaps in his knowledge that Gavin felt compelled to address.

Don't mind the professor, Bev laughed.

The white man's burden, Roddy quipped. Where would I be without the help?

Gavin was irritated. Why behave as if South Africa had not lost its pariah status? He said out loud, Why not take your cue from Mandela? Heard of ubuntu? Gavin had just that day read in *The Times* an English political commentator ridiculing the word, citing its transliteration as so much meaninglessness, so that he, Gavin, for once would refuse to instruct, refuse to be the source of information, as the young man looked blankly at him. This time the boy – who with tilted head seemed to be waiting for an explanation – could look it up himself. But Bev, who often got the wrong end of the stick, frowned and said that it would not be necessary. She seemed to be taken in by the young man's shallowness. There was something about him that Gavin couldn't fathom, couldn't put his finger on, except that he was irritating in a quiet, needling sort of way. Roddy had provoked him into saying that the imagination is overrated, that writers' 'work' cannot compare with the thinking required for historical or philosophical research. Which he supposes is an extreme position that he does not actually, or fully subscribe to, although God knows it does contain an element of truth. And they only have themselves to blame. Even at the University here in Cape Town the writing of fiction and poetry is now called 'research'. It should keep the travel costs and library budget down, plumbing the depths of their own psyches, he recently joked with a sceptical colleague in the English department.

Still, in spite of the arty fellows, the Study Centre had been a wonderful gift. It was good to meet other scholars, and without the concentrated period of writing, the uninterrupted days and the world warded off by a phalanx of efficient staff, he would not have arrived at such astonishing insights, and finished the work in the short sabbatical. And now the monograph on nineteenth-century European settlement in the Eastern Cape has, just as he expected, won a well-deserved prize. For the truth of the matter is that there's so much shoddy scholarship about – the universities in this country are simply no longer the places of learning that they once were.

Gavin loves Saturday evenings like this. Bev cooked a superb dinner of kingklip for just the two of them, and after his customary clearing of the dishes, he settled in his chair in this comfortable sitting room where, looking out onto the garden, they read or listen to music. The rain in winter may be relentless, but in summer there is nothing to beat this house. Last year he had the entire wall replaced with sliding glass doors so that the frangipani and nicotiana waft into the room, and the brook around which the garden is structured babbles cheerfully. Now, as they listen to Beethoven in the twilight, inside and outside slide into each other. He lights a citronella candle, just in case. There is nothing like watching from the comfort of upholstered chairs a pale moon mature in the sky. Just the two of them.

Gavin wishes that Bev had not left the magazine section of the newspaper on his chair. *The Mail & Guardian* had printed the short-listed story from *The Guardian* competition. He supposes they are short of news. He has flicked through the story, gratified to find his views on contemporary writing confirmed: passable, if predictable descriptions of the setting at the Italian Study Centre – the roar of the sea competing with that of the traffic, the rustle of pine trees, the grand house and elegant lunches at the large perspex table on the terrace, the mildly diverting exchanges between characters. And, predictably, the Ligurian trompe l'oeil. Are writers not supposed to use their imaginations, invent, for god's sake? What is the point of simply transferring from the everyday, from what happens to be within view, or hearing, to the page? Gavin shakes his head. It is the same problem he has with photography, and as far

→

as he can gather no one has yet satisfactorily explained how such documentation succeeds in illuminating the human condition. The discussion in the story of colonial genocide is marginally more interesting. Roddy's character, much given to shaking his head vigorously, says:

No, no, no, such speculations are painful to those of us who know something about history. Let me take you through the arguments.

Gavin must hand it to him – the positions are surprisingly well-presented, logically argued. But where is the art in that? He chuckles at the dialogue, not least because, for all the sardonic tone, young RP has clearly learnt some lessons in history from their dinner-table discussions. But all through the Beethoven sonata, something has been niggling, and now Gavin finds himself picking up the paper once again.

Bev, who is doing the crossword, looks up to see Gavin shaking his head. Oh dear, she should not have given him the Arts Supplement with RP's story; she is not in the mood for a diatribe on art and knowledge. It had been such a joy having Roddy at the Centre. Nearly two years ago – and Bev still savours his frank interest in her, his careful consideration of what she so haltingly had to say. You should write, he said, which made her blush. And so she tried, sat down with pen and notebook, and forced herself to write, but that precisely was the problem – it was a matter of forcing out the words so lacking in flow that such a business could not be called writing. She ought to have found the courage to talk to the young man about it, but the time never seemed right. Then, after realising that she had struggled for two consecutive nights to find outfits with which to wear again the necklace that he had complimented her on, she felt ashamed, and for a few days avoided him. I'm old enough to be his mother, she said aloud to herself, and felt even sillier. Of course she needed no such admonishment. Was it because of the mother, the woman from the tip of Africa, more or less Bev's age, that he took such a kindly interest in her?

Pass the mulk, he mocked at breakfast. You sound just like my mum.

How often she wished that she could ask about the woman, the revolutionary mother, but it would have been too difficult. All she could hope for is that he had not read it as indifference, that he had understood how she was trapped by all that complicated history.

Does Bev really expect Gavin to read the story? She knows what he thinks of contemporary writing, of the hype, as he calls it, the media-driven culture industry. Perhaps she wants him at least to believe that the boy is well regarded, that she had not been stupid in admiring him. Now, looking up again, she notes his frown, the livid colour, and feels a shiver of terror.

Gavin is a celebrated historian who, before the end of his first year as a student, had already earned the label of 'bright'. From the start he was considered a star, a catch, and Bev was certainly envied for having been chosen by someone with the unusual combination of being bright, handsome, and a rugby star. Envied when they married. She lists the things that others must have foreseen: for bearing the name that appears on the cover of the well-reviewed books, for foreign travel that comes with a prestigious Chair in History, for the issue of marriage, their lovely boys, both away at university – all these things must have been there as embryos, little bloody specks, contained in the albumen of brightness. She tosses the word about and summons its synonyms: vivid, luminous, brilliant, blazing. Blazing, as in blazer.

It was the summer of 2000, when arguments were trawled out once more on whether the new millennium does not actually start in 2001, and the magazines offered yet again advice on new resolutions, starting afresh, on new directions and new wardrobes, and on how they had escaped computer meltdowns by the skin of their teeth, so that, when Gavin received his letter of acceptance from the Italian Foundation and invited her along, she looked upon it as a beginning. At least for herself.

Oh, you should come, he said, it could be something of a holiday for you – no cleaning or cooking – and besides, what on earth will you do with yourself, kicking your heels here for two months on your own?

It is true that she is often lonely. After all the chores, the reading of a novel, a newspaper, and the planning of dinner, the afternoons stretch endlessly, forlornly ahead of her. Then she wanders through the house from room to room, sits for a while surveying what is hers, theirs. So much stuff – chairs, cupboards, framed prints, beds, rugs, crockery, so many different patterns to memorise and recall, and Bev would wonder: What to do? What to do with it all, what to do with herself? When the children were still there, at school, she had on occasion asked other mums what they do when all the chores are done, but it turned out that chores are never done. Afternoons of pacing the floor, waiting for the hours to pass, could, it turned out, be avoided, but she lacked the necessary imagination, was no good at thinking up new forms of housekeeping, and Gavin certainly did not think her amiss in the running of the house. They have never had servants, and after the children left, they dismissed the char who came once a week for three hours. They would not be typical South Africans, Gavin said, though Bev worried about the hungry women who knocked on her door for bread, and who offered, in exchange, to wash the windows she had just buffed into gleaming mirrors. She could not say with pride, I've cleaned them myself; instead, she said that she already had a cleaner. Bev found that peeling potatoes in the early afternoon for dinner that night, or kneading bread for tomorrow, or pickling lemons for the summer, simply shifted the dark hole of time further on into the days, the weeks, the months ahead. The hours remained so many beads stuck on a rusty abacus, unwilling to slide along. There was no escaping the time in which she floundered, in which her spirit grew thin, spread through the house, spread effortlessly over all the dust-free surfaces of cupboards and chairs and beds, seemed to evaporate, leaving her light-headed so that she would have to sit down and sternly summon back the Bev who sorted out the laundry into white and dark, cooked balanced meals, and settled electricity bills.

Gavin's suggestion had made sense. She would view the fellowship in Italy as an experiment with unpunctuated time, unmarked by chores, which would settle things for good. She would read novels about other mild-mannered women; perhaps try poetry; read up on the history of the area, the architecture and the dazzling trompe l'oeil of Liguria, in which, maybe, a lesson lurked. Bev, who managed to get lost in Cape Town in spite of Table Mountain, toyed with the idea of day trips to other towns. Would she have the courage to take such risks? She took lessons in Italian, which for some months guaranteed the shift of an abacus bead from 3 to 4 p.m. Gavin smiled distractedly at her preparations.

Did he really want her to come to Italy? Would she not be in his way, cramp his style?

He deplored the vulgar expression. Of course he wanted her to come. She had never been in his way and he knew he could rely on her to be sensitive to his needs. Of course – he had no misgivings at all. Few women your age look as good as you do, he said, having thought about the expression and decided there was an entailment that warranted the reply. But what was his style? He supposed himself to be a solid, old-fashioned sort of man, a family man, who dressed soberly in a navy-blue blazer, and perked up remembering that actually, his hair was rather fine, no loss there, so that he did not have to worry about styling strands across a thinning patch as so many men of his age do. Gavin, struggling with the story, is not surprised that his thoughts have wandered. Nevertheless, he will read on. Bev will be disappointed if he doesn't finish it. Fortunately it is the sort of thing that one could easily skim, skip a phrase, a sentence or two.

For all Y's authority, the child, the palimpsest of a boy who is afraid of pigeons, persists; it rises like a blush below the elegant silver hair, so that the fleeting look translates into a message of panic, a plea to his wife. Who will act, will leap to his side to steer him away from menace, from the portly pigeons that strut self-importantly, or the cool, comprehending look of the gauche young man who will not take his word, who tries to interrupt. I'll check it in Brewer's, the young man stutters, when Y has already explained the mythological origins, has given a fuller explanation than any contained in a dictionary.

Bev yawns. Through heavy eyelids she watches Gavin wriggle in his seat and reach for his drink before he turns back a page to re-read.

At the Study Centre, Bev did not find it easy to be a spouse. She ought to have been used to the condition, but there she was something like an uninvited guest, a freeloader, a charity case, or so she thought the serving staff viewed her. They grimaced at her poor Italian and made no effort to speak slowly, but Gavin said that she was imagining things, that her sensitivity was a symptom of the colonial cringe.

And how did Madame spend the day? the Czech historian asked.

She giggled, oh this and that, explored the gardens; she did not believe that he really wanted to know. Already his eyes darted about in search of escape. She was grateful for the writers and artists who brightened the evening dinners. They did not seem so serious, and Bev thought, why not? Why not try her hand at writing, nothing serious, of course, just a bit of fooling around with words, see if she could sketch a scene. But the words she knew were dense forests through which a path had to be beaten and Bev lacked the strength. One evening before dinner, after a tiring day with pen and blank paper, she sought out Roddy; she would talk to him about writing. He had just joined a group standing around awkwardly with their drinks. He said that such an affair where you were expected to circulate was called a stonneroonie in Glasgow. The drink in hand would loosen their limbs and tongues and steer the prattling partygoers about the room, and he demonstrated with a silly walk and a flash of teeth that got everyone laughing, so that Gavin too rose to join them.

Gavin said that he had read that day that so many million works of fiction were published per year. Did they not think it terrible, all this production of novels, with which to fill the world?

Roddy smiled. Publishers would not publish books that they did not think they could sell, he said.

Well, I call it shameful, wasteful, Gavin persisted, the sheer amount of pulp produced, tossed into a benighted world – I am of course not speaking of great literature – and then others have to read it all.

In the larger scheme of things where men join armies and go out to shoot people they don't know, the harmless, solitary pleasures of reading and writing could hardly be called shameful. In fact, they should be encouraged. And not many of us are able to read or write great literature. We have to make do...

No, no, no, Gavin interrupted, but Roddy, the conscientious fellow, turned away with drink in hand to circulate according to the rules of the stonneroonie.

It turned out that the spouse's unstructured time at the Study Centre was only such within the fixed parameters of set mealtimes and Gavin's working routine. Saturday and Sunday afternoons were reserved for sightseeing. Bev spent her free hours lying on the dirty beach where the seaweed had started rotting, staring aloft at the growing white line drawn by departing aircraft, the bright point of a pen driven inexorably across the blue slate sky. Purposeful. Leaving behind a clear message. That was what it ought to be like, she thought. The notebook by her side was a mess of half-finished sentences, vigorous scrubbing out, and so very little left of her efforts. She would have to tear out the pages, destroy them; she kept her labour with words on the beach a secret. If only she could knock up something like the trompe-l'oeil window on the narrow building that she passed on the way to the shore. The building, wedged snugly into the fork of two streets, boasted a window whose lime green curtains were captured flapping gaily, and permanently, in an imagined breeze. Momentary deception of the eye – that was all she aspired to. It was not as if Bev imagined herself a Virginia Woolf or a Nadine Gordimer; she had nothing of importance to say; she didn't expect any more of her own attempts than to brighten up a street corner or to help one forget the stifling heat for a brief, illusory moment. And still writing eluded her.

Three meals per day spent with other fellows was trying. Gavin preferred Bev to sit by his side at lunchtime, so that he could report on the morning's work, and that was preferable to making small talk with the professors. But were they not expected to circulate? Who cares, he said loudly, about couples having to separate at table. He didn't, he added in the silence that followed. He had chosen her, Bev, to share his life with, so stuff the rules. And over lunch he discussed a trip they would have to make to the Eastern Cape, a matter of research that had cropped up. Damn, he would have to leave that chapter for lack of evidence, but he had no doubt that he would find it, that things would work out as planned. Bev hoped that there would be a chance to talk with Roddy about the trompe l'oeil of the region, but sitting as he did across the divide of the large table she did not have the courage to raise her voice.

How extraordinary, Roddy said after dinner one evening, that you two should do everything together, that after all these years you still seem to like each other. A good advertisement for marriage if ever I saw one. You must know everything there is to know of each other.

He was single; nothing so far had worked out for him. No one to cramp his style, Bev thought. Gavin took the young man's expression of surprise for admiration or envy.

Thirty years at the end of this month, he proffered, so it isn't surprising that we are so close, that we do everything together. We had a wonderful time in Genoa today – the Palazzos Rosso and Bianco, San Lorenzo cathedral... Bev feared that he would list all their sightseeing, so that she interrupted, murmured that yes, they've been so lucky, together for thirty years. But Gavin shook his head emphatically.

No, no, no, not lucky. It takes some thought, some backbone to keep a marriage working in these pressured times.

Y shakes his head. No, no, no, he says.

He has two ways of starting. If not the multiple Nos, his opening would be: Of course, of course, which involves an equally vigorous shaking of the head, and really there is no way of knowing how the man chooses between the two since both are followed by an invitation to infer that his knowledge and understanding are boundless, that the other person's naivety is a given.

X frowns thoughtfully while the lecture on cultural difference is being delivered. The new Père Ubu, he thinks, blazered, and buffed by the academy. 'Bunkum' – delivered in his mother's no-nonsense guerrilla style as she looks her interlocutor straight in the eye – that's what he ought to say. Instead, he smiles. Perhaps it's all about personal vanity: Y shakes his head to draw attention to his handsome, full head of once-blond hair now elegantly silvered with age. Common vanity, a vigorous nod at Mother Nature who has always been kind to him, whom he has come to rely on.

Gavin would like to stop reading this odious story, but something over which he has no control drives him on. It is the same morbid fascination with which he examines in the mirror his mosquito bites, the swollen sacs of poison that drag his face into skew-whiff distortions, the same absorption in something that he knows to be temporary. Like mosquito bites, this story will eventually disappear without trace. There is no need to be upset by these facile words, by the ravings of a limited mind. But something niggles, a sense of something unspeakable woven into these sentences that Gavin can't bring himself to draw out into the light. And a monstrous sense of shame creeps up lividly from the open neck of his shirt to his very brow where it settles in the luxuriant hair. He steals a look at Bev. Does Bev know of the thing hidden in this story? Bev sits with her hands in her lap, her eyes glazed, her head tilted. Most likely she has not yet read it, or not read it carefully, in which case he must protect her from it. He must find a way of hiding and destroying the paper. Gavin wonders if RP has interrogated his own use of initials – X, Y, Z indeed, instead of naming his characters. Pathetic. No doubt such cowardice passes for postmodern ingenuity. Speed reading is all this story deserves. His eyes skim across a couple of paragraphs until he is held spellbound.

The suites are partitioned at the bathroom wall, which ensures privacy, protects them from each other's sounds. Except in the bathroom itself where the partitioning wall is less solid than one would expect. There, occasionally, above the sound of rushing water he witnesses the lie that is Y's perfect marriage. He lies rigid in his bath and tries not to splash, the better to hear that voice of reason bark at Z, laugh cruelly at her quiet, timid explanations. She would be cringing at the menace that rises above the angry rush of water. X hears the wife's whimpers of fear or her clipped anger, and finds himself inventing a dialogue around which to weave a story. More than once the stifling of dry sobs like hiccups. The bathroom is also a place in which to retreat, he supposes, but then the entry of another, the unmistakable no, no, no and the slamming of doors. So much for that smiling marriage.

Gavin sits bolt upright in his chair as the monstrous thing claws its way out of the print, and hisses. How low can a writer stoop? He is not surprised to find that the chap eavesdropped on their conversations in the bathroom, but how dare he misrepresent their marriage in this way? How dare he be so cruel to Bev, poor gullible Bev who wouldn't harm a fly, who had shown the chap every kindness, and who had listened attentively to his pretentious prattle? The thing slithers under Bev's chair where it hides. The young man simply has no sense of morality, of decency. If Gavin has never balled a fist in his life, he is close to it; if he were to walk into Roddy What's-his-name now, there'd be no accounting for his actions. There is a bitter taste in his mouth. Fiction, my foot, he snorts with disgust.

Why did Bev give the offensive story to Gavin?

She had read it whilst making the dinner. That afternoon she started early, intending also to get the bean soup ready for the following day, and whilst she stirred the onions, making sure that they caramelised rather than burn, she read the paper held aloft in her left hand. When the beans had been added and the stock heaved energetically in the pot, Gavin came into the kitchen, so that she folded the paper in half, put it on the wooden counter and swiftly transferred the bubbling pot of soup onto the wad where she continued stirring. There was some spillage but never mind, it didn't matter, she would bin the paper anyway. And now watching Gavin grow red with rage, she can't tell why she hadn't binned it after all.

Bev expected the story to be about something real, in fact, to be somehow connected with Roddy's mother. Would that not have been why it was printed in the *Mail & Guardian*? Once, he asked her about the Eastern Cape, where he said his mother had known Steve Biko and spent some months in gaol. He hoped to visit the region early next year, a research trip, although he hoped also to meet family – he owed it to his mother, he muttered. So, was the mother dead? Bev wondered. She nodded; she felt for him. Why then was she unable to ask about the mother? Instead, she waved at the Czech historian hovering under the great palm tree, who rightly read it as an invitation to join them. Her voice was thick with shame as she said, poor Pavel, how lonely he seems to be.

Even a cursory look at the story must have given Bev an idea of the thing, Gavin decides. He understands her hurt, her need for him to explain the ugliness away. That is surely why she has left the paper on his chair.

You know why he hates us? Prejudice. We are white South Africans of a certain age, the ready-made pariah. Gavin's voice is unnaturally calm.

But he doesn't hate us, Bev says, oh no, not at all. We spoke quite a bit in the end, quite frankly of the bad old days, you know.

Which goes to show how innocent Bev is, how simple and good-hearted, so that a rush of affection mingles with the bile in his throat. He would like to place both hands around the chap's scrawny neck and slowly squeeze the life out of him. Not that he cares about the pathetic characterisations, the heinous misrepresentation. No doubt the story has been short-listed as an act of positive discrimination – they have strict quotas in Britain these days and of course South Africa, ever the colonial mimic, is following suit in that direction. The meanness of it all, the folly, beggars belief. Gavin's bile subsides. Why should he care about such badly written nonsense, a story so patently devoid of imagination? He will skip to the last paragraph, just see how the artless thing gets wrapped up, check on the direction of the man's malice. Actually, Gavin often sneaked a look at the last page of a novel, even if across the unread pages the words did not mean much.

He is transfixed by her. The lovely red hair tumbles in luxuriant waves in the lamplight that pools above her head. Her eyes are half-closed as she listens to the Moonlight Sonata and her hands, still youthful, lie serenely in her lap. Her face is composed, which gives her the beauty that she does not quite manage in daylight. As the music moves into a crescendo he watches, spellbound, her left hand rise slowly as if in a trance, watches it move mechanically to the coffee table by her side where it falls precisely upon the glass paper-weight, cupping it in the dome of her palm. It has a green eye in the centre, and from the pupil rays of colour shoot into the glass. He watches her lift her hand, in balletic slow motion, the weight of the glass palpable in her dreamlike movement. Her arm is raised, stretched well above her head when she leans back and, like the skilled netball player of her schooldays, aims for the centre of the French window, drawn across into a double pane. It shatters into a million pieces as the glass eye crashes into reinforced glass, the mosaic spreading and crackling eerily, and beyond it a full trompe l'oeil moon disperses into a million fragments before it skids away across the sky. Her arm is still raised and the glass jewels are still dropping like hailstones out of a clear sky when he rises, crosses the jewel-studded threshold to find some air for his choked lungs from which an eerie sound escapes.

Outside the sky is spangled with stars. There is also the pointed red light of an aeroplane finding its way expertly across the chaos of lights and stars, straight as a die as it dips towards its destination.

Bloodier than Blood
Doug Johnstone

SHE HUNCHED FORWARD in the driver's seat and squinted. Stupid wipers were just smearing the snowflakes across the windscreen. Her finger hovered over the lights, waiting to flick off full beam if they met someone coming the other way. The snow wasn't heavy but the flakes splatted on the glass like crystal bugs committing suicide.

The seatbelt cut across her belly. She needed to piss. The baby dug a foot into her bladder. He was always awake at night. Three weeks to the birth, if he arrived on time, but first ones were always late.

The radio sputtered and crackled. Rory was pushing buttons with his stubby fingers. His head lolled like a Thunderbirds puppet. 'Drinking for two,' was the joke he trundled out every time he came back from the bar tonight.

She'd hated the whole wedding. Her ankles were swollen and she worried about wetting herself most of the night. Everyone kept coming up and touching her stomach uninvited. The smell of caffeine and alcohol on their breaths made her queasy and jealous.

They were his friends, not hers. Landed gentry half of them, Findlays and Lachlans, overgroomed private school girlfriends and wives traipsing behind. Everyone glistening with booze, slavering homespun wisdom about pregnancy at her.

So tired. The baby keeping her up at night. Elbows and knees, toilet trips and heartburn. And Rory snoring. Worse when he'd had a drink. Tonight would be a nightmare.

He was still punching between stations. Static pulsed through voices and music. She'd read that one percent of radio noise was the echo of the big bang. Sound from the beginning of time. Big deal. She had her own big bang coming in three weeks, time resetting to zero.

She'd had all the tests, even the amnio, which hurt like hell. They were clear for Downs, sickle cell and spina bifida, despite her age. She lifted a hand to her face, pushed at the lines on her brow, traced the creases at her eye. She ran her hand through her hair, wiry now since pregnancy. Her body reacting to the alien sucking life from her. Piles and incontinence, eczema and acne. A humiliating surrender to someone not even born yet.

Headlights blinded her for a moment, then dimmed. She lunged for her own lights but they didn't dip, instead the fog lamps came on. She panicked at another switch and the indicator began clicking. By the time she dipped her lights the other car was past.

She breathed. Her heart gradually slowed. She hated driving country roads at night. She was going too fast but she wanted to be home. Piss, Gaviscon, hot chocolate, bed.

The snow blurred on the windscreen. Crap wipers. The car looked fine from a distance, shiny black BMW with leather seats, but things were falling apart. Central locking on the blink, steering that pulled left, a sticky clutch and a slack handbrake.

They needed to trade in, get something more suitable for the baby, but Rory wouldn't have it. This was his big metal cock and he liked to show it off.

He was always flirting when drunk. He'd

danced with the bride's teenage niece tonight, then bought her a drink. Flirting was the extent of it, as far as she knew, but it made her sick all the same.

She'd been invisible to him tonight, which was fine. She had a new man in her life, currently drawing nutrients from her through a pulsing umbilical cord. A little man she could love forever. One that would make things right.

A burst of static made her teeth clench.

'Leave the radio alone,' she said.

'I'm just trying to find something decent.'

Music emerged from the blizzard of noise. A strained voice, singing. 'Something in my veins, bloodier than blood.' The baby did a somersault and her stomach lurched.

'It was a good night tonight,' said Rory.

'For you, maybe.'

That made him perk up. 'I know it's not easy for you at the moment.'

'Do you.' It wasn't a question.

'Not drinking and all that.'

'It's not about alcohol.'

His hand squeezed her thigh. Through her thick elasticated maternity trousers, it hardly felt like anything.

She glanced at him. He put on a woozy smile. She loved that smile once. But things change. Who's to blame for that? No one, that's the worst thing.

He let go of her leg.

'You're just all over the place,' he said, 'what with the...'

'I swear to God if you say "hormones" I'm going to kick you out the car.'

She saw a flash of something through the rush of snowflakes, empty eyes reflecting headlights, then there was a heavy whump, a metallic crack and crumple, the car juddering as she kicked at the brake. They swerved and were thrown forward in their seats, her belt cutting under the bump and into her bladder, making her piss herself.

They lurched to a stop and were jerked back against the headrests.

The slash and squeak of wipers. The thin rasp of the engine. Scratchy music. The stench of urine from her soaked trousers. The alcohol on Rory's breath.

'Are you okay ?' he said.

She opened the door and vomited onto the tarmac. The rush of snowy air made her lungs sting. She straightened and looked in the rearview mirror.

'We hit something,' she said.

She could see out the corner of her eye he was rubbing his neck.

She undid her seatbelt and heaved herself up using the doorframe. The piss on her trousers was already cooling in the freezing air.

'Come on,' she said.

A dark mass was sprawled out behind the car. She walked towards it. There was movement, flailing legs scraping at the road.

Pine and fir crowded the roadside. Snowflakes disappeared as they landed. Everything red in the taillights.

Steam rose from the body on the ground. A primal moan, the sound of trouble.

She sensed Rory behind her as she walked. She was almost at it now.

A deer.

Its neck was broken, its head at a horrible angle. Eyes rolling, breath billowing from its nostrils. Back legs bent and crushed under its body, front legs thrashing the air. A deep gash down its flank, matted hair along the wound and blood pooling beneath its body.

'Shit,' said Rory behind her. 'It's fucked.'

She wanted to slap him. She stared at the deer, its eyes wide in terror.

She went to the car. Opened the boot and took out a fire extinguisher. Felt the heft of it in her hands. Walked back to Rory and held it out to him.

'Kill it,' she said.

'What?'

'Put it out of its misery.'

He stared at her, then at the extinguisher.

'Why me?'

She laid a hand on her distended stomach and raised an eyebrow.

He hesitated, then took the extinguisher and walked to the deer. Its whining increased and it snorted in panic.

He knelt by its body, clear of the scrabbling

legs. Eventually he lifted the extinguisher above his head and smashed it into the deer's skull. Its legs jerked and it gave a sickening wail.

Rory looked up. There was a fleck of blood on his cheek, a thin trail down his shirt. She felt the baby kick, thump-thump against the wall of her womb.

Rory raised the extinguisher again then pummelled it into the deer's face, mashing the eye, crushing the skull. He swung it again and again, throwing his weight behind it, puffing with exertion, blood spattering up his shirt and across his face. The deer's legs stiffened them slackened, but still he heaved the extinguisher up and down, up and down, until the deer's head was nothing but a flat mess of hair and bone and brains and blood.

He dropped the extinguisher and put his hands on the animal's torso, gasping as he got his breath back. He was smeared with blood.

He raised his head.

'Happy now?' he said.

She felt the cold urine sticking her trousers to her thighs.

She turned and walked to the car. The baby nudged her insides, trying to tell her something, and she rubbed her belly in reply.

'There, there,' she said.

A Fairy Story

Frances Corr

SHE SAT INSIDE for outside was too big. A bumbly came in and left. She'd put on socks to make her feet feel secure, and chaffies carried on.

Bored with putting nature into words she was looking for something else. Under buckets and bins, behind doors. Destitute of thought she presumed that those who travelled back and forth in a car daily to work were to be respected more than she. She thought even the long nosed dog would look down on her.

So she ate. And she couldn't feel her way out. She wished she could coax herself out like a chaffinch with crumbs. Or whisky. She couldn't find herself. She'd been shouting through drawers, in the mirror, in a bottle. It was a most disorientating feeling. Frantic. Like a sheep without a lamb. And she wished she could have that lovely mumsie woolly feeling of unification.

I have nothing to show for my day. Nothing physical or tangible is in my hand. Bar an empty whisky glass. Is this a crime fit for the gee-o-teen?

Square me up someb'dy. Deck me out in a suit and hand me a career where there are forms and folders and ungenuine talk. A minefield where the quaint or bewildered shall be waded in upon. No mercy.

As one of the bewildered she decided to take shelter in a den far from the words of the Harsh World, and quietly live out her life as a fairy among biorachs. Peeping out from time to time and awaiting change, and trying to fit bluebells on her head for fun and frolics.

She wasn't sure if she cared for chaffies' toes. Hard and tippety tappy. Give it a hat and a stick. Her own toenail was black and horned due to frolicking in footwear too tight. Such was the frolic that the foot's condition was forgotten. There are some things that take priority. Euphoria was one, eckies being, as far as she knew, unheard of among the fairies. Who needs it man, she'd heard one utter.

She stayed in there for years. Like some she'd heard of hiding in the jungle till the war was over. Only being in the jungle they hadn't heard it was over. Or was it. Sometimes it's hard to tell. Cos there's things that sting the fairy. That crush her and hurt her bad. And it's peasy. Peasy weasy. Like holding a gun to the head of a buttercup.

But still she finds it hard to hate. Silly they call it. Could be the name of a grass, such a shrill weak name. Grass will be looked down on in the Harsh World for being unable to look after itself. And for being unable to hold a folder.

There's plenty shelter from torrential rain under a big Scots pine.

The ups and downs were colossal. But it was worth it when she found merriment. It wasn't always easy but she felt empathy for those who feared being singled out and something written on their door. Thoughts would have labour pains attached, still she couldn't help but have them. Full o fun and mischief. Full o fun and mischief.

On occasions the fairy had lost days as she tried to recollect herself after maybe chatting with a person who, whilst friendly enough, may

➳

have walked by her world and missed it. She'd try and compensate for the gap, emptying her admiration on to others and becoming viscous. Fairy instincts thankfully led her home for her eyes would be big and useless. The very spores of people got into her like asthma. Bending this way and that she'd try and get life into herself till a smile came easy again, and maybe take a notion to play on her pipes.

Call me a tool of lightning she thought, but there's something afoot. She pished wickedly in a tin pail. She hastened to breathe, remembering that in death you don't, when a fairy boy popped by and told her not to fret for the chaffies who fly against a hard window. You get worse ones yourself he scolded, as she worried that they might give themselves a headache.

One of the worst things was the thought of Slump on the pavement outside the pub. It gave her that gutsick feeling that others would move house to avoid, to a bungalow with a high hedge. Fairies will not thrive in the bungalow. Just one o those things. No point in sheddin tears. But the fairy spouts water like a kettle so don't tell her it's wrong to care.

Later she would build a fire, dragging twigs and scratching her shin. Scratching her shin bothered her less than the thought of having to run a small business selling gifts to tourists. Her smile would very quickly burn out, she feared, like that of a rave casualty. As it was a chirp came easy. Should it fail her on wakening it would not be long gone, resuming with the taking shape of chores. Why sweeping her floor and setting her bed to rights were as important as a world summit, for they set another fairy day.

Some cunt's gonny pay for this, she angered as she came upon an uncovered crap in the woods, and hacked at her curls. There is something about the helpless feel that's the saddest of all. To walk in where you want and do what you will and tear down someone's curtains and leave them bare when there is no defense.

Some mornings she'd wake as if with a bootlace round her neck, stiffened and choked. She was feart for Big Mannies when they were angry. Sometimes Big Mannies weren't even sure they were angry and they'd just go gruff. Their moods were kingsize. So big they couldn't see the end of them and presumed there was nothing more.

She sat upon a stone with a tummy full of oatcakes and considered her day a vacuum. She was neither here nor there nor up nor down. Good job the word malingery was absent from the fairy vocabulary. She'd heard from a friend via a mobile on their way to work, so she had, the folderless fairy. Folder-ree folder-ro folder-ree folder-ro-ho-ho-ho she burst into song.

I don't know how you have the patience to live like that, said the friend. I don't, said the fairy. It's just I can't think of anything else. Without the hills and the moths around me I'm like a thinned out neep. I just keel over.

Aah bless you, said the friend. And drove off.

I've never been so pleasantly lost in all my days, said the fairy, skipping from stone to stone with no strong emotion to drive her to anything. In out in out the weather drove her though. The day was one part cloud to one part sun.

She jumped a rope swing suspended from a tree and swung back and forth buffeting and bumping in her issue-less world. Till a staved pinky or a bellyache would bring her off.

Get off me get off me she gnashed at her curls. I don't like there to be much between me and the elements. I tell you what, promised the fairy to herself, but she kept on getting bruised. Thoughts from the Harsh World still rippled and made her go quiet. Very quiet.

Go away I want to be on my own she said to herself. I'm limp and I canny be bothered.

She began to worry about her day. Each morning she'd continue to wash panties and hang them out, eat breakfast and dook in the pool. But her routine could often be interrupted by a desperate urge to scrape her head along the side of a log. The fairy struggled hard to state something that others found simple. She thought perhaps she should buy and read a reputable paper.

With that she began to build a fire and ponder her lives. One that required combed hair and one that didn't. At least it was only double. Over warm flat stones went her feet by the river, as she bent and gathered enough twigs to make a black bundle. Some too bendy, but could be folded and shoved under the oxter of a more mature log to burn compact. Even a short burst of flame was always welcome.

The fairy fair needed to have majestic pines swaying in her eye-view. Anything less sent her swirling into the world of the ga-ga, where she would become next to useless, regardless of what she had on. Don't take me down that road she instructed her head. Down mad street. Don't take me there. I'm not fond of the shops and I have no timetable for buses back.

She wondered if everyone's head be like this. A museum full of curios to name but one. Or perhaps she just needed a job. In the Harsh World she might find herself in a big new electronics factory. In the manager's office being told off for being unable to follow the simplest of instructions. For being a diddy. But she wouldn't let on that she knew how to build pyramids.

On the fire pine branches went up like fairy lights. It was better at night when the sky was black and the stars were out. Some were afraid of dark and rocks. Not afraid of sinking the toe of a boot into a fellow's skull but afraid of high cliffs and mountain tops.

She bust up some more twigs and cooried for all she was worth in the hope that the mist might clear and the two lives meet like randy bastards.

The next day her back was sore and she couldn't hear waves. This was not the seaside. Hot hot went the sun. Baked fairy was the order of the day. A day to keep your cap on. The flies buzzed, a nut fell from a tree and a moth stood silver as a stick, perfectly in line with the grain. A moment preserved in vinegar.

There was something about flies. When in amongst you wished them all to fuck. When not, you wanted to step in just to see, just to have a keek at what might be there. To stare deep into a dark ribcage like an old house to see if there was dust or a bible or a pair o false teeth or a cat under the floorboards wi a scream on its face. And she thought of Slump outside the pub. Left long enough the flies would be round him too. She wondered if there might be a pink heart.

The fairy needed fed. She upped and found a cowpat to stand in and nourish herself. Like other Scottish creatures she survived well on the bleak landscape, a little nourishment going a long way. She decided to tidy up. The fairy would not shy away from turfing out old notions and spent ideas. Her arms were strong from much emptying and she'd sing in the space till something new came. Folder-ree! Folder-ro!

She put on her dress for play. Glass beads bangles and butterflies. Bright orange and vivid yellow were to be found in her own ribcage should she stretch. And her curls would ease soft as a tiny waterfall. There's a lot of beads in the world you must remember, she reassured herself. And velvety petals so don't despair. They shine in the grey and dust. Amethysts and iron ore, quartz and cairngorm marble. Get happy and paint your toes. Get red.

When the fairy danced she opened like a flower. Should someone offer her bottled water she'd puzzle and say why I have a whole river of the stuff. The whole body immerses, blasting the system further open. And she danced and danced and danced.

She also enjoyed a warm wind on her fairy body. Big Mannies would not appreciate this, seeing it only as a berry for picking.

There's a jobby in the woods and there's even fuckin bogroll stuck tae it man, said one of the flies. And they all laughed the plundering laugh of four boys in a Fiesta with the windows down.

The fairy sat stone as one on a park fountain, for not only did she know her world, she knew what she was to that laugh. Should a friend call her now on a mobile she'd sound like a hostage. So clouted, in the Harsh World she'd go find something to hurt herself with.

Stretched panties hung silent over birk branches. They would be dry as a biscuit in no time. Not a breeze. Not so much as a fairy breath. Came only a waft of sadness.

Big Mannies like the look of a fairy. They like to pick her up like King Kong and make her dance and tell her she's a good girl. They like to play with her and poke her up the skirt and tell her this is how a fairy should be. And when she's got the hang of it, they'll queue for days to see her.

Slice yir fuckin belly open and scrape ye out. Scrape the guts out o ye. Scrape the fuckin pison out and sluice you out wi a hard toxic chemical that'll dye you blue. That'll bite hard into yir surfaces and leave yir organs squeaking like balloons. Then rinse.

An exotic beastie landed with a donk, smaller in sound than a shuttlecock hitting a racquet, and left the same way but in reverse.

In the Harsh World the only cloud she found was a flat one in a book. There was scant air here, only a charged soup of many people in and out of each other's space like dusty bluebells gone wrong. Mixing and mashing till nobody knew who they were anymore. As if all had been blindfolded and birled, then questioned. Applause would be due if you could remember at least that you were a person and not a section of traffic or a gameshow.

She gathered leftovers and put them in a dish, keeping only the essence of an era, arranging it decoratively in a suitable vase, and placing it on an altar, suspended in a spanking new atmosphere. She could wear her past as an earring, condensed to a point, a little cherry or charm. A little cairn exhibited on top of a brand new mountain.

A cat had pished on her doormat. Its big marmalade body travelled a wall. Just like a cat. Cats here man, she thought. Don't give a fuck. It's probably steamin.

At home the cat confided in another cat. It's the remorse he said. Knowin you've puked on someone's floor.

If you don't feel the remorse you'll never get away fae it, said his friend. Cause there's no reason. One drink and yir back to laughin at the barmaid.

Outside the pub the flies buzzed round Slump. From a distance she could hear them. Where've you been ya cunt, they said. It's your round.

Astronomy 101

Pippa Goldschmidt

ONE DAY, A woman appeared in the Observatory canteen and sat next to Jeanette. The woman didn't slouch down in the low-slung chairs like everyone else; she sat upright with her back straight, her hair so glossy in the sunlight that Jeanette couldn't see what colour it was.

The woman explained to Jeanette that she'd come to work at the Observatory for a few months, to finish writing a book on the cosmic microwave background. Jeanette always pictured this remnant of the Big Bang hanging through the whole universe like smoke from a fired gun.

The woman told Jeanette about her plans to release a detector on a balloon high into the thin air above the South Pole. The balloon would fly for three weeks, pointing at the sky and collecting information before sinking back down to earth.

As they drank coffee out of the Observatory's chipped mugs, the woman talked about life in the Antarctic, and the thousand variations of white in the snow. 'The only colours you see are artificial. Human life is artificial there. It's like living in outer space.'

'How long have you spent there?' asked Jeanette.

'Six months.'

It was summer now in Edinburgh. The woman would be going back to the Antarctic in the autumn to fly her balloon.

'Where do people here go in the evening?' The woman wore an ivory-coloured scarf tied around her neck, and Jeanette watched her skin pulse as she spoke.

'There's a pub nearby, at the bottom of the hill,' Jeanette felt shy, as if this might be inadequate. The pub was a grotty students' drinking den with bad beer. But Jeanette didn't think the woman drank beer.

'Good. I'll see you there at seven?'

Jeanette nodded, and the woman turned around to talk to someone else. Jeanette's supervisor waved at her from across the room, he had some feedback on her thesis. He also wanted her to proofread the exam paper for the undergraduates. When she went back to her office, she realised she didn't know the woman's name.

1) What is the observational evidence for the expansion of the Universe?

(50 points)

Jeanette sat waiting in the pub, her whisky and water reduced to a slick on the bottom of the glass. Finally, the woman arrived and bought a glass of red wine.

'Cheers,' Jeanette said, but the woman didn't reply.

Silence. Jeanette wiped her sweaty hands on her jeans and imagined herself somewhere dry, still, safe; on the moon.

The woman inspected her hands. 'So,' she said, finally looking at Jeanette, 'you want to fuck?'

The sex wasn't particularly interesting that first time. The woman's body was oddly anonymous; her skin seemed exactly the same colour and texture all over. She behaved as if she were used to being naked with strangers, as if they were doing this in public.

It was very dark in the woman's hotel room; the curtains were pulled tight shut against the rest of the city. The woman said she couldn't sleep when it was light. In the Antarctic summer, days crashed up against each other with no gaps in between. She said there was nothing to do but work. Everyone worked night and day.

At coffee time the next day Jeanette saw the woman on the other side of the canteen. She felt the woman glance at her, once or twice, before she left. She had a lot of work to do on her thesis.

Later, the woman appeared in her office. 'So this is where you're hidden away,' she smiled, 'I'll see you this evening?'

Jeanette nodded and continued reading her supervisor's feedback. He had found gaps in her analysis; she had made too many assumptions. The last chapter was going to have to be completely reworked.

2) Explain how we can see galaxies at distances of more than 20 billion lightyears, when the size of the Universe is only 14 billion lightyears.

(50 points)

This time Jeanette found a cluster of freckles at the base of the woman's spine, only fractionally darker than the rest of her skin. This time the neatness of her body was admirable.

The woman kept saying, 'You are so fair,' as she stroked Jeanette's breasts. 'Like ice, like snow.'

It was nearly Midsummer eve, and sunlight managed to slide its way into the room, in spite of the curtains. Throughout the night, the woman kicked at the sheets and sighed, as Jeanette tried to sleep.

The next day, she found it difficult to concentrate, so she went to find the woman. But her office; a clean, bare box of a room with whitewashed walls, high up in one of the Observatory's towers, was empty. Just a faded star chart idly flapping in a draft near the window.

It was the same all through the summer, the woman was never in the office. Sometimes Jeanette would find evidence of her; the pattern of the room would be disturbed by her jacket flung over the chair. A rich dark plum-coloured jacket that made the rest of the room seem even paler in contrast.

During the next night, Jeanette felt almost dizzy surrounded by the black space, her head floating near the ceiling. The woman's hand in hers was the only thing that tethered her to the bed, to the surface of the earth. She didn't fall asleep until the early morning, her sleep an afterthought to the night.

The woman said, 'I couldn't sleep last night,' but Jeanette knew she had. Jeanette was trying to work, her fingers lying inert on the computer keyboard. The woman stood behind her and kissed the nape of her neck, very lightly so that all Jeanette felt was dry lips on her skin. Or perhaps the woman didn't kiss her at all. Perhaps she only touched Jeanette with her fingertips; Jeanette wasn't sure exactly. On the screen, the woman's distorted image walked away.

Later, when Jeanette went outside for some fresh air, the full moon from the night before was still just visible, low on the horizon. It seemed to have no substance, moth-eaten with holes so she could see right through it to the rest of the sky.

Back in her office, she printed out the revised version of her last chapter. But when she went to the printer, something was wrong. The pages were blank. There were faint scratchy marks on a few of them, but most were pure white. No warning lights flashed on the machine, no indication of what had happened, or where her work had gone. Her supervisor refused to read the electronic version. She didn't know what to do. She just wanted to sleep.

3) In 1964 Penzias and Wilson discovered the cosmic microwave background radiation; experimental proof of the Big Bang theory. They initially thought this radiation was caused by bird shit. Which one of them shot the pigeons nesting in the telescope?

(50 points)

One morning just before the equinox, when day and night were almost equally balanced, they lay parallel on the bed, tracing the edges of each other's bodies. Jeanette dared to ask, 'Will you email me from the South Pole?'

The woman didn't reply.

Now the nights were taking over the days. Jeanette climbed the stairs, knowing the woman's office would be empty. But it was a good place to sleep, and her supervisor wouldn't look for her there. She wandered over to the chair and sat staring at the blank screen. She reached out and jiggled the mouse, bringing the screen back to life. She looked closer, there was an email:

Darling, have missed you so much this summer. Can't wait to see you again.

That night, Jeanette pretended to fall asleep straight away. The woman was sprawled in the middle of the bed, snoring gently. Jeanette opened her eyes and stared into the darkness, as thick as black coffee, for the rest of the night.

4) Draw a Minkowski space-time diagram. Now plot on it the precise points showing when and where you first met your ex-lover, slept with her and then cried yourself to sleep over her.

(1 point)

A few days later, the woman gave a seminar. It was the last week of her stay in Edinburgh. Jeanette arrived late at the lecture theatre and had to squeeze into one of the few remaining seats.

The woman started talking about her last balloon experiment, two years before. Jeanette didn't know about this previous experiment. She'd only been told about the future one. But here, in front of everyone else, the woman talked about the balloon lurching out of the sky and tumbling to the ground. She showed a photo of the balloon's skin slumped on the ice. It reminded Jeanette of crumpled bed sheets. The data collected during the balloon's flight was lost somewhere in the vast expanse of the Antarctic, and would never be found. The audience sighed as the woman told them that years of work had depended on this one short flight.

Jeanette's eyes filled. She looked down and a tear splashed onto her left shoe, exploding into dark water. She waited until the spot faded away before she dared look up again.

The woman left. It took some time before Jeanette started to sleep better.

Perfection, extract from the novel *Lost Bodies*
David Manderson

SLIDING SHADOWS ON metal and glass. Touch of hot metal, the wind flicking his rolled-up cuff.

Over the junction, through the traffic, up the flyover. Blast of air on the side of his face.

The roads quiet. The river, the city spread out. Cranes and warehouses to the east. The new bridge with its arch. Tower blocks, hotels.

Tyres moaning over a grid, his indicator clicking. Pumping the brake, slowing, letting the slip road take the edge off it. The sun lancing in the windscreen.

The south side: like a foreign country. Looping roads, derelict buildings. Hardly any traffic. Glints of steel and glass from what few cars there were moving in the distance. It went like this when there was a match on. A ghost city.

A railway bridge, cash and carry warehouses, a pub like a box standing on its own. The main road cutting a swathe through everything. New schemes going up, old ones coming down. Road signs for places he'd only heard of. Turning his head looking for landmarks. It had to be this way, into the sun. Stick to the major roads, see if they brought something back, jogged his memory.

Just the Sunday before last when he'd come over this way, two weeks ago yesterday – but it felt like years. Every day since then searching the papers for news, getting more and more jumpy.

He hadn't planned it, hadn't set out for anywhere, just parked in a city centre multi-storey and jumped on the first bus that came. The best plan to have no plan, go for it when the chance came. He'd sat up front on the top deck, heading over the river, through the waste of the old Gorbals and then along this way, looking out the windows for a likely-looking place. He'd felt like he'd gone for miles. And then he'd seen it, a line of railings. A gleam of water, tree-covered slopes.

Never try the same place twice, and never go back: rules he'd made for himself. He hadn't known then he'd have no choice.

The car bonnet steady, a solid sheet of metal sticking out, the engine almost silent. One of the things about these old Rovers, the way the engines ticked over so quietly you could hardly hear them. The tyres making a wet sound on the newly-laid surface. Shells of new buildings beside derelict ones.

His stomach churning. More tenements: fabric shops, boxes of vegetables and fruit out on the pavement, charity stores. Women in veils, long dresses over trousers.

A touch on the wheel, on the pedals. Turning his head, using the mirrors. That pub with blue-painted walls and gold lettering – he'd seen that from the top of the bus a fortnight ago, he was sure of it, its carved doorway and dark frosted windows... but even if it was the same place, he might be going past it in a different—

Humped-up tenements on the right. A dome at the cross ahead. An open area opening out on his left. He leaned over the wheel, steered into the bus and taxi lane, scanning it as he went past.

The long stretch of pavement, the railings with spikes along their tops, joined with a collar at their necks. The flat pond and the green flanks of hills, the bushes and trees going up them.

He stood looking up and down the street. Rubbing his nose, breathing into his hand, standing there a moment. Walked round to the back of the car, opened the boot, and took out his blazer.

He shrugged it on, jerking his shoulders. Slammed down the boot. Stood for another second with his hand on the hot metal then went round to the passenger door. The sunglasses in the glove compartment, with the mirror lenses. He unfolded the legs, fitted them over his nose.

His heart beating.

Walking back the way he'd driven. A narrow tenement street with a double row of parked cars, nobody on it. The vehicles with their tyres up on the pavement, just space enough down the middle for traffic to squeeze through.

He'd walk right past the place if there was any sign of trouble, or too many people.

He went over the road, headed up to the cross. So quiet. This place would be packed later. There was a nearer entrance to the park this way, behind a grand-looking building, but he'd go on to the next one, the gate he'd used the last time, to keep things the same as then, duplicate them.

This was the way he'd come that day, past the cross with its four facing roads, past the five-a-side courts and the old toilet with the banked-up bushes behind it. He'd stood at this pedestrian crossing waiting for the green man, not knowing what was going to happen, but knowing that something was, his heart pounding, shaking through him, and at the very second he'd been about to cross, at that exact instant she'd come out of one of the streets on this side, and hurried over the road in front of him. A small, youngish, dark-haired woman in a dark skirt and a white top, one hand up at her shoulder holding a bag-strap, walking quickly in high-heeled shoes with white straps, going in surges, taking a few quick steps and breaking into a trot, then slowing to a walk again, as if she was late for wherever she had to get to.

Her top had a collar, a stitched pattern down the front. She'd had a short black jacket over her arm. Her chestnut hair had been cut in a bob, darker at the back of her neck than on top. It hadn't been so close then – fresher, just at the start of the heat-wave – but he could see how hot she was.

All the way down this road, trotting, walking, half-running – where'd she been going? He'd wondered about that then and the whole two weeks since. Out of the city? But she'd only been carrying that small shoulder-bag. She kept glancing at her watch, a flash of gold, trying to do too many things at once, running and trying to think about her route, heading along the line of railings stuck in their concrete mound, sometimes glancing round as if she sensed something. But she hadn't noticed him, not the whole way along here. The street had been busier that day. It could've been anyone. She'd stopped only once, at the end of this long part, by the park gates, and looked back – he'd changed the line of his walk, looked away from her.

She'd turned into the park, a short-cut to wherever it was. It'd been easy for him to keep up.

This was where she'd gone in and he'd followed, the heat radiating off these railings at the end of the road, dust swirling in circles on the open part by the entrance, between these wrought-iron gates pushed back, the black cast-iron flaps made to look like curling leaves between the bars, fifty yards or so behind her, and his heart had been in his mouth. He could feel it beating through every part of him.

She'd gone past this still sheet of water. Towards the winding paths. Past the terrace of smashed greenhouses behind rhododendrons. The air heavy with the noise of traffic from the junction, but fainter. Limp sunlight. Almost no-one about. Children's swings: tyres on chains, slides and walkways built like fire-engines.

His blood beating in his chest and arms and legs that day, he'd felt like a furnace – but today he felt hollow, paper-light, his arms and legs like stalks, all the way down to his fingers.

Two full weeks and surely *something*

➸

should've happened? One half of the path curled away to the open park, the other towards the pond. He was walking towards the water. A few people up on the hill, flat out on towels. Bare feet and chests, rolled-up jeans, skinny city pallor. The stillness that fell during a big game. Later there'd be the hangover, the bars full, the slopes crowded, everybody keeping out the shadows.

A boy squatting next to the pond, staring into it. A fat-bellied man with a poodle on a long lead, his hand up, wrist cocked. Past them. The sweat rolling out of him. Not a breath of wind. Burn in his throat, clench in his balls.

Sunken rubbish and coils of weed. A mat of twigs and rubbish in one corner. Sweat on his cheeks. He pushed a knuckle up under the glasses. Smeary wet feeling. Don't pause to take off the jacket. A man strolling, no one to remember.

He moved towards bushes, the path going behind a half-burnt shed. Dark stones worn smooth, shiny, leading down. This was the way she'd come – she must've known the path was here, used it before.

He stopped on the hidden stretch. Blood-roar in his ears, listening for anything – a scrape, a crack. Darkness under the trees. His skin crawling.

The path going down, a hedge on one side, a slope on the other. His foot kicked a loose stone. He stopped, listened, went on again. Rubbish among the tall grass, stuck in the hedges – everything browner now than before, more burnt. His mouth dry, full of the taste of copper.

What was he scared of? Whistles? Dogs? The bushes full of uniforms? They'd never be allowed to, there would be an outcry – but *somebody* would've come this way since that day, stepped off the path and—

The track bent round a bush. Here was the old derelict house, some kind of lodge or maybe a gate-house, the bushes growing right up to it, its windows boarded up. The path, angled bricks marking its edges, leading round it. Patches of sunken gravel, the trees a canopy on both sides, above. A greenhouse tilted against the old stonework. The track dipping down by the side of a wall. He stopped again. Ahead of him the slit-shaped gap in the trees at the end. He couldn't look at it.

A gate in the hedge on his left, something he hadn't noticed last time. He looked at it, tense – some sort of trick? Ridiculous, it was just a gate. Long iron bars, with black paint splitting in cracks, open red seams. Red flakes of rust and trodden-in bits of glass on the ground.

Some kind of old laid-out garden in there, overgrown and neglected. A bin on a post just inside the gate, rubbish spilling from it. His heart thudding.

Almost silent, the air dead, grey between black trunks. Only the thinnest noise of traffic, and another behind it, further off: children in a playground.

He scuffed his foot on the moss, a slithering sound, to make a noise, break the silence. His face, palms and back wet with sweat. The sunglasses slipping down his nose. Opening his mouth, breathing in shallow pockets.

It'd gone like clockwork, not a single thing he hadn't thought about. Except one, a tiny noise, out of place, meaningless, like a finger click. The knife, the broken bit of steel. He hadn't even thought about it at the time – that cheap light metal he'd never liked, snapped in two halfway down the blade – he must've trodden on it.

Another step. Shaking badly on the outside now. Inside too. He could almost see through the arch. His face was dripping off him. He'd found the mattress in the bushes nearby, filthy and ripped and full of rat-holes, dragged it out afterwards. Two more steps.

His body heavy and numb like it was made of lead, the sweat trickling down his back, his legs. Even his eyes sweating. The slit, the thin trees bent in their middle, the darkness, he was right in front of it. He couldn't bear to move. Like he was cast in bronze, solid joints that would crack. He put his hands out, pulled the branches back.

She'd changed. Still on her back, in the same position, one arm out, the hand curled up, the other across her stomach. He'd hauled the mattress up and jumped back with a shout, expecting something, a shock of something, he didn't know what. But not this.

The way she'd changed and stayed the same, her body on the leaves and churned earth, separate from it, but marked by it. She'd swelled like beef, almost black, unrecognisable – but it was her, the same person, different and identical.

Something had been at her face. Some of it was gone – but nothing horrifying about it: you could still see, turned sideways, the delicate profile, the shape of the nose, the line of the cheek. So simple and human lying there, her sides and flanks on the crushed brown grass, her skin laced with earth. She didn't seem naked. Her toes pointing up and slightly forward, her legs a little apart. But protected somehow. Clothed in bareness.

She still had something on, the remains of the top with the collar twisted up round her neck. It looked like a bandage, the way it had pulled and thinned over her left side, stuck to something discoloured. He stood over her, breathing through his mouth, looking at the neck and face, not lower down at the mess. Her lying there, him standing over her. Something ancient about it, something right. Nothing to be afraid of. Things starting to grow around her, tips of new grass starting to show through the earth, clumps of green fern.

He started to move around her, looking at the ground. This strip of rough ground between the path and the park railings, cut off by dense walls of saplings, so close together you couldn't see in, couldn't tell the place was here unless you were in it. Kicking the stems of taller plants apart. He hadn't realised the place was so overgrown. He'd thought it was a clearing, an open space, but now it seemed like there was cover everywhere. Less than three thin inches of steel, it could be anywhere. They might've moved it, him and her, after it broke, trodden on it, shoved it deep, or kicked it into the undergrowth.

Moving out in wider circles, trying to be methodical. The place was so big. This was useless. He stopped, straightened his back, looked round. Started to walk stooped, his hands trailing the ground, fingers sifting the clots of fern, the leaf-mould. The heat trapped in here under the hanging trees. The rotting fern-smell, and that other smell from where she lay. The feel of the dirt under his nails. He was right down at the bushes now, where he'd dragged the mattress from.

Totally fucking – he ripped up a long frond of fern, pushed his finger and thumb along it, stripping it. The sweat rolling off him. Breathing in shallowly through his mouth. Grainy stuff under his shirt, in his eyes, his nostrils – the kind of muck he couldn't stand. He threw away the stalk, went back up the slope. The lines of her jaw, her collar-bone, her hips. The sweet smell seeping in through his mouth. He stood over her.

La casa dei doganieri
Eugenio Montale

Tu non ricordi la casa dei doganieri
sul rialzo a strapiombo sulla scogliera:
desolata t'attende dalla sera
in cui v'entrò lo sciame dei tuoi pensieri
e vi sostò irrequieto.

Libeccio sferza da anni le vecchie mura
e il suono del tuo riso non è più lieto:
la bussola va impazzita all'avventura
e il calcolo dei dadi più non torna.
Tu non ricordi; altro tempo frastorna
la tua memoria; un filo s'addipana.

Ne tengo un capo; ma s'allontana
la casa e in cima al tetto la banderuola
affumicata gira senza pietà.
Ne tengo un capo; ma tu resti sola
né qui respiri nell'oscurità.

Oh l'orizzonte in fuga, dove s'accende
rara la luce della petroliera!
Il varco è qui? (Ripullula il frangente
ancora sulla balza che scoscende...).
Tu non ricordi la casa di questa
mia sera. Ed io non so chi va e chi resta.

The Customs House

Translated from the Italian by

Allan Cameron

Do you recall the customs house,
high on the cliff above the rocks and sea:
lonely, it has awaited your return from that evening
in which your thoughts swarmed in
and restless lingered there.

The salted wind whips against the ancient walls
and your laughter no longer carries carefreeness:
the compass spins and madness calls,
no longer do the dice then add
to a figure where they fall.
You remember not; other times divert,
disturb the unravelling thread of recollection.

I hold the other end; the house moves far away
and on the roof the blackened weathercock
spins in restless disregard.
I hold the other end, but you are alone
nor do I feel your breath within the dark.

Ah, the horizon is in flight to where
the occasional light of a tanker
drills the hard cover of night air.
The breach is here? (the teeming froth
breaks upon the ragged wall of cliff...)
You remember not my evening's house nor the day's.
I do not understand who goes and who stays.

L'agave sullo scoglio. Lo scirocco

Eugenio Montale

O rabido ventare di scirocco
che l'arsiccio terreno gialloverde
bruci;
e su nel cielo pieno di smorte luci
trapassa qualche biocco
di nuvola, e si perde.
Ore perplesse, brividi
d'una vita che fugge
come acqua tra le dita;
inafferrati eventi,
luci-ombre, commovimenti
delle cose malferme della terra;
oh alide ali dell'aria
ora sono io
l'agave che s'abbarbica al crepaccio
dello scoglio
e sfugge al mare da le braccia d'alghe
che spalanca ampie gole e abbranca rocce;
e nel fermento
d'ogni essenza, coi miei racchiusi bocci
che non sanno più esplodere oggi sento
la mia immobilità come un tormento.

The Agave

Translated from the Italian by

Allan Cameron

The wind of the desert gusts
and cruel burns the jaundiced earth;
in the sky of fading lights there pass
some tufts of cloud,
and then they're lost.
Enigmatic hours, shudders
of a life that slips
like water through the hands,
ungraspable events ungrasped,
light and shadow, movements of the unsettled
objects of this earth that move the soul;
oh the dry wings of the air,
now I am the agave whose roots
reach into the riven rocks,
I slip from the sea's embrace
of sodden seaweed, clammy
it encloses jagged points,
then fast reveals deep narrow shafts.
And in this turmoil
of every being, my buds unable
to release their load, close tight,
today my static state torments me.

Out Of Magma, The Moon: A Witness
Alexander Hutchison

Early that evening
as soon as I stepped
out, I saw a little
patch of peach and rose-
coloured light spilling
on the snow of the mountain's
sloping ridge. I had
my coat and scarf, but
not the new *coppóla*
bought next day
in the *fiera all'aperto*
of nearby Randazzo.

Bareheaded in the chill
I leaned back in
along the wall and let
the wind blow by.
Though the mountain any
time is still composed
of ruinous fire, this
was no vented flame.
It was the moon.

It was the moon: not
reflecting from a cloud
but gradually rising
slowly like something
flowing from a forge
in a nimbus of silvery
rouge: something made
new like skin and flesh—
misshapen, yellowish
pale *mandarino*—
echo of fruit and fire.

Within three minutes
or four or so it had
assumed more usual
form (rounded, white
blue-silver) this
night beyond the full.
No one else to see,
to tell, to point, to say.

But the white quick cat
with ginger-spotted coat
stepped out from a hedge
quick, quick, quick
across the cooling crust.

Snakes, abductions, golden
days and *suino nero*
make our stories rise
and flow, give bite
to life. But listen.
Each night the moon
charged with pale blood
rises from a fumarole
on Etna's fiery flank—
out of the earth's deep
fissured core, I swear—
there '*from out the dark
door of the secret earth*'.
And the wound is
healed straightaway.

Secure that cat
and it will tell you.
Just as I have
told you now.

Blustered
Nalini Paul

The evening's in a foul mood.
Spirits blow from across the sound,
howl in the hollows
of dry stone walls

with memories of countries
on landscape paper,
borders scribbled in blue pencil crayon
a fall-off-the-earth edge
before water.

The path twists rock-hard, Achilles-swift.

At the bending crest,
rain stretches like washing on the line
from Hoy to the Black Craig.

The landscape invites from a safe distance only.

Wind lashes my face:
I'm a martyr, of sorts,
trudging through mud that shines
in fading lilac light

until gravestones cut the sky
and the sea brings life
so close to death;
the two sit comfortably together
as polar opposites would
where day refuses to die
and shines in waves too animated
for words

until the darkness of country roads
and lapwings electrifying the night
take flight
before the silence

and the window glow of houses,
standing still.

Six St Kilda Poems
Donald S Murray

ST KILDA – APOCALYPSE

After his retirement, Alexander showed
signs of how his early years on the island
had affected him. He would spend days
at the town's infill site, seeing gulls skirl
above debris. Sometimes, he'd watch a
DVD of Hitchcock's *The Birds,* smiling as
wings smashed windows and windscreens,
terrifying school-children with their swoop.

'The day is coming,' he'd say.

But what horrified his wife most was the
morning she opened the freezer. Seabirds,
wrapped in plastic, were stacked upon its
shelves. Icy beaks and heads glittered.
Frozen feathers sparkled.

'Best to be prepared,' he explained.

ST KILDAN FLIGHT

Marissa thought Domhnall was no longer
eating because Gormel had been whisked
away by a great skua while her two children
played in Village Bay.

'It's grief,' she said, 'sorrow.'

He was refusing food he normally gorged
upon, his round features becoming hollow.
She frowned, thinking of how the bird passed
over Domhnall that afternoon, choosing his
smaller sister for prey.

'A terrible ordeal...'

But then came the morning the skua
returned, its wings hovering over the now
slender, spindly boy before lifting him high.

'Great!' Domhnall shouted. 'The bird can
manage me now!'

→

LOVE?

'Dare you climb the Mistress Stone,' Judith said arriving in Village Bay. 'Prove how much you care.'

He laughed at his wild, fair-headed companion, so unlike the grim, Presbyterian family from which she came.

'We'll see...'

But when he reached that rock and saw how it framed sea and sky, he faltered. He was supposed to tip-toe on a ledge to show he wished to marry her – a dizzy, precarious place.

'Go on,' she prompted.

He looked towards her, seeing for once her mother's stern jaw, her father's unflinching gaze.

'No,' he said.

A ST KILDAN SEES A PLANE

It thirsts for oil
it hoards within
a skeleton of iron
before stirring into movement,

the instant wing-feathers whirl and revolve
and the long cry of its mating call
skirls out across abandoned fields
following a dark path

like the one
the solan goose
might etch out on a wave
its wings have smashed and splintered,

after swallowing those
who once shoaled towards it,
now tucked below the plumage
of its breast,

and we watch it hoisted higher
than those cliffs
our sea-birds used to orbit,
taking flights as far-flung

as the albatross
that once tumbled down
to visit us
on shores that we called home.

THE DEATH OF THE LAST GREAT AUK

(The last Great Auk ever found in Britain was killed by St Kildans who believed its witchcraft to be responsible for a particularly violent storm that struck the island.)

And so we descended on it
– that strange bird –
and cried it for a witch:

As if its flightless wings
could summon up
the strength for storms;

As if head and beak could break
clouds free of their ledges
and bring rain tumbling
like eggs
shelled and shattered on these rocks.

A mistake, of course,
and when the flap was over
we looked down
into that great bird's sightless eyes,

Where could be read
our future –
black as nightfall,
boat slipping away in darkness
as it carried
the remnants of our race.

ST KILDAN AT EDINBURGH ZOO

When he steps near the aviary, he wonders
at the scarlet ibis, Eurasian eagle owl,
delights in the kookaburra,
crowned crane, vulturine guinea-fowl,
the rock-hopper penguins, too, which he compares
to seabirds flicking plumage dry on boulders
near his old home, stretching wings like feather boas
wrapped coquettishly round their bare shoulders.

He also longs to set them free,
see sirocco doves flap high above
their cage, the black stork mingle with the business-crowd
stepping out to work. Yet most of all he'd love
to see these rainbow lorikeets claim for their own
each window-ledge and roof-top on these streets
and summon him to breakfast with the songs he's missed,
a symphony accompanied by a chorus
of bright and luminous wing-beats.

Mystery shopper report, with conclusions

Richard W Strachan

Abstract

To assume the guise of an 'ordinary' shopper, and, through a series of pre-determined scenarios, test the training and sales competence of various retail establishments and their staff. Extrapolating from this, the same approach is then used in a 'real-world' encounter, with the data subjected to a comparative analysis[1].

#1 Retail

The first case study was researched and undertaken at an 'average' high street retail establishment[2]. The author attempted to purchase an item of the establishment's basic stock, through the intercession of a sales assistant[3].

In this instance, the author decided not to approach the staff directly, but to determine if their training was such that they would recognise a potential customer in a state of confusion and spontaneously offer assistance. To this end, the author adopted what he considered was an appropriate expression[4], and wandered vaguely between the four points of the shop floor, staring, mumbling etc. The author picked up items, examined them as if unsure what purpose they could possibly have, then replaced them. Shop staff, gathered around a sales point, at first seemed more concerned with their conversation, detailing unsavoury aspects of their social and sexual lives, punctuating each anecdote with much raucous laughter[5]. Enhancing his performance, the author soon became convinced that the staff members were studiously ignoring him. The author decided to employ the 'Brusque' manner of address, as outlined above [see note 3]. The response garnered by this can only be described as nakedly impertinent, and needless to say after a series of reciprocal exchanges, the author was summarily asked to leave the establishment minus what he had entered it for,

1 Undertaken without commission; data has been collated on the author's own initiative. Objectivity has been retained, but this has also resulted in a considerable and unremunerated outlay of funds. Passim. Invoice for funds to be submitted at a later date to the appropriate companies.

2 'Average' calculated in this case through a formula of the author's own devising, taking into consideration median cost of products and relative position on the high street, the location of nearby train/transport hubs, fast food outlets, and weighted by average earnings etc. This pre-case study research was to have been appended to the report, but as it took a considerable amount of the author's time and money to collate, the appendix, to do it any kind of justice, would have run to many tens of pages and would have significantly outnumbered in terms of pagination the report itself. In addition, field work within this retail establishment, surreptitious note-taking, tasting, and so on, deflecting challenges of staff etc, should be taken into consideration when drawing conclusions from the case study and from the report as a whole.

3 The styles in which a sales assistant can be hailed vary. Examples: (Brusque) 'You there!' (Obsequious) 'Excuse me – sorry – I was wondering if you wouldn't mind helping me find something?' (Businesslike) 'Excuse me? I'm looking for [insert as appropriate]'

4 Bemused, open-mouthed, etc. Confusion is most effectively conveyed if accompanied by a smile.

5 This seems to be an occupational hazard for businesses that persist in hiring younger people for their staff, and where those businesses serially reject applications from more experienced individuals, rack and ruin can surely only follow. Is it any wonder that for those blessed with or fortunate enough to have access to an 'internet' connection, the prospect of purchasing goods online is more favourable to them than taking their chances with rude and obstructionist staff?

to wit: the basic item of stock.

Conclusion

Staff in this establishment are only prepared to treat potential customers 'pleasantly' if customer adheres to certain societal norms[6].

In this case, therefore, the philosophy of the 'customer is always right' is dependent on other conditions, and based primarily on a perceived ability to pay.

#2 Wholesale

Some companies operating on a wholesale rather than a retail basis still require detailed investigation of their branches and staff in order to ensure that branches/staff adhere to company regulations in terms of quality, service, etc. The author picked a large regional wholesale chain, focusing on a branch in an industrial estate on the outskirts of a major urban conurbation[7]. Funding by this stage had become an intractable issue, so the author decided to challenge the basic security arrangements in place, rather than the chain's customer service.

Entering the wholesale establishment, the author proceeded not to the aisle where alcoholic drink was stored, observing that this area, as it was no doubt subject to attempted theft most often, was patrolled by a security guard[8]. Instead, the author picked an aisle relatively obscured from the till/payment area, in this instance the aisle where bathroom/kitchen items were stored. With stock sold only in bulk, it was not possible for the author to conceal individual items on his person. On consideration, the author decided that his best course of action was to attempt to leave the premises while carrying a box of items (in this case, a bulk purchase of prophylactics), exchanging furtiveness for brazen unconcern[9]. The author was not overly surprised to be stopped before he was able to reach his parked car, but puzzled that it had taken staff quite so long to notice the deception. However, he was not expecting the level of unprofessionalism displayed by the staff members who had pursued him into the parking area. The author defused the situation through a firm explanation of his purpose, showing relevant identification, and congratulating staff on their robust response. Releasing him, after heated debate, the assorted staff members[10] told him in no uncertain terms that he should remove himself from the firm's property and should demonstrate a reluctance to return at any future date. The author complied, expressing thanks and gratitude. The author then retired to his parked car.

Leaving the parking area, the author passed by the loading bay area of the establishment, observing that the security shutters were open, and that several items of stock were on full display, apparently unguarded. Reasoning that the establishment's management would appreciate further testing of their security arrangements, the author parked by the loading bay area and rapidly filled the boot of his car

6 Eye contact, basic personal hygiene, coherent speech etc.

7 An aside; most wholesalers seem to operate in areas of the most extreme urban degeneration. In this instance, the author was forced to walk through a car-park littered with used prophylactics and broken glass, and in the furthest corner observed some extremely furtive men who were, for some reason, blowing thin vaporous smoke through plastic bottles and drinks cans.

8 The wholesalers, in common with most establishments of this nature, had evidently banked on the mere presence of the guard in his ill-fitting uniform as a suitable deterrent to attempted theft, rather than the guard's physical alertness, physical presence, age, fitness, build etc. (Aside: in this sense, most companies that deal with the sale of goods and the potential of these goods to be stolen, have a touching and perhaps semi-mystical faith in the power of symbols to guide and moderate behaviour. Possibly a fruitful area for further research.)

9 Observation has confirmed that this is the style most often employed by the more successful shoplifter.

10 In addition to the elderly security guard, who brought up the rear, it appeared that the majority of the branch's staff had come out to apprehend the author. On reflection, their excitable disposition was probably a side-effect of the relative tedium of their day-to-day occupations. The author was aware, when apprehended by the staff members, that the branch was fairly isolated, and that coupled with the staff members' bellicose frame of mind, the author was momentarily in a state of possible danger, viz. his personal safety at the hands of those who had apprehended him.

with stock items. These included alcoholic drink, tins of meat products, and several boxes of household cleaners. The author then drove away from the establishment, leaving the industrial estate, and proceeded home. The author will forward on a copy of this report to the establishment, FAO the manager, with an explanatory letter, and will await further instructions re: the return of the stock items. An invoice will also be presented for the reimbursement of unforeseen expenditure[11].

Conclusions

Possible correlation between the relatively isolated location of the wholesale establishment compared to the high street retail establishment, and the vigorousness of their response?

Response wholly disproportionate to the 'crime', but must take into account deterrent value of this for repeat offenders.

#3 Real World

The author determined that, after the examination of retail and wholesale standards, it would be no great leap to submit 'real-world' standards to the same type of examination[12], due to the prevailing employment model[13] currently ascendent in this country. To this end, the author chose the pursuit in which relationships of power, transaction and negotiation are most prevalent, although generally subterranean; to wit, the attempted seduction of a member of the opposite sex.

Deciding against any venue[14] specifically tailored for this purpose, the author instead chose to undertake his experiment in a neutral location[15], relying on the favourable examples witnessed in most television programmes aimed at a broad-based demographic[16], and believing that the potential recipients of his attention would, through prolonged exposure[17], be well versed in the grammar and style of such encounters and therefore more amenable.

Financial issues[18] rendered trains and coffee shops out of bounds for the purposes of the experiment; supermarkets and bookshops appeared to encourage browsing to a degree, but, as the author had experienced elsewhere[19], supermarkets not indefinitely.

A bookshop seemed the most profitable venue for the experiment; not only was browsing positively encouraged, but the imaginative level of the member of the opposite sex to be potentially approached would be higher in this environment; the exalted and transformative nature that the author has been led to believe Literature possesses would render the recipient of the author's attention less judgemental, more open minded to differences in conventional appearance, hygiene, and so on, and less likely to raise the issue with the authorities if the author's attention was not appreciated. The author picked a large branch of a major national chain and made initial observations.

At first the author felt he blended in well with the median customer – of a certain age, dressed plainly, male, unconcerned with the censorious glances of various staff members

11 Expenditure included plasters, antiseptic cream, dry cleaning bill for jacket/trousers, and minor repairs to lining of hat.

12 Increasingly, in the author's observation, "real-world relationships" are subject to the same transactional nature as retail and wholesale relationships. The industry of the real operates according to the same rules as the service industry, and, as Thomas Carlyle noted (the author could not find the correct reference for this, public libraries being what they are – see "Libraries and the decline of public decency" report, with conclusions) human relations cannot and should not be governed solely by the notion or virtue of "cash payment".

13 With a negligible manufacturing base and an economy based mostly on credit, retail is not just the symbol but also the actuality of the economic structure. Aside: If the majority of people in this country work in some capacity within the service industry, what effect does this have on public standards? A prolonged relationship of this nature, where servitude breeds contempt in the server and arrogance in the served, can only have the most detrimental influence on the population, which would explain the welter of rudeness and discontent that the author has seen unashamedly displayed, and would not feel it an exaggeration to describe himself the victim of, on many, many occasions.

14 Convention guides this pursuit into specific areas of social interaction – public houses, 'nightspots', discotheques, and so on – areas which have in common the ready supply of alcoholic drink. Alcohol appears to be used as a means of removing the barriers of inhibition, embarrassment, shame, etc.

etc. Most of these customers had gravitated to an area of the shop secluded from general sight, where the shelves were stocked mainly with texts that formed part of the 'erotica' genre. The author joined them, but soon left after being challenged[20] by another customer. Wandering between floors and pausing at various sections, the author before too long observed a girl browsing the shelves and tables at one particular section who gave every appearance of being open, imaginative, unbiased, and so on. She was also in no particular hurry, possibly occupying her time on a 'lunch hour'. Moving rapidly and with animation between the tables, the girl seemed enthusiastic and pleased at the range of books on display. As the temperature outside was characteristic of the season, she was wearing shorts that revealed a significant portion of her lower limbs, and a plain t-shirt. The author also took this immodest level of dress as an indication that the girl was not unwilling to countenance an approach from members of the opposite sex.

After the surreptitious taking of notes and photographs for the report, the author made his approach to the girl, but had got no further than the initial, casual laying of a hand on her shoulder in order to effect an introduction, when several members of the shop and security staff, as well as the girl's mother and father, physically intervened. The girl was by this point crying, possibly at the ungentle treatment being meted out to the author, and was being calmed by the mother through the application of toys, colourful books, etc. Apparently the author had been under observation since entering the establishment. Aspersions were liberally cast by the shop and security staff on the author's sexual proclivities, and the author overheard frequent claims that some form of capital punishment would in fact be too lenient a measure for 'the likes of him'. The author was taken through to a secure location in the back-room area of the shop, where he sits now compiling this report and awaiting the arrival of the police.

Conclusions

Very difficult to make any specific conclusions about this experiment, as it was interrupted in no uncertain measure before it could be properly undertaken. Suffice to say that it is not as effortless as it is made to look on television.

Report Conclusions

Retail, wholesale and 'real-world' areas are governed by certain rules and conventions in terms of the transactional relationship between staff, customers, and other members of the public. These rules can often seem opaque to the uninitiated, which puts them at an immediate disadvantage when negotiating these conventions, and this can frequently result in substantially unpleasant scenes, with an attendant risk to physical health, bank balance, criminal record, etc.

In retail, the relationship is one of

[15] Bookshops, coffee shops, supermarkets, and train compartments seem to be the most common locales for this sort of encounter.

[16] 'Soaps', early-evening terrestrial 'situation' comedies.

[17] See note 12 regarding condition of libraries etc. With the lack of alternatives, television provides the most widespread form of culture available. Noting also the prevalence of advertising on most channels, correspondences can be drawn with general report thesis, i.e.: broadly transactional nature of interpersonal and social relationships.

[18] See above, passim.

[19] See report "The contrast between supermarket advertising and the experience on the ground", with conclusions.

[20] Or possibly propositioned.

'cash-payment', where the ability to pay for one's purchase appears to trump all other considerations, but where the much-vaunted phrase 'the customer is always right' is exposed as less than comprehensive when the customer does not adhere to societal norms.

In wholesale, the system is broadly the same as in retail, but with less pleasant physical surroundings, and a franker style in interpersonal dealings between staff and customers. It could be tentatively posited then that the more you buy, in terms of bulk, the less valued you are on a personal level. Formula – buy less, and be treated better?

Conventions in the 'real-world', such as they are, seem too malleable and shift too easily, and it has not been possible to come to any firm conclusions about them. As the author finishes his report, to be filed with the others, he is informed that the police have now arrived. He fervently hopes that they will be able to explain aspects of the 'real-world' to him.

Bags I Go First...

Vivien Jones

ABOUT MIDDAY THE sun broke through. By one o'clock the lawn was dry enough to send the little boys out to play. Even though he was a head smaller than Ollie, Jimmy took the lead. Through the window their mothers could see Jimmy's arms directing operations and Ollie rushing back and forth from the play room to the sandpit where Jimmy presided. Jimmy's mother clucked her tongue and shook her head.

'He's so bossy!' she said, not without fondness.

'Ollie's very accommodating.' Ollie's mother responded. 'Very popular at playgroup. Always helping.'

'The thing is, Jimmy's so quick, he's always there before the others.'

'Ollie thinks about things.'

'You have to have leaders though. Even at playgroup.'

'Nature will out. That's true.'

The mothers made sandwiches and came back to the window. By then the little boys had made a kingdom around the old rhododendrons. Jimmy was strafing the sky with an old rolling pin, wearing a cloak of old blanket and a fireman's helmet while Ollie patrolled the perimeter armed with a red plastic hammer.

'Does Jimmy ever play with girls?'

'There aren't any in our street.'

'Ollie has a bit of a fan club at playgroup. He's so gentle. They like that.'

'Bit soft, do you mean?'

'As opposed to?'

'Well, proper boys.'

The little boys became bored and tired and hungry and abandoned their kingdom and came to look for their mothers. Finding them engaged in a shrieking fist fight in the living room, they watched for a while then Ollie picked up a plate of sandwiches and offered it to Jimmy.

'Your mum's a wimp.' Jimmy said, taking a sandwich.

'Yours is a bully.' Ollie responded, stuffing one too.

For a moment they stood looking at the two dishevelled, sweating women.

Then the little boys went to the playroom and worked some more on a 1000 piece jigsaw they had started earlier.

I Am Not My Body

Allan Cameron

(with apologies to William Makepiece Thackeray and to the readers for retaining his Pumpernickels and silly surnames)

Maeve King has the sad face of a spaniel, as her slightly swollen jowls sag under a hidden weight. Her body too appears unequal to the struggle against gravity. Her head and slim shoulders are the point of a triangle whose base is her wide hips, standing on the other smaller and inverted triangle of her heavy thighs running down her short legs to her dainty feet. And you, my reader, have already dismissed her – have you not? – in spite of all your 'politically correct'. You would never call her a 'dumpling', 'hefty' or, good heavens, a 'lump of lard', but with all the delicacy of your class – you are middle-class, aren't you? we are all middle-class now that the Thatcherites in both parties have declared the working class no longer to exist – you might suggest a better diet and the odd work-out at the gym. There is no real excuse for being fat. Obesity is an optional condition, we are told. Surely we can all make the effort? Why were we put into this world, if not to look after our bodies – to ensure their enduring attraction and longevity, no matter how many pots and potions it takes, how many trainers and track suits always shiny new and how many days lost in sweaty activities we detest or in thumbing through glossy mags in search of the latest advice.

You think she looks a fool and cannot keep on top of life. Well then, you have made the same mistake as many others. Take another look. Maeve's piercing eyes express a real intelligence and energy. Those who believe success to be associated with such virtues most likely fail to notice them, because of Maeve's timidity and reticence.

That was Ms King when she started to teach German literature at Southdown University, an oasis of learning, tolerance, good manners and the occasional sit-in, situated in a pleasant, affluent but rather uncultured county. She did not work out, it's true, but she did work (the foolish girl). Her young colleagues in the department were two ambitious men with Scottish names and pronounced English regional accents: Harvey McBride and Cameron Murray. McBride was permanently outraged over many things big and small: from the lack of appreciation afforded some minor women writers of Pumpernickel in the eighteenth century to the lack of appreciation afforded himself after having made his discovery of them. Indeed his outrage in a world of wars and starvation appears to have pivoted around a peculiar mismatch between the objects he most appreciated and those appreciated by almost everybody who stubbornly persisted in their ignorance after he had produced more than three kilos of learned articles. Nevertheless the head of department was happy enough with the research points.

McBride was also considerably aggrieved that the human generality failed to appreciate his selfless parenting: when the train pulled into the university station one morning and he had to button up the coats on his small herd of toddlers, he lectured the impatient students who wanted to get off and did so by addressing his prodigious progeny in the following terms: 'You see these people, they're always in a hurry; no time for anyone but themselves. But we don't have to be rushed. No one can make us rush. No one. You might well ask why they're in such a hurry. Their classes? I don't think so.' The guard was now moving down the train and slamming any unclosed doors as he went. The surprisingly numerous offspring for so young a man stared at their father uncomprehendingly, but the students understood well enough. In part they felt impatient and in part resigned to going to the next station, where they would have to take a train back in the opposite direction. The departure whistle was surely imminent and the whole scene had something theatrical about it. All things considered, this was more amusing than the average morning journey to their studies. But McBride had not finished: 'These lads and lassies are going to be straight off to their various coffee shops to loll around and talk indescribable rubbish to each other.' Now he was becoming abusive and his rhetoric was strangely old-mannish for someone who had only just completed his first score and ten. The students were becoming more restless. Some were heading back up the carriage to the other door, some were eyeing the door he was blocking as though they were about to rush it, and some were just enjoying the spectacle.

'You have to do up every last button,' grinned one of them. 'When it comes to children you can never be too careful. That's a fearful cold wind out there!'

'When I want you advice, I'll ask for it,' said McBride rather weakly, but then he stiffened, 'and don't think you know how to look after kids; you're no more than a snivelling little kid yourself.'

If it was intended to wound, the barb bounced off uselessly. The student, who now appeared more determined to stay on the train than McBride did, had a taken up a more permanent position leaning against the back of one of the chairs with one foot propped up on its toe, like an Edwardian gentleman at his fireplace. 'No one understands children, least of all their parents. The child a parent sees is a mere construct in the parent's addled brain, and has nothing to do with the reality of the child. By the time the parent becomes aware of his or her own idiocy, it's too late: the child has grown up and is ready to challenge the parent.' At this stage, the student disentangled himself from his Edwardian posture, leant right down until his mouth was close to McBride's ear and hissed, 'And then the fun starts!'

'Watch yourself,' replied a startled McBride, 'watch your behaviour. I'll have your name.'

The young man was unmoved and resumed his gentlemanly pose, 'Of course, when it comes to understanding children and always admitting that they remain pretty impenetrable for us all, I believe that the closer one is to childhood, the slightly easier it is; having witnessed your performance this morning, I am absolutely convinced that this is the case.'

At this stage, McBride had had enough; gathering the living proof of his fertility around him with a protective gesture that suggested the student's words could be construed as offensive to those of tender age, an implication belied by the children's continued expression of complete bafflement over the entire exchange, he opened the door and took them with him. The station-master's whistle blew, as the students piled out, and he began to wave his arms about in a state of extreme agitation. Health-and-safety was being ignored, and the culprit, wearing a highly fashionable long raincoat of the kind used by American sleuths in the thirties, slipped away like the Pied Piper. You have now been introduced to our heroine's tormentor – not a demonic one, and in the end he turns out to be not all bad. That is the thing about tormentors, they are very rarely all bad, which confuses matters considerably.

But Maeve was not alone. She had a champion and a very remarkable one at that: the tall, dark-haired and attractive Anne Bartlett, a German historian. She immediately understood that Maeve not only had a fine mind but, also and more importantly, a very good heart. They enjoyed each other's company, and what little social life she had revolved around ➻

her protector. Anne was one of those people whose intelligence never interferes with their profoundly decent instincts. The white charger was always waiting and, when she mounted it, her own self-interest was entirely disregarded. When it came to Maeve, it was an open and shut case. Here was a woman of undoubted talents whose execrable colleagues were pushing her around and worse: their put-downs were articulated with the slightly weary tone of people who are trying their very best to be kind and to show understanding. Maeve, whose mind ran along strictly rationalist lines, was of course utterly outsmarted and unable to understand exactly where she was being wronged. In heroically holding them at bay, Anne did not use the sword of truth and the trusty shield of fair play so beloved of some right-minded politicians; such weapons would have been far too heavy for her, but she was handy with the rapier of sarcastic comment and a virtuoso with the very down-to-earth broomstick of common sense, which can be used for prodding or simply lateral beating around the head – a very humane instrument of warfare as it causes no lasting damage to the adversary.

Like so many of her kind – her wonderful kind, Anne was less adept at running her own life than at running other people's. She did everything on impulse and considered her own innate decency to be found amongst most people. She had an asymmetric love-affair with a young Czech called Lech, who was intermittently studying for a degree in German literature. He would occasionally come over to England to get drunk, an experience that differed from getting drunk in Prague only in this respect: in England he could complain incessantly about the poor quality of the beer, which undoubtedly added to his pleasure.

Unwittingly Lech was to bring about changes in Maeve's life: such is the fragility of the threads that hold us together. The timing of this momentous event was that season of drunken silliness, that Yuletide whose ebb leaves behind a clutter of empty wineboxes and beer cans. But its place was far more complex, and it requires me to make a little detour.

A few years earlier, the university had decided that it needed to catch up with the more entrepreneurial times. They appointed a go-getting vice-chancellor to further the successes of our illustrious, liberal and, might I say, candid seat of learning with its dreaming towers and cloisters of poured concrete and ceramic pools of shining water, redolent, I think, of some Mediterranean marvel – Venice perhaps. Why not? Well, perhaps because they had to fill in so many of these pools that tended to catch all the falling leaves that Autumn brought and then began to turn all shades of brown before blooming in mid-winter into a bright algae green.

And this genius of business management they hired was none other than the now infamous Lord Brown of Envelope. He was a Tory in those days when Labour life peers were lagging behind in the corruption stakes, and Lord Envelope was leading the pack: not for him the odd night at the Paris Ritz and a few thousand the tax man knew nothing about. No, he was a man of taste and couldn't possibly restrict his life of luxury to weekends. I will not tire the reader with the details which kept three KPMG accountants working full-time for two and a half years. For our purposes, I must only mention the wine. The university was the owner not only of large structures in reinforced concrete and endless 'villages' of student accommodation that must have kept the London Brick Company busy for several weeks or possibly months, but also a sixteenth-century hall it rather neglected and had allocated for post-graduate lodgings. No sooner had the building come into Lord Envelope's vision than he started to dream up the most perfect dinner parties in a refurbished version of the hall. And so it was, much to the anger of the post-graduates turfed out of their eccentric accommodation and those pedants at English Heritage who thought his porch with Doric columns not in keeping with the ancient Tudor build. But as Lord Envelope constantly liked to point out to the university authorities, they needed to pay the 'going rate for the job', if they wanted a well-run institution with an international reputation. He always drove this important point home by telling them that he had turned down a much more lucrative job in America as the Chief Executive of the Coca Cola Corporation, and had done so solely out of his great love of learning instilled in him by his mother, a writer of popular who-dun-its who had been unjustly neglected in favour of Agatha Christie. The good men and women of the senate committee were very impressed and indeed cowed by his generous sacrifice and kept opening the university's purse wider and wider.

But I have promised not to burden the reader with all the dismal minutiae of greed, and restrict myself to the one element that was to affect the fate of our plain but unhealthily virtuous heroine, Maeve King – unhealthily for herself, of course, and not for society, which would be much improved if there were more plain Maeves around.

An old Elizabethan hall has, of course, a cellar, and a cellar has to be filled. In the case of Lord Envelope, it had to be filled with the best. In all, the accountants sent in after the vice-chancellor's arrest, found 9,738 bottles of the finest claret, mostly _____, and the invoice that went with this modest drop of hospitality was considered so scandalous that the senate decided to sell the entire collection of claret (we won't mention the whites and the other reds here) to an enterprising young French historian called Tom Viticult for 25p a bottle (I will leave you to do the sums and choke with envy).

Tom did not have a wine cellar, but his terraced house in Brideton, Southdown's seaside capital, did have an unused coal-cellar, which certainly helped out but did not suffice. The surplus was distributed around the house at the bottom of wardrobes, under sinks, in the cupboard under the stairs, beside the cold-water tank in the attic and underneath almost every item of furniture: beds, tables, desks and the TV stand – much to the irritation of his wife, Claire, another scholar of French culture.

Such a quantity of wine could not be drunk by Bacchus in a lifetime – nor by Tom in spite of his comparable thirst for the red liquid full of dizzying dreams, vivacious conversations, happy palates and the odd sore head. There was nothing for it but to organise the mother of all Christmas bashes, and what better place to hold it than in the Elizabethan hall which was having its Doric columns removed, a cost the university was defraying by renting it out to the public. The cleverness with which we manage to keep wealth circulating around our advanced western economies is something we never fully understand or appreciate as we should. Thus a small part of the booty was earmarked for immediate consumption, much to Claire's approval as she saw an opportunity for re-deploying part of her invaded wardrobes. By now, the reader must be aware of how fate was manipulating persons and the concomitance of events in order to deprive Maeve of her one support.

So the time was Christmas and the place was the Elizabethan Hall with the partially dismantled Doric columns. Lech was feeling that life was a good adventure. The stifling regime that had run his country since shortly after the war was staggering towards its end. He was abroad again, and as yet such visitors were uncommon enough to attract great interest. He had a beautiful girlfriend, although a touch serious for his liking. A childhood full of rank moralising did not endear him to her stern principles. Good fortune, he thought, is like a woman, and you will do much better if you take her forcefully – none of that namby-pamby sensitivity for her feelings. Sensitivity is something we leave to women; it is not a male virtue. And good fortune, like a woman, loves youth – vigorous youth that doesn't think too much – youth with a good hard body that makes her slightly fearful. Lech had steeled himself with a few foul-tasting English pints before thinking these princely thoughts that can be found in any of the back streets of our towns and cities when the night clubs empty on a Saturday night, but also in the works of our great European philosophers, lovers of knowledge and civilisation. Lech had the feeling of being elected to great deeds and happiness, which he mistakenly believed to be interconnected.

The entrance to the hall was guarded by

➸

the austere head of the Italian Department, Professor Pino Pinguino who must have got up at five in the morning to present the world with such a well-ordered appearance ranging from polished black shoes to a beautifully coiffured head on which it looked as though each hair had been laboriously placed in position to match a perfect cascade of thatch. There are worse ways to waste one's life, but few that express so compellingly the inanity of our vanity fair. Lech waited for the tall professor to make eye contact with a guest requiring a double dose of sycophantic effusion, and then boldly ducked under his line of vision. Fate must have arranged that too.

As Lech got drunker and discovered the English right-thinking classes to be stuffy, puffed-up and, worst of all, unnaturally incurious about Lech himself, he became increasingly obsessed with the idea of reciting the bawdy poems of the infamous satirical poet from Pumpernickel, Otto Pornovsky, considered a degenerate by the Nazis, not least because of the suspicious ethnicity suggested by his surname and not sufficiently redressed by a Christian name harking back to four Holy Roman Emperors no less, and one of them garnished with a 'the Great'. What Lech could not possibly have known was that during the eighties feminism had passed from its virtuous radical stage to its tiresome finger-pointing one, in which deviation from the new norm could not be tolerated. Pornovsky is famous for his unremitting depiction of women as mere bodies and objects of male desires, an attitude that was not exclusively Pornovskian and could not be banned by diktat. The cheerless Doctor Joyce Graves also of the Italian Department started to bang doors to broadcast that her finest sensitivities had been unpardonably affronted, even though she had been known to eye up the talent amongst the first-year students at the beginning of each year and then report every physical detail to the diaphanous Doctor Cecilia Atrophy from English Literature who looked as though she didn't have the energy to eat her breakfast, let alone make love to one of the sturdy lads depicted by the good doctor of philosophy and defender of our new morality.

As the Czech boyfriend could not be summoned before the school committee, it was Anne Bartlett herself who had to respond for his bad behaviour. Anne, of course, could have made short work of that committee, and many a time she had done just that on behalf of other people, but on this occasion she felt that a grand gesture of solidarity with the part-time student and full-time drinker was in order. It was difficult to reconstruct the exact course of the senate proceedings after the event, as the reports were conflicting, but the result was that Anne handed in her notice. Lech repaid her loyalty a few months later by marrying Sophie Witleston who, as far as bodies are concerned, was very well endowed with the upholstery required to set the male hormones racing. The content of her cranium was somewhat limited, unlike her bank account which had been overflowing since her father had sold off his razor-blade company to an American corporation. And all of this, of course, was fine by Lech who knew a good thing when he saw it. Besides the contents of Anne's cranium and bank account had been the other way about, and that can be tedious for a man, particularly one who wants a quiet life and freedom to indulge his pleasures.

But the greatest loser in this tragic end to Anne's academic career was Maeve, who lost her closest friend – and worse, that rare friendship that stimulates and keeps the mind alive.

Anne would marry a doctor – a real one who cures patients – and during her happy years of motherhood, something she had never really hankered after, she started to write a satirical novel about a Northdown University and characters not that dissimilar from the ones we have encountered here. After lying some ten years in a drawer, it has now become a huge success. Anne appears on Newsnight Review, and seated on their low and uncomfortable chairs, she can be heard to reel off inanities in clipped tones to the grinning assent of the presenter whose mind is elsewhere of course – on such matters as who should be the next speaker, who would best enliven her programme, how to make the speakers perform and, God, the desperate urgings of her producer channelled directly to her ear. Anne, meanwhile, falls prey to belated ambition and resentment. Her treatment by the university, which she had rarely thought about for more than a decade, became an obsession, and more inexplicably, she feels that she has wasted her enormous talents on an ungrateful family, which in reality is both grateful and admiring of her success. So it is clear: the vanities of our fairground world can even corrupt the best and brightest of our sons and daughters, so what hope for us, we lesser mortals?

But what the reader really wants to know is Anne's opinion now of that Lech for whom she sacrificed her career. But don't you know? – We, the vainglorious *homines sapientes*, would lay down our lives for someone whom in all probability we would detest six months later in the happy (or perhaps unhappy) event of our surviving. We are motivated by vanity and impulse, although we dress up our vain and impulsive acts in all sorts of fine clothes. And as for the past, we are forever rewriting it.

So now we come to the really weepy part of our story. Our heroine has been deprived of her *caballera* in shining armour (I'm afraid we have no word for a woman knight in our native tongue, which is no less lacunose than any other language, despite chauvinistic beliefs to the contrary), and is now defenceless against ruthless men who do not want their way with her body but are quite capable of stealing her research results and impugning the integrity of her academic work (in no other field of human endeavour have so many been so dependent on the rumours of so few). I hear you objecting that you hear very little about Maeve; what a predictable lot you are! It is sufficient for a heroine to be virtuous. That is her principal task, but you have to admit that supercilious academics, wayward Czech students and corrupt university vice-chancellors are much more fun to read about.

As the most junior member of faculty in the department, the now unprotected Maeve was summoned to the offices of both Cameron Murray and Harvey MacBride, descendents of a people who could never distinguish between forename and surname or foreboding and surly moaning. Cameron Murray was to see her first and had her waiting for three-quarters of an hour while he interviewed students. 'So sorry to keep you waiting,' he would say, with that sly, mock solicitousness he had so expertly mastered. But stop, I'm not a military historian and I'm not an academic. I would never tire you with a battle scene, and describe the clashing steel, the parrying shield or the copious bleeding from fatal wounds, so why would I discuss the even more monotonous cut and thrust of an academic single combat with its purring niceties, wicked jokes, subtle sarcasm and brutal demonstrations of the will to power (and power over what)? We know the outcome: Maeve was put upon. Ah! you say, what a middle-class form of oppression; she was hardly breaking up broken bricks for aggregate on a Bengali roadside. You're right; evils may be relative, but they are all evils. Leave criticism to the critics and let me introduce you to one last character.

Letizia Rubicondi looked like a beauty in a sixteenth-century Italian painting, and such beauty terrifies most men, except for the occasional oaf who has not the sensitivity to fear it or, at the opposite extreme, refined and self-confident natures such as that of MacBride who made her an offer she could refuse: promotion from lettrice to permanent teaching staff in the following academic year in exchange for allowing him to share her bed – his being occupied by the stout, agreeable and extremely loyal lady who was his wife and mother of the well-buttoned offspring. Letizia was a new friend – not a replacement for Anne, as she was not inclined to quixotic demonstrations of solidarity, but she had a fiercely independent character that Maeve admired and learnt from.

One day, Maeve plumped herself down on an armchair in Letizia's study and said, 'These shells, our bodies – what an effort it is to lug them around, and they need such pampering even when, like mine, they're overweight and unattractive. Fed, watered, scrubbed, clothed and covered with all sorts of pongs and potions.

How many industries flourish, how much commerce feeds the assets of wealthy men, and even how many wars are fought to secure the safety and comfort of these fragile bags of flesh, which must wither in all events?'

'Well, off you go like the anchorites into the desert to eat berries. You'll forgive me if I don't join you,' laughed Letizia Rubicondi.

'But it's all right for you,' said Maeve, indicating not without a little distaste, Rubicondi's well-styled and well-garmented form. Why, she thought, are Italian feminists allowed to dress like man-killers in tight shirts and high heels, with perfectly made-up faces and manicured nails? 'Look at what I have to drag around. And why do all men, whether ugly or good-looking think that all of us, unclad and defenceless to their amorous needs, should resemble the latest Hollywood anorexic.'

'Defenceless to their amorous needs? Oh dear, you are fucked up,' Letizia passed sentence. 'Personally I have always thought that they would like to put it anywhere, and find making love to us only marginally more attractive than doing the same thing to a watermelon.' Letizia demonstrated once again that, contrary to popular belief, Northern Europeans are more romantic, while if you want truly unromantic and indeed cynical attitudes to sex, you need to go to the south of the continent. 'Although it has to be admitted that a watermelon is no good when it comes to decorating a bar stool. That is why I never go out in the evening accompanied by a man: they always want to parade you like a trophy. That's why I keep my sex life and my social life entirely separate.'

Maeve, who had been to bed with very few men – all fumbling, awkward encounters, and had never known one who wanted to parade her like a trophy, blushed at her friend's explicitness and self-confidence. It wasn't just about sex, and she decided to take the conversation in a different direction.

'Look, the brain is some kind of computer, but you just switch a computer on and as soon as it gets its electric current, which is instantaneous, it starts to work in an entirely reliable fashion. But the brain is so fussy and so dependent on a healthy body. It gets tired. It doesn't like your drinking habit. It absolutely hates your insomnia, and becomes uncontrollable in the face of over fifty undergraduates.'

'Well, for starters,' came the smiling reply from Letizia, who always finds complex subjects reassuringly simple, as her brain contains one of those old-fashioned filing cabinets, the wooden ones with tiny drawers for holding index cards: everything has a category and everything can be filed away. There is no room for doubt or *crossover*. 'Well, for starters, our brain is not a computer (it is filed under 'b' and not under 'c', she presumably meant), and it has intuition, which is simply jumping to a conclusion before you have sufficient evidence. A computer doesn't do that kind of tomfoolery. It applies absolute rigour, while our brains are, at best, dysfunctional computers.'

'I don't know about that,' said Maeve, uncertain as to where she should start her response. It struck her that Letizia was much more impressive when she was talking about sex. 'All that defragging business: isn't that a bit like sleep – and dreaming? After all what is sleep, if not sorting out our brains and getting them ready for the next day, but computers do it so quickly; they defrag in a couple of minutes, whereas we lose a third of our life. It is the terrible inefficiency of it all that irritates me.'

'So we're in agreement. The brain is at best a dysfunctional computer.'

'Well, not really! The brain, like everything that makes up a human being, is both remarkable and rather clumsily constructed. Yet another demonstration of how we must have been designed by evolution, although designed is not the right word. 'Designed by evolution' is an oxymoron.'

'I'll argue against myself here. Computers, if they were designed from scratch now with the knowledge we have accumulated – with hindsight, as it were – would be designed differently from what they have become. Because they have evolved step by step, and the design of each generation of computer is constricted by the format of the previous one. That is a bit like evolution, isn't it.'

'You're right, Letizia, but I was only using a metaphor when I first said that the brain is a computer. It isn't really a computer, because it contains the ghost of consciousness.'

'Now, you're being silly. Next you'll be believing in God and all that tomfoolery,' Letizia said, displaying that endearing habit of people speaking a language that is not their own: the over-frequent use of a low-frequency word for no other reason than the speaker's irrational pleasure in articulating the word in question, often because that word would be quite inconceivable in their native tongue.

'Is it silly not to know?'

Letizia sat on Maeve's chair rest and put her arm around her. 'You are far too serious, my dear,' she whispered. 'That is why I find you so entertaining. You're coming out with me tonight. I'm going to show you off and give you a good time.'

Maeve suddenly felt a little weepy. 'You wouldn't find it so entertaining if you knew what I have to put with. If you had colleagues like Harvey MacBride and Cameron Murray...'

Letizia removed her arm and stood up. 'Come off it, Maeve! What are you looking for? A knight in shining armour. They don't exist and never did.' Maeve's eyes began to burn and she thought to herself that Letizia clearly didn't have an index card for Anne Bartlett. 'MacBride's a jerk,' Letizia continued, 'and so is Murray. So what? They're like the weather: you have to put up with them as part of reality. The storm comes in, and then it blows itself out. And you're still here, working away as you always do. I'd put my money on you, any day. You'll pull through, but stop feeling sorry for yourself. You need *le palle* – balls. What you call *guts* in your language. What a strange lot you are! I tell you what: you're coming out with me tonight and I'm not taking no for an answer.' And so a kind of friendship grew stronger. Letizia would continue to push Maeve into having a more relaxed relationship with her own body, and Maeve would continue to resist, because her resistance came from her nature and could not be overcome by intellectual argument.

And we might have been a little too hard on MacBride, as who can blame him for the inconstancy of his values, the hypocritical manner in which he displayed them, his bullying of faculty and students alike, and his ruthless exploitation of Maeve as I have described, albeit somewhat summarily? We have to admit that his behaviour was perfectly adapted to survival in the delightful and enlightened environment we categorise as academia. In no other sphere of activity is reputation so important and carefully cultivated or projected onto society like a magic lantern. In no other trade are personal politics, committee-controlling, grand gestures and conspiracy so important. What? Even worse than politicians? you ask incredulously. Well indeed, politicians are more dangerous because they have real power; if, however, the world were run by academics, there would very probably be more war and mayhem, not less. So we should be thankful that our ingenious societies have found the means of channelling these people into careers where their cantankerous rivalries can do no real harm or lasting damage to society at large.

And the proof of what I say can be found in the history of Doctor Harvey MacBride himself. His self-help book, *Shit on Everyone Else, or How to be a Great Writer or Artist*, so touched the spirit of our times that it became a 'runaway bestseller'. In it he explained what had already seemed an established fact: everyone has a novel in them or in the drawer or in their soul or in some other place. Presumably we all also have a marathon, a sculpture and a very successful business enterprise in us, if only we could find the right success manuals and be bothered to follow their advice carefully, thus unleashing on the world huge numbers of frustrated writers, runners, sculptors and businessmen. That's already happened, you say. Quite right, but there is still a market for this stuff. MacBride followed a tried and tested formula: success is reliant on self-belief, and it is interfered with only when you start to weaken and take other people's feelings into account. Success is a matter of focus and ruthlessness, and the object is to sell oneself as one would any other 'product'. This populist treatise was followed by the equally successful

➳

Being a Bastard Gets You to the Top or How to Be a Successful Politician or Captain of Industry and the slightly more original *Method Acting as a Way of Life*, which explained how the skills of dissembling anger, moral outrage, concern and sincerity can be used to further almost any career. He too was invited onto TV chat shows and was such a success that he became a permanent fixture. Of course, his colleagues no longer took him seriously: how could they? – he had written books that everyone wanted to read. To his great credit, he too started not to take himself seriously. He continued his academic career in a very desultory fashion, dropped off all the committees and didn't finish his monograph on whether Goethe visited Pumpernickel for one afternoon in the autumn of 17__. His bank balance grew and he became very relaxed, but the bank balance was not that important as he showed great generosity and gave half of it to a charity drilling artesian wells in Africa. When Cameron Murray, who shortly afterwards would succumb to an unpleasant accident involving a plate of *strozzapreti*, stopped him in the corridor and provocatively said, 'You do realise that those books of yours are crap!' he replied, 'You're wrong. They're complete crap,' and bounced off laughing at his own feeble joke. In short, a bad book liberated its author and made him a better man.

But you the reader and I the writer of these lines have not led blameless lives, and if fate had landed us in one of those pleasure gardens of learning, might we not have behaved just like him? Surely our professions account for ninety per cent of what we are. Our contribution is slight, although we do not like to think so. And one final word on this subject: when it comes to writers, translators and all those who push a pen for no other reason than to turn an elegant phrase or shape an original thought (if such things exist), keep a very wide berth but read our books as we are on the whole a penniless lot and our egos are made of material fragile to the touch of reality.

And so in the end Maeve became head of department and, wonderfully, was reunited all day long with the studies she loved. She took joy too in the successes of the staff she recruited, even when they eclipsed her own. And they rewarded her by relaxing into their work and putting aside those university politics of which we spoke. And they loved her dearly and few would countenance the idea of leaving because, although we humans consume our lives in bickering and plotting and spreading false rumour 'to better ourselves' and our families, the thing we really desire is to work in harmony and concert with each other. It is circumstance, shall we say, that makes us do what we do aided, no doubt, by that weakness we so often call strength or ambition. But always we want for something better.

And how uplifting are these light satires? I am weeping while I write, as I seldom indulge in happy endings, as you will find out if you persevere with this book. What's this? You're not happy? You say that her emotional life is not complete. I am not writing for Hollywood, and not every happy ending requires a man and a woman to get together (or two men or two women, for that matter). Look, if you want heterosexual heaven along with an estate and an income of three (hundred) thousand a year, forget it or read one of the classics.

For us sweet cynics of our modern age, the emphasis has changed – and for the better I would say: a shred of progress now that progress seems an unlikely claim.

This short story is part of a collection, *Can the Gods Cry?*, which will be published by Vagabond Voices on April 4th 2011.

&

Django Ross

& WELL, SAYS I, the wee Balfron shop where Mother always used to buy the flowers has stopped selling them &. & never mind let's try the Co &

& yes &. & not only yes, but chrysanthemums, as Mother always used to take &. & more, 20% extra free &. & oh, good, says Mother, they'll last that wee bit longer &. & the logic's suspect, but the intention sterling &. & wull Ah take thi price aff? says the boy &. & naw, says i, doant boathir yirsel. Thir baith deid – they cannae read the price &

& yes, the cemetery's as impeccable as ever &. & gauging where I might be laid to rest, when I am laid to rest, I look at the consecration plaque for the extension &. & more, I see the note attached to the dedicatory tree &, says I, must tell wee Maggie this one &. & this one's that said tree was planted by Councillor Colin O'Brien &

& so to the grave, & the hellos, & the careful spacing of the chrysants & how's that &. & that'll do fine, son, says Mother, a nice even job &. & the latest news is passed &. & they're sorry to hear of Jack's death, but even sorrier that I didn't know until after the funeral was over &. & never mind, son, says Mother, you did your best &

& then the picnic, for the sun's shining, & only the gentlest of breezes wafts &. & what does that mean? says Father. Wafts. I mean, when you come to think of it &. & ach, Alex., says Mother, away & don't be daft &. & this is home-made bread &. & you've done a great job there, son, says Mother &. & this is wild gorgonzola, & now you're talking, says Father &. & this is home-made wine, & that's just dandy, Sandy, says Father, & no, I can smell the spirit, says Mother &. & this is Glasgow water, says I, & the best in the world, says Mother &

& aye, says I, I'll better away for the 'bus - one an hour – I'm on the 'bus pass &. & get away, says Father, you're never that age already & aye, says I, so Ah mur &. & aye, says Mother, it's just a generation passing &. & we fair enjoyed your visit, son, says Mother &. & me, too, says I &. & but just before you go, says Father, you seem to remember your mother's speech patterns very well &. & aye, says Mother, and your father's, too &. & aye, says I, you'll never be dead while I'm alive &

& cheerio, the noo &

& cheerio, says Father &

& cheerio, son, says Mother &

& it wiza dubl-dekr omnibus oan thi wey oot, bitit sa singil-dekr coach oan thi wey hame &

Dirty

Patricia Ace

Wish my wife was this dirty – written in dust on back of white van.

O white van man
my name is Anne
I'm single and I'm flirty
I'd like to find
a kindred mind
who likes his women dirty

My flat's a dump
my sink's a sump
my bath's all foul and scummy
I haven't showered
since they cut the power
my sheets are grey and crumby

My neck is mank
my armpits rank
my legs are dark and fuzzy
my nails are black
my teeth have plaque
my make-up's stale and scuzzy

My clothes are stained
with old chow-mein
my hair you could fry an egg on
and that's not all
my feet appal
and my gut you can rest a keg on

O white van man
my name is Anne
I've crossed the mire of thirty
if you've got time
for a life of grime
come round and let's get dirty

The Ladies of B-Wing Topless Calendar

Andy Jackson

Miss January (infant strangler)
loves Madonna, Chinese food and shoes,
talked around to posing for the camera —
that arse, those legs – nice stocking fillers,
if you get my drift. You'd hardly know
the things she's done, her skin so smooth,
her tan lines fading into tide marks.
Bikini straps hang down like limp spaghetti,
eyes not blank and sullen like a killer
but shining with the power of her body.

Miss June (the Preston Poisoner)
likes Ronan Keating, keeps Alsatians,
puckers up and looks at the photographer,
perhaps at me, or maybe at herself,
imagining the jolting rounds of hand relief.
Great idea, something for the lads
while pulling in the fivers for a charity,
cheques pinned to death threats in the mail.
Her grand concealments, all her simple plans
which could not fail, refracted by the lens.

We need to see more. Would you move your hands away?
We've been a bad, bad boy. Now, you must pay.

The Master

Olive M Ritch

Did he awake from a dream
with the taste of her scream
on his lips? Great wings beating
still in his head. Did he admire

that feathered glory whose knowledge
and power she might have donned,
mastered by the brute blood?
Being so caught up, his fierce hands

fixed words on the page, pen
loosening thighs, engendering there
a stage for all the daughters
        of the land.

The Annabel Chong Documentary

Janette Ayachi

I am broken into pieces like bread
passed out, shared amongst the men;
they take me between their teeth
tasting my consistency in relief
kneading my body back to dough
positioning shapes that they know
to savour the places with surprise
where I rise where I rise
or slowly they break in where I bake
scavenging crumbs as my body numbs awake.
Fucking two hundred and fifty
men on tape for ten hours
this is my celebration
of a new woman's liberation.
Messalina you were my muse
you too had appetite to feed and prove
even Scylla could not succumb
to how many men you won,
staining your name in history.
And now this my documentary
which to declare equality I endure
as Woman, Asian, Feminist, Whore,
– the truth of me has been said
I am broken into pieces like bread
passed out, shared amongst the men.

Deil Tak The Hinmaist
Alexander Hutchison

'I think ye ocht t' pit the pillywinkies on t' him...'

The girt yett kickit in, an lo! – they liggit: *scummers o pŏts*
an skĕlpers o cuddies; jaws that cleikit, rhymes that reikit; Kerr's Pink
tatties biled in their jaickets; deedle-dabblers in cytoplasm; virtual
realtors swickin an swyvin; daddy-lang-legs; dirlin Dodies;
hoodie-craws cracklin fae the tippy-taps o trees:

Deid-loss or Daidalos
fit's it gaan tae be?

Pooshin pumpers, coonter-jumpers, cairpet fitters birslin wi a moo-fae
o tacks; tomcats; corncrakes; shilly-shally sharn shifters; couthy bicuspids; aa the wee glisterin
anes; aa them that wid grudge ye one jow o the bell.

The neist yett swung, syne mair wis kythit: tethered tups,
draigelt yowes; the slalom loons fae Dandruff Canyon; wheepers
o candy-floss; footerin futtrets; the hee-haw-hookum o hystet hizzies; foosty fowk lik Finnan
haddies; Buckie blaavers wi the full wecht o blaw.

Shouther tae the third yett, an jist as ye micht expeck: sornars
an sooks; herriers an haverers; gran chiels in blue corduroy, fantoosh
wifies; r.p. flannel dinkers; parkins, merkins; secont-sichtit seannachies
wi hunkies clappit t' their snoots; flunkeys; junkies; buglers; shooglers; Methuselahs wi nips an
tucks; trashtrie shotten aff the shelf.

As douce a set o creepy-crawlies
as ye're ivver like t' see.

Here-am-ur; hempseed; fushionless tail-toddle:
Daith's on the fussle lik the win throw the widdy.

Roon the corner, an doon the stair: polyglot thrapple-stappers;
chirpy chairmers; mingers an moochers; bracken for brakfast, neebors
for lunch. Lest bit nae least: flees in putty, wersh wicks in seas o wax.

Coda: Scoor it if ye fancy intil ae muckle plum duff –
plooms, suet, orange peel – simmert slaw an slaistert
in slices, faa's t' say it winna lest for years?

Glossary:

Hinmaist: hindmost; *ocht*: ought; *pilliwinkies*: finger or thumb screws, an instrument of torture; *girt yett*: great gate; *liggit*: lay; *skelpers*: strikers, whippers; *cuddies*: horses; *cleikit*: caught, hooked on to; *reikit*: stank; *tatties*: potatoes; *deedle-dabblers*: dilettantes; *dirlin*: reverberating; *Dodie*: George; *swickin and swyvin*: cheating and screwing; *daddy-lang-legs*: crane flies; *hoodie-craws*: hooded or carrion crows; *pooshin*: poison; *birslin*: bristling; *moo-fae*: mouthful; *couthy*: cozy, homely; *glisterin*: shiny; *sharn*: dung; *jow*: peal; *neist*: next; *syne*: then, subsequently; *kythit*: revealed; *tup*: ram; *draigelt yowes*: bedraggled ewes; *loons*: lads; *footerin*: hesitant, exasperating; *futtrets*: weasels or stoats; *hee-haw-hookum*: an indeterminate mischief; *hystet*: hoisted; *hizzies*: women-folk; *foosty*: fusty, mouldy; *fowk*: folk; *Finnan haddies*: a type of smoked haddock; *blaavers*: braggarts, boasters; *wecht*: weight; *blaw*: wind; *shouther*: shoulder; *sornars*: importunate scroungers; *sooks*: flatterers; *herriers*: robbers, plunderers; *haverers*: gabblers, people speaking nonsense; *gran chiels*: VIP's; *fantoosh*: extra fancy; *wifies*: women; *r.p.*: 'received pronunciation', posh spoken; *parkins*: large, round, ginger and oatmeal biscuits; *merkin*: a pubic wig (some say) or the *sine qua non*; *seannachies*: wise men; story-tellers; *snoots*: snouts; *shooglers*: shakers; *trashtrie*: rubbish; *douce*: proper, respectable; *fushionless*: limp; vapid; *tail-toddle*: intercourse; *fussle*: whistle; *widdy*: wood; *thrapple*: throat; *stapers*: stoppers, stuffers; *mingers*: ugly wasters; *moochers*: cadgers; *flees*: flies; *wersh*: dull; *scoor*: scour, scrape; duff: pudding; *plooms*: plums; *slaw*: slow; *slaistert*: slathered; *faa*: who; *lest*: last.

In search of Duende

Christine Williamson

They looked for me
in the Royal Albert Hall.
I was not there.

They looked for me
in the Sydney Opera House.
I could not be found.

They looked for me
in Paris, Rome, New York and Buenos Aires.
I was nowhere to be seen.

An old shepherd chews memories,
weary boned and leather skinned
from decades given to his mountain flock.
He invites hot liquid
into small cups
and smiles.

The Clangers on Acid
Patricia Ace

We were young, in our twenties, living in the country,
on the dole and trying to be artists. Unfortunately
we'd chosen Perthshire, a cultural dearth, the only people
nurturing any kind of creative urge were retired from careers
with the Council, Hydro Electric, Norwich Union.
So we continued to feed our hollow souls with the usual
suspects – drink and drugs – the baby in bed, Brookside
on the tele, a spliff on the go and Ian dropping in from over
the road to show us how to make a chillum out of a carrot.
The three of us huddled round the coal fire like the Fates.

But soon enough we got bored of that and invited friends
from the city for a dinner party, dropping a tab before
we sat down for starters – the beef in red wine went largely
untouched – really I shouldn't have bothered. Within half an hour
the wallpaper was crawling, the rag-rug a Lilliputian orgy,
embryos bobbed in the lava lamp. An hour in and the girl I hardly
knew but always liked, had hoped, in fact, would enact my
lesbian fantasies later that night, was telling me about the
miscarriage she was having in my kitchen. I took a long hot bath
and tried to get a grip. It didn't work.

Within minutes it seemed the sun had come up and the baby
wanted breakfast. We watched *The Clangers* on video.
I was strung out for six weeks after that trip, suffering
delusions of grandeur, convinced I was the next Sylvia Plath,
ready to stick my head in that oven. And the rest?
Mostly we grew up and settled down, got mortgages and proper
jobs at the Council, the Hydro, Norwich Union. The dealer
got MS and died young and that girl, she moved to London,
never carried a child to full term.

Manuscript
Andrew McCallum

(i.m. Edwin Morgan)

In this sense I am not writing any sort of autobiography, but my writing is my autobiography. There is a difference.
Umberto Eco, *The Paris Review*, Issue 182, Summer 2008

Look what has happened
to the truth
and to the facts
and to the past:
you have transfigured them,
humanised them,
brought them at last to poetic justice.

Look what has become
of your pleasure and your pain:
you have changed the names
and shuffled the particulars,
made something of what is forever gone.

As it was, there was no form.
As it was, there was no rhyme or reason.
As it was, there were only chance meetings,
chance love affairs,
a chance of rain
and no chance of anyone sharing your strawberries.

But now, when they read your manuscript,
as makar you can sincerely say,
Of course – don't you know? –
none of this is true.

Diasporran.
Catherine Baird

Diaspora ma arse.
Why don't yees aw jist come back
bring whit yi've learnt
and pit up wi the damp dreich weather like the restae us.

Contributor Biographies

Patricia Ace's pamphlet *First Blood* was published by HappenStance Press in 2006. Recent poems and stories are appearing in *Orbis*, *The Rialto* and THE SHOP. Her portrait is currently displayed at the Meffan gallery in Forfar in photographer Chris Park's exhibition, *Dualism: Portraits & Poems*. She is looking for a home for her first full collection, called *Fabulous Beast*.

Janette Ayachi has a Edinburgh University Masters in Creative Writing. She is published in *The Edinburgh Review*, *Velvet*, and the current editions of *The Red Wheelbarrow*, *Poetry Salzburg Review*. Two poems were short-listed in the Mslexia poetry competition 2009. She is a member of Words On Canvas writing group at The National Gallery. Her chapbook *A Choir of Ghosts* is published by Vision Street press.

Catherine Baird writes poetry, short stories and drama. She is currently working on a novel. Her work has appeared previously in *Gutter Magazine* and she was recently a runner-up in Glasgow's Scotia Bar Poet Laureate competition. Her experimental novel, *The Responsive Mood*, in reply to Padgett Powell's book *The Interrogative Mood*, will soon be available to buy online.

Nick Brooks is the author of two novels, *My Name Is Denise Forrester* and *The Good Death*. He is currently completing a third, *Millionaire's Shortbread*, and writing a collection of poetry and illustration, *The Tenant Ghost*. He is also working on a PhD, and has plans for another novel.

Larry Butler was born in Illinois and has been living in Glasgow since 1981. His day job is teaching tai-chi in healthcare settings and leading life-story groups at the Maggie Cancer Care Centre. His current big project is creating an arts-eco village in Scotland: bodhi-eco-project.org.uk. He is convenor for Lapidus Scotland (creative words for health & wellbeing) lapidus.org.uk.

Allan Cameron is the author of two novels – *The Golden Menagerie* (2004) and *The Berlusconi Bonus* (2005 and 2010), a book on language – *In Praise of the Garrulous* (2008), and a collection of poetry – *Presbyopia* (2009). His collection of short stories, *Can the Gods Cry?* will be published in April 2011. He is also the translator of twenty-five books, most recently Alessandro Barbero's *The Anonymous Novel* and Ermanno Cavazzoni's *The Nocturnal Library*.

Niall Campbell, 26, from the Outer Hebrides of Scotland graduated from St Andrews Creative Writing Mlitt in 2009 with a distinction. He has had poetry published, or forthcoming in: *Poetry Review*, *Cyphers*, and *The Red Wheelbarrow*. He currently lives in Glasgow.

Jim Carruth's first collection *Bovine Pastoral* was published in 2004. Since then he has brought out a further three collections and an illustrated fable. In 2009 he was awarded a Robert Louis Stevenson Fellowship and was the winner of the James McCash poetry competition. In 2010 he was chosen for the prestigious Oxford Poets anthology. jimcarruth.co.uk

Margaret Christie lives in Edinburgh. Her pamphlet *The Oboist's Bedside Book* (HappenStance) was shortlisted for the Callum Macdonald Memorial Award.

A C Clarke has published *The Gallery on the Left* (Akros) 2003, *Breathing Each Other In* (Blinking Eye Publishers) 2005, *Messages of Change* (Oversteps) 2008. She is currently working on a collection of poems on the atheist priest Jean Meslier (special thanks to Donny O'Rourke for his encouragement in this) and a pamphlet inspired by the Anatomy Museum in Glasgow.

Frances Corr began writing in a community group in Glasgow's Year of Culture, 1990. This led to writing plays for the Lone Rangers, the Ramshorn Theatre, Dogsbodies, 7:84 and a drama documentary for Schools Television. She has had short stories published in *The Big Issue*, *Cutting Teeth*, *New Writing Scotland*, *The Research Club* and *Sushirexia*. She also writes poetry and paints.

Jason Donald was born in Dundee, Scotland. He grew up in Pretoria, South Africa and now lives in Switzerland. His first novel, *Choke Chain*, was published by Jonathan Cape in 2009.

Rodger Evans was a music journalist, a speech writer, and a member of the children's panel. Much like Zelda Fitzgerald he wishes to write a beautiful book to break those hearts that are soon to cease to exist: a book of faith and small neat words and people who live by the philosophies of popular songs.

Hazel Frew's poems have been published widely in magazines and anthologies including *New Writing Scotland*, *Orbis* and *The Rialto*. Her poems have been translated into German, Arabic and Italian. Her chapbook *Clockwork Scorpion* was published by Rack Press in 2007 and *Seahorses*, her first full length collection, by Shearsman in 2008.

Graham Fulton's collections include *Knights of the Lower Floors* (Polygon) *This* (Rebel Inc) and *twenty three buildings* (Controlled Explosion Press). His most recent publication is *Black Motel/The Man who Forgot How to* (Roncadora Press). A major collection *Open Plan* is published in February by Smokestack Books. *Full Scottish Breakfast* is also on the way in 2011 from Red Squirrel Press.

Ewan Gault's short stories have won a number of awards and have been published in various collections including previous issues of *Gutter*. He's currently editing a novel set in a Kenyan running camp in the week before the violent elections of 2008.

➳

Pippa Goldschmidt used to be a professional astronomer and is enjoying being in the *Gutter* gazing at the stars. She's interested in using fiction to explore science, and the story published here is adapted from her soon-to-be completed novel. She's a writer-in-residence at the ESRC Genomics Policy and Research Forum, based at the University of Edinburgh. See pippagoldschmidt.co.uk for more of her work.

Rodge Glass is the author of the novels *No Fireworks* (Faber, 2005) and *Hope for Newborns* (Faber, 2008), as well as *Alasdair Gray: A Secretary's Biography* (Bloomsbury), which received a Somerset Maugham Award in 2009. Recently, he was also the Editor of *The Year of Open Doors* (Cargo, 2010) and co-author of the graphic novel *Dougie's War: A Soldier's Story* (Freight, 2010).

Barry Gornell lives on the West Coast of Scotland. He is trying to grow up with his children, supported by his wife. Screenwriter, ex fire-fighter, trucker and book shop manager, his fiction has been published in *The Herald*; *Lets pretend, 37 stories about (in)fidelity* (Freight, 2009) and *Gutter 03*. His first novel is *The Healing of Luther Grove*.

Kirstin Innes is a writer and journalist, and co-runs Glasgow spoken word event Words Per Minute. Her short fiction has been published in Cargo anthology *The Year of Open Doors*, and the EIBF anthology *Elsewhere*, and she's performed her writing all over the country, on BBC Radio Scotland, and at HydroConnect Festival. *Fishnet* is her first novel, looking at sex work and Scotland.

James A Irvine was born in Edinburgh in 1960 and now lives in Tranent, East Lothian. Since retiring from 'normal' work for health reasons he at least now has the time needed for his writing. He writes poetry and prose in English and Scots and is currently completing *Changing Light* – a novella in English.

Nick Holdstock's work has appeared in *n+1* and the *London Review of Books*. *The Tree That Bleeds*, a book about China, will be published by Luath Press in Spring 2011. nickholdstock.com

Alexander Hutchison grew up speaking north-east Scots and various registers of English in Buckie and thereabouts. Shot off to Canada and the US after university; came back after 18 years, and after a spell in Edinburgh settled with his family in Glasgow. The link to Sicily is one of several Italian connections: eg at informadiparole.it – and his website is alexanderhutchison.com

Andy Jackson was born in 1965 in Manchester and moved to Fife 20 years ago. His poems have appeared in *Magma*, *Northwords Now*, *Poetry News*, *Rising* and *Blackbox Manifold*. His first collection *The Assassination Museum* was published by Red Squirrel in 2010, and he is currently editing an anthology of poetry inspired by TV & Movies.

Vicki Jarrett lives and works in Edinburgh. Her fiction has appeared in several anthologies and been broadcast on BBC Radio Scotland, Radio 4 and Radio Somerset. She was shortlisted for the Manchester Fiction Prize 2009. She is currently writing more stories and working on her first novel.

Brian Johnstone has published two collections and two pamphlets. His second collection is *The Book of Belongings* (Arc, 2009). His work has appeared throughout Scotland and in the UK, America and various European countries. *Terra Incognita*, a collection of his poems in Italian translation, was published in 2009. He is the poet member of Trio Verso, presenting poetry and jazz.

Doug Johnstone is a writer, musician and journalist based in Edinburgh. His next novel, *Smokeheads*, will be published by Faber in March 2011. He's had two novels published by Penguin, *Tombstoning* and *The Ossians*. He is currently writer in residence at Strathclyde University. Doug is also in several bands including Northern Alliance, who have released four critically acclaimed albums.

Vivien Jones lives on the north Solway shore in Scotland. Her short stories and poetry have been widely published and broadcast on BBC Radio 4 and Radio Scotland – her first themed collection of short stories, *Perfect 10*, was published in September 2009 by Pewter Rose Press. In August 2010 she won the Poetry London Prize. She has been awarded a Writer's Bursary from Creative Scotland for her next fiction project on the theme of women amongst warriors. vivienjones.info

Arthur Ker studied at Glasgow School of Art. After a stint with the BBC, he worked as a design lecturer and now writes full time and lives in Argyll. He has had short stories and poems published in magazines and anthologies. If all goes to plan, his first novel *Crossed Wires* could be published by the end of the year.

Jenny Love went from teenage mother to mother of teenagers and wanted to change the world but couldn't find a babysitter. If you hunt hard, you'll find her work online and rumour has it, on old fashioned paper and ink. There may even be a book in the offing. She lives just outside Glasgow.

Micaela Maftei lives in Glasgow.

David Manderson is a writer and academic. He's published short stories, articles and essays in many anthologies, small magazines and journals. He lectures in creative writing and screenwriting at the University of the West of Scotland, where he also supervises creative writing PhDs. His novel *Lost Bodies* will be published in 2012. His agent is Edwin Hawkes of Makepeace Towle Associates.

Andrew McCallum lives in Biggar, works on the margins of Edinburgh and writes by the light of a cigarette when he should really be in bed. He never ceases to be amazed that what he writes occasionally escapes into print. He enjoys a growing reputation as a scallywag and, to the despair of his teenage sons, has recently discovered goth metal.

Lesley McDowell is an author and critic, reviewing for The *Herald* and *Independent on Sunday* among others. Her first novel, *The Picnic*, was published in 2007 and *Between the Sheets: The Literary Liaisons of Nine 20th-Century Women Writers* in 2010, described by *The New York Times* as 'full of juicy details'. She is currently working on a retelling of the Electra myth.

Ross McGregor lives and works in Kilmarnock, Ayrshire. In 2008 he won the Scottish Book Trust New Writers' Award and went on to write his first novel, *The Fair Fortnight*. Ross is now writing his second novel and a series of poems. He recently had his poem 'Cup Final Day, 1997' published in *New Writing Scotland* 28.

Anneliese Mackintosh has had short stories broadcast on BBC Radio 4, as well as published in various literary magazines and anthologies. Currently she is working on a 30-minute play for BBC Radio Scotland set on a train, and is writing a novel about terrorism and baked goods. She is also editor of Cargo Crate. Go to anneliesemackintosh.com, it's great.

JoAnne McKay was born to a family of slaughterers in Romford, Essex. Reived to Scotland by a red-haired man, she now lives in a small Dumfriesshire village where she combines motherhood, work and a Masters degree with mixed success. She has published two pamphlets, *The Fat Plant* in 2009 and *Venti* in 2010. Poet Hugh McMillan says they are 'absolute stoatters'.

Gordon Meade lives in Fife where he divides his time between his own writing and running creative writing workshops for vulnerable young people. During 2008/2010 he was the Royal Literary Fund Writing Fellow at the University of Dundee. His sixth collection of poems, *The Familiar*, will be published by Arrowhead Press in Spring 2011.

John Douglas Millar is a writer, he was born in Scotland in 1981. He lives and works in London.

Jason Monios lives in Edinburgh. His poetry has appeared in *Acumen, Magma, Poetry Scotland, New Writing Scotland, Horizon, The Warwick Review* and *The Guardian*.

Anne Morrison lives in Sutherland and works as a copywriter. Her children's novel *Uamh nan Cnàmhan* (*The Bone Caves*) was published by Stòrlann in 2009. She is a winner of the Highlands and Islands Short Story Award (2004) and the Neil Gunn Short Story Prize (2007). In 2005, she came second in the Scotsman Orange Short Story Prize.

Donald S Murray comes from the Isle of Lewis but works in Shetland. A full-time teacher who is also a poet, author and journalist, his books include *The Guga Hunters* (Birlinn), *Small Expectations* (Two Ravens Press) and *And On This Rock; The Italian Chapel, Orkney* (Birlinn). He has appeared at various events, including talking about St Kilda at the Edinburgh Book Festival in the company of the celebrated writer, Will Self.

Duncan Muir grew up on a small Hebridean island where he spent his childhood riding horses on the beach and terrorising small furry animals. He is a graduate of the University of Glasgow's MLitt Creative Writing.

Stephen Nelson is the author of *Flylyght* (Knives, Forks and Spoons Press), a chapbook of minimalist poems. He's also had a chapbook of visual poems published in Dan Waber's *this is visual poetry* series. His work will be exhibited at the 2011 Text Festival in Bury, Manchester. He blogs visual poetry and other delights at afterlights.blogspot.com.

Nalini Paul has recently completed a one-year post as the George Mackay Brown Writing Fellow in Orkney, where many of the poems in her new collection, *Slokt by Sea*, were written. Her first poetry pamphlet, *Skirlags* (Red Squirrel Press, 2009) was shortlisted for the Callum Macdonald Award. She was born in India, grew up in Vancouver, and has been living in Scotland since 1994.

Andrew Philip was born in Aberdeen in 1975 and grew up near Falkirk. He lived in Berlin for a short spell in the 1990s before studying linguistics at Edinburgh University. He has published two poetry pamphlets with HappenStance Press, *Tonguefire* (2005) and *Andrew Philip: A Sampler* (2008)— and was chosen as a Scottish Poetry Library 'New Voice' in 2006. His first book of poems, *The Ambulance Box* was published by Salt in 2009.

AP Pullan was born in Yorkshire now well looked after in Ayrshire. Poems previously published in *Iota, Poetry Scotland* and *New Writing Scotland 28*.

Fiona Rintoul is a writer and journalist. Her fiction has been published in anthologies and journals. She is a past winner of the Gillian Purvis New Writing Award and the Sceptre Prize. She has been short-listed for the Fish Short Story Prize and the Mslexia Women's Poetry Competition, and long-listed for the Bridport Poetry Prize. She completed a Creative Writing MLitt at Glasgow University and has just finished her first novel.

Olive M Ritch is an award-winning poet in her final year of a PhD in Creative Writing at the University of Aberdeen. In 2003, she won a prize in the National Poetry Competition; in 2006, she was awarded the Calder Prize for Poetry at the University of Aberdeen. She is currently completing her first collection and has been published in a number of literary journals and anthologies.

Cynthia Rogerson is a novelist, short story writer, closet poet, mother of four kids and two grandkids, and programmer at Moniack Mhor Writer's Centre. She is still trying to write a great work of art.

Django Ross is a Very Unimportant Person (VUP).

Helen Sedgwick is a writer, editor and tutor who moonlights as a scientist. This used to be the other way around. Her website is at helensedgwick.com

Mark Ryan Smith lives in Shetland with his wife and two young children. He works in the Shetland Archives and is a part-time PhD student at Glasgow University, studying the literature of his native isles. His writing has appeared in the *New Shetlander*, the *Herald*, and PN *Review*. His pamphlet *Midnight and Tarantella* was published in 2008.

Richard W Strachan lives in Glasgow and has had stories printed in *Markings*, *Sein und Werden*, and online at the *Human Genre Project*. He writes for *The Skinny* and the *Scottish Review of Books*, and is the co-editor of the journal *Free State*. He writes a blog at richardstrachan.wordpress.com

Simon Sylvester was born in 1980. His short stories have been published in magazines including *Smoke*, *Gutter* and *Fractured West*. His nanofiction collection *140 Characters* is published by Cargo Crate, and he writes new stories daily on *twitter.com/simonasylvester*. He lives in Cumbria with the abstract painter Monica Metsers, earning his crust as a teacher, journalist and labourer.

Colin Will is an Edinburgh-born poet and publisher with a scientific background who lives in Dunbar. He has served on the Boards of the Scottish Poetry Library and StAnza. His fifth collection, *The Floor Show At the Mad Yak Café*, was published by Red Squirrel Scotland in 2010. His own publishing house, Calder Wood Press, specialises in poetry chapbooks.

Zoë Wicomb was born in South Africa and now lives in Glasgow. She is Emeritus Professor in the department of English studies at Strathclyde University and Visiting Professor at Stellenbosch University, South Africa. In addition to two collections of short stories, she has published two novels, *David's Story* and *Playing in the Light*.

David Whelan is a fiction writer and journalist. His fiction is available at *3:AM Magazine*, *Cellstories*, *Deadman's Tome*, *SNM Horror Magazine*, *Pulp Metal Magazine* and *Tengen Magazine*. He has some words pending publication by Shortfire Press and *Stymie Magazine*. He's about to write a novel. He is 22 years old.

→

Christie Williamson is a poet from Yell in Shetland. His translations of Lorca's poetry into Shetland, *Arc o Möns*, was joint winner of the Callum MacDonald Memorial Prize 2010. He lives in Glasgow and is the proud father of two beautiful children.

Graeme Williamson is a writer and musician; he was born in Montreal and lives in Glasgow.